Praise for
The Topography of Pain

Usually we don't know the past, we don't understand the present and we don't dare to imagine the future. But Ivan Lesay knows and understands and he also dares to imagine, when in his extraordinary triptych he takes us on a journey through time from communist Czechoslovakia through Slovakia's transitional present to the futuristic world of tomorrow, in which people can finally live out all their fantasies, precisely those that the past forbade and persecuted, and the present promised their fulfillment, only to cruelly crush its promises. *The Topography of Pain* is a surprising narrative about the worlds of yesterday, today and tomorrow, a brave writing odyssey by a talented writer that demands an equally brave and talented reader.

—**Goran Vojnović**, writer, screenwriter and film director, Slovenia

Part critical portrayal of life in present-day Slovakia, part sobering look at the country's recent past with the euphoria of the Velvet Revolution replaced by growing cynicism, and part chilling depiction of a dystopian future, Ivan Lesay's ambitious debut novel deftly switches perspectives, letting the reader guess the relations between its three protagonists: the beautiful student Naďa, the aspiring journalist Jaro, and Adam, a young man who falls down to earth from dizzying technological heights.

—**Julia Sherwood**, translator, United Kingdom

Once upon a time there was a land where an authoritarian regime held sway over the nation. But one day revolution ignited, and the system broke down. The country broke in two. The people broke in pieces. It hurt, and the pain endured as they started searching their path forward, some striving valiantly, others less so. *The Topography of Pain* unfolds as an intricate narrative that delves deep into the torment spanning three generations, unveiling its myriad facets, whether surreal, hyperrealistic, or postapocalyptic. At its culmination stands a man named Adam, who has the chance to cut the chain and bring himself, the family, the country back to the joint. In the end there is hope.

—**Alexandra Salmela**, writer, Finland

Someone who just wants to be left in peace is being hit hard by destiny and biology. Ordinary people have extraordinary lives. Periphery happens to live the very essence of the history. Is it because of the time and the place? Generation between two eras, country between the big worlds. All kinds of division here! Plus lots of love and alcohol, very naturally present.

—**Jānis Joņevs**, writer, Latvia

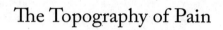

The Topography of Pain

GUERNICA WORLD EDITIONS 83

THE TOPOGRAPHY OF PAIN

Ivan Lesay

Translated by Jonathan Gresty

Slovak
Literary
Centre

This book was published with financial support from SLOLIA,
Slovak Literary Centre, Slovakia

GUERNICA
World
EDITIONS

TORONTO–CHICAGO–BUFFALO–LANCASTER (U.K.)
2024

Original title: *Topografia bolesti*, Ivan Lesay
Copyright © 2020, IKAR
Translation Copyright © 2024, Jonathan Gresty and Guernica Editions Inc.

Guernica Editions Founder: Antonio D'Alfonso

Anna van Valkenburg, general editor
Michael Mirolla, editor
Cover design: Allen Jomoc, Jr.
Interior design: Jill Ronsley, suneditwrite.com

Guernica Editions Inc.
1241 Marble Rock Rd., Gananoque (ON), Canada K7G 2V4
2250 Military Road, Tonawanda, N.Y. 14150-6000 U.S.A.
www.guernicaeditions.com

Distributors:
Independent Publishers Group (IPG)
600 North Pulaski Road, Chicago IL 60624
University of Toronto Press Distribution (UTP)
5201 Dufferin Street, Toronto (ON), Canada M3H 5T8

First edition.
Printed in Canada.

Legal Deposit—Third Quarter
Library of Congress Catalog Card Number: 2024933651
Library and Archives Canada Cataloguing in Publication
Title: The topography of pain / Ivan Lesay ; translated by Jonathan Gresty.
Other titles: Topografia bolesti. English
Names: Lesay, Ivan, author.
Series: Guernica world editions (Series) ; 83.
Description: Series statement: Guernica world editions ; 83 | Translation of:
Topografia bolesti. | In English, translated from the Slovak.
Identifiers: Canadiana (print) 2024032854X | Canadiana (ebook)
20240330536 | ISBN 9781771839181 (softcover) | ISBN 9781771839198 (EPUB)
Subjects: LCGFT: Novels.
Classification: LCC PG5440.22.E83 T6713 2024 | DDC 891.8/73—dc23

BODY

pro-topia

The water falls down, flooding the corners of consciousness. It appears blue, although it is not. The colour changes according to its volume. A small amount is colourless. As the amount of water rises, it becomes harder for the red, orange, yellow, or green wavelength of light to penetrate—only the blue one has a chance to survive. However, the blue is not visible through the dark rain falling from the grey sky.

"Let's get under cover before we're soaked," she said. He pressed her whole body against the wall, creating a shelter from both sides so no rain would fall on her. His breath was hot and she had goose-bumps. He pulled back his head and they stared at each other for a long time. The rain was coming down hard, there was no wind, and he was drenched to the skin, all except for his face. But he was in no hurry, not planning on leaving any time soon. The moment their lips met, a drop of water as big as grape fell on her cheek, directly hitting her birthmark. Both of them were startled as if they had got walked in on. But all it was was just a few drops of rain on the sheet metal eaves which had coalesced into one, making it weigh just enough to separate and drop down instead of hanging on.

She remembered this moment the day before yesterday, as she was lying on the bed next to someone else. Sweat, breath, and heartbeat on naked bodies in decreasing frequencies. The bustle from the street, the sounds of approaching thunder, the first drops hitting the metal window sill, and the smell of the lunch menu from the restaurant on the ground floor, fried meat: all of this penetrated through the window into the otherwise empty room. Through the closed curtains only a narrow strip of dim daylight entered the room, hitting her legs. They hurt so badly just a week before, even the thought of it sent a shiver down her spine. She pulled her legs to her body; the shadow now cleared the way for the light so it could shine on the sweaty shaved back of the neck of the man next to her. She checked her watch—his time was up, let's hope he wasn't asleep.

The thunder rumbles again today. The wind rises, the dust rises, the black clouds gather, and cover the last bits of setting sun. They barely made it. It started to rain as soon as they got into the car where it was still warm from before. Now they silently watch those who are still outside in a hurry, looking for their way to their cars and tents. Jackets and plastic bags over their heads, swearing, blood alcohol content, loud laughter, all noises muffled. It is thundering non-stop, the ground is shaking, lightning flashing. The storm still hasn't shown its full potential.

They've been together for a long time and they have already talked through all the important things. Without a word, they watch the start of the havoc. She peeks out in all directions, an energy drink in her hand, and a straw in her mouth, looking for the next place where lightning will strike. She straightens her back and stretches her stiff muscles. He looks straight through the windscreen, arms outstretched, squeezing the steering wheel.

When she first got off with him, she had no idea it would last this long. Her classmates started dating the boys from the next class, so she thought she should also find a boyfriend. He came in handy—it was the path of least resistance. He wasn't ugly, and he wasn't one of those crazy teens who kept roaring with laughter like crazy and blabbed everything out to their friends. He was sort of unexceptional, and ideal as an extra. Trustworthiness—it wasn't the quality she was looking for, but she was happy to find it in him.

Her friends were breaking up and starting new relationships, and she found out she was happy with her life—she did not need any drama. They stayed together.

His sharp profile with the raindrops flowing down the car window in the background made him look like a drenched, proud, and sad eagle—he will fly away as soon as the sky clears up. He looks five years older than her, even though they are the same age. She strokes his eyebrows with her finger, runs over his eyelid and nose, fondles his chin. He is handsome. Though he is shorter than she is, she doesn't mind: he doesn't talk about his height. In fact, he does not speak much in general. She sometimes addresses him as: "My little autistic boy."

The festival is bathing in torrents of water and no one can be seen out in the downpour anymore. She keeps twisting the wheel on the side of her seat until she is almost able to lie down. She leans over, trying to unbuckle his belt. The rear windows of his Volkswagen Polo are covered with dark foil, no one would be able to see them. But he is not in the mood, he just caresses her hair and smiles. He puts his hand back on the steering wheel and grips the leather covering fastened with leather straps.

After half an hour, the rain slowly subsides. About eight drunken bodies with bottles in their hands stumble out of the car next to them, dancing on their shaky legs in the mud and screeching. It seems that the festival is going on. She rolls down her window and hears other performers being called on stage.

* * *

When he came out of the bathroom with a confident smile, he asked me how I liked it best. He was only wearing socks (: -O), and his grey pants splashed with water were tight from all the excitement. He looked pretty handsome, but oh, how I hate smug guys.

"With my boyfriend!" I lied on purpose to pull in his horns.

The smile faded from his face. All he said was that in that case we were probably unlucky that day. He tried to lighten the situation, but I put on an obligatory smile. I knew he was just one stop—my market segment would look different.

I asked him if he wanted to talk. He shook his head. I didn't want to pester him anymore, so I just pointed to his boxers, blinked, and said we wouldn't get far with them on. Then everything went smoothly, basically a routine. I started to jerk him off, he squeezed my breasts and ass. He was moaning loudly so I sighed too—I tried to sound authentic. Then I applied lube to make it go smoothly and we got it on.

I haven't been in this business for long but it surprises me how similar the clients are to one another. How schematic men are. I don't know, for example, how a guy can think I'm doing this just for fun. Not only a macho like this one but also some slimy, fat, bald clerk thinks I'm trembling with eagerness to fuck him. Oh, God, I do it for money. You mix mortar, you tap on the computer, you study, you retire—I fuck. Mystery solved.

As he was banging me, I only focused on a single part of his body. I always do it like this—either I think of something completely different, a totally different situation or I focus on a single subject. An object in my rented flat or on a guy. My eyes seem to be outside my body, my mind seems to be outside my body. His fingers, that's what I was focused on that time. They are rough and scratch my skin, and they look awfully big and raw as well. They are so different from mine as if they were separate limbs. He must have scrubbed them for a long time before coming here. But one does not wash the ingested dirt, and the smell of work away so easily. Who knows, maybe it's visible on me, too. When I buy a large package of liquid soap for my flat do people suspect that I work in the sex business? Can others see it in my eyes? Does my body radiate it?

At first, I was in a bad mood and sarcastic and hard on him, and then he was hard on me in return. He wanted to get back at me, but he was insecure, disgruntled—he thrust my hips roughly like a jackhammer. He must have felt that I was elsewhere, that I was absent, that I was not with him. He was no longer aroused, he just wanted to get through with honour. As soon as he finished, his sweaty body dropped next to mine on a bed covered with a blanket.

I'm in a better mood usually, and also nicer. When the standard question of how I like it comes up, I say "hard and from behind." Honestly—I don't even care, but guys always get turned on by that. Another advantage is that I don't have to look them in the face and can get lost in my thoughts or check if my nail polish is peeling or not. Just the day before yesterday, there was such a modest guy, he was quite nice. I smiled at him, stuck my butt out, and imagined how I was going to spend the money I was about to earn in a clothing store. I had to buy something new. I saw a beautiful coloured blouse. And a beautiful dress! As he approached climax, I sighed aloud a few times, as if I was too, and after a while, it was over. We said our goodbyes, kissed both cheeks, I don't think either side was unhappy. I know it sounds weird, but I feel good quite often when I do the job right.

* * *

Modern hospitals are no longer painted white inside but green. White causes stress, green calms people down. Her body slowly slides into the tunnel, she breathes shallowly. She fits into place like a coffin in a cremation furnace heated up to one thousand degrees Celsius.

They told her the procedure was going to be uncomfortable. She didn't sleep well and had been shaky since morning. She bit the inside of her cheek as she chewed her yogurt and corn flakes with fruit too hard and too fast. She could not finish her breakfast and still has a swelling in her mouth which she is running her tongue over continuously. Actually, didn't they tell her not to eat before the procedure? Fuck!

And also, the taxi driver didn't help. When she told him which hospital she wanted to go to, he asked where exactly. He had no other reason apart from curiosity—there was only one entrance to the hospital. Surprised, she answered him.

"Ahhh, em-ar-i." Nodding his head the taxi driver expertly acknowledged the receipt of information. She was surprised by how much he knew about the procedure. Until then she thought it wasn't very common but from the way he was talking, it seemed that every other family member or customer had undergone it. He knew everything. That all the metallic things had to be removed— "maybe even your bra, if it has any metal parts," he squinted at her through the rear-view mirror, and her imagination added a sleazy grin to his look—that it would be banging in the tunnel, as if they were tearing up the asphalt with a jackhammer, that they would play music through headphones on request and also give her an emergency button to use if needed. He said he knew of cases where people panicked and clambered out after just a few minutes.

"Claustrophobia, hallucinations, and so on, literally anything," he said. The tree-shaped aroma wrapped in rosary bounced and smelled pungent, just as the Wunderbaum inscription implied.

"Those who can avoid it are the lucky ones," the taxi driver said tapping his forehead as he turned to the hospital.

She had to remove her make-up. That's what the assistant told her when he found her standing only in her pants in the hallway of the examination room. She really had metal underwires and hooks in her bra, but there are also metal components in makeup. With downcast eyes, the assistant handed her a green piece of papery clothing and gave her a minute to remove the thick layer of make-up she had applied barely an hour before without knowing that she was putting metal on her face. Then he glared at the large birthmark on her naked face without even hiding it. Finally, he scanned her with a hand-held metal detector as they do at an airport. It beeped somewhere in the area of her lower back, but she was sure there was nothing in her pants. She prayed she wouldn't have to undress completely because she didn't shave, and what if the paper poncho rolls up? He asked her if she happened to have a metal implant or a prosthesis. Shaken, she was unable to answer.

"I guess it's fine; sometimes it plays up," he said, shrugging and opening the door to the examination room.

After the stress of the previous days and months, she enjoyed this strange solarium. She had everything, things were happening to her but she didn't have to do anything, just lie still. Parked, she breathed deeply; only pale green light penetrated her wide-open eyes from the periphery. There was silence in her headphones, maybe she told them she didn't want any music, she couldn't remember. The banging was not so loud. The staff busied themselves in routine movements, everything went smoothly, according to plan. It was a little cold until a contrast medium and heat began to flow into her body. The emergency button was warming in her hand, but she was not going to squeeze it. She was amazed—after just a few minutes in, she felt relaxed and safe during an examination she had feared so much; she started praying that it would never end.

With almost no ambitions, she had always had trouble seeing herself in the future. She could imagine grey hair, even wrinkles. But what she would do for a living, what and who she would be, was not so easy to imagine. Now she almost felt the physical proximity of a milestone of some sort. She was not happy to be a patient and have a body that did not listen to her. On the other hand—she faced no dilemmas, the horizon had narrowed, she was fully focused, had a clear goal. If she survived, she would be new.

* * *

"Wait, you can't be serious!" Naďa doesn't ask Kristína, she just announces it. She stops, takes a step back, frowns. Maybe she just imagined it. "I would never ever expect this from you!"

Kristína shuffles her feet one step ahead of Naďa, looks at the ground, bites her lip, and probably regrets not keeping her mouth shut. Against the background of posters and grinning graffiti faces, they stand still like statues obstructing the flow of crowds of students in the underpass between public transport stops in front of the school.

The two of them also hurried to the lecture, but now it is clear that they will skip it. Their heels slowly tap on the names of fresh economics graduates painted on the sidewalk. The asphalt is cracked and resealed; the whole city is full of scars, on blocks of flats, on sidewalks, on roads. Can't things be done properly the first time?

They sit in a café a minute later, eating a toasted sandwich and drinking cappuccino.

"What the fuck? What the actual …?" Naďa asks, again and again, refusing to accept the information.

Kristína, a petite girl from the East, explains the situation with downcast eyes, but in a straightforward and surprisingly simple way. A small cross on a gold chain beats rhythmically after each completed sentence. They discuss the fundamental issues and sensitive details for a long time. Naďa is already slowly digesting the news and becoming more and more curious.

She walks, among trees, along a path covered with branches that fell there during a night storm. Other times it is full of runners, cyclists, couples, dog owners, and families with children over the weekend. There is almost no one here today, though. Swearing, a cyclist turned back—even his fancy bicycle was not fancy enough to conquer big branches. Naďa also left a retired dog owner behind who decided to throw some of the broken branches off the path.

She had wanted to come here for a long time—ever since she started going to university and learned that there was a river nearby. Now was the right time to do so. She doesn't have proper clothing or shoes. Her heels sink into the soft ground, she is cold, but she desperately needs to move. She is already at the Danube and desires to go down to the water, at least dip her palm into the river, but after she slips twice, she abandons the thought. She persistently continues on the path. She looks around; no one else is there. Is she crying? She doesn't know. She sniffs deeply and spits clumsily, saliva and mucus stick to her tongue, and hang on her chin, *fuck!* She forgot her handkerchiefs.

What upset her so much? The conversation with Kristína: of course, she plays back fragments still very fresh in her memory. Why did Kristína tell her now, when the shocking news is almost a year old? Naďa told her about her health condition a few days ago. Did Kristína want to return the favour, tell her something too, repay her in some strange way?

And another thing—Kristína asked her what *she* thought of herself, what kind of person *she* was. She flipped out when Naďa, still in shock, asked her friend how she was coping *morally*. What kind of a person does she want to be after all this? She did not intend to judge ... Or did she?

"Of course, it's not all right, of course, I'm not okay with that. Morally," she drew quotation marks with her fingers in the air, "or otherwise. If anyone finds out, I'll fucking end myself right away. So, I hope you're not planning to tell anyone. But what the fuck do you think of yourself, that you are … perfect? Just because you look great, have good grades, have a nice hipster part-time job, a nice boyfriend, you go home to see your mother every weekend, you are nice to everyone. The perfect girl. Have you ever made a mistake? Look at you—you're like a robot! What is inside you? Who are you? What kind of person are you? Sorry."

Nada was not offended. She had been asking herself similar questions since she started seeing doctors. Others have always thought she was perfect, yet she found herself more-or-less annoying—like an empty cement mixer switched on. She was just surviving, not living; she made a little effort here and there. This resulted in a run-of-the-mill existence. Until now, all she had done was survive.

She no longer wants to smile and be friendly to everyone. She often gets sudden attacks of tiredness—she just sits down and stares into the void, at the children in high-visibility vests holding hands, at the smoker in stretched and baggy briefs on the balcony opposite their window, at the arguing homeless people at the station, at the warm wind that stirs the puddles after the rain, at her mom dancing in the kitchen, at her own face in the mirror. She is both bored and entertained by herself, she doesn't have the strength to get up, she is empty. What kind of person is she? What is inside her? *What does the lo-co-what does the lo-co—what does the locomotive dream about?* the old song plays in her mind against her will. Why is it raining again? It was only drizzling a minute ago. And why the hell has she walked this far?!

* * *

What causes a cold? Is it coldness itself that turns the nose red, gives you a sore throat, swells the nodules? Or do some viruses or bacteria—always portrayed green in adverts—lie in wait for a body weakened from the cold weather and attack insidiously from the side? Hollow reflection, yet the fact is unequivocal—the organism behaves differently, sends signals of discomfort to the brain and sets the nerves tingling. She is, like every weekend, at home, in her mom's hometown. She won't be helping her this time. On the contrary, her mom will be taking care of her as if she were a baby. The corners of the blanket do not let any cold air in, mom tucks every single one under the diseased body, her daughter becoming a pupa. There is an old ten-litre pot full of infused, ground, hairy rosehips in the kitchen, slices of lemon and pips floating in it. Naďa will either piss herself or get diabetes.

Nothing has changed here. There is a memory in every corner, an image or a smell that awakens a neuron which shifts the excitement to the archive and eliciting an old scene along with emotion from the depths of the gallery. Photos in memory are not black and white, but brightly coloured, screaming. That hole ... she made that hole in the wall two decades ago—she was playing with a bubble that wasn't supposed to be under the wallpaper. The exposed piece of the panel that still looks almost like a map of Czechoslovakia is still there. Old jumble lies in the larder in white plastic bags with the logo of a grocery store which no longer exists, they now sell stylish bicycles which are supposed to look old. Mom does not change things, she does not throw anything away, but the apartment still looks in good condition, cozy, and clean. Like that of a true housewife.

Her daughter inherited patience only for selected situations and illness is not among them; a cough, sore throat, itchy nose, sneezing, high temperature—these are undeserved wrongs and have lasted since prehistoric times. She uses the toilet for the third time in an hour, slams the door, flips through the newspaper. She curses silently—why do they have to write about every tragedy that occurs in Slovakia? Nevertheless, she flips through it with shallow breath and can't take her eyes off the photo of the compressed car with the exact time of exit 22:45, numbers in digital form, and the names of the victims: Pavol (34) and Martinka (22). Death can be very *schematic*—a disco, alcohol, safety belts left to hang safely, a bend on the bad road between villages, a skid, a tree, injuries incompatible with life. On the next page, Igorko (11) drowned and a family from Revúca lost the roof over their heads due to their debts. Naďa was never immune to horrifying ideas. Death, disease, misfortune: they always scare and immobilize her. However, she cannot resist their temptation. And at the moment of her own body's physical failure, she feels a certain satisfaction. She does not have to worry anymore, it is here—she can finally be horrified in the first person, she is shaking.

"Come see this, it's adorable, it'll make you laugh," her mom calls from the drying room. There is an ironing board, a clothes-horse and a comfortable guest bed—when Naďa comes home, it is always nicely made, even though she still sleeps in her childhood room. There is also a table with an old computer in the drying room. The light from the screen is shining on her mom's beautiful face, she does not seem to age. She only degenerates from the inside under the influence of the huge e-mails from her active friends, who probably get paid for forwarding them.

"Zuzička sent me this." She talks about her friends as if Naďa was also on the closest terms with them.

Mom is touched by the PowerPoint presentation of sleeping puppies. Then, with tears in her eyes, she goes to the bathroom; the washing machine has finished its cycle. Her daughter dumped one week's worth of dirty clothing out of her suitcase; by Monday there will be catharsis and a rebirth via fabric softener. Last weekend, in the same place, at the same time her mom showed her a video (friend's video!) in which a refugee from Eritrea climbed out of a suitcase in front of Swiss customs officers. Terrible world. People send in equal measure pictures of animal happiness and human suffering.

Naďa sits at the computer, automatically opens a folder with her name. Her whole life has been arranged in it over the years. Still in high school, she digitized old photos, and the folder grew to more than twenty folders. She likes order, and she needs system now more than ever—maybe when she looks at the photos one by one, she will be able to create a structured idea about herself. Because when Kristína asks her who she is, she cannot stutter out an answer. Can she live without knowing what makes her who she is, not knowing her essence? Can she die like that?

* * *

She was born and did not cry. The doctors were surprised, her parents were afraid, but everything else was fine. The photo was also fine, normal. Mom pink in the face, dad laughing and a bit scared, baby kind of squished, with a protruding chin and detached expression. It's the only photo she has with her father. When she calls her mom, her head immediately appears in the doorway.

"What else would you like to know, my love? I'm sorry, but he left us. It was autumn, he'd been hanging out somewhere for a few days, then came back, all wet, packed a few things, kissed us both, and stepped into the rain. That's all."

"But why?"

"I don't know exactly; it's been a long time. He was sick, he couldn't live with us, he kept saying he didn't want to hurt us, but I had never understood him."

"He left … and he's still alive, are you sure?"

"Of course, he's alive. He lives somewhere in Prague, at least he says so."

Naďa has her doubts. She does not understand how her mom could have dealt with it, but she does not have the strength to repeat a conversation which has led nowhere a hundred times before.

A long time ago, she was maybe eight or ten years old, a man visited them. Mom gave her a treat from the tin box and told her to go and play in her room. She almost never gave her sweets and Naďa never asked for them. She was sitting in her room: the toys were still, she was still, the sweet was still, tucked between her cheek and teeth, breaking the enamel and sowing the seeds of tooth decay. She was listening to the whispers of two voices.

When the man left, she asked her mom who it was. Mom said it was just a friend.

* * *

She does not have as many memories as she has photos from the nine years of primary school, and there weren't many of those either. One old classic: a girl with twin pigtails, a smile with an incomplete set of teeth, a spelling book on the table. Mom definitely had the original somewhere—a photo in a large format, name, class, white mounting, translucent cover paper. Like a cobweb. Memory covered with dust. Or maybe it never actually existed.

Another iconic photo—little Nadenka sitting by the piano. She is clutching at it like a drowning man at a straw. The piano was tense too, as she stiffly sat behind it.

Nine school reports with straight A's, a few shallow friendships, she would no longer recognize most of the class. Memories of classmates are as flat as cut-outs from a children's magazine, like the chest of their Geography teacher. Mornings—breakfast and school, evenings—dinner, homework and sleep. Over and over again, then summer holidays, then Christmas, then repeat. Maybe two deviations from normal—a broken arm in plaster or the week in the isolation ward alone without mom. Small traumas, a few joys, nothing special, just fast years of slowly flowing fog.

Empty, she goes to the kitchen to eat something. Mom automatically heats milk for her, *my kitten*, and refills her mug of tea. Both mugs are standing on the table in front of her; she can mix them together.

"So, are you feeling better?"

Nađa shakes her head. She will not lie to her mom or burden her too much.

"Hopefully, it's just flu, it'll pass, you'll see." She doesn't know anything yet.

Nađa gets up from the table, hugs her, scrunches her face to stop the tears.

Mom offers her dumplings dipped in egg. Always slim without having to restrain herself, she never understood the concept of diets.

"Have you been looking at the photos?" Mom has a beautiful smile and Naďa nods tersely, munching a pickle. She sits down at the computer again with her stomach full. She is barely breathing, her nose is blocked by a cold and her lungs are squeezed by a stomach filled with three dumplings, three eggs, and three pickles. She breathes through the calorific triathlon with her mouth open as in childbirth.

"You know which one I like best, don't you?"

She knows. She still feels embarrassed about it, and if she had to show it to anyone, she would blush. She let her friend talk her into making a "portfolio" in the photo studio. The photographer hinted that, perhaps, the album might get noticed by a modelling agent, to whom, for a small fee, he himself could pass it. The surcharge was a trivial amount of money compared to the amount paid for the photos; together it was a small fortune. The version for her mom talked about a skilful and ambitious friend who wanted to be a photographer and just tried out her skills on Naďa.

Until then, she had not taken her body as an object subject to aesthetic criteria. She brushed her hair so that she would not look tousled, offend the school rules and the taste of people around her. She wore clean clothes, but most importantly she wore whatever she had. Her mom did not use Naďa as an outlet for her own sartorial self-expression; her fashion was dictated by habit and purpose. Classmates began to wear outlandish things but pointlessly and too soon in her opinion. She was not a Puritan nor did her mother lead her to religion; she knew exactly what adult women looked like. Not from textbooks, though, but from porn magazines.

Sometime at that age—one particular day, at one point, coming out of the tub stripped of her clothes—she realized she was sexy, that she looked like a woman from such a magazine. She did not want what they were doing there: such contortions repelled her. She just dryly realized that she was an adult. And from then on, she too "wanted to look good."

She clicks on the photo, although she remembers it in detail. There is a fifteen-year-old girl on it already very similar to her current self. A dark figure stands out against a tacky pale blue background as if cut out from somewhere else and glued to the drawing. Unnaturally leaning over, exactly as instructed by the photographer who told her to hang on. Slightly parted legs, her butt sticking out, her left hand resting on her left side, a gentle forward bend to the right. Young, lithe and lively. Hot. *Fuckable*, commented her classmates later. She was offended because the narrow meaning of the word spoke of only one purpose. However, both boys and girls began to use it often and without restraint, so she pardoned it and thought of it as something similar to *peach, cutie* or *doll*. In a broader sense, she was flattered.

She is evaluating her fifteen-year-old version on a computer screen with today's view. Eyes completely wrinkle-free, original chestnut brown hair colour, her acne smeared over with a fine layer of make-up. Nice work, but there is one big mistake—her neck has a completely different shade. At that time, no one had yet advised her that it was not enough to only apply make-up to her face but also necessary to smooth it down her neck and dissolve the border between mask and reality.

Despite minor flaws, everyone liked the result. Naďa did not regret that she had spent almost her entire earnings from the horrible summer job at the brewery. No-one else probably even noticed, but the photographer allowed himself one minor touch-up. He blanked out the birthmark under her right eye, next to her nose. She had never liked it, it was ugly, she wished for it to not be there. It was pointless for everyone to tell her that it was a beauty spot, that it suited her, that it was proof of her uniqueness, that no other girl had one like just like hers, that Cindy Crawford had something like it too. As if beauty could be objectively argued. She just never fucking liked it and that was it. She looked in the mirror and repeated that "*otherwise,* she's pretty". But she was not. She had a black mark on the notice board. And then suddenly the photographer came and, without asking, erased it at the drop of a hat. How come she had not thought of trying the same procedure in real life until then? Why did she not simply cover this conspicuous but flat birthmark with a thicker layer of make-up? How much time in life does a person unhappily waste in distorted self-perception? And can all problems be solved just as easily?

Life is stored on the timeline of the photo viewer program—the past is to the left. She moves the cursor in the opposite direction from her mom's favourite photo and stops it at a not much older photo. It is a group shot from her first school year with innocent, frightened faces, demented aliens after captivity and admission to their internment camp. On stage in the school hall, in front of a velvet curtain, she stands in the middle, above a poor bullied girl with a 1.A. sign. She wears a blouse with a floral pattern and glasses.

Left, right, hundreds of other photos from secondary school, life documented and stored on media in hundredths of seconds; a personal history in myriads of pixels. A pointillist Nadenka, almost like the real one; shots showing either her or a twin who lived her life for her.

"Are you going to drop dead for me too, you bitch?" she quietly asks the unmoving smiling face of a girl on the lookout platform of the Empire State Building, high above New York.

Next to the girl is her boyfriend, frightened as always when he found himself outside a familiar environment. Work&Travel was the biggest stress ever, he still has not forgiven her for dragging him across the ocean to sell hot dogs at an amusement park. He masked his uncertainty with lessons and quotes from movies and tv serials.

"Fear of heights is illogical. A fear of falling, on the other hand, is prudent and evolutionary," he said stiffly quoting Sheldon Cooper from *The Big Bang Theory*. And then he tried to smile.

"Acrophobia, that's what it's called … professionally … if you didn't know. Fear of heights." Naďa did not respond to the monologue.

"And do you know what *contraphobia* is?" he asked continuing the lecture, moving his back to the wall. Naďa shook her head, even though she knew both the question and the answer.

"When a person does what they are most afraid of. Imagine that I would do high-altitude work, washing the windows on this building, for example."

An inventory of the photos has not given her an answer to who she is, yet. What actually defines her: her visual identity? After all, she looked quite different years ago. Only the birthmark has remained the same. What if she had it removed? Original Naďa, fundamentally changed Naďa, reborn Naďa?

How does he see her? She does not ask him, they have never bothered with things like that, he is not the type—neither is she. Analysis, reflection—that is what her mom and a few friends are for. Having a guy equals having security. Love for her semi-autist is a non-aggression pact.

"Mom, am I normal?"

"Of course, you are, my little girl, why shouldn't you be?" her mom asks, pouring herself a finger of port. Her eyes ask her daughter if she wants some too. No, she thanks her.

"I'm completely normal, so completely ordinary, is that right?" Sickness gives rise to aggression, doubt, self-reflection coated in offence.

"No, you're the most extraordinary being in the universe, you're my treasure." With her face in her mom's palms, Naďa laughs till the tears run. 'Normal' and 'a treasure'—she can choose which.

She has never chosen anything in her life, though. If she leaves out small stuff and practical banalities, she has never had dreams. She wanted to be a good daughter, to *get along* with everyone. Like wine, she did not want to offend. But that is not a dream, is it? Even in primary school when they were asked what they wanted to become, she felt abashed. She repeated after her classmates—a doctor, a lawyer. In order not to be conspicuous, she sometimes hammed it up and wrote "veterinarian" in full. So that no one would think she was fake.

She had no real interest, not even hypothetical ones, in any of the part-time jobs she had. She worked to make money. In the brewery, the bakery, the hypermarket, the car plant. Now she makes coffee and knows the difference between ristretto and espresso. As for the difference between the jobs? Money and level of comfort. Better to work in a warm than in cold place, better to carry lighter things than heavier ones. More money for less music—she'd take that. She was good at maths.

After some calculations, she figured out she would go to Economics University. With its wide range of job opportunities and potential for a decent salary, everyone nodded at her pragmatic decision. Her mom supported her, and although she could imagine a different field for her, in the end, as expected, she just said *whatever*. Maybe she would have told her the same thing even if she had killed someone. She was everything to her mom, including *whatever*.

On the far right is the most recent photo in the folder. It is of her, Kristína, and three other classmates at a student party two weeks ago. They are holding plastic glasses with the Fernet logo—it was a promo event. All smiling, slightly drunk: obligatory entertainment. Like sisters, one sports team with one purpose. Naďa is one of them, a student of economics, averagely self-confident, ambitious but without vision.

Who does she take after? Who is she a product of? Of a father whom she knows only by voice and with whom she has only one photo? If genes can overwhelm upbringing … Of a dreamy mother? That would not be fair to her nor even to herself. Is she a product of the times? Times were different. Her past fits on one page that can be graded B at best, formally correct, but without a hint of imagination. Her present is confined to the languishing and sick body that wants to defend itself so badly but does not even know against what. Only the instinctive ability to plan for the future lives on in her brain. She doesn't turn the computer off with the mouse but instead brusquely hits the reset button on the hardware case.

* * *

"Is your name really Mercedes?" A man that weighed about hundred and fifty kilograms and had a hairy back asked me amusedly as he drew a circle with a three-pointed star between my breasts.

"Mmm," I said, slowly and flirtatiously in a way guys love. The client kept asking—how did I come up with the name of a luxury car, or whether I consider myself of a higher, 'luxury' class. No, not yet, I thought. So far, I'm lolling around in a rented flat with a brute like you, for thirteen hundred crowns for half an hour, so I'm definitely not high class yet. But as soon as I map out the market of desire a little, I will be.

While I was thinking about my business plans, I told him a story about how my father came here from Argentina where Mercedes is a common girl's name. I already knew that this business was not (just) about sex, but also about hidden worlds, about ideas, about disguises, about fantasy. About everything but the truth. There is enough truth in everyday life, truth is boring. Officially, guys rent my body, but to 90 percent of them, I am a parallel story, an escape from reality.

He didn't want to believe that, in Spain and Latin America, girls are called after dream cars. That's what I was expecting. I already knew, when Chantal (also a fake name, of course) was creating my profile on the web, that I was going to try to attract attention with something special. I didn't want to be cheap and easy like those colleagues with catchwords like: no. 5 silicones … special offer: oral sex au naturel … escort service included … an inexperienced beginner or, alternatively, an experienced MILF. *It may be a cliché—even Chantal said it was embarrassing—but the connection between the car and the woman seemed like an ingenious combination of men's desires to me. It might have been embarrassing if twice the number of clients hadn't asked for me the following week ;-).*

Anyway, the most interesting thing is that guys want to know my real name. They feel that, if they find out my real name, they will get under my skin, that they are not with a whore, but with a lover, that they are gods, and that I don't only care about their money but also about them. Everyone wants to be somebody to someone. And penetration is not the peak of pleasure, not even for men.

There is no reason for me to be pathetic at work. So, I kept to my plan, didn't reveal my name, and only told my client what I had studied on the web before. Mercedes means mercy. Really? *The name comes from the name of the Virgin Mary—Santa María de las Mercedes.* You're kidding. *The car brand is called after a girl, not the other way around.* You're making an ass out of me. *And my witty joker grabbed mine.*

Apparently, I did it—I caught his eye, he hung on my lips and he was immediately more curious. He didn't want to show it—he didn't come here for this. But I knew that me being quiet for a minute would work the magic.

"I don't believe you. What's your real name?" *He could not stand the weight of the most ordinary secret, exactly as I expected.*

"Five hundred crowns," *I began my planned experiment.*

At first, he didn't understand, but after a while, his mouth widened into a big smile; he thought he had won. Maybe he was disappointed I did not want to tell him for free. Just because of how amazing he was. That would be an even bigger honour, a real trophy. On the other hand, nothing good or nice is free, and he knew that. And in front of a woman, no man wants to look like a cheapskate. If I offered him, I don't know, oral or pissing for an extra charge, he would probably tell me to go to hell. And maybe even call me a filthy, disgusting and greedy whore. But in this situation? He wanted something from me, he was the one asking questions. I just set the price.

Dear readers, have I lured you in? Because I lured my client in a lot. I already had him hooked but I wanted him to swallow a sinker too.

"Or you know what, let it be. It's probably not a good idea anyway. I shouldn't let you into my private life."

"Don't worry, I won't tell anyone, I have no one to speak to about it anyway. So, what's your name?" *He reacted quickly so I wouldn't have time to change my mind.*

Silence. The silence I enjoyed as I listened to it melt.

"Don't worry, I'll pay!"

Bingo!

"All right, but I don't do this usually, just because it's you." *Extra personalized service, a sense of exclusivity cannot fail. The satisfied customer was already smiling triumphantly. Finally, I told him my name. My second, made-up name.*

"Mária …" he said devoutly. And after a while, it dawned on him. That's right, Santa María de las Mercedes. *Everything fit together and he was part of the story. He had no doubt about the authenticity of my "real" name. It was perfectly ordinary, even ridiculous for a woman who sells her body. I was tempted to tell him that my full name was Mária Magdaléna, to give his experience biblical proportions, but that would be too suspicious. Mária was enough for him to leave with the impression that he had fucked a saint so well that she even told him her name.*

The experiment came out quite well, what do you think? I will be very happy if you write your comments here in the comment section on mercedes.blog.cz, or rate my article. Remember, I'm developing my unconventional business and you can become a part of it. I will be grateful for any criticism and recommendations.

Your Merche (a diminutive a Mercedes and what my dad called me ;-)).

* * *

She is tiring fast. What's going on? Angry, she tries to fool herself into thinking that it's just her imagination. She is fighting it, ignoring that feeling; she is disappointed, she wants to feel sorry for herself, but most importantly—she is angry. Angry with herself. Because she is tiring fast. She feels like an old neighbour who, in the block with no lift, had to rest at each floor before reaching the third.

"Wait, slow down. I'm not twenty anymore," he would shout at her grandson, panting, sweaty, leaning against a wooden banister rail, hidden under decades of paint.

But Naďa is only a little over twenty. And she is tired. And her legs hurt!

"Two espressos, one latte, and a raspberry cheesecake. To table three."

She goes from the large copper coffee machine to the table in the corner by the window and she barely makes it. Her legs are heavy, hurting, and she has a stitch in her side. She discreetly skives off for the rest of the shift, holed up in the kitchen, in the restroom. She can see her colleagues are aware of it, but what else is she supposed to do?

She has never refused to work. Not that she enjoyed it, but she has been used to having part-time jobs since high school. They lived alone, her mom's income was no great shakes. She had to work.

* * *

In her final year, she worked in a bakery. Her mom knew the foreman, so Naďa could choose shifts and which section to work in. He did not recommend her to go to the sweet department, he said that it was conveyor belt production, fastpacking, and palletization—quite strenuous stuff. So, she spent a couple of afternoons during the week in the savoury department looking in the oven, waiting for what came out of it, sorting the good sticks from the burned ones, then placing the packages of savoury sticks in boxes and sticking labels on them at the end of the cycle. These three activities were performed at hourly intervals, then repeated, with two rounds per shift so the staff did not go completely nuts.

The foreman was strange from the beginning and she preferred to avoid him. But once he surprised her by the oven—she was turning round to head off to the boxes and he was about an inch behind her. Frightened, she bumped into him, he lost his balance and had to catch himself on a metal baking sheet sticking out of the oven. He burned himself, hissed softly and she apologized; he then composed himself and concentrated, showing her how to properly scrape off the burnt pieces of the sticks with a spatula. He slowly guided her movements, as if teaching her to dance. He clung to her from behind and smelled of wine. During each subsequent shift, he always found a few minutes to "pay attention" to her—one day he grabbed her hand lightly, another he brushed against her ass gently, smelling her from behind. To top it all off, he often mentioned what good friends her mom and he were, as if harassing her daughter was part of some agreement. She clenched her teeth and vowed to hold on for a few more months until the end of August. She didn't feel like looking for a new job; if it wasn't for him, that one wasn't that bad.

On one hot July day, he smelled of alcohol even more than usual. In her mind, she was preparing what she would tell him: To let her be, or she was seriously going to tell his wife and her mother! She watched him peripherally for the entire shift. About an hour before the end, when a colleague went to the toilet, he walked towards her. She whispered her little speech to herself quickly, but it happened so fast and she didn't even know how: in just a second, he lifted her cloak, slipped his hand under her leggings and panties, and stuck his finger in her ass. The adrenaline was coursing through her body so much there was no room left for her little speech, she was shaken by animal fright and anger. Although he pressed up against her aggressively, she leaned forward, her legs spread, found her footing, and—more instinctively than intentionally—as she was turning towards him, split his brow with an elbow aimed between his eyes. He stood there, surprised, blood pouring down his face. A female colleague who was standing in the doorway saw Naďa kick him in the crotch, covered her mouth and sobbed as the foreman bent forward in pain. Naďa briskly walked away—and home.

* * *

"Mom, I have something to tell you," she sat in the kitchen, still shaking. "You know, your acquaintance ... the foreman ..." Mom was doing her nails with a nail file, small shavings falling on the synthetic tablecloth. She didn't react. "Mireček." Naďa reluctantly uttered the name by which her mom knew him.

"Yeah, Mireček." Mom's face lit up. "Just the day before yesterday, I met him in Kaufland, with his wife and children. Such a beautiful family. It was very kind of him to get you that job, we should be grateful. Or was it yesterday? I can't remember anymore."

Naďa couldn't react. What exactly did she expect her mom to do after she found out about the incident?

Should she tell her boyfriend instead? Either he would do nothing, and maybe even accuse her of provoking it, or he would go to the factory and beat up the foreman and break all his fingers, systematically, one by one. Both scenarios were equally likely—even after all those years, she could not guess which outcome was more probable. She was afraid of both of them, so said nothing.

Two days later, she went to the shift as usual; she didn't want to give the bastard the feeling of victory and not show up. She needed the money and it was he who should be ashamed, not her, she kept saying to herself on the way to work sobbing. She bumped into him sooner than she expected—already at the entrance turnstile. She looked him straight in the eye, her buttocks clenched and her heart in her mouth, almost in her head, pounding with the cadence of an assault rifle. He could not handle her stare for long and was the first one to look away. He frowned, a small piece of thread sticking out of his brow: he had had it stitched.

* * *

After arriving in Bratislava, the same day as enrolling at university, she also registered at a temping agency. She took the first offer she got—in a hypermarket. Before starting, she quizzed her acquaintance who worked there about it. He said the worst job was at the cash register, stress and material responsibility for every single Euro. She would not have objected to sitting at the cash register and billing, but no one asked her. And so she worked in the frozen food section, the second worst option according to her acquaintance. She had to keep moving back and forth between the shop and the sub-zero temperatures of the freezer rooms.

"Building up her immunity to the cold," she said, jokingly.

But she wasn't lucky with her superiors again. This time no one put a hand in her pants, but her bosses—on the day shift a woman her mom's age, at nights, a guy a few years younger—neither would get off her back. She'd take a sip from the mineral water she left by her metal cabinet in an area called the "changing room"—just a

corner in the warehouse where both men and women changed—
and they were already on to her, telling her not to mess around.
She went to the bathroom, it did not take her longer than a minute
together with washing her hands, but either he or she was already
waiting for her outside. They were like twins asking her why she
messed around and if she couldn't wait for the break or till the end
of the shift. She quite admired them—to keep dozens of scattered
employees in constant anxiety about getting caught somewhere—
well it takes talent. They neurotically ran around the shop with
telephones glued to their ear, walking dozens of kilometres per day.
When a colleague told Naďa how much they earned, she was surprised. She thought that people in their position had to earn much
more, but apparently they only earned about two hundred more
than a part-time worker who worked all month.

* * *

"What are you doing here?" Naďa's memories are disturbed by
Winona, a colleague with a lisp and piercings under her lower lip
and in her tongue, two in both places. She removes the translucent
hygienic gloves she wears for working with food. She sits down
next to her on the radiator, both lost in the shade of the food shelf.
At this hour, not so many people go to the café, two more hours and
they will be closing.

"Are you all right?" she looks at Naďa carefully, placing a hand
on her thigh. She runs her tongue around the inside of her mouth,
grimacing, smacking her lips, creating suction—she always looks
ridiculous when she fights the leftovers of sticky white bread
between pieces of metal.

"Yeah, sure. I'm probably coming down with something again,"
Naďa says. "I know it looks suspicious, three sloppy shifts, off sick
for a week, and now this. But I don't want to skive off. I felt so ill I
couldn't even move. Don't tell Kamil that I'm not feeling well again,
okay? It will pass in a minute, I'll stay in bed until tomorrow, take
some Paralen and sweat it out. Don't tell him anything, will you? I

really don't want to lose this job." She grabs her hips, straightening her lower back.

"All right, I won't tell anyone. But it's not such an amazing job." Winona scans the room sceptically, staring at the bar through the door. "Don't worry, even if Kamilko wanted to replace you, you'd find something else without any problems—there are enough jobs around here." She puts a savoury stick from a megapack in her mouth and offers one to her colleague. Naďa wants to be nice so takes one and they both put them in their mouth as if they were cigarettes. They sit and pretend to let the salt fall down as if it was ash.

"Sure, but what kind of jobs? I haven't had a better one so far." Naďa remembers the bakery and, disgusted, throws the stick butt under the shelf. "Compared to the previous ones, this place is heaven and Kamil's an angel. Seriously," she says as Winona laughs. Naďa also starts laughing at the idea of Kamil, the angel.

"Was it really that bad in Tesco?" Winona asks. She has never experienced a typical Slovak store; she and her parents lived in a big house in Kittsee, Austria, from her early age, and only ever went shopping in Hofer's or Spare. Naďa told her about her job in the freezer one day after Winona complained about having to slice a kilogram of cold turkey to make sandwiches. It seemed like a great injustice to her: her fingers were almost falling off because of the cold, she grumbled. Naďa was amused.

"Probably not that bad, hard to say. I don't want to complain, but they kept bossing us around, even though we did what we were supposed to. Students were their main target. Those idiots didn't even know how to express themselves properly. For them, Tesco was their whole world, they lived for their job and nothing else."

"I can imagine … Plus, that freezer."

"Though there are worse things …"

"Such as?"

Winona keeps asking—she probably doesn't want to leave the warm radiator. Should she tell her about the pervert who harassed her and ended up with stitches in his eyebrow? Better not. It is not something she really feels like sharing. She can already imagine

Winona looking appalled, feeling sorry for her, asking endless questions. Naďa could not bear that amount of interest. But she could tell her about the previous job before that one, in the car plant.

"So—you come to reception, they take your ID and return it to you when you leave the shift. It's probably not even legal. Secondly, you don't sign anything, no contract, you have nothing. You work through an agency, you have something signed with them, but not with that car plant. When you arrive, you have no idea if the shift will last eight, ten, or twelve hours."

"Christ!" Winona says quietly, "I'd tell them to piss off."

"You can, but you won't get paid. Plus, they'll accuse you of costing them by not showing up. You'll always get the short end of the stick in a place like that."

"And what were you doing there? Was it at least possible to muck around a little?" Winona blinks, pulls the mozzarella out of the fridge, slices it, and pours olive oil over it. "Take some, that's what Kamilko gets for exploiting us," she says with her mouth full, struggling with her piercings again.

"This is far from exploitation," Naďa says, smiling. "Do you know what a *hajzelpucér* has to do? You do. So, I'd rather do that than what I had to do there on my last shift. In fifty degrees, I had to scrub the fucking cylinders. First the floor and then the black sediment on the ceilings with concentrated acid. It ran down my arms, it burned, I almost lost it. And the foreman said he wanted it shiny like grandma's silver cutlery. And that he won't let me leave if he finds a trace of condensation. That he'll make sure I won't even get paid."

"The sadistic fuck, I'd throw the acid in his face."

"It did cross my mind. But I stuck to it."

"Did you hand in your notice?"

"We didn't even sign a contract, I already told you. I just didn't show up anymore, either in Volkswagen or the agency. Fuck them. I took the last pay check and ciao."

"And didn't you at least complain to the agency? For fuck's sake, it's not normal to abuse a person like that."

Naďa smiles and stays silent.

"Well, all's well that ends well, right?" Winona says, licking mayonnaise from her finger. She makes two wholewheat tuna sandwiches and pierces each triangle with a palm tree pick dramatically. "Tra-da!" She hands one to Naďa, though she refuses. She is not hungry and still not feeling well. But she is in a better mood now.

"I'm telling you when my classmate told me that they were hiring in this café, and when I made a deal with Kamil, and it was absolutely great after the first shifts, no problem. I was about to kiss Kamil's feet, that's how happy I was," Naďa says.

"I sucked his dick once," Winona says without thinking. She pauses, surprised by her own honesty. "And once I screwed him, on that table." She points to the stainless-steel work unit. The second confession indicates activity and self-will, even dominance. Giving a blow job, a waitress to her boss—that doesn't sound very dignified; but to screw someone, it's almost like using someone, to be literally and figuratively on top. Naďa can't exactly imagine, after a brief inspection of the crime scene, a place where they usually cut vegetables and pastries, how Winona could hump Kamil there. She frowns. Winona knows the position was different, and she knows Naďa also knows. They both blush.

"Why?" Naďa asks after a while. Neither of them had another topic for conversation, no bridge.

"I don't know," Winona says. "I really have no idea …" She shakes her head. "I guess I just wanted to … I guess I …" She is looking for a reason intensely. "Fuck! I don't know. I guess I'm just fucking dumb."

* * *

"Girls, why aren't you working? You've got to be kidding me. I was looking for you all over. I've told you a million times that even if there are no customers you should find something to do, wipe the tables, clean the coffee machine. Christ, I didn't think I'd even have to mention putting things away …" Kamil closes the lid on the mayonnaise and puts the rest of the food in the fridge and on the shelves.

When Naďa first met him, she was not enthusiastic—another boss, another guy. He was younger than her superiors before—in his mid-thirties, dark, his forehead growing at the expense of hair, belly hanging over his belt, a brushed leather jacket. She only had a female boss once, in a hypermarket. No jackpot, but at least she didn't humiliate her. At first, she wasn't sure about Kamil—mafia boss manners, she walked around him on tiptoe. But the longer she worked with him, the less she was scared of him—he was basically harmless. Even when he bent his subordinates' ears and reprimanded them, they were not stressed; they even openly pulled his leg.

Working in a café was also better in terms of money. Unlike the agency, Kamil paid her on time and did not cut the margin. Of course, it was only a minimum wage on paper—he gave her the rest in cash, the swindler. The tips made it worth doing.

"There are two customers at the bar who want to pay, at table six they already finished their food half an hour ago. Pepo can't manage it by himself. Should I go do your job for you? What the fuck do you think you're here for?"

"I'm coming, I'm coming." Naďa smiles at Kamil through the grimace, holding her lower back, scuffing her feet.

"Why are you bossing her around? Can't you see she's sick? She should be at home and you want to keep her here? Don't you want to give her acid, and let her polish the whole place? And then what, polish your dick as well?"

Kamil clearly does not understand Winona's outburst, nor does Naďa. The same goes for the rest of the people in the café—they all heard and look even more confused. The music stopped just at that moment; only one customer coughing at the cash register breaks the silence. Then, when he realizes he is the only one making a sound, he tries to silence the cough with one hand and raises the other to apologize. Kamil looks at Naďa, waiting for an explanation. Naďa is about to shake her head, to show him that she doesn't understand either, but she senses that the outburst may have helped her, so she just stares at Kamil. Under the growing pressure of glances, he stutters in a whisper: "I mean, if you need to, sure, go home. I told you one last time to come when you feel better. I thought you already did."

* * *

The problems began on Tuesday. It was the end of the exam period, the semester had not started yet and she planned to work as much as possible. It was just her legs that hurt, though she hoped it was nothing serious. She was just tired after only a few hours as if she had finished a 12-hour shift. She was just yawning, though just a few times a minute, hoping no one would notice. She did not sit down on the tram so she would not sleep through her stop. At home, she found her boyfriend reading. He saw she was not feeling well and wanted to help her, asking her what was wrong. Her body felt heavy; soon she could hardly stand his incessant questions. She was not getting enough oxygen, she could barely see through the yellow haze, she always perceived the disease in yellow shades, dryness, old skin, acid, bile. She felt faint and crashed into bed helplessly, without showering first, without brushing her teeth. She wouldn't even notice it if she died.

She went back to work on Wednesday. Her vision was poor and she felt sharp pain in her hips and ankles. About two hours before the end of the shift, one customer asked her if she was okay. At that point she gave up and made an excuse about having her period. Kamil was surprised but did not object; he just said "okey-dokey"— his voice pitched higher than usual.

On Thursday, she saw from the new work schedule she'd been given time off. Thank God—she would sort herself out. She spent the day lying down, alternating between her bed and the couch. She poured hot drinks with paracetamol down her throat, sweated, napped, prayed to get better quickly. She felt fine from time to time, but as soon as she got up to do something—to wash the dishes or even read something on the Internet—she had to go back into a horizontal position, to not move, take her foot off the gas pedal, just breathe, just breathe. In a daze, she mused about possible causes. She had rarely had flu, and never with such strong symptoms. She hadn't been working more than before, and the job was better, too. Stress—everyone always mentioned that first. Was she experiencing it? Or had she caught something? Where, from whom? How long was it going to last? What should she do? Should she go to the doctor when she was just tired? All day she hibernated in the nooses of such hollow reflections.

Friday's shifts were always the hardest. She never quite understood why, the café was not a disco or a nightclub. You wouldn't think that the consumption of coffee and cakes peaked at the end of the week, before the weekend. But it does. People come together, preparing for the weekend as if it started for them in the morning. *Expresso, latte, cappuccino, cheesecake, today I'm having a cheat day, weekend around the corner, hahaha, what kind of soup do you have, where can I find the cinnamon, what takes them so long, that's a slow-food, heehee.* She did not go out for coffee in her spare time.

Images of carefree customers ran through her head on her way to work. Like yellow-brown clouds of a sandstorm which irritate the eyes, fill the lungs, and grind meat down to the bone. Doped up with analgesics and caffeine, dig deep, dig deep, she had to go through till the end of that day. *You are rested, you have been lying around all Thursday.* Ironic smirk. *Rested? Are you fucking crazy? I am dy-ing.* She got on a half-empty tram and later, as more and more people crammed in the closer it got to the centre, she was looking out of the window. *Grannies, children, pregnant women, disabled, today you are going to stand. I'm not going to let anyone sit down in my place, over my dead body.* Her heart was pounding from the coffee, but her eyelids were drooping and so was her mood—from minute to minute like a submarine in free fall in the Mariana Trench. Determination too—with each stop the unpleasant audio signal announced that they had sunk by another kilometre.

When the door at her penultimate stop closed and the recorded woman's voice announced the location from where the sign of her workplace was already visible, the light bulbs of the logo hanging in the window, she almost stopped breathing. The ceiling of the tram was falling, the bang of the tracks was getting stronger, pouring into her ears like wax; people were growing and filling the space, pressing on her. Her insides were trying to force themselves out, she pushed them down. For a while, she didn't hear or feel anything, as if time had stopped. That image cheered her up for a brief moment, but the next moment "Vysoká" was announced. As if an usherette had called it out in front of a large audience, quietly awaiting a performance in which Naďa was supposed to perform Solo. But Naďa didn't get off. Her head sent a signal to her body, but it was too weak: her body was like a 10-ton statue of Buddha and sat completely motionless in an overheated plastic chair. From all the nerve endings that were supposed to set her leg muscles in motion, maybe three or four answered, rather reluctantly, embarrassed that they were going against the grain. A few minor characters were more successful in getting off and getting on. The mistress of ceremonies cold-bloodedly announced the end of the show, the curtain fell, only the tram moved and Naďa, still behind the scenes, felt relieved. She stayed on until the terminal and watched people leaving her in the warmth.

The driver parked the machine on the turn at the end of *Rača*, licked a cigarette, and shouted *get off!* The view of the wagon—at the back sat a homeless man wrapped in a puffer vest and long coat, even in his sleep tightly clutching the ends of yellow plastic bags, and in the middle, hunched Naďa. The driver raised her eyebrows: a nicely made up, beautiful girl, had she forgotten to get off? Naďa looked desperate, so the driver just waved the lighter in her hand and went out. When she returned from the break, she asked: "Wanna go back or what?" As if she was a taxi driver and Naďa could choose.

* * *

She is sitting hunched up in the dark and struggling to breathe. If she had to estimate the proportions of the gases entering her nose, she would give 1 to oxygen, and 8 to perfume. And yet Kristína only had a few items hung up here to dry! Naďa assigns one part of the smell to the washed and badly dried stack of towels, next to which she has curled up into a ball. *Aviváž*, it sounds so French and smells so homely, so Slovak. As soon as this crazy event is over—let it be soon!—she is going to tell her friend not to pour so much perfume on herself and that it is better to wash towels without fabric softener. *God, what is taking her so long? How much time has passed?*

A few minutes before, the bell rang; they looked at each other with a question in their eyes and both nodded their heads briefly: they were going for it. Kristína went into the hallway, Naďa squeezed herself into the closet in the bedroom. Finally, now she hears some noise. There is a conversation going on in the hallway, a few sentences. They are entering the bedroom. Her heart starts beating so loudly she is almost certain it can be heard in the room. In panic, she gasps for breath, no longer doubting they'll sense her presence. Both her hands are over her mouth and nose, her eyes are bulging. However, the two characters she sees through a small crack in the closet door are too intrigued by each other.

"So, is half an hour enough?" Kristína asks. "I am free for the next hour, that is, if you can last that long," she says coquettishly, professionally, provocatively. Naďa does not recognize her; if she wasn't nervous as fuck, she'd laugh.

"And even if you don't last, I can massage your back," she says, winking.

"No, half an hour is enough, thanks," he says, mumbling. He is maybe even younger than they are.

"Okay, as you wish," Kristína says. "It'll be fifty euros." The boy has the banknote ready; he was crumpling it in his hand. Now he is quickly stretching and straightening it, handing it to Kristína. She steps towards Naďa—moves the closet door and hides the fifty euro note in a drawer next to her crouching friend. Naďa is on the verge of fainting.

"Here you go, the bathroom's this way." Kristína hands the young client a towel.

"Do I have to? I took a shower before I came." He reluctantly takes the towel and holds it as if it was mouldy.

"I understand, but those are the rules. So, please." She is holding the handle on the open bedroom door and points her other hand towards the hallway, to the bathroom.

The lad goes, closes the door, they can hear him locking it and starting to shower.

Kristína rushes to the closet and nervously, with a forced smile, asks, "Well, what do you say? It could be worse, right? Around lunchtime, there was this fat man, almost retirement age. Even after the shower he still smelled like a tramp. I can smell him even now; can't you?" Kristína sniffs around with scrunched eyebrows, completely unfocused. Naďa smells and feels a lot of things, but panic dominates.

"Are you crazy?! He'll find us here. Get out!" And she pushes Kristína away and closes the door. She already regrets getting into this foolishness and cannot even blame her friend for it. She does not remember exactly where the idea originated; they probably figured it out together. And maybe she started it herself—she was curious and asked Kristína how the business was conducted, whether it was hard, what kind of guys were coming to her and stuff like that. It makes her feel worse; this bizarre situation is a joint responsibility. She is sitting in a closet like a spy, her neck and face burning red; she is exhausted from stress, her breath is shallow, she is looking through a crack at her friend who is about to get fucked for money. Kristína, it occurs to her, might even be regretting that she is going to have an eyewitness. A witness to an activity that no one else knows about and one she can't brag about. *Screw it, we are done!* Naďa says to herself coming to a conclusion that suddenly seems so clear. But though she wants to suggest it to her friend and slip out quickly, at that very moment, a showered young man enters the room and the sliding doors of the closet slowly close again.

Kristína quickly switches into role, sighing and mewling strangely, perhaps relieved that the moment she could change her mind has passed, perhaps trying to ready herself for the physical contact that is about to happen.

"Ready, handsome, are we going to do this?"

She sheds a short satin gown with Chinese patterns of flowers and dragons and leads the boy to bed by the hand. She kneels down on the mattress only in translucent underwear and pulls off his shorts. Naďa almost gasps when this releases an erect penis now just a few inches from Kristína's face. She remembers magazines from mom's drawer from a long time ago. Since she started sleeping with her boyfriend, she has not seen porn. And with her boyfriend, it was different than what she sees right now. They have always been in a darkened room; she does not even know why.

Meanwhile, Kristína has stripped herself and her client without embarrassment, they are already lying side by side. She is giving him a hand job, he's stroking her between her legs, trying to get his fingers in. "Ho ho ho, sweetheart, not so quickly, we didn't agree on this, fingering is not included." It's like she's a saleswoman in a greengrocer's saying we don't have tangerines. Naďa's friend has told her that sex in a private flat is a pretty standard business. The web goes into some detail about what and for how much. When they were sitting on the couch with her friend a few minutes ago, she really didn't mention fingering on the phone, Naďa could confirm that. She imagines a crazy situation—she would now step out of the closet, like a deus ex machina, and, like a referee, caution him for a prohibited action. *Yellow card for fingering—against the rules.* Of course, the issue could be solved by a surcharge. "Anal, pissing and cumming on face at my discretion and for an additional fee." When Kristína recited this on the phone half an hour before, Naďa almost choked on the mixture of nuts and raisins she was chewing. She knew where she was and what was going to happen, but all these details, and especially the matter-of-factness with which they were related shocked her.

This client is not interested in the 'above-standard' services. He is just starting to perform *basics* on Kristína, and they are included. No innovation, Naďa is looking at an absolutely basic form of mating. Kristína lies on her back with her legs spread out, supporting herself on her elbows, looking uninterested, as if she was sunbathing on the beach. Her head is tilted and she is looking in the opposite direction, not at the sliding door, but out of the window. In the end, she cannot resist, she checks on her client—he has his eyes closed—and then looks at Naďa. There is a subtle shade of red on her face. Maybe she is blushing with shame, maybe it is a natural reaction to the physical activity or to the excitement of having a spectator. Looking into the eyes of her friend, Naďa also feels something close to excitement for the first time since she's been here. *This isn't normal what am I doing here,* she tells herself, but at the same time feels a tingling in her belly not caused by stress. She wonders what it is like to experience an orgasm with someone.

The client turns Kristína onto her knees, and after a minute of thrusting from behind, slows down and straightens up, tilting his head back. Kristína confirms the end of the act, giving a series of very convincing sighs without taking her eyes off Naďa, who can no longer stand it and closes her eyes.

The fact that she came here showed the confusion that only recently but very quickly took over her life. Now, however, she is even more confused—she feels it in each cell of her body. Opinions, feelings, values, urges, fears, desires, shame, excitement—all of this is now mixing together and she is drowning in it. Like a stratospheric balloon, she soared quickly upwards, the earth soon hidden by clouds. The sky is wide, though, and dizzy, freezing, cracking, she is spiralling down to the ground again. The sexy costumes and towels in the closet circle around her; tensed, she holds the hanger rail until the part of her brain responsible for balance calms down. However, her heart is still racing, the heart of an assistant in the box of an amateur magician—waiting to see if the sword bypasses her or if fate ordains it to pass through the centre of her chest. Through a crack, she sees two actors of her private peepshow getting dressed without a word. The images engrave themselves into her life. Can she choose how? She is sweating.

* * *

"Oh hell, how I sweated." Kristína attempts a relaxed conversation as she crouches in the bathtub with the showerhead washing her armpits. Naďa has given up on usual standards of privacy and intimacy. After what she has just witnessed, sitting on the closed lid of the toilet and watching her naked friend taking a shower does not seem strange to her. She would like to make conversation, casually, but she cannot think of anything to say.

"Did you mind me?" she asks after a moment.

"What?" Kristína pauses for a while.

"Did you mind me being there? Watching you ... doing it."

"Not really," Kristína replies too quickly before even thinking about it. "Actually, yes, at the beginning. I was more nervous than during my first time. But then I relaxed. I guess I'm a pervert or something, but when I looked at you ... you know, during the act ... it was kind of hot. Certainly, hotter than having that rabbit on top of me. I'm actually grateful to you that I am not alone in this anymore; the secret was weighing on me. And I don't have to tell you about it in detail. I mean, how would you describe something like that? Embarrassing, isn't it?" She smiles and gets out of the bathtub, wrapping a towel around her body.

Naďa nods but stays silent, pushing a clothes horse with towels on it from out of Kristína's way. No wonder the towels are stiff when they hang here, in the bathroom without a window, with no form of ventilation.

"Half an hour ago, I couldn't remember how we got into this situation. But now I'm glad we did," Kristína says. "How about you?"

"More or less." Naďa is sorting out her thoughts. "One second I feel like it's totally, absolutely normal. You've got something a guy wants, you give it to him, he pays. And that I was watching—so what? I haven't seen anything unusual. No massacre, no science."

Kristína puts more mascara on her lashes and runs a wine-red lipstick over her lips; they walk into the living room and sit on the couch in front of the TV switched on all day. A stupid courtroom TV show is on. Both stare at the screen, Kristína taking handfuls of peanuts and nuts from a bowl on the coffee table and stuffing them into her ever-full mouth.

"But I'm also thinking about why you're doing this. And you know, there are millions of arguments against it. Risks, safety, health … Forget morals, but you know that you're going to have to keep it a secret forever, from everyone. When you find a man, you probably won't tell him. And then one day you'll be walking around, I don't know, maybe shopping somewhere with your kids, and you're going to run across the man who just came inside you. You're not going to expect it, neither is he. You're going to stare at each other in panic. Do you think your husband's not going to figure it out? Do you think you can hide it forever? And then you'll ask yourself if was worth the money." Naďa is trying to imagine such a life, to calculate the chances, the probability, the intensity of the tension. No result. "And why I assisted you in doing this today … oh boy, I really don't know. It probably isn't really normal, is it?"

"Your eyes didn't pop out, did they? So what? And don't worry, no one's going to figure anything out, I'm being careful." Kristína is in high spirits, just smiling and staying silent for a long time. She has earned some money and just got rid of part of the burden without having to awkwardly put the experience into words and sentences. It flashes through Naďa's head that she herself now has more torments and dilemmas than her compromised friend. But before she can think about it more deeply, Kristína interrupts her.

"I have something for you!"

She goes to the hallway to get her handbag and pulls out a packet, tears up the wrapping paper, and hands a book to Naďa. "You like to read, so have this." *Belle de Jour.*

* * *

There's a handful of people standing in front of the building. They talk, laugh and sneakily glance outside their groups wondering who else has come, whether they know someone—acquaintances or celebrities. A few individuals here and there light up and fill the air with smoke. A tram passes in close proximity. It no longer rattles like the old ones, but its weight on the bend still makes enough noise to catch their attention. Passengers look out, trying to decide what's going on, what concert is taking place today; the spectators outside look back at them, see the tunnel lit up from the inside, eye the tram until it gets lost around the corner.

She's not an ordinary listener. She is not in the group nor a lone smoker. It feels uncomfortable for a while—as if she had no reason to just stand outside on her own. She chases that idea away. She does not have to apologize for anything; she does not have to explain anything to anyone. She closes her eyes, breathes in, slightly bends her head back, and straightens up making a few vertebrae crack. Her protuberant chest attracts glances; several men look at her. Today, however, she is alone and will remain alone. As usual—she doesn't need company at a concert. She stopped trying to talk her boyfriend into going with her a long time ago; he hated going to concerts of classical music. And she didn't know how to be silent with other people which she needed to be. She can't imagine standing here with a friend and talking about school, clothes, men, anything. Not even about music. She wants to focus on the music, not anticipate it or analyze it afterwards. She wants to have physical communication with it. She's looking forward to it with her whole body.

* * *

She hated Music lessons but blamed herself for ending up there. She didn't have any expectations. It just sounded good when two of her classmates left after-school club sooner to go *to Music lessons,* and they articulated *Music lessons,* so tunefully, putting stress on the first word, making it sound almost like magic. So she also wanted

41

to attend and asked her mom to enrol her, and what wouldn't her mom do for her? At first, she asked Naďa what instrument she would like to play, and when she saw that Nadenka hadn't really thought about it, she laughed. *Piano*, the soon-to-be musician spat out angrily and without hesitation. She thought of it first because one of her classmates referred to it as a "royal instrument", and probably because she knew it from her mom's stories, too—she had danced with a piano playing in the background when she was young. Naďa had seen photos and a video; the quality was poor and there were weird streaks of colour in it, but it was still clear that mom could move beautifully and let the sequence of hammered tones guide her perfectly. When her daughter realized, she was even angrier—it was not her goal to please her mom. She should have thought more carefully before making her choice. She should have bitten her tongue or said bassoon, oboe, tambourine—literally any-thing but piano.

"Nadenka, you can't even imagine how happy you've just made me!"

Stress, however, came with her first public performance. When little Nadenka imagined that she had to play the most common beginners' folk song in the class, playing for people other than her teacher and her mom in the class, she thought she would pass out, not once, but *whenever* she imagined it, several times a day, for about thirty days before the performance. In her imagination, she saw it a hundred times: herself sitting on a high chair by the piano, unable to find middle C, let alone play anything. She played perfectly in class or at home, practising constantly. But the idea alone, just the idea of strangers' eyes looking at her in silence, at her and no one else, made her gasp for breath. It didn't matter that her teacher kept repeating that only a few people would be there—just parents of pupils and teachers. It didn't matter that her mom told her that even if she made a mistake by any chance—not that she would because she could play it perfectly—nothing, absolutely nothing would happen. Just the thought of making a mistake made her panic.

She didn't eat the day before the performance and didn't sleep well that night. Her ears had been ringing since morning, a red band halfway between two radio stations. All that remained in her memory was a collection of scenes: herself in different places at different times as if someone was transporting and exhibiting her. And then, finally, they exhibited her in an improvised concert room at a village school.

She and her mom were the first ones there. Naďa stood by the wall, staring at the door, praying that no one would come through it. She really wished cars would not start, that bus would overturn into a ditch on the road, that Maruška's grandmother would break her leg and Jurko's father get gastric flu. With each person coming in, her shoulders felt heavier and heavier, and the floor parted beneath her. She turned away as the tenth spectator walked in, she couldn't stand looking anymore nor bear counting. But the opposite wall was completely covered in mirrors—young ballerinas practised there—casting a reflection of other arrivals (in the end, there was about thirty of them) and of herself, a small, pale, stiff, miserable creature in the Red Sea. She almost lost it once she saw. From that moment on she only looked at the toes of her worn-out shoes.

Resignedly, she waited for her moment—when they called her name, her mother let go of her hand, stroked her back quickly, and Nadenka walked up to the piano. Her perspective had changed, she looked at herself from above, as if she was experiencing clinical life or clinical death—what was the difference anyway? She saw herself playing, her mom sitting in the second row, raising her clenched fists as high as possible so that her daughter could see she was keeping her fingers crossed for her. Her play was impeccable, completely automatic. The teacher later told her that she played too fast, but otherwise nicely. And that she could see now that there was nothing to be afraid of and that next time she could do it without stage fright, ok?

She wanted them all to be right and wished only to get used to performing in front of an audience. But her stage fright persisted and the same pattern kept recurring: pre-concert anxiety, partial paralysis, stress, an out-of-body experience—and then relaxation with mom in a cake shop eating dessert. After each concert, she was completely worn out, as if a thousand volts had passed through her.

She had played in eleven concerts and at the twelfth, she made a mistake. Not a big one; laymen in the audience probably didn't notice at all. But she did. Just before the end of the étude, she relaxed slightly, just a tiny bit, in the belief that she was almost done—and that's when she slipped up. Suddenly, everything changed. She came to herself immediately, in the strict limits of her body, all her senses turned on, the lighthouse lit up between her eyes and painted everything red, she watched the faded keys, already cracked at the edges, her sweaty hands, her mom smiling encouragingly, visibly forcing herself to do so, her teacher, who she played a four-hand étude with—she looked at her protégée and urged her to tune in, deliberately slowed down, nodded to indicate when the penultimate bar started, when the last bar started, but only two hands finished.

Her mom bought her two pieces of punch slice at the cake shop, repeating over and over that nothing had happened, that even the best people make mistakes, that she hadn't even noticed and other things that contradicted each other and—both of them already knew—were completely useless. Naďa was sorry she wouldn't please her mom anymore, no matter how much she wanted to. For several days she remained non-communicative or even catatonic. She answered in monosyllables, lying around, not playing, life popped out of her. On Tuesday morning the following week, the day when her daughter went to music lessons, her mom said with no preamble "You don't have to go there anymore."

* * *

Particles are gradually separating from the static groups of people and lonely individuals, the dynamics heading towards the entrance to the concert hall. Left hands are being raised, eyes checking the time, mouths signalling, heads nodding: they need to get to their seats.

Nada joins the throngs at the entrance, a mixture of perfume and tobacco in the remnants of summer sultriness, the clinking of jewellery, and incomprehensible speaking. Men act like gentlemen, guiding their partners with their arms, some of whom really need support, acting like ladies and seeking balance in their high heels.

A soft carpet leads her up to the first floor where she looks for a toilet, but sees a long queue, as usual. Without hesitating, she heads to the men's. One questioning look from the urinal, but most importantly—free toilet cubicles. Could it be one of the men smiling at her outside a while ago? Nada locks herself in the cubicle and silence follows. Locked from the world, even a square metre of insulation gives a sense of security: the body exhales, muscles relax. She does what she came there for, tears off a piece of toilet paper, dries herself, flushes, and goes outside. As she washes her hands, from the corner of the small room, just behind her, a voice says: "What a brave young lady."

Startled, Nada concentrates on the soap on her hands and tries not to show her fright.

"Are you here by yourself?" The deep voice resonates even in a small space.

The light of the lamp above the washbasin is dim, Nada does not even see a silhouette in the gloomy room. She focuses on the mirror but doesn't see anything without her glasses. She's mustering up courage to say something and opens her mouth, but at that moment another man enters. Taking advantage of the situation, she then gives the unknown figure a defiant look, shakes her wet hands in his direction, and leaves. In the lobby of the concert hall, her phone tells her she still has eleven minutes to forget that asshole: he must not spoil her experience. She breathes in, she can handle it.

* * *

For more than ten years music only brought her suffering. Radios in cake shops, swimming pools, fairs, annoying buzzing everywhere. Amateur bands, concerts full of untuned guitars and mistakes, the smell of beer and toilets, sticky floors, blue stage lights, potato chips scattered on the table, sweat and acne on the bartender's face, cracked Jack Daniels advertising boards, music from the bar, music from the concert hall, a cacophonous mix which although she wasn't the one playing still brought vicarious embarrassment. Every music associated experience burned indelible images into her brain.

Munich, however, changed everything. The city, spick and span on the outside, but smelling like a decomposing body on the inside, like the swill which she had to toss out in blue plastic bags several times per shift. She felt disgusted. How can people waste food like that, order something and then only take one bite?

Munich was hell. A huge *Bräuhaus*, always full of guests, constant stress. The chefs were mostly Germans, but the ancillary staff were from Eastern Europe—some Polish women and then *Yugos*. At the bottom of the food chain, Kurds and Ethiopian guys from a refugee camp near Nuremberg who worked there illegally. She never understood how it was possible in Germany. Her image of the country had been so different: she expected order and respect for the rules.

Her neurotic boss flew around the bar like a whirlwind, spitting commands out so fast there was no time to negotiate, *bitte, danke* and he was already gone leaving nothing but a draught and the smell of cologne and hormones behind. The German chef did his best to be nice, but he ignored problems and avoided conflicts. His aim was to please the customers and give them their food; he wouldn't have cared if there had been carnage in the kitchen. The assistant chef was from Slovenia but pretended to be German: serious and silent most of the time, so his accent didn't betray him. The other German cook was fat, with a dragon tattoo on his back which sank into his rolls of fat and emerged out of them elsewhere. It was said that a Vietnamese couple had once worked in the restaurant and the fat Dragon had had an affair with the woman. Her partner had then jealously stabbed her with a professionally sharpened kitchen knife, waited for her to bleed to death, then jumped out of the window. When Naďa worked there, the Dragon lived with another Asian girl and looked happy. It didn't take much for the biker Uwe to flip his lid, though. When a Bangladeshi colleague called him *Schwule* after they accidentally bumped into each other, they were immediately like fighting dogs who had been waiting the whole shift for this particular moment. They beat each other with huge wooden spoons used to stir soups in cauldrons, striking each other on their shoulders and heads until they bled over their ears and brows. The Yugoslavs, Poles, Kurds, and dark Ethiopian boys were okay and she got on best with them. She was sad when Yonas from Addis Ababa told her that he had a doctorate in electrical engineering from the Soviet Union. He had been doing well, but now was without his wife and three kids for the fourth year: he sent them money and called them once a week. She was disappointed to learn that he was sleeping with Ewa, a colleague from Poland, understood but at the same time, didn't. She felt sorry for the woman on the other side of the world whom she knew only from the photo in Yonas's wallet. He showed it to her proudly with a loving smile.

In this hole—in a place that seemed completely different on the outside—in this marasmus, in this gloom, the gleam of music shone on Naďa once again like a nova, its glitter bouncing off all the shiny shop windows of the main street and shaking the bells of the late Gothic Frauenkirche cathedral, bombing it for the second time, and rebuilding it—even more beautifully! The whole city was more beautiful when sound added intensity and flexibility to its shapes. Buildings were bodies, leaning, dodging, grimacing, shivering from the cold rain, exposing its cold walls to the sun.

* * *

The Skype call exhausted her once again. It was never easy to communicate with her boyfriend, but long-distance communication was a complete failure. She would call him from Munich's main station; there was a good wireless internet connection there. His expressionless face creature always stared at her from the cell phone display. One sentence answers and topics ran out quickly. He always waited for her to come up with something. She had gone, it was her doing—let her put the effort in. After she hung up, she exhaled, closed her eyes, and for a moment listened to the bustle of the nearby café, the footsteps of the passengers, announcements about platforms and train departures. She would happily get on one that would take her in any direction for at least a day.

She didn't take the usual route back from the station but hung around, postponing her return to the dark lumber room in the restaurant attic. She wandered until she suddenly heard the sound of an accordion suffusing the narrow street like a lure. She had encountered street musicians before, but this time it was different. Even the mournful tones sounded happy in the noise of a big city street, long before she even saw the musician. And when she noticed him a mixture of joy and wonder shook her. He wasn't handsome. He was an older guy with grey hair in a ponytail, jeans, and a waistcoat, with sleeves torn from his flannel shirt. But his smile was beautiful. Maybe he was drunk, maybe high on coke; his white teeth and glassy eyes were shining. She watched him for a long time; he played familiar and unfamiliar melodies, improvised, played around, did whatever he could think of—both with the instrument and with the listeners. Naďa devoured his music and stood there until he stopped playing. He looked at her: maybe he wanted to talk to her after he put his accordion away but she turned around and walked away quickly.

She went to see him whenever she could, stood as close as possible without him noticing. She fell in love. Not with a person, a guy, his music but with his symbiosis with the instrument, the barely discernible boundary between him and his accordion, the perfect union of the animate and inanimate. With his movements, of which the music was only a beautiful accompanying phenomenon. With his hands, pushing and pulling, fingers pressing on the keys and buttons, his bends of body, stamps of feet, posture, the unerring connection between mind and flesh, a sound achieved. He was tuned perfectly. He was not a brain, bones, veins and intestines but a single string that sounded into the endless space fearlessly and without stage fright, far beyond the horizon of this God-forsaken city.

Until one day he didn't show up. Nor did he in those that followed. It surprised her how fast she dealt with it. The lover of tired summer evenings had lifted the curse and she was no longer afraid of music.

She discovered a Mongolian trio of belly singers, an Irish guitarist, and a petite slant-eyed flautist from Asia in the streets of Munich. She even pardoned the reproduced music. When her African lover visited Ewa, her Polish colleague, she turned the volume on her old player up, until the tones of Radio Klassik were louder than the sex noises behind the thin wall. She went to the CD store and listened, mostly to classics and jazz: Rachmaninov, Górecki, Britten, Boulez, Coltrane, Lacy—she knew all of them by name. She also knew the faces of the sales staff, happy to let her use the well-thumbed CD player. While listening to music, the production of which she could not see, she indulged her imagination, visualizing musicians—whole orchestras of them—as they handled wood, plastic, metal with their body parts, fingers, mouth. From the music she was able to deduce their movements, the most important thing for her. Movement and body control were the greatest art. She found it out in a foul place and was happy. That was what fucking Munich was good for, that and the money she earned.

* * *

She finally sits in her seat, breathing deeply. Everything around her goes silent as the performance is about to start. It is now she puts on her glasses in order to see the artists properly. On the way to her seat, inching down the aisle, she was greeted by an elderly gentleman and replied in a nice manner. Maybe he was a professor, maybe a client. She straightens her back, stretches her neck, she is happy. She can see the whole space around the wing above a small bald guy in the first row. She imagines the movements of the tiny pianist, listens to the tones of the piano in her head. She can feel it as if it was live already—she has spent the last few days continuously listening to her music on YouTube. What will it be like when she finally sees and hears it for real?

The entrance—her efficient movements—precise steps, a smile, a bow. That poise before pressing the keys—waves of pressure dashing through the air, causing goosebumps, huge and bulging like scars. The 100 percent control. Naďa is about to burst out crying or laughing. Today, she does not have to worry about the concert failing—the tiny pianist convinces with every single cell of her body. The energetic first piece: the pianist riding a motorcycle, Naďa joining, wrapping her arms around her waist. Supersonic speed, curves, under pressure, but at the same time complete safety and faith; they rejoice and whoop a hundred times louder than children on the rollercoaster in the American amusement park where she spent a dreary summer with her offended boyfriend. Today there is no history, there is only the present. The second piece is slower, the ride is calmer, the motorcycle replaced by a boat. Meditation, Naďa falls into hypnosis, the rollercoaster becomes a temple. The music is sacred.

How she enjoys the piano! Asymmetrical instruments disturb her, hurt slightly, even when virtuosos play them. The accordion is on the edge, but the violin and flute trouble her. As does the cello: she loves the sound of it, but the movements of those playing it sometimes upset her. However, the little Japanese pianist is excellently symmetrical: she repeats Glass's figures over and over again, slowly unwrapping them. The Earth spins, the melody begins, develops, ends and does the same once more, slightly modified. The rainbow rises, the semicircle of colours becomes a full circle, coloured stripes rotate through the concert hall like the decoration of the old cake shop, smelling of Linz pastry, soft just right, neither brown or black, yet. It is easy to make a mistake and Naďa can tell when something goes wrong, can smell the burning. But tonight, no one is going to get burned either on the stage or in the audience.

Suddenly, an electric current passes through her. A man sitting in the row behind has put a hand on her shoulder and broken the circuit. She falls from her other dimension back into reality, flying at supersonic speed, the sonic boom deafening her. As if she had just woken up, she is disoriented for a while, wondering what it was. Her mind probably flinched more than her body because the people around still have their eyes on the stage and have not registered her fright.

"Are you telling me you really don't remember me?"

She looks around, there is a man behind her, leaning towards her but the angle and his immediate proximity make it hard to see his face.

"No," she says, answering the first part of the question—she doesn't want to tell him anything; her *no*, however, sounds more like a reaction to the second part—that she does not remember him. She is not sure. The voice seems familiar, as does the perfume, but who would keep all that in their head? She has only been in business for a few weeks: a wheel of dozens of faces, bodies, odours spins in her head with no intention of stopping.

"No? But I do remember you, you whore. Are you pretending to be a lady from a higher class?"

* * *

It's like a scene from an adventure story for teenagers—she devours the content of the pages under the blanket with help from her mobile phone light, enjoying the forbidden reading. When she lived with her mom, she didn't have to hide: she read whatever she wanted to. Even now she could theoretically, but she hides the book from her boyfriend.

"What are you thumbing through?" he asked when he found her lying in the crumpled bedding in the afternoon, magazines and books all around her.

"Nothing ... just some ... women's rubbish," she answered surprised. She hadn't even noticed him coming home. "*Vogue*," she shouts more calmly, hiding the book in the locker and grabbing the first magazine at hand.

She is approaching the end of the story—it is exciting, believable, perverted in the civility with which it describes the work of a luxury call girl in London. Kristína got her present just right, probably not even knowing how much. Or maybe she did. The notes of an intelligent young woman who, out of need, began to earn money in the sex business and then wrote anonymous blogs about her work until she was eventually forced to reveal her identity. In the book she describes with consummate ease the route to a job that good society despises: the unsuccessful search for a job in her field of study, debts, diminishing financial reserves, a sequence of coincidences. *A sequence of coincidences?* Every story is a construct based on selected, cherry-picked facts. We stamp excuses on all the shreds of our past. Life is a choice.

Life is a choice, Naďa tells herself quietly, in order to weigh the sentence in her mouth as she moves the centre of her gravity from one elbow to another. Her hand is numb and her back hurts, so much it burns. She does not know how she *chose* her health problems—this area is not included in her newly formulated concept of choices. But how she will face them *is* a choice.

Society despises prostitution, but Naďa's conscience is quiet. Maybe she should at least have some inhibitions or feelings of guilt. But she does not. She only feels physically that morality is something that has stuck to her from the outside, but does not belong to her: she has not signed the acceptance certificate. Culture, society? Naďa shakes her head, feeling no debt. She is well-raised: knees together, downcast eyes, greeting nicely, saying thank you, not answering back, not being rude, being polite, saying sorry, here you are. She has learned good manners. But with a shot of stabbing pain in her lower back, she can only think of one thing.

"Fuck it ..." The vulgarly expressed conclusion surprises her and she frowns, wondering if it really came from her. But after a short while, fully identifying with it, she nods to herself and replaces the three dots with a definite full stop. She is sure of the fact.

"Fuck it!"

She googles *Belle de Jour. The Intimate Adventures of a London Call Girl.* In addition to the cover of the book she has under her pillow, photos of an ordinary-looking woman pop up. Confident, a trace of melancholy in her eyes, pretty, but not exceptionally so, acne scars on her face. A normal woman who looks ... exactly like who she is—Dr. Brooke Magnanti, a renowned researcher with a doctorate in biology. Another photo, the same woman but known as Taro—on all fours, in erotic underwear, with a provocative smile. This is how she was photographed in her other role, on the website of the agency for escort services. This is her, too. Even after everything Nađa has read in the book, she does not condemn her, on the contrary, she feels tenderness and sympathy. And thirdly, video recordings of lectures—sessions with a now successful writer and political activist. This is another of her incarnations.

She puts her phone on the bedside locker. She would like to go to sleep but can't do it. She needs something to drink. With great difficulty, she climbs out of bed and limps into the kitchen. A passage that she read about five times resonates in her head. Belle de Jour/Taro/Dr. Magnanti answers a client who asks her why she makes a living from sex. "Well, I guess I'm one of those people who are able to do something just because they can't think of a reason why they shouldn't." She reads the sentence for the sixth time—*to be able to do something just because she doesn't know why she shouldn't.* Such a stupid and clumsy argument, but there's something about it.

The sight of the fridge depresses her. Invoices lined up in perfect symmetry hang from it with the help of magnets. Unpaid ones, naturally; paid ones are ticked off with a green marker and placed in a desk drawer; the ratio of unpaid ones is increasing. There are only a few things in the fridge, all a *Value* brand from a nearby supermarket. She opens a litre carton of orange juice and drinks the last of it. Overly sweet, no pulp, disgusting. Even the cheapest juice sold in plastic gallons in a Colombian store in New Jersey tasted better.

She is pissed off. Not that she expected her boyfriend to provide for her—she has never had chance to get used to a man's care in her life. But he could have contributed more. At the beginning of his university studies, he worked part-time at a state-owned firm, ran a network and helped older office workers discover the basic functions of Word. To this day, Naďa does not know why—when was it, a few months ago?—he quit. Since then, he has only been doing casual work at intervals that are getting progressively longer. Sure, she has been cancelling shifts recently, but for good reason. She can barely move. But what's his excuse? Always behind the computer, he won't even look at her.

She breathes in deeply: there is cracking in her upper spine and the joints of her ribs. She walks back to bed, but even routine activities require effort now. She cannot feel her legs; they are swollen and feel heavy; the floor feels like it is no longer there and she can barely keep her balance. Her mattress is sagging. There are days when she doesn't even get out of bed. This is the second several-day long period of rheumatic pains, the first was a few months ago. Then she got better and hoped it would not happen again. But the weariness and bone-stabbing came back a week ago.

She closes her eyes and wants to think about something nice. She was watching a documentary about Norwegian fjords; she would like to go there sometime. She wanted to share the idea with her boyfriend—just to mention it, she knew they didn't have money for it—but when he came home, there was no opportunity for it. Now she imagines him on the deck standing by the Norwegian flag: postcard scenery, fresh air, seawater splashing alongside the boat, he poses stiffly. He doesn't like to travel, but he would probably like it there.

Her sleepless mind replaces the idyll with a scene from her second visit to the stuffy, overheated doctor's office.

"Doctor, tell me, what's the worst scenario? What do we want to rule out?"

The young doctor with red spots on her face, dressed in a pale green fleece sweatshirt on sweaty white scrubs, furrowed her brow.

"Right now, it's hard to say exactly. It could be some kind of virus, an orthopaedic disease, I don't want to scare you or suggest anything. Let's wait for the results, then we'll be wiser."

A nameless threat is a challenge to the imagination. Cancer? Defeated patients in bed with tubes up their nose and other orifices. Something worse? What could be worse? She grabs her phone from the bedside locker again and wants to google something, but pauses—what is she going to tap in: "terrible diseases"? She puts it away quickly and turns around. She is just a short distance from her boyfriend's face. He is always so eerily quiet when he sleeps. When they spent their first night together in his parents' cottage, she got scared in the morning and, following TV stereotypes, put a watch under his nose to see if he was still breathing.

She has been lying in bed for seven days. A week is not very long, so she is surprised how quickly a person lets go and leaves the old routine behind. She wakes up, then after a moment of boredom, falls asleep again. She does not keep track of the day. When she is awake, she reads anything, forgetting about the content almost immediately. She hobbles around the apartment, counting the floorboards. She can recite the order of television channels both in ascending and descending order. She made a pact with a pensioner from the ground floor; together they stare out of the window at the street. She has found out that it is possible to spend hours doing that. She analyzes the rules of regularity and deviation of life on the street in front of the block. She drinks something, although she's not thirsty; at least she'll have to go to the bathroom. She waits for her boyfriend, waits for him to distract her then gets angry when she sees him sitting at the computer for hours. He asks her if there is anything he can bring her, if she wants anything, to eat, to drink. He cleans, he does the shopping. He is practically perfect. But as soon as he has done all the housework and fulfilled Nada's biological needs, he clocks off and sits at the computer. It's stupid to reproach him: he's doing everything that needs doing. But how about doing a little extra? He could lie down with her, touch her, simply talk to her. Or he could read something interesting from the paper out loud and they could discuss it. They could watch a movie together, he could entertain her, he could simply do something beyond the call of duty, just on his own fucking initiative. It would be nice if he wasn't just like a hospital orderly!

Hospital. That risk has been hanging in the air since her first visit to the doctor, after her first absences from school and work. Now, after her first "relapse"—as the doctor called it—the likelihood of hospitalization increases. Even though they don't talk about it, they both feel it coming. He is stressed more than she is. He limits contact to the bare minimum and escapes into the world of electronic networks.

* * *

I have just said ciao to a 20-year-old client. Sporty, fair-haired, tall—it could be worse ;-). Despite that, I prefer older clients. Younger ones are either overly timid and need to be led by the hand, and I myself am more nervous with the nervous ones. Or they're like this one—they mistake the private flat for a gym. My crotch has been pounded, once again I'll be sore for two days. Hard-earned money, I really feel like I deserve it.

The rules don't apply one hundred percent, but basically, older men are more perverted. I don't mind, I've got used to it. On the other hand, they are less performance-oriented. They are often nicer, they want the pleasure to be mutual—which is impossible in most cases, but it's the thought that counts, I feel more dignified. There have also been a few real gentlemen who treated me like a lady. They took me to dinner, held the door open, slung their coat over my shoulders before the cab arrived. I didn't deny them sex, how could I? After all, that's what they pay for, I'm not naive. Business rules must be accepted by both sides.

What I like most is that older gentlemen often want to talk. Without communication, this job would lose its meaning for me. If I couldn't write about my experience, I would have to quit. And it is easier to write when I can talk. And getting paid for sex is easier when I can use my experience to add to my blog. Anyone can be a whore. Working in the sex business to create a brand that will appeal (and not just a sexual one) sounds better. My rationalization? Maybe. Does it bother you? It doesn't me :-)

* * *

The cursor flashing on the screen hypnotizes Nada and she does not know how to continue the blog. She started it intending to tell two amusing stories about older gentlemen, the Inspector and the Coach, as the girls call them.

The first one was a regular who used to come every month after the pay-check. A recent retiree, employed in a private security service, he always came in a different garb: once in a shell suit, once in a trench coat à la Columbo, once with a hat and fake moustache, another time in an orange suit worn by road repairers. The girls were looking forward to Inspector and had fun guessing what he would be wearing next time he showed up. When he arrived, he leaned on the inside of the closed door—*I made it!*—and chose between the girls like a sultan, a wide smile on his face. He was generous; every girl fussed over him. A legend, a talisman—rumour had it that the one he selected would be lucky for a whole month.

Coach was less popular—and violent. Nothing terrible, far from the limits of unacceptable, but still. Plus, he put negative reviews on the girls' profiles. He posted them anonymously and thought the girls didn't know, but they worked it out based on details he gave. In addition to his aggression, he spoke weirdly using football comparisons and sports terminology during sex. They found him on the web—he managed the national youth team.

She wanted to present the mini-profiles of these two in a blog post about older men, but it was Belly that was really on her mind despite her not wanting to write about him. When she met him, he was a customer like everyone else. He came, no extra demands; he paid; he left. The same scenario the second time. It was common for clients to return. During their third time together, he asked her what her real name was. *Nada,* she replied in spite of the unwritten rules. She herself was surprised. Nice name, he said. She felt the urge to break the long silence, so—again despite the rules—she asked him the same question. Belly, he told her and she burst out laughing. She was expecting anything else, a first name or a rather more flattering nickname.

"They really call you that?" she said. "You're not obese."

"It's my last name—well almost. And everyone calls me that. Even my ... You can call me that, too."

He had disarmingly big eyes, a big sad dog.

Naďa averted her gaze, pulled herself together. She left the challenge unanswered; healing lonely hearts was not on the agenda. She escorted him to the door, but when he arrived a few weeks later, she unexpectedly greeted him—*Hi Belly!*—with a smile.

Handbooks in the field of the sex business are not published. If they were, they would certainly contain a strict ban on any other than commercial customer relationships. But in practice, all kinds of things happened; Naďa even heard about a marriage resulting from it. A few times she wondered if she wasn't letting Belly get too close—figuratively speaking. But she did not know the answer to that. Anyway, she could not like all her clients equally, could she?

Belly always paid for an hour. The first round went very quickly, the second took a little longer, but otherwise, they spent maybe forty-five minutes talking, joking, teasing each other. He was an excellent listener; he reacted with honesty, questioned with interest—and sometimes didn't even have to ask. She lost her professional vigilance. They developed a relationship that was certainly not lover-like, but it was intimate. He stroked her cheek, traced circles around her birthmark and kissed it. She giggled at his ticklish stubble like a schoolgirl.

"So what exactly do you do for a living?" Naďa asks, counting in her head how many times they have now met.

"Oh, I'm in the media." Instinct also works on the client's side; Belly goes into his shell for a while. He thinks, he evaluates—what kind of risk is he taking when he answers?—finally, he does: "For a newspaper, I'm an editor. I've never done anything else in my life."

"Why didn't I guess? I confide in you like in a priest during confession … and you actually tap me for information. I hope you're not going to write a feature about all this."

"And what would I write: that I have second-hand info from a friend? From a cousin?" They laugh.

"I write too, a little." She is skating on thin ice, but she misses having someone to talk to about it.

"And what do you write?"

"Stories. Well, short stories to be precise." She turns her face away. She's afraid she's making a mistake.

* * *

He waits for her at the table, as always when they meet in a restaurant, which means he has arrived early, because Nađa is usually punctual. Pieces of ice are melting in a whisky glass; he is only sipping cold water now. He considers it courteous to wait for a lady to order wine: whisky doesn't count, a man can't stay thirsty.

"What do you feel like drinking today? Semi-dry as usual?" Nađa smiles slightly, still unaccustomed to the familiarity. She nods. She likes semi-dry wine. The waiter sits her down formally at the table, its tablecloth reaching to the floor. They study the menu without a word. Mineral water, rolls, butter, and three miniature bowls with spreads are brought in the meantime.

"You know what I'm thinking about?" she asks, without looking up from the menu. He raises an eyebrow and shakes his head. "What I'm imagining?"

"Tell me."

"All the delicacies in my mouth that I'm going to order from this incomprehensible menu."

He looks mystified.

"How they'll mix with my saliva, how the soft texture will roll over my tongue, bring my taste buds to life and send signals all over my body. How I'll close my eyes and feel pâté in my little finger. I will shake from all that traffic in my body, so much excitement, so many impulses."

He does not even bother to pretend anymore; he clearly does not understand where this is going.

"The chewed-up mass in my mouth slips down my throat, fills my stomach. The stomach is an important organ, you guys know that. It purrs quietly when it's full and pours poison into the whole body when it's empty. I'm hungry, shall we order now?"

Today, she does not want to be a nice accessory who just smiles. Today, she does not have to let herself be led by a leash like a dumb cow all evening. She will not be a bimbo without an opinion who is astonished by a man's awesomeness and blinks so that her eyes don't burn from the dazzle. She is here to eat well and to have a nice conversation. And she wants to set the direction and tone of the conversation for a change. That's why she provokes him.

"Of course. Go ahead, what do you fancy?"

"Pumpkin soup. Butter fried zander. Green salad. And what about the wine?"

"Yes, semi-dry. Anything specific? Are you going to choose, or should I?"

"You choose, you've drunk more than me after all," she says, laughing. The equilibrium at the table has now been set; the evening may begin.

Today is their fourth time together in a similar situation. They switch in choosing restaurants and always go to a different one, trying them out. He chose the first one—an upmarket establishment near the centre with classic Central European cuisine. It was a strange evening, but after an uncertain first half-hour and a few decilitres of Frankovka from Limbach, they had a great time. He paid. She was also hunting for her purse, but he shut her down with one gesture and said: *Your turn next time!* with a cocky smile. Two weeks later she insisted: *Today is my turn to repay you!* They were in a Japanese restaurant which she had chosen and though he hurried to pay again, she honoured her word—she was in charge that night.

The third time they went to a Hungarian bistro between Bratislava and Šamorín. Today, they found themselves in a restaurant in the city centre, which, according to information on the menu, "fuses the world's cuisines."

He has been caught off guard, surprised by her sharp *entrée*. She is sorry, but it's time to cut the umbilical cord of a relationship they are pulling from the recent past. The fact that she paid the other day was not enough; he still acted like her benefactor. She didn't like it anymore and wanted him to understand that their relationship had changed—they were no longer a client and a girl from a private flat; he was not paying her; they were not having sex. It was not clear what kind of bizarre relationship they were cultivating, but she wanted them to be equal.

The last time they met in a private flat was when she told him she was writing. He was curious; she was defensive.

Of course, she was—the readership of her blog had grown exponentially. Clients who were interested in her articles started contacting her and wanted to meet.

"Good afternoon. I just … I don't know whether I have the right number … I am looking for Mercedes. The one writing a blog about … I only found this number, on Aphrodite or something. Is it you?"

Naďa quickly hung up. It should have occurred to her. She blogs about the sex business; she wants to catch their attention. She is good at that and that leads to men trying to track her down. They google Mercedes and private sex; it doesn't take a genius.

She changed her phone number and also deleted her profile. She had to alter tactics and divide her identities. From now on, Mercedes existed only on the blog. Her experience and finances now come from a private flat where she is Sara.

"Sara? Really? Don't you want to change it for something more original?" Kristína asked her, as she uploaded Naďa's new photos onto the web. Her blurred face was standard, but she had also had her birthmarks retouched, and her hair dyed dark black. Naďa was thorough in her identity change.

"You're right, I don't!" Naďa had done her research and Sara wasn't a random choice—probably this name was the most popular in her field; she needed to blend in.

Only Kristína knows her double identity. Maybe a few more girls would remember her but the turnover at the private flat is high: she and Kristína are the oldest ones in the "business". New colleagues already know Naďa as Sara. Theoretically, there are clients who had been with Mercedes and might see a resemblance between her and Sara. Naďa will never completely eliminate the risk. But she has done everything cosmetics can do to minimize it.

Anyway, she has no intention of widening the circle of insiders, not even in the case of Belly. The last time they lay in bed, he massaged the sore spots between her shoulder blades and spine and tried all sorts of tricks to learn more about her writing. He was a good masseur, psychologist, and probably also journalist—but she resisted. She kept changing the subject and inventing things!—how as a child she wrote a diary then a few short poems for a school magazine. But what does she write now? He wouldn't let it go. Some rubbish just to go in the drawer afterwards, she replied and changed the topic—she began to talk about her father. How he too was a journalist, that she probably inherited it from him. She talked about where he worked and how he ended up where he is now.

"I knew your father, we worked together," he said at the very end of their first dinner while looking into a tall crystal bowl even though he had already scraped from it the last of his Somlói galuska.

"I figured that out the last time we were together," Naďa said, offering him the rest of her dessert. She held her stomach to indicate that she was full; he shook his head and exhaled.

"How come?"

"You stopped massaging me. You froze and got lost in your thoughts."

"That's right, the idea chilled me to the bone." He smiled and shook his head. "And I still find it bizarre, don't you?"

She shrugged her shoulders and finished her dessert after all.

* * *

Her father was buried deep in her subconscious. She knew his voice intimately, but was it possible to have feelings for a man whom she hadn't actually met? To relate to a voice recording? Mom always spoke highly of her husband, even when she talked about him leaving them. Almost as if she felt sorry for him, instead of herself. She often said, *after everything that happened to him.* Naďa made a legend out of her stories. She fantasized about him as about a fairy-tale character; he dubbed himself on the cassettes.

However, with each new story, her father comes to life. Mom had never told her the stories she heard from Belly during their dinners. Motion is added to his static voice; two dimensions become three; fantasy unfolds; memories that she didn't even know she had emerge. A real person takes shape in her imagination, her biological father, a person whose decision meant she was born and exists, one of her two most important people. He lives somewhere far away, he is passive towards Naďa, and yet he is now crawling to the centre of her attention from the periphery. He shouts at her on a grassy meadow: "Let's play, Nadenka, catch me!" Is it for real that such a memory comes to her mind right now? Or does she just deduce, stylize, overidealize? The smell of an old leather waistcoat of his left in the cottage suddenly blends with the image. She would wear it over her coat during freezing winters. When the snow on it melted, the leather released smells and aromas. Only after decades does she match them with her father. Her curiosity is aroused.

* * *

She went home for the weekend the week she had dinner with Belly for the third time. She didn't even take her shoes off. Just ran straight into the drying room. An old wooden chest, a suitcase, her mom called it, had always stood right behind the door; the paint, once wine-red, perhaps, was now cracked and peeling. The chest was not very useful: her mom always just went around it, put the laundry on it, bumped into it. When little Nadenka first opened it and went through its contents, she only found a bunch of yellowed cuttings, tapes in plastic wrappers, a small cassette recorder and a Walkman with leaking batteries that the whole chest smelled of. Dad's stuff, was all she was told whenever she asked.

Whole months passed when she didn't even touch the case but there were moments when it turned into a magic box. There had to be treasure somewhere inside, Nadenka was sure of it. She plugged the recorder in and listened to her father's voice and the weird noises on the recordings—at first just because she was bored. Later she wondered if they were codes and if there was any key to them. When she learned to read, she studied the cuttings and learnt them by heart.

She hunted amongst the heirlooms—but what exactly did she want to find? Could she look for answers without questions? The identity of a growing person is unstable at crucial moments, fidgets a lot, has to be calmed down. She had nothing else to do, so once in while, she went through his artifacts, quoting texts she didn't understand, soaking dry roots in water.

"Mom, where's that tape?" Naďa systematically unloaded the contents of the chest.

Mom took a deep breath, maybe hoping to buy herself some time by asking what tape? But when their eyes met, she gave up.

"It has to be there somewhere, Nadenka. And why are you looking for it anyway?" The small wrinkle above her eyebrows deepened and curved.

"No reason, I just remembered something."

"And what might that be? Is something wrong, darling?"

A child notices such things—the only cassette among hundreds taped over with layers of brown elastoplast. Nadenka always held it in her hands, studied it against the sunlight, but in the end put it down and listened to the others instead. It wasn't until she was fifteen that she asked her mom if she could listen to it.

"All right then," Mom said with resignation, picking up a knife, carefully cutting through the tape in one stroke and unlocking the plastic lid of the cassette.

* * *

She sits opposite her father's old colleague, unfolding and folding her napkin over and over. There are yellow stains from turmeric and Hokkaido pumpkin on it, plus red ones from her lipstick. She stares into her plate, using a fork to smear it with her leftover sauce. A fusion of which national cuisines was this food? she wonders. Does Belly visit other girls, too? There is a draught here—where is it coming from? She takes a deep breath, reaches into her handbag and hands him a Walkman with headphones.

"Listen to this."

* * *

My dearest, dearest Nadenka!

I have been sitting here, alone at the cottage since lunch, wondering where to start. I don't even know if you will ever listen to this recording. A pathetic goodbye, isn't it?

/longer silence, creak of the tiny oven, raking of a fire poker, cracking of dry wood/

I keep thinking of you. You're at home now, with your mother, helping her make sandwiches. You're looking out of the window and asking when the sparklers will appear in the sky. And maybe you're also asking where your daddy is. And instead of being with you, I'm here alone, dozens of kilometres away from you. I have my reasons, and I believe they're good ones. Hopefully one day you will understand and forgive me. Otherwise, it wouldn't make any sense, sweetheart. Just the idea of it destroys me.

/he sniffs and blows his nose into a handkerchief/

Ivan Lesay

*Let me clarify my reasons—well I'll get to them soon and tell you
everything, just give me a moment, just a little longer. Let me remember
all the nice things. As you know, your name is from the Slavic word
for hope and we chose it deliberately in the belief that a new era would
begin after your arrival. I confess I had no idea what to expect from
parenthood. I even remember not expecting anything. When your mom
told me she was pregnant, I was happy. Death is mourned, conception
and birth are celebrated, right? I was looking forward to it, but it all
came from the outside. Inner joy? Well I was hoping that would come
with your birth. But it didn't. I looked at you, a crying ball of flesh, and
felt nothing, only regret. Not about you but about the whole of humanity.
How ridiculous and defenceless we are when we come into this world!
And how ridiculous and defenceless we are when we live and also when
we die.*

/a chair moves, footsteps can be heard, he sits down again, there is
a crack and slicing, he is probably cutting an apple/

*And then it happened—I slowly began to love you. Our relationship
grew stronger with each new day. I, a stinky, pot-bellied, hairy fellow /
his voice cracks/ And you a tiny, sweet-smelling, rose-coloured, toothless
pet. I felt like a sculptor. But when I think about it now, I was the one
posing and you the one creating.*

*With your mom, I felt love immediately. With you, I received it in
doses that grew stronger every day. The most beautiful thing was to discover fun with you. How does something like that come alive in such a
small human being? We'd hide a bootee under the blanket and pretend
we didn't know where it had gone. It was such a silly game and yet we
had such fun. You couldn't talk back then, but you could laugh and cry.
You understood the essence of life. Learned words … learned words only
dissect reality and mask perception. There is really nothing more than
laughter and crying in this world.*

*Two years, a drop in the ocean of eternity. But two years of memories
with you that could hardly fit into two eternities. Is it really only two
years? When you listen to this, you're probably a big girl. How old are*

you, sixteen, eighteen, twenty? I'm trying to imagine you. It's not easy to stretch the features of a two-year-old girl in time. I know you are beautiful—what a shame I can't see you!

/a click, the recording stops, and after a while starts again/

I wonder whether it is really necessary for you to hear my defence. I'm sure your mom has told you something about why I left. I have no reason to question whatever she told you. Her version is certainly closer to the truth than mine—and that is my problem. I just want to explain how hard it is for me to leave. To leave you both.

I am sick in many ways. I am bad. And lately, kind fate has turned its back on me. I'm not bitter about it, because before this, my life used to be happy and its highlight was, and in fact still is, you. That's more than enough.

There's something that has been growing on my tongue for a long time. It hurts more and more but I don't mind the pain. I fear that it might be cancer and that it might consume me. Well, I'm not afraid, I'm sure. What else could it be? Your mom begged me to have it examined, to see if it really was cancer and if something could be done about it. And I told her that I'd gone that it was cancer and that no, nothing could be done. But I lied and never went to see the doctor. I don't need anyone to tell me that the sun is yellow, that day is followed by night that the lump on my tongue is cancer.

I have fewer and fewer ideals these days. There were times … I was convinced that I had them deep inside, that they were the essence of me. But I was probably wrong. They are just veneers, labels. I stand in the flow of a mountain river and they peel off me and float downstream. They don't keep me warm and the water removes whatever heat they gave me; I'm getting colder and colder. Ideals are contagious and harmful. You acquire them at an early age, guard them, fight for them. You believe you can live a better life with principles, be a better person. You believe you have something to hold on to, that you have a compass. And then, you have absolutely no idea from where, a gale force wind comes along and snaps you in half like a tree. In a second. And you wonder whether it wouldn't be better to be a weaker but more malleable tree which can withstand such a wind? Sometimes you have to bend, to move out of the way. Look at me, making all these excuses for myself. The truth is, I sold out. Yes—I cashed in on what I know best: words. I'm not a bendy tree; I'm a weed. Oh, my girl, why am I telling you this? It's hard—I want to explain my decision to you. At the same time, I don't want to shatter your illusions. Ideals—I'm afraid mine will all go. What kind of person would I be then? What kind of a role model would I be for you? It didn't work out for me, but with luck and courage, it might for you.

Have I ever wanted anything else than for you to be happy? Memory is crooked, you can't count on it. I could swear I wanted your happiness even before I knew your mother. And I wanted to safeguard you both. But I made a mistake though. I don't want to bother you with details.

Your mom ... we loved each other, and still do, at least I think so. But we didn't always behave nicely to each other. I imagine you with a baby face, but as you listen to this, you are definitely grown up and know a lot about the world. You must know that people sometimes seek pleasure, recognition, joy, and other things in the arms of other people ... outside their primary relationship. God, it sounds so embarrassing, but how else do I tell it? Believe me, I've been thinking hard. Well it happened to us ... though neither of us planned it. And I suspected that one of my very good friends was involved, someone who meant a lot to me.

/glass clinking, sound of tap, loud swallowing/

I drink. Well, I did. And I drank a lot, believe me. The strange thing is that I've been dry now for several weeks, even without having to try. Since I decided to go, I've been peaceful somehow, even optimistic. I don't need to drink anymore. Water's enough.

/two glasses clink together/

Only now though ... Sometimes there were whole days that I couldn't remember, especially after I started taking medication. Painkillers—my *tongue hurt; my soul hurt. I took all kinds of pills just to fill my mouth with them. Once I read one of my articles and couldn't even remember why and how I wrote it. The editor called me to ask if I really wanted it published and laughed, thinking it was just a joke. I quickly went through all the papers on my table and found it there: my language, my diction, my signature. There was no doubt about the authorship. I could barely breathe and was pouring with sweat. I hesitated for a second, forced myself to laugh, then tried to make out it was just an April Fool out of season—I got you!*

I had mental blanks. And when I found out about my behaviour— by chance, later, from others—it was inexplicable to me. I'd become threatening! Someone else had come to life in me and I'd lost control. I don't know if you remember this ... now, when ... if you are listening to this. You were surprised when I came home one day from a long walk with Duňka—she was covered in bandages and badly bruised. I told mom and you that she was hit by a car and I had to take her to the vet. You stroked her carefully, and put Pukino, your favourite teddy bear, in her bed. She was hurt and looked sad but at the same time, she was happy that everyone was paying attention to her. She bit the bandages, played with them, and looked at me with those eyes of hers in disbelief. She hadn't been hit by a car. It was me; I beat her in cold blood for some-thing trivial, I don't even remember what anymore. I guess she got in my way. So, I kicked her. She whined. I kicked her again and she whined even more. I shouted at her to make her stop, but she kept yowling even more and I beat her and kicked her like crazy. The way she was cowering, hiding her tail, too afraid to look at me, how she watched what I was doing from the corner of her eye, it made me so angry. I have no idea how long it lasted, maybe a few seconds, maybe a minute. Fortunately, no one saw it.

I would never hurt you, never! But I won't forget the look in your mother's eyes when she came home the day before yesterday. I was almost done, only a thin strip of hair remained on your head. And then mom snatched the shaver from my hand and asked me what the hell I was doing, quietly but emphatically. So, I told her you had lice in your hair and it was the best way to get rid of them. Are you crazy? she asked me about three times. While there were just the two of us there, you had a lot of fun looking at yourself, at your bald head. But after your parents' argument, you cried when you looked in the mirror. In the end mom cut off the last of your hair to prevent you from looking like an Indian. That was the moment when you started yelling. As if she was scalping you. I just stood there, baffled, but I realized I shouldn't have done it. And I realized that mom wasn't just reacting to this one episode. She didn't ask if I was crazy metaphorically—she meant it. And I can't blame her.

That's it, it is time to stop bothering you. These are my reasons. But back to your happiness—there is nothing I want more. It's exactly what I said when your mother's older sister, Auntie Péťa, once paid us a visit. She cut me off and said that a two-year-old doesn't need happiness. A breast and a dry diaper are enough. I disagree. I know that, even at such a young age, you are already very perceptive and can feel what's going on around you. And I, sadly, am a disruptive factor, someone who upsets the apple cart.

So be it. I fought and lost the battle and now I have to rest. Suffice to say it makes me happy to think that part of me will stay alive in you ... who will be happy ... all your life. I love you, Nadenka!

* * *

His eyes water, he is lost for words. He listened, stopped the tape clumsily several times, looked at Naďa, took off his glasses, rubbed his face. Then again put his glasses and headphones on and continued listening.

"Everything all right, sir?" the waiter asks, a cloth napkin draped over his left hand, leaning too close to Belly, his back as straight as an ironing board as if he was trying to make sure he really did have tears in his eyes. Belly moves away, dismissing him with a gesture of annoyance.

There is silence for a while. You can only hear muffled conversations from the neighbouring tables and the clanging of cutlery, Strauss's *On the Beautiful Blue Danube* is playing quietly through the loudspeakers. Naďa is pretty sure it was on when they came in; they probably play the same CD over and over again. She wonders if it was a good idea and doesn't even know what she was hoping for, what she expected from him. What can she expect from this pathetic guy who happened to be her father's colleague and also happened to be paying her for sex? She is angry with herself because she can't work out her own motives. Today, she came intending to be the dominant one, to redress an unbalanced relationship. *Relationship?!* God, what is she thinking? He is an ex-client; is she going nuts? If Kristína or the other girls knew, they'd make such fun of her!

At the same time, she is experiencing something new, and—although she is shaking and unsettled—she is grateful for it. The man looking at her compassionately from the other side of the table has helped her find a shaft of memory and identity that was buried until now. She is indebted to him for every piece in her history. It is not his fault that he knew her father, it is not his fault for choosing her in that flat and that, in some deviant way, they suited each other. There was no malice behind their becoming acquainted: it was just a coincidence. Belly has a few annoying manners—he patronizes her—but he's not a bad person. So, it's okay, Naďa reassures herself, that she is redressing their relationship tonight—their *platonic* relationship—while repaying him for all the details of her own story she wouldn't know without him. She reflects on her choice of words—*redressing ... platonic ... shaft of memories.* If she was writing a blog, she would put quotation marks around every word.

"I don't know what to say," he says, sniffling.

"You don't have to say anything." Naďa takes the Walkman back and shoves it into her handbag. Her head is bowed and her hair covers her face. "I don't have a lot of friends, you know." She thinks about her boyfriend, Kristína, her ex-colleagues from the café, her current ones from the private flat; she thinks about mom too. No one knows her true self; she does not confide in anyone about everything. How does this guy happen to know more about her than anyone? In fact, apart from her connection with the blogger, 'Mercedes', he knows pretty much everything.

They fall silent again. They have finally changed the CD: behind the bar, an old jazz LP with the crackle of vinyl is playing, probably Dizzy Gillespie, though she's not sure. In Munich, she took a liking to his *Night in Tunisia.* Now she imitates the jazzman from the album cover, swelling her cheeks to the maximum. She blows out towards Belly and the flame of the candle between them flutters until it almost dies. Now a trumpet with a mute is playing, together with double bass, piano, and drums that don't really drum but just rustle somehow. She feels like she's had ECT. She's never had the procedure, but this is how it must feel with muscles weakened, tension released, her breathing slow and deep, a slight shiver. Only the shine in her eyes is something extra.

She chews the tender fish with eyes half-closed. It crumbles in her mouth; just pressing it against her palate is enough. There are some bitter leaves in the salad which taste great. As children they would pick such leaves from damp ditches, chew them and nod their heads self-importantly: *sorrel, sorrel,* they would cry. She's hungry, and if she didn't have to restrain herself in this high-end restaurant, she'd throw huge pieces of food down her throat and wash them down with mouthfuls of white wine. But there is something good about such self-restraint—at least she can enjoy the food and drink more. She's not going to gobble it down like Duňa. She can control her desires and has to listen to her body, has to know what's doing her good and what is important. No diet is required, only tasty, wholesome food, in moderation, in small bites. Fully conscious, here and now, not at home in front of the TV, in such a way she doesn't even know what she's eating. She cannot be sad and wipes her tears. Then she places another piece of white fish on her fork, puts it in her mouth, closes her eyes, inhales, chews, and purrs like a cat, shimmering.

The break also suits Belly. He ingests food, but mainly information. He keeps going back to the tape and whispers something to himself. He looks closely at Naďa, superimposing her adult face onto a story from two decades ago which is now fresh and raw to him again. He shakes his head, playing with the tape case in his hands, opening and closing it. Finally, with a loud sigh, he closes it for the last time, and reverentially, with both hands, returns it to Naďa.

"I remember when his problems started. But I never experienced him in that state. How could he leave you like that? What could have happened to him?"

Naďa doesn't know the answer but knows the question intimately.

"Well, the main thing is you haven't taken after him."

"How do you know?"

* * *

Heat is the worst for SMs.

The value of this information in this scorching city: zero. She unscrews the cap of the sunscreen, the whole thing is greasy and the bottle slips in her hands. She spreads sunscreen on herself again, from head to toe. The shadow of the bush she lay down in two hours ago is getting ever smaller as the sun is now almost directly overhead, reducing the space where life can be enjoyed.

Nearby, three boys have sat down on the grass, all in their late teens. They sit in the heat without protection and finish their beer, their shoulders burning red. They don't mind, they laugh, steal glances at Naďa and keep nudging each other. Another friend joins them, carrying four beers in frosted plastic glasses.

"You chose the best place to sit, you pricks," he tells them, nodding towards her. Somehow they find it funny and roar with laughter.

They throw their empty glasses behind them and a wasp immediately flies into the one closest to Naďa. It jerkily circles over the rest of the beer but there is little room for manoeuvre. It then sits but its legs stick and it instinctively flaps its wings, drumming the plastic a few times before finally flying out.

Yesterday, in an overheated flat, with open windows but no hint of a draught, she watched with her boyfriend a documentary about a desert somewhere in Africa. There's a lizard there that has to dance to survive up to sixty-degree temperatures. It lifts its front right and back left leg into the air so they don't get singed, cools down for a while, then switches legs, repeating the action over and again. When even this doesn't help, it buries itself deep in the sand to cool off.

There's nowhere to escape. From the flat to the swimming pool, but it's worse there than she expected. She showers, not wanting to take chances with the pool: what if she caught? Along the way, she kicks a discarded beer glass, which flies toward the group of rowdy boys, hitting one on the arm he is leaning on. They go silent, look at her, trying to decipher the gesture, yet there is none. Naďa isn't sending any signal by it, at least she doesn't think so. She passes them as if they didn't exist, can feel them looking at her butt, watching her as she takes a shower. It's not unpleasant but she cares nothing for them. Naďa turns the shower on to maximum and stands under the torrent of water letting it run all over her body, isolating herself in it, cooling down like a dead chicken in a plastic bag. Between the cascades of water, she sees two people standing in line and waiting for her to finish. Naďa turns round and remains in the icy embrace for a few more minutes until she starts shaking. She comes out with a map of blue spots on her body, her teeth chattering behind her blue lips. She walks barefoot across the lawn to the snack bar, already looking forward to it. They make fantastic fish here.

"Heat is the worst for SMs."

It was gloomy and cold out when she read that sentence in a leaflet or somewhere on the internet. She couldn't have imagined then it would be such a big problem. Now she can, though. She'd kill him, the tight-fisted fucker. The owner of the flat she and her boyfriend rented had promised last year he would fix the air conditioner. But he'd done fuck all about it. Of course he didn't have to sweat buckets in there. Why should he care?

The heat slows down the flow of her thoughts: instead of brain matter, there is dough in her head. The cold of the shower has gone and in fifteen minutes, she's on fire again and can feel the heat in her muscles and joints, the soul of the grilled fish having moved into her body. It is not working. Naďa looks up at the sun, so dramatically dry, it has conquered this part of the day, vanquished the last remnants of shade and hammered them into the ground. She too has to bury herself. It's a degrading survival strategy compared to the desert lizard's: she takes a taxi to an air-conditioned shopping mall to cool down.

* * *

So, what do you say, my sweetie, are we going to do some SM on Thursday? :-P Don't get too excited, you perverted bitch. It's stabilization/mobilization I've got in mind :-D

The text message from Kristína cheers her up. Naďa sips the last drops of iced coffee through a straw.

Only if they close the windows and turn the air conditioning on at the gym! Not like last time. :-O Can you arrange that? ;-*

In the early days of her new career, she had a hard time coming to terms with it. It was her 'godmother', Kristína's fault. If it wasn't for her, she could now calmly answer her mom's question about what exactly she does for a living. Gradually, though, she realized that it was not Kristína's doing. Naďa has come to accept her life. *This* is her path. This *is* her path. *Hers.*

Shared secrets can bring people together. Kristína went to church every week. She also went to discos and liked to dance until the morning. She wore distinctive jewellery—in size, in price, in lustre. She hated sports and loved the heat, the south, the sea, ultra-modern hotels. Everything which she liked or didn't like was the perfect counterpoint to what Naďa liked or didn't like. Even so, they bonded like sisters. It was a surprise to both of them and they enjoyed it.

There were men in some of the private flats, mostly pimps and security guys together in one, but Kristína ran their place on her own. And although she had never had a really bad experience, she insisted that there were always at least two girls in the flat at the same time. So, she and Naďa spent a lot of time together—especially in the living room, while clients came and went. They spent hours in front of the TV, watching the dumbest programs, swearing, and laughing. One of them would put towels and bedding in the washing machine while the other one cut cheese and fruit or knocked up some instant meal. Then they hung the towels on the clotheshorse in the living room, ate, took a nap. Kristína took the phone calls, answering questions about prices, practices, available girls, rolling her eyes, in a low voice with grimaces hinting to Naďa what kind of guy was calling and what he was asking. After the clients left, they always evaluated them. Sometimes they weren't worth talking about. Sometimes they were funny. Sometimes they were disgusting.

Shared suffering brings people together even more than a secret. Kristína discovered an altruistic instinct and would come up with endless free-time activities for them both.

"I have to take you for a walk, you tar." She goaded Naďa. "I'm not going to let you lie around at home, staring at the ceiling and feeling depressed!"

She entertained her in an organized way—sometimes even a week in advance, Naďa received invitations in her phone calendar. Like *a walk-cinema.* After the movie, they always rebuked each other—Kristína loved Hollywood children's movies, Naďa preferred horror and thrillers. Kristína told her she was a sicko for watching such stuff voluntarily and forcing her to do it too. They both liked and disliked working out equally—but sweating was easier together. Dance—Kristína. Bicycles—Naďa. Slovakia Ring car racing—Kristína. Ballet—Naďa (Kristína fell asleep). SM—Kristína.

* * *

"SM," a sweaty client stammered in the hallway of the private flat. It was Saturday evening; he was wearing an ice-hockey jersey and a scarf. He smelled of alcohol and was shaking nervously.

"Excuse me?!" Naďa exclaimed and put her hands on her hips. Was it possible that her disease was so obvious a drunk guy would notice it in a single second after looking at her from the door?

"You know whether you do … yooooou knooow. Sssado-mmmaso," the Slovan Bratislava fan said. They were both relieved.

"Yeah, yes, come on in. I only do light sado-maso. And for an extra charge, okay?" She led him to the room. When she didn't hear his agreement, she looked back and saw him taking a breath wanting to say something. Their eyes met; he quickly nodded.

While she lashed the naked guy's back and butt with a leather whip, she wondered how hard the two letters were burned into her identity. She was a girl for sale, yet S and M didn't evoke sado-maso to her, but sclerosis multiplex.

When she heard those words from her GP for the first time—just as one possible explanation of her symptoms—nothing specific came to mind. She may have caught the words before, but had had no reason to pay attention to them. On her way out, she let them roll around in her mind and on her tongue. They reminded her of many different things—forgetting, inferiority complexes, multivitamin juice, a large shopping centre. A magic formula! But what would a formula used to reverse the pain coming from demented nerves sound like?

S-M, three forms of pain:

Unsolicited pain, free of charge in one packet together with the disease;

Chronic pain from which you escape—in a gym with rubber SM belts that "stabilize and mobilize" the spine;

Exciting pain, fake punishments, and positions of power and domination between two or more bodies.

Have you eaten? A message from her boyfriend lights up on her phone. It's 1 pm, he's extremely punctual and faster than technology—only after his message does the reminder *Lentils/egg* appear on her phone screen. It was he who put it there, too. She breathes in, her rib cage cracks, she feels pain in the small of her back.

* * *

"Have you eaten?" her boyfriend asks at the door instead of greeting her. She's all drenched having been caught in a summer storm. You cannot hide from something like that. You see darkness on the horizon and tell yourself you are going to take cover but within a second you are as wet as a drowned rat.

"Sure, lentils and egg," Naďa says, lying. The fish at the pool which she ate outside of her meal plan filled her up. And she can't digest food well enough to handle two meals in a row. He wouldn't understand such a deviation from her schedule. Just as he doesn't understand that she'd appreciate help at the moment—he could hand her a towel and some dry clothes so she doesn't wet the whole flat.

"Where?" he asks doubtfully. The last time they looked for such food it wasn't easy at all.

"At the restaurant near the bowling alley," she replies, hardly hesitating. "They had lentils with smoked meat on their lunch menu. I persuaded the waiter to give me a hard-boiled egg instead of meat." That doesn't sound so unlikely and hopes that he won't check it on the internet though is almost certain he will.

Since she entered the flat and drank a glass of water in the kitchen, he hasn't looked at her once. He stares stonily at the computer, only his hand and index finger moving. Naďa is taking a breath, okay. It will be she who takes the first step then. She goes up to him and sees how he quickly closes the windows on the screen until only his inbox is open.

"How did your day go?" She kisses him on the neck. It's cold and salty with sweat.

"Fine. And yours? Have you had something to drink?" He looks at her and the fridge alternately.

"If you paid attention to me a little bit, you'd notice I've just had some water," Nada says. How can she love him when she hates him five times a day? She answers like she always does: Her boyfriend doesn't want her to cover her mole and says that she looks much better with it than "some plain Jane hidden behind make-up."

"I heard, but you know one glass isn't enough," he says, glancing at the fridge again.

"You know what, I'm going to take a shower. A cold one, okay? To cool down. I can do that, right? Is it on the list?" She turns on her heel and wants to slam the door, but there are only beads between the living room and hallway, which rattle softly.

"They didn't have lentils at the bowling place today," she hears him shouting from the living room as she steps into the shower.

"What …? If you want to help me," she murmurs, turning the blue tap, "then why do you piss me off me so much?"

She wanted to be grateful for his care. And she was. Everyone told her the same; it was written everywhere. A routine is key to managing the disease. A system. She had one, she was never messy. But he, he is a systematist with a big S. He's had autistic traits since she met him, back in high school. There was something cute about it at the time. But later, especially when they started living together, his obsession began to annoy her.

"Right away, honey, I'll put it right away." Of course, she'd forgotten about her nail varnish on the sink. She dried her nails; putting the varnish away didn't look like a priority to her. But when she later searched for it, it wasn't on the sink anymore. Had he seen it? did he know where it might be? He had and it was somewhere "where it belongs." She found it in her handbag, open, spilled. She later found a "not put away" comb under her pillow that evening. Only ten minutes after she tried her evening dress on and hung it over the chair, she found it scrunched up between dirty laundry. When she did the dishes and left the water running for a few seconds, her boyfriend repeated "water, flood, water, flood …" in an uncomfortably high and loud robotic voice which only stopped when she turned the tap off. The situation was similar in the case of the kettle on the gas stove—she turned the gas off only after pouring water on her coffee. Unacceptable! An alarm "fi-i-i-re, fi-i-i-re …" rang around the kitchen. She knew it probably wasn't his fault. In the end, it made more sense to adapt to him. There was no alternative. He couldn't be otherwise. She had a nutjob at home, so what? He's got other qualities, she loves him.

And still does, but since she fell ill, she's been worried. That's right since *she* fell ill, she's been worried about *him*. He has obsessively studied everything about the diagnosis. When they were at the appointment together, he added information and corrected the doctor. He has compiled the optimal menu and daily routine for Naďa based on hundreds of internet tutorials. Although he claimed—because it was also stated there—that the patient (he called her that, his own girlfriend) must above all be in good mental health and not under stress, he was irritated when she deviated from the routine he had "set" for her and it was hard to talk to him. Like right now.

She comes out of the shower; he is sitting at an empty table which, compared to the rest of the furniture in the flat, is disproportionately large. Walking around the flat has basically become walking around that table. There is a large lava lamp in the corner of the room. Although it is not turned on it seems to Naďa that a wax ball is slowly coming to the surface in the blazing furnace of their flat. Her boyfriend is peeling an orange, trying to keep the peel in one piece, as always. Naďa approaches the fridge and for the millionth time looks at the list of tasks downloaded from the internet:

- *maintain a positive and realistic approach to life, even with the help of a psychologist or psychiatrist,*
- *take an interest in your illness and treatment options,*
- *listen to your body and try to understand its needs,*
- *do not isolate yourself from friends and family,*
- *speak openly about your feelings, confide in your doctor as well,*
- *try to avoid injuries and getting hurt,*

- *avoid overheating, heated swimming pools, overheated rooms, prefer a cooler environment,*
- *try stretching, working out or exercising in the swimming pool on a regular basis,*
- *drink plenty of water, i.e., 2.5 litres a day,*
- *increase your zinc, fibre, and linolenic acid intake by eating oily fish and fish oil, sunflower oil, pumpkin seeds, fruit and vegetables, wholemeal products, cranberries, lentils, wholegrain rice, peas, cheese, eggs and sesame seeds,*
- *exercise your memory by doing crossword puzzles, reading, playing cards and doing jigsaw puzzles together.*

General instructions and tips have been highlighted in green, whereas those which need to be repeated are in red. Next to the latter is a box with dates which Naďa can either put a tick or cross next to every evening. Of course, she doesn't *have to*, but she can.

Her boyfriend also has the list—a list for her, of course. It is a result of thorough study and consultation with doctors and SM interest groups. All possible medicaments and treatments are summarized on one page. These are categorized on a grid: clinically tested v. experimental; covered by insurance v. paid in cash; for relapses v. long-term immunomodulatory and immunosuppressive; first-line versus second-line, western v. alternative. When visiting her GP or a specialist, Naďa feels like she is between two millstones, with a second figure of authority at home who is becoming less a partner and more of a nurse and carer.

"Which specialist recommended this procedure for you?" her doctor asked once. What was she supposed to say? That it was her boyfriend who never completed his studies at the Faculty of Business IT?

If she had to read all those case studies, keep all of those names in her head, analyze reviews and go through recommendations written in Slovak, Czech, Hungarian, Polish, English, and German in order to develop an ideal strategy, she would go nuts. It took some time before she could even remember the name of the disease properly. She is in denial, which makes it impossible to remember all those names—all those copaxones, corticosteroids, solu-medrol infusions, interferons, zumab infusions. When she sees them all together, she thinks she would almost rather have cancer.

She *is* grateful to him! Or does she just not want to be ungrateful? He is helping her. Into *the grave* ... Her face reddens as a result of the involuntarily malicious replica. She knows she can only beat the disease if she is meticulous in her lifestyle and eats and behaves correctly. At the same time, she feels from the very depths of her oft-subdued soul that she will only survive if she is mentally well and enjoys her life.

* * *

"When you say *enjoy*, does it involve *having sex* with another guy?" he asked emphasizing both verbs as if Naďa had used them together in one context and he was just quoting her. They were lying in bed, all sweaty, and she complained for the first time. She told him that she liked him, but didn't want to be a slave to his regime. He countered.

"What do you mean?" she asked without looking at him.

"Am I right?"

She only hesitated for a moment. He leaned on his elbow as he lay on his side, studying her closely and slowly nodding his head.

"I could taste a condom when I was licking you."

A long silence followed. He waited. She wondered what she should tell him and how. Several options were on the table, but none of them seemed like a good start. The longer she thought, the more she was convinced that there was no such thing as a good start to this kind of discussion.

"Who is it?"

She wasn't ready for the most ordinary question and assumed her *whole* secret had been uncovered. Unable to react, she remained silent, her eyes downcast. Her disconcerted mind started making bizarre calculations on the topic of *economies of scale*. You kill one, you are a murderer; you kill millions, you are a conqueror. You rob one, you are a thief; you rob millions, you are a bank. Could *economies of scale* work with infidelity as well? Hundreds of anonymous paying clients compared to one lover.

"Is it the one you have consultations with? The Englishman?" What? She might have once or twice mentioned her thesis supervisor from Nottingham was nice.

"You don't have to say anything, I knew it. You kept raving about him."

Pure nonsense, but why argue?

* * *

She lies with her eyes closed and only gets up after hearing the door slam. She doesn't know where he has gone; it is not usual for him to leave before she does. He has left a letter to *Miss Nadežda Migešová* on the table, right in its geometric and hard-to-reach centre. The words *Subject: Personality Technicalities* are written in the top left of the A4 paper. There, he tersely writes about his disappointment. If they are to continue together, she has to promise that "IT" won't happen again. He may be an autistic dick, but he is not a complete idiot; he has feelings and felt something wasn't right for months. Years of living together taught him that, he felt the slightest change in vibration, she had suddenly starting broadcasting on other frequencies. He is sure that it is not a result of her disease; he feels the influence of *semen (of another)*. He didn't want to ask at first; he has no right. Every man for himself, even in a relationship, he always claimed that. It was her talk about the *pseudo-enjoyment of this pseudo-life* that finally provoked him.

The disease must be difficult for her, the confrontation with pain and *possible death* probably led to her *urge to seek escape from a good man*. Therefore, he insists that she signs up for a consultation with a psychotherapist, that's his only condition (!!!). Footnote—*the need to seek psychological help is also mentioned in the list on the fridge.* This is so she doesn't think he wants something unheard of from her.

* * *

"I have a hard time falling asleep." Naďa examines the framed certificates from completed courses. They do not sit face to face, but in chairs with axes intersecting at right angles—easy to meet the eyes, easy to look away.

"What happens after, what do you think about?"

"I don't know. I review the day, things which happened to me. I wonder if I'm tired as a result of the disease coming back or whether I am entitled to simply feel tired."

"You have to be entitled to feel tired?" A pair of mischievous eyes stare at Naďa, a curly wisp of hair in their way. Regardless of the time of day, Mária always looks like she has just come out of the shower. Is her hair wet or is it something she puts on it? It's a funny look for someone with such a discerning eye—she looks like an elf crossed with a fairy.

It wasn't easy for her to talk during their first sessions; she couldn't speak fluently and felt embarrassed about having to complain. What was she supposed to say? That she felt betrayed? That she had always believed in justice—that if she didn't have great ambitions and lived modestly, fate would not notice her and would leave her alone? Should she have named all the nonsensical things she was ashamed of to Mária? That she was afraid of offending someone, disappointing someone, of making a mistake which no one would ever fix, of doing something bad and irreversible?

"Sometimes, when I'm almost asleep, I feel I am going to fall down from somewhere high. The place where I am about to fall from always surprises me. Sometimes it is scaffolding on a skyscraper, sometimes the balcony of our old apartment, other times a crane, a window. Weird. And whenever I am about to fall, when

I can almost feel the fall coming, I freak out, wake up, and cannot fall asleep again."

"And what do you think—why does this happen?"

"I don't know. Sleep is like a small death. I have no control over myself, I don't know if I will wake up."

Mária pauses her speech and movements as well. After a while, she starts to nod slowly.

"I didn't want to interfere with that thought. Let's talk about it some more. What exactly do you feel then, what happens to you?"

"I freak out and try to chase away that thought, I try to think about something else."

"Okay, but what do you feel at that precise moment?"

"Fear."

"Of what?"

"Of the fact that everything I ever cared about is futile because everything will end. The lives of my loved ones, my mom's life will end. And mine too. And there is absolutely nothing I can do about it."

Mária pours water in Nađa's glass, even though it is almost full.

"I rarely have clients who open up so quickly. And the things you talk about are so great, so fundamentally human, that I honestly have nothing to say to you. Let me share something with you. I struggle with similar feelings myself, more often than I'd like. And believe me, in my whole career I haven't met a person, nor heard of one, who was really able to deal with the feeling of finitude. It probably won't comfort you, but it is an eternal struggle."

Nađa carefully takes the glass and sips from it. What would her boyfriend be like in therapy? What would he talk about? How would he talk? What would he bring? Would they discuss the same topics or completely different ones? She has no idea.

"But you can work with fear." Mária smiles again.

How? Nađa's face asks instead of her mouth.

"Close your eyes and imagine it's evening, you're in bed and trying to fall asleep."

Naďa relaxes her eyelids and slowly tunes out, until—like almost every night—she shudders awake at the horror of falling. She then sees Mária with her head in her hands, concentrating on her own thoughts no longer observing Naďa. So, she tries it once again. It works.

"Where are you now?"

"I just fell then panicked and am now trying to think of something nicer."

"Focus on the present, what are you thinking about?"

"About my boyfriend licking me down below. I've never had an orgasm with him, but it feels nice. The intimacy calms me down like an anaesthetic, melts me somehow."

"Nice," Mária says, and one can tell she is smiling based on the way her voice sounds. "But let's get back to the fall. Even if it's unpleasant, try to go on, don't run away. What happens when you are falling?"

"I'm afraid, I'm falling, the ground is getting closer, I'm gonna die."

"Really?"

"I guess ... why?"

"Let's fall together, shall we? How high are you right now?"

"Do you mean in metres?"

"For example."

"About a hundred metres up."

"One second has passed. How far from the ground are we now?"

"Fifty?"

"Okay, now?"

"Ten."

"OK, now? Where are you?"

"On the ground."

"Alive, dead, injured?"

The blinds rustle and fresh air comes in.

"No, I landed on my feet, I am standing. I am all right."

She rubs her shoeless feet against the carpet; she can feel the structure through her stockings.

"But … it doesn't make any sense," Nada says, though the muscles around her mouth twitch upwards.

"It does, actually! If we were really standing a hundred metres up, it would be normal to be afraid of falling. But our imagination is free, physics doesn't apply to it. Do you want to try it again?"

"Yes," she says carefully.

"So, how did you land?"

"I didn't. I stopped just above the ground."

* * *

"Would you like some melon?" she asks.

He mumbled something from the table but she cannot decipher whether it was a yes or a no. So she will cut it, put it into a bowl, leave it on the table and see. She thrusts the long kitchen knife into the middle of the watermelon. The fruit is so warm from the sun beating down on the market, so ripe from water, sugar, and heat that its tense rind cracks all around its girth. Nada's finger slides into the crack that has just formed, and the knife, already in motion, cuts into the skin of her index finger just below the nail. Nada has a prescience of sharp pain and sees a hanging piece of skin and a nail both flooded in blood just a second later. She hisses, jerks her arms and drops the knife, both halves of the watermelon then falling and breaking into smaller pieces after hitting the ground. Her blood drips onto them.

He gets up from the table. "Jesus!" At first he is scared and wants to help. "What are you doing?" he asks rolling his eyes in disgust. "Into the bathroom!" He drags Nada as fast as possible to stop her splattering the whole flat.

Nada pulls her hand away from him.

"What are you doing?" he asks standing in the bathroom looking alternately at her mad face, bloody hand and wide nostrils that barely manage to supply her pumping chest. Blood drips onto the floor creating a stream between the tiles and a cross at the intersection of four of them. Will it come off?

"What are you doing?" he asks once more, this time less in surprise than in reproach.

She stands in the hall, not feeling the injury only her blood boiling. He is in the bathroom and has turned the cold water on, waiting for her. There is so much she wants to say to him. She wants to yell at him, she wants to explain, she wants to cuddle him, ask for his forgiveness, to thank him, to kick him. But all she does is snort, her nose running. She finally enters the bathroom but stops by the door still. She then pulls the key out of the lock, steps back, and slams the door before locking it.

"What are you doing?" he asks a fourth time from behind the door.

She sucks on her cut index finger and the blood tastes sweet. She keeps it in her mouth for a few minutes, until it stops bleeding completely. It looks chewed up, like a tenderized cutlet in colour and texture.

She goes to the room and sits down at his computer. She lets her injured hand hang, as if removed from her body, grabs the mouse with her healthy hand and navigates it to the history icon. She can feel she is on to something and yet the names of sites shock her: murdervideos.sk, torture.x7.cz, deathtube.net. She plays a video and breathlessly watches a man in a mask—well, probably a man, she cannot see the face—cutting the neck of another man who is tied down and kneeling. He does not stop until the victim's head is separated from the body. As if it was never alive, it looks like a failed dummy from a movie studio. Naďa opens more and more videos, unable to watch any of them till the end. A worker crushed by a fork-lift truck, motionless, dead. A boy somewhere in Asia, stabbed in front of a shop by two children with long knives in their hands. A mulatto woman repeatedly raped in her ass, detail on the bleeding hole, crying, asking for mercy. A Russian teenager, with innocent smile for the camera beating another one's nose: about ten punches delivered with all his might—a smashed blue-red meatball in the middle of the face of the other one, who is no longer defending himself.

The internet is an endless testimony of everything that happens in the world. Everything is there, she knew it theoretically. And she probably expected to find something twisted in his computer, but this brutal stuff has shaken her to the core: a world of death and suffering lives within her reach, right in front of her. Why would he watch anything like that? She doesn't know him at all.

"Naďa, open up, I know what you're doing!" he shouts from the bathroom. As if she were the one who should be ashamed for what she was doing.

"Naďa, stop fooling around, I would never hurt you ... I've never ... Are you crazy?"

She opens the fridge, takes out white bread, and spreads a thick layer of pork lard over it. She chews a large bite, without vegetables, without anything.

"Naďa, what are you eating? You shouldn't ..." He doesn't finish the sentence; the locked door holds his words back.

With her mouth full she returns to the computer. She has no intention of watching any more videos; the folders on the desktop are her main focus now. There is one named SM but she knows it perfectly, it has become folk literature in their apartment. The other folder is labelled *Pain&Neuro*. A double-click opens a sea of documents in various formats. Articles from professional journals such as *Journal of Pain Research; Journal of Neurological Sciences; Nature Neuroscience.* Scanned or downloaded professional books, *Pathophysiology of pain; Wall & Melzak's Textbook of Pain; Pain, Its Anatomy, Physiology and Treatment; Understanding Pain: Exploring the Perception of Pain.* Although this discovery is not as visually shocking as the videos before, Naďa is still amazed by how deeply her boyfriend has delved into the subject.

She has stuffed herself with two large slices of bread covered in fat and now feels sick. She runs to the bathroom, remembering halfway that she has locked her boyfriend in there. If it wasn't for the door, she'd puke directly all over him.

"Naďa, Nadi, what's going on, what are you doing? Are you okay?" He kneels, knocking on the door.

The key in the lock turns, Naďa opens the door.

"Why?" Covered in vomit and blood she scans her boyfriend

with a half-empty look. He sits on the floor, the water he turned on is still running.

"Why?" she asks him one more time.

"What do you mean why, what's wrong with it, why do you even ask? It was you who showed me this world."

"That's bullshit."

"You got sick just like that … what was I supposed to do?"

"Wait, what? You really think that—that I got sick on purpose? Just to be a burden to you?"

Her boyfriend doesn't answer, just gets up and turns the tap off. Now the water is just dripping.

"But I don't mind it that much," he says quietly in the end. "Despite everything, living with you still has more advantages than disadvantages."

"Are you kidding me? You're now counting the pros and cons of living with me and I'm supposed to be happy that I come out with a plus sign?"

Her boyfriend furrows his eyebrows. Is he supposed to object? Is counting so abnormal?

"You? Someone who enjoys the pain of others? In the warmth and safety of your home, you take care of your obligations, hand me medication, keep an eye on my daily routine, check things off your list feeling good about yourself. And then you watch some poor guy get his head cut off with an axe or burned alive in a cage?" Naďa carefully dries the weeping wound, wipes vomit from her lips, rinses her mouth with menthol mouthwash.

"You don't understand it, you don't know how things are," he says waving his arm. He averts his eyes and stares out of the window.

"What is there to understand? Come on, tell me what I don't understand."

He clenches his teeth, his lips create a perfect line, he's still looking outside. His neck is sticking out of the top of his polo shirt looking longer than normal; he gives a dry swallow.

"Tell me, what am I to you—some kind of experiment?"

He has never hurt her. Not even during sex, when she wanted more and whispered to him to bite her nipples, to spank her. He was conservative, Nada now has enough experience to compare. However, the contents of his computer are like no other. She doesn't know if she can demand confession, repentance, an explanation.

"What's wrong with it?" he suddenly replies in a quiet and thoughtful voice. "Seriously. So I look at clusters of pixels in motion that create an image, a reproduction of reality. But tell me, what difference does it make if I watch it or if I don't? This is what happens in the world. Regardless of whether we choose to avert our eyes or not. It's sick. It's a sick world. And to understand it you have to understand pain and to also see this side of the world. That's why I look at it. So I don't forget, so I remember."

It is really hard for Nada to decide whether she can't react or simply doesn't want to because she is so tired. When she listens to her boyfriend, when she looks at him, she knows that their trains have long been moving in opposite directions and they can no longer see each other over the curvature of the earth. They could yell at each other but they can no longer hear. Her lower back has been aching for two weeks now, she's having blackouts, and he's voluntarily dumping all the depravity of the world onto himself to remind himself of what it's like. Why?

"Suffering has to have a reason, it has to have some deeper meaning," he says, as if he knew what she was going to ask. "When your problems started, when you were sleeping the whole time and could barely walk because of the pain, when you kept dropping things and were tripping over nothing, do you think you were the only one suffering? Do you know what it was like for me? Until then, you were independent, confident, I could lean on you. Do you think that I didn't know what an impractical idiot I was? You've been my anchor for years and then you started to fall apart in front of my eyes. I still can't get over it. Don't think I've always been like this. But when you got sick—when you introduced me to pain—I was forced to ... I don't know, look for answers. To questions about suffering. I started studying pain to be able to understand you."

Naďa is surprised but says nothing. She is carefully putting a plaster on her finger, the square tabs in her mouth. Has pain really become the quality that fundamentally defines her?

"Has it helped? Do you understand me better now?" Naďa asks without looking at him. She takes a rag from under the bathtub and wipes the blood and vomit up. Soon the bathroom is as clean as if nothing had happened.

"No," he replies, standing over her like a piece of furniture.

They stay silent for a long time. Thunder is starting outside again and the window bangs in the draught. But they're too drowned in themselves, each on their own, to stir. Through a window, a neighbour is yelling at her children to come in so they don't get wet.

"Can you move a bit?" Naďa points to the toilet. He steps aside, she lifts the lid, lifts her summer jumpsuit over her shoulders, and pulls down her pants.

"But do you know what I found out?" he asks her, while she gets up and flushes the toilet.

"I have no idea."

"When I see the evil that we, humans, are capable of, I can't help but see the parallel. The whole world, its entire central nervous system, is chronically ill. Like with SM, no one knows why, but we're ruining our ways towards each other. Through hardened optic nerves we don't see that every person is fundamentally the same. That you're just like me, that he's just like her. The abandoned space between us is getting filled with the scars of emptiness, scattered among all the people in the world. The pain and suffering of others become invisible for us because we are blind and surrounded by scar tissue, and so we can torture and kill. The nation elites, those who should be brain stems, and their decisions should be spinal marrow, are dull and non-renewably sclerotic. They destroy what could bring us together, they let everything become necrotic and perish. The myelin of love dissolves in the acid of our own hatred. No wonder we have severe neurological symptoms. Society malfunctions.

We don't coordinate—we're lazy, crooked as a whole. We destroy ourselves. We destroy our environment. Fuck, we're masters in this world but at the same time total invalids disabled."

Naďa is too tired to think about whether she agrees with him or not. "You know what? I may be selfish, but I couldn't care less about any of that right now. I have my own problems, massive ones."

One, in particular, is what things will be like in the days ahead. The practicalities of finding a new place and moving out after many years of knowing each other and several years of living together.

She has no choice. *He* is the scar impeding her free movement and struggle for self-preservation. It's time to say goodbye to Little Braňo.

* * *

The most important thing was to learn how to breathe. A person takes in air in without a break from birth until the last time they exhale—they should know how to do it perfectly. But they don't. Naďa breathed shallowly and quickly. And it was also how she lived.

Now she stands in a meadow near a housing estate with her legs apart; she feels the river flowing beneath her, the wind blowing through her hair, her lungs filling with air. She breathes, she finally breathes properly. One of her arms is behind her head, the other is stretched in front of her; they are neither tensed nor relaxed. She tunes into the world, harmonizes with it, absorbs its rays. And she concentrates all of her energy on two things—deep and controlled breathing and surgically precise movements. She is becoming the owner of her own body; only now does she feel at home in it. She moves onto the next position, slowly moving her centre of gravity and rotating her hands, slowly winding up the silk yarn as if it was almost there.

She first went to a tai-chi group in Zbraslav, now she prefers to exercise alone, in the meadow near her apartment in Troja. Even in the cold she will do it but not in the rain. She doesn't wear a special kit, just comfortable everyday clothes. Movements liberate pathways in the body; that is all she thinks about. She even smiles—how easy it is to direct the mind through movement and focus it on the here and now.

She sits on the terrace she always goes to after exercising; they have Kofola there. You can smell the past inside the bar—it does not smell great but at least it is there—and has been for decades. Right next door is a new café clad with wood from pallets, the emphasis of its glass display on *tradition* and *location*—and on *coffee roasted in Holešovice*. But she'll never set foot inside: it wasn't there a year ago nor will it be in two years. The fleetingness of locality, that is the only thing typical of metropolises these days. Trendy shops are like mushrooms—they grow quickly, then get snatched away. Or they dry out completely, become wooden, disintegrate. New ones grow in their place: meadow mushrooms, toadstools, toothed toughshanks, jelly fungi, oyster mushrooms, sheathed woodtufts, roundheads, truffles. Fungi are parasites, closer to animals than plants. Everything feels huge to her. The city is changing, too quickly to find its character. Nothing takes root, nothing's traditional, nothing local, everything just pretending. Is she in the right place?

It is going to rain, the parasols are fluttering in the wind blowing through the terrace and a coaster just flew off her table when she lifted her glass. A canvas sign advertising the ZOO is flapping on the railing by the roadside, on it a gorilla galloping like the wind behind a giraffe. Guests get up from their tables to take shelter inside; others go to the bus stop. The waiter quickly takes down the parasols so it's just the two of them outside now. Large drops make grey spots on his white shirt, adding to the yellow spots of sweat under his arms, there are no more colours. The colours give way to sound, the street is dark and noisy.

"Miss, it's raining, you should go inside," the waiter says as the rain sticks his fringe to his forehead and a hairy wrist with a silver chain pulls it back in place.

"You're going to get wet," he says as if she was listening to him, as if the problem was that Naďa didn't understand the notion of cause

and effect. But she understands everything. That's why she just sits still and breathes deeply. The waiter doesn't dally, waves his hand and trots inside. Naďa gets up with eyes half-closed and adopts a *tai-chi position*, flapping her hands outwards to fan herself and drive away demons. Two waiters stare at her through the glass door. The hairy one shakes his head and fixes his fringe behind the glass; the other one laughs so hard he leans backwards, pointing his finger at her.

* * *

A large area in front of a pale blue building made from marzipan, maybe a parking lot, Naďa is a figurine, one of many in a long line. They don't walk, they just move on the tracks like figures in an astronomical clock. There is a mini lift on each step, in front of the entrance gate, moving smoothly up, along, up, along, up, along, three steps. They briefly nod at the figurines going in the opposite direction. The doors open automatically, the right half sliding to the right, the left to the left, revealing a long geometrically perfect tunnel. Everyone inside is sharpened, planed and sanded down with a file until they are smooth. Buratino at the reception bows and points to the corridor with his jointless right: you may proceed.

She has been here before, it should be familiar. But everything is alien—as if it was not a hospital but a factory producing something rare and intangible. You cannot smell nor hear anything; no smells, no noise. There is just a silent hum as the greased figurines glide in two rows against each other. The air is cold and fresh; you can see huge green slender trees through the glass and the ventilation here is so good, all the oxygen is giving her a headache.

There are two arrows at the end of the long angular tunnel; she approaches them slowly and knows that she has to take a risk. She picks the one pointing left. Only now does she stop being a figurine and become herself. All those flat mechanical toys that haven't taken a turn fall into an immense hole at the end of the tracks until their shrinking dots are out of sight. Naďa, now three-dimensional, takes short steps to the door at the end of a corridor which, for a change, is narrow and dark.

She's opening a drawer, there's the body of a little girl in it. It's blue, unmoving, but it's not dead, just sound asleep. She caresses the body, touches the girl gently to wake her up. She calls out to her, whispers in her ear. *Wake up, sweetheart, what's wrong, what's happened to you?* She tries to slap her gently, to pinch her, nothing. *Just you wait, I'm not letting you get away with this. You cannot do this to me now, now that I'm here, now that I've found you. Don't worry, I'll fix you. Show me where you're broken.*

Without a scalpel, she opens the girl's body, sinking her hand into it, at which moment she wakes up.

* * *

The day after the dream, she went to the hospital. She listened to her intuition—she had no reason not to.

Poorly dressed for bleak weather, white on blue, a red cross on her breast, in some sense it was a uniform. She paid the taxi driver, stood in front of the building, and stared into the windows. She had been there many times, but something was different this time. As if she expected an invitation. As if she expected a conveyor belt to come on and take her through the automatic door. But there was no such thing, just a large area with lots of pavilions, one big human ZOO. All the pointing arrows made her dizzy; her eyes were betraying her. So she let herself be guided by other senses— the sound of a fountain, the scent of flowers replaced by the smell of food, of mayonnaise salads and fried meat. She went to the canteen cash register to enquire.

"Go to the second floor, that's where you'll find it, or ask some-one else." The woman behind the register didn't even look up but went on tapping the food list on the screen.

"No, there is a pathology institute on the second floor," a tall man in white called from the queue. "If you are looking for where they do autopsies you have to go out, around the parking lot and up to the Na Šafránce bus-stop. There's also a place where you can get information for the bereaved persons. What or who are you looking for? What department are you from? What a strange uniform."

"Naďa is that you? What are you doing here? Have you had a relapse?" another man said and his voice was familiar. From neurology on the fourth floor.

"Naďa what's wrong? Why are you dressed like a nurse?" The doctor left the queue and came towards her.

She narrowed her eyes, wanting to go back into the darkness and remember the details, to get her bearings back in a slowly fading dream. *Where are the fucking arrows?* She was coming to her senses. How does she look like in the erotic nurse's outfit that she wears for her clients? Short skirt, suspenders, tits out. She wanted to run away quickly and abandon this desperate idea, but her stiff legs and high heels didn't let her. Instead she crashed into a table and chairs and ended up on the floor. She tried to get up, picked up a salt cellar and some toothpicks, but then gave up. Instead she just stayed sitting on the ground, exhausted, almost catatonic. All that advice from doctors and psychologists, to relax, to let your intuition guide you. To listen to your dreams! To dissociate from yourself, to look at yourself from the viewpoint of others, those who love you or care for you. None of it worked. Nothing worked.

* * *

Her pulse rate goes from two hundred to a hundred then from zero to a hundred in three seconds. Then back to two hundred. Blood is pulsating in her neck, her head is spinning and her legs shaking. It's as if the rest of the body didn't need blood. Why is all of it rushing into her head? Think!

Coordinates: the family cottage. Since Naďa finished school and started living in Prague, mom has been coming here more and more, for longer periods. Naďa is here too, with her near-heart attack and itchy scabs after her latest tattoo. *House of Pain*—the name of the tattoo studio amused her.

Mom: out, gone to gather some herbs. She's will turn into a witch one day. Elderflower, hawthorn, comfrey, nettle, the entire cottage is going to smell of them. Naďa is looking forward to it but it is still a long way off; for now there is a problem that needs to be solved.

Problem: an open envelope on the table. His handwriting on it. Son of a bitch, what right does he have to send things to her mom?

Solution: Solution?

How to deal with the consequences of her mom reading a transcript of an interview with her for a feminist magazine? Naďa was sent one part to authorize. It was easy for Little Braňo to hack into her inbox, wasn't it?

How to deal with the consequences of her mom reading a copy of *Cosmopolitan* in which—in order to avoid any trace of doubt—an interview with Naďa has been highlighted with a marker pen. In fact, an anonymous interview with Mercedes. Mom's a lot of things but she is not stupid.

No solution, resignation. She sits on the steps in front of the cottage, chewing a sour apple while she waits for her. There is a stream of thoughts and images in her head none of which she tries to stop. Paťa and Káťa were graduates of gender studies, one Slovak and one Czech. They spent more time arguing with each other than asking her questions. She now laughs at the memory; they were sweet.

Dad: he lived in this cottage. After he went mad, he was found by a neighbour naked and frozen down by the brook. Dad and his tapes: tangible records of an intangible inheritance. The sounds of the past. The cottage is full of them. The cottage is full of him. What kind of dilemmas did her dad have? Naďa never understood them from the recordings and no longer has the strength to listen to them. How could he be alone when he had mom?

Mom. She can already see her; she smiles, and nods, the basket is full.

* * *

Paťa: Mercedes, at the outset I want to say that we are not here to moralize or somehow re-educate you.

Naďa: Okay, so tell me why you are here. Feel free to ask whatever you are interested in.

Paťa: Well, first we would probably like to know how and why you decided on the sex business.

(...)

Naďa: Is something wrong?

Káťa: No, no, please, answer. I just wouldn't ask this at the beginning, but don't worry—I don't want to complicate things.

Naďa: What would you ask?

Káťa: Well, certainly not that. Such a question already suggests that we consider your choice 'problematic'.

Naďa: And don't you? Would you have contacted me otherwise?

Paťa: Yes.

Káťa: Yes and no.

Paťa: The sex business is problematic, but not because of people like you. It's because of the system.

Káťa: In our studies, we don't only deal with the sex business. In terms of gender, lots of professions are problematic; to be honest, I can't think of one that isn't. But perhaps problematic is not the right word. Anyway, we didn't want to meet just because you work in the sex business. We are also interested in teachers ... managers ... house maids.

Naďa: OK, it doesn't matter. Anyway, so you know, I really didn't get into it just for fun ... I'm not a nymphomaniac. Sex has never been the most important thing for me if you're wondering. There were certain circumstances, so I reacted to them. But isn't that what life's about? About reacting to circumstances?

Paťa: Exactly! According to research, it's people with a limited supply of career choices who go into prostitution. The male-dominated system abuses the economic, social, political, and legal status of women. We're seriously disadvantaged.

Naďa: Oh I don't know about that. I've had many bad experiences with men doing part-time jobs but ... What's important for me is that I am not unhappy with my career, no matter how I got into it. It actually suits me. I don't want to quit. I provide sexual services, I'm original ... I have no plan to give up. And I could if I wanted to! My disease is under control, more or less. I have savings, I've invested some money and started another business. So I don't need to sell my body anymore, I just want to.

Paťa: Maybe you feel you have to say all that ... You've got a high income, a creative approach to the industry, you're reconciled to your job—all that is okay. But it doesn't mean you're not being exploited and not a victim of male superiority and female submission. He is the one buying you, not the other way around. Plus, if you were to quit, it would be like you questioning your original choice. Living with that isn't easy. But once again, just to be clear, I am not accusing you of anything, I'm simply criticizing a system which you are a victim of.

Káťa: Paťa, it all makes sense to me. I look at Mercedes, listen to what she says. She doesn't seem like an oppressed woman; I don't feel any stigma attached to her.

Paťa: I don't want to psychoanalyze, I really don't. But what she says still strikes me as being a kind of rationalization. But let's get back to your health. Were you healthy when you made your decision?

Naďa: No, I wasn't.

Paťa: Did you have a job?

Naďa: Yes, I did, but ...

Paťa: But you couldn't continue with it and your income was low anyway. Sorry, for interrupting you there.

Káťa: And forgive me my next question—if you had to quit one job because of your health, how come you could start working in the sex business?

Naďa: There are various phases of the disease. When it was bad, I didn't do anything, I couldn't. During better times, I was able to see my customers.

Paťa: It is a perfect example of how a bad situation literally forces you to do something you would otherwise not do.

Naďa: I don't deny it! I was frustrated, incredibly disappointed by
… I don't know what. By life. I didn't have a father. Mom has been
such a brilliantly straightforward person all her life, I still can't see
inside her head. I lived by the rules, my main goal was not to upset
anybody—the world would thank me for it. But what did we get for
it? Nothing! Nobody gave us anything in return for our kindness.
We weren't starving but had to count every penny. And then I got
sick. My boyfriend and I couldn't settle the rent, payment demands
came in thick and fast. It's humiliating to wait and see whether your
insurance company will approve injection treatment for you or not.
I was so tired and in all that worry and shame, I wondered what
to do next. Okay. After a period of bad pain and ideas that got me
nowhere, offering sex for money turned out to be the best of lots of
bad options.

Paťa: The capitalist society gave you no choice.

Naďa: I was pushed into a corner where there were only bad options.
At one point I just told myself: fuck it, I don't owe anyone anything.
Fate had turned its back on me, I felt cheated and terribly disappointed. Everything I'd thought and believed in until then—I don't
even know what it was now—suddenly none of it mattered. All I
knew was I either give in or do something fundamentally different,
radical.

Káťa: Do you regret your decision?

Naďa: I had a dilemma making it, but never afterwards. Paťa, you
claim that capitalism exploits me. But now, I am the capitalist. I
create desires and then, for selected clients, satisfy them for a lot of
money. From that point of view, I regret nothing, genuinely nothing, I just provide a service like any other.

Paťa: There is one difference, though—it is a sexual service. It means
you are commodifying your own body.

Naďa: I'm sorry, what is it I do?

Káťa: You take your own body to the market. Páťa wants to say that
it's wrong to think you're providing a service. She says you provide
goods, your own body. You're selling yourself.

Naďa: Well I suppose I know what I'm doing. I've repeatedly had clients wanting me to take care of them in every possible way, to be their mistress, friend, even a sister or mother. But when I wasn't in the mood, I told them … I was clear about it—it's my pussy I'm selling. If you seek devotion, go home to your wifey.

Paťa: Are you really able to separate the two? I can't imagine it. How do you detach a body having sex from the identity of the person. How can you dissociate from your own sense of self? If you can, then sorry, but it almost seems like a mental disorder to me.

Káťa: What kind of statement is that, Paťa? Are you saying that women in the sex business are mental cases? That doesn't sound very feminist. Do you think that a professional boxer who earns a living letting other men punch him in the head until he's unconscious is mentally ill? A hockey player, a masseur, a surgeon, a pathologist? Why should sexual behaviour be so important to a feeling of identity? Isn't that rather conservative? There are so many occupations which involve working with your body. People do sell themselves and often it's a problem. But what makes the sex business so special? Are the reproductive organs sacred or what? That's closer to religion than to your Marxism.

Naďa: ???

///the end of the recording, for now, we will send the rest ASAP///

* * *

A Scarlet Woman or a Business Genius?

Even autumn can be kind to our bodies—the pleasantly cool air might foretell winter, but it is still warm enough to sit outside. I sip ginger tea in a café on the banks of the Vltava and wait for her. Cosmopolitan readers already know her, even though they don't really know who she is. Her reasons are understandable but it's unbelievable how she has managed to protect her privacy and identity. I watch girls and young women passing by and try to guess what she might look like, which one of them could be her. I recognize her agent in the crowd. We've been in touch for over a month. The terms of the meeting were absurd but we wanted to have an exclusive interview first, so the management of our publishing company finally agreed to signing a five million crown penalty clause in the case of any secretly taken photos or personal information leading to disclosure of her identity being leaked.

"Alone?" asks the well-known agent, a man with a bald head, Ray-Ban sunglasses, and a checked scarf around his neck.

Alone, I answer truthfully.

He nods his head to someone behind me and a moment later Mercedes is standing there. The most luxurious call girl, blogger, businesswoman. At first glance, she seems inconspicuous. Nicely tanned, she has a delicate tattoo on her neck you can see under her blouse. But for legal reasons I cannot describe it in detail. Before she greets me, she takes off her sunglasses. She is beautiful and I feel like she has seen through me in a second with her super-intelligent eyes. She is smiling.

Although I have been preparing for this interview for a long time, at that particular moment I don't exactly know how to start. She sparkles with naturalness so I don't want to start the conversation on a false note. I ask her how I should address her.

She laughs.

You've caught me off guard there. I don't even know, you are probably the first person I've met in this setting, both as a civilian and as Mercedes.

I can't remember the diminutive of Mercedes that you used in your blog.
Merche. That's a good idea, feel free to call me that.

So, Merche, you are one of the most widely read bloggers in the Czech Republic, your blogs are published regularly in Cosmopolitan, and you plan to publish a selection of them in the form of a book. Our readers, in your case both male and female, would certainly be interested

to know who this mysterious author is, where she comes from and what else she will surprise us with. If you were to introduce yourself briefly, what would you say about yourself?

They are all difficult questions and I don't have answers to them all. But writing helps me in my search for answers. I could say that I am just an ordinary girl and woman. I definitely am in some ways. At the same time, no, I'm not ordinary. I would be embarrassed to lie and be falsely modest. I used to be ordinary. But things have happened in my life that have changed me. I was studying and I got sick—and I had to look for a way to make a living so I started working in the sex business and then started writing about it. These are all facts. When I talk about it like this it makes sense but at the same time, the sequence of events sounds ... crude. It was much more complicated than that and I didn't plan any of it.

So, did you plan anything else?

It depends on how you look at it. I didn't formulate my future in the form of plans. At the same time, I did do things that would prepare me for some sort of future. I did them automatically.

What were you planning to do? And why?

I had no clear idea. After university, I would see what job opportunities there were. Working for a company, perhaps. Maybe in a bank?

You don't sound very enthusiastic.

That's the thing. As I say, I was being matter-of-fact and pragmatic. As with my choice of school. I wanted to be able to find a job, to make money, to make a living after graduating.

It sounds really pragmatic. Did you just want to please your parents?

No, I wouldn't say so. My father left us when I was little. I only grew up with my mother. And she probably had no great expectations of me. Or at least she never let me know about them. She tried to make an artist of me but that soon fell through. I wouldn't say my parents were *behind my plans. I guess I'd developed my own ideas about how I should live properly. But I was probably just deluding myself.*

And what made you stop doing that, what changed your plans?
Illness.

I know it's probably hard for you to talk about it but can you be more specific?
You know I can't. It's a chronic disease and I have good and bad days … fortunately it's not contagious. When I got sick, I had to quit my very conventional part-time job, I wasn't able to stand up for a long time. At the same time, I had expensive treatment to pay for. The insurance company doesn't cover all the experimental and alternative part of it, so …

… so, you got into the sex industry. It probably wasn't an easy decision.
It wasn't. But it wasn't a hard one either. Sure, your first thought is a mixture of shock and disgust. You react negatively to the idea. But when I thought a bit more about it, it got so rooted in my head that in the end it seemed quite normal. A classmate told me that maybe one in ten students earns money this way. I looked it up on the internet and surveys have proven it. I was really surprised. I remember looking at the girls at school all day, trying to guess which of them did it. After a few days, maybe weeks of reflection, it struck me as being an interesting alternative with many perks. I was basically on the other side already.

But from your blogs, we know that in your case it wasn't just about the sex industry.
From the beginning, I knew that I didn't want to be just a whore. Even though I was going to be paid to have sex, I wanted more, I wanted some added value. I don't know, maybe I just needed to ease my conscience somehow. And then it all came together and started to make sense. The moment I came up with the idea of combining work with writing about it, I knew it made sense.

You described your very first job with a lot of humour. Was it really that much fun?

I was very nervous and my heart was pounding, I could barely breathe. The client immediately asked me if I was a beginner. I denied it but I guess he could see it on me. Maybe that's why he was so considerate and it all went so smoothly. A few minutes after he left, it seemed like the most ordinary thing in the world. I had no remorse, no moral dilemmas. And with each new client, it became more and more of a routine.

Let's talk about writing. Did you have any previous experience of doing it? Your writing style is very entertaining, spontaneous and natural.

I had absolutely no experience. Maybe I have an aptitude for it. If you can inherit it in your genes, I may have it from my father, who was a journalist. The very first day, after my first client left, I sat down at the computer and the words gushed out of me like a waterfall. It was as if I could hear the keyboard breathe, as if it was saying "So here you are at last." I could feel life flowing through a cable connecting the keyboard, my fingers, my head, and my body. It was like being thirsty and having something to drink, it was a wonderful, joyful feeling. Sometimes I looked forward to the client only so I could then share what he was like and what feelings he aroused in me.

Gradually, however, something more emerged from your writing. You've now made an exclusive business out of your services—how did you manage it?

I started with the most common marketing questions, really the most basic ones they taught us at school. Do I want to be one of those anonymous girls on a website with a masked face and an awkward fake name? No. How can I compete? What more can I offer? First I gave myself an unusual name. Then the blog. Readers who wanted to meet me started writing to me, and there were a lot of them. I had to set up a filter. Again, I didn't have to think hard for long and just followed the textbook—soon demand exceeded supply so I increased the price. I could even *plot it on a graph if you want. I soon started to enjoy it. Have you ever been to Berlin?*

Yes.
So, you've probably heard about the club called Berghain, right?

Is that the one where they only let a few lucky people in?
Exactly! People will wait there for ages in the hope of being let in—and there's no explanation for if they are or not. And yet, perhaps because of it, there are always lots of people queuing there. Because when you suddenly find yourself inside after waiting for an hour out in the cold, you've won and every drink tastes better. And while you dance, you think of the poor people who've not been let in and are stuck outside in the cold, thinking about the next best option. And it makes you happy.

And the same goes for your clients ...
I hope so, you should ask them. But yes, this is the way I thought about it. For example, I've been doing auctions recently. Whoever offers the highest amount wins an evening with me. At the same time, according to the agreement that the guy has to make with my agent beforehand, I do not commit to anything. When I'm interested, I go to bed with him and fulfil his every wish. If not, there will be no sex at all. For rich men, the possibility of rejection is such a challenge that they have trouble resisting.

Wouldn't it be much cheaper for them to seduce a young woman at a disco?
Probably. But they don't need to save their money. They need to spend it. And I am more than happy to help them with that. The second difference is that rich men are often married, busy, they don't have time to hang out in bars and try their luck there. And the third difference is that with me, they are guaranteed intelligent company. And if they have a little bit of confidence and I am interested in them, they will have the kind of sex which, with all due respect, a less experienced girl from a disco would probably not give them.

And what about those who fail the "auction"?
I don't just do auctions. I also offer standard appointments. Interested parties should send me a motivational email, anonymously, of course. I'll read it and if I'm interested and have time, I'll reply.

A motivational email—fascinating! It is no secret that you earn more than most in your business. But, if I may ask, how much do clients have to pay for an hour with you?
There is no fixed price. Only a voluntary contribution.

Really?
That's right. In the most luxurious restaurants and clubs, the rich also order food and drink without knowing the price. They have so much money that they are willing to pay almost anything. And it helps makes the experience exceptional. Only once has it happened that a man paid me less than what my theoretical, market price would be. In other cases, they overpaid, often massively. Rarely do men want to look like cheapskates in such a situation.

You obviously have a way with men. And there another special thing about you that excites them. Is it true that you've never ... come?
Yes. I was close a couple of times but I've never had an orgasm. Well, except when I did it myself. I am looking for a man who will make me feel at least as good as I can make myself feel. I wasn't even able to climax with my boyfriend.

Do you have a boyfriend?
I did have. It was a long-term relationship but we recently broke up.

Did he know what you do for a living? Did he find out?
Kind of but it wasn't that that destroyed our relationship. It was more complicated than that.

How about your family?

I don't talk about my job. That, I think is clear. Society is not ready for that yet, unfortunately. But if my mother found out, I don't think it would be the end of the world for her. We spend less and less time together—she lives far away.

What about your future plans? You revealed that you are preparing a book, even suggested that you'd like to bring your own brand of perfumes and fashion accessories onto the market.

I'm keeping the details to myself for now, but yes—I'd like to do all those things at the same time.

And then—maybe the new business will earn you so much money that you could eventually quit the ...

What? Prostitution? Feel free to say it. Why does everybody think I should want to quit the sex industry? Do you think I don't enjoy doing it, that I'm only doing it out of necessity?

No, but I assumed you wouldn't want to do it forever. Maybe you'll meet a man and your job won't be compatible with life with him. Maybe there will be children. Maybe ...

Maybe I'll be in a wheelchair in a year from now! But seriously. I wouldn't ask you whether you want to be a journalist for the next ten years. Could you even answer that question? Honestly, I have no idea how long I'll be doing anything for. But I'm not planning on quitting, even if I got obnoxiously rich. Everything I do brings me satisfaction. I made this choice and haven't changed my mind since. I'm not the type to adapt or apologize to anyone. I want to ride the wave as long as I can.

Where do you want it to carry you to?

To the top! I am already a celebrity in my branch. You're interviewing me; you might as well ask me about my favourite colour or dessert. People want to read such things. I'm doing great, I'm making money and I want it to stay that way as long as possible.

109

You are confident, successful, ambitious. You are famous. And yet— almost no one knows what you look like. Aren't you sorry you have to remain anonymous?

Not at all, quite the reverse. I've invented and developed something mysterious and independent of my everyday identity. I've created a concept, a brand. Other women in the industry are already trying to copy my business plan but I'm not afraid, there is only one original. Men are willing to invest time and money just to schedule a meeting with me. Not with any woman but with me specifically; they want to see my face and they are rewarded. I love the moment when they see me and their faces light up because I am even more beautiful than they dared hope. I am a legend but no one bothers me when I go shopping at Palladium. I have everything.

* * *

It's a deep dark night. My heels creak against the tarmac, I plod along the white road verge. It is so straight, so symmetrical and so long. The distance between the lamps seems short from the inside of a car; it seems endless while walking. The road narrows in the distance, perhaps the lights will be closer to one another at the end.

Why is it foggy? The moon is shining. The sequins on my skirt reflect its glow, only a tiny amount of light penetrates through to my joints. There is a dull pressure in them as if they didn't even belong to me. They move and bend but the lubricant is missing in them. My hips and knees are squeaking and my bones cracking: cartilage is a weak shield. It may sound weird but can pieces of clothing and shoes hurt? I take off my high heels, look at the bow over the hole for my toes, and wonder how it can hurt so much. A good thing my eyesight is getting worse, at least I won't see anything anymore. I stick my head out in the fog so that I don't see the tarmac, the barriers, the weeds that break through in the space between the tiles of the drainage channel. So that I don't see anything, so that the whole world doesn't start hurting.

I shouldn't have gone there. I should have listened to my intuition. A bad premonition was not the product of a fading relapse. It turned out to be true. Shit.

I got off at the services and he asked me whether I'll be all right. But that wasn't the main subject of his interest. I shrugged. He asked me whether I will keep my mouth shut. There is no one to talk to at the motorway. And this night is not made for confidential conversations.

A truck driver stops near me but I tell him to *fuck off, you motherfucker*, the worst vulgarity I can think of. He certainly understands, he has to be Ukrainian or Polish based on those few words he said, I cannot see the licence plate properly. Does he think I am some street whore?!

Men!

What do you call a duel in which three people compete?

The last of them, the one who drove me here, gave me some kind of powder. Supposedly for the pain, I had to lick it off the paper square in which it was wrapped.

What do you call a duel where there are four people, three plus one?

I don't recognize the surroundings at all. It was a short ride. Or a long one? Five minutes, half an hour? I wasn't sober. I don't normally drink at work but in this situation, I poured one drink after another. There are no colours at night. There are only black and white, shadows and shades. Light falls from the streetlights, a little from the moon as well; somewhere up there are also stars but they are tired tonight, their light does not break through the light smog from the motorway next to the town. Their light does not break through the fog which fills the holes in my retinae.

At the very end of the road, I guess rather than see a regular spot, a white quadrangle. What can it be in this region? I walk closer, the surface increases.

A blank sheet of paper. A high school journal, experiences, and reflections. Shallow and embarrassing even without the course of time. I finished one block, bought a new one without ever writing a single letter in it. I opened it. I examined the blank paper and studied the structures, the cellulose, I remembered the visits in the pulp mill; they showed us the mash from which the paper is poured, dried, and cut. I closed it.

I quit the diary overnight. It was the only real form of writing anyway. Fake keyboard tapping and uploading on the internet doesn't count. The letters are ground into electric shocks, into signals, which are spread through the air even without a wire, anyone can steal them and ravish them in the virtual interspace. Even now, thousands of sad messages, lies, and fictional stories fly around me. Signals of despair blow right into my face, my hair blows in them as well, microscopic particles of delusions and rumours cut into the eyes. I am all alone here, surrounded by ghosts. A digital cloud paints *The Scream* by Munch up there. I look away, I feel dizzy.

The white rectangle is closer, I can already recognize the outlines. It is a hospital built of pure cold. Translucent without a living soul inside, only the dummies from the shop-windows are in there. Each one has a red target representing the source of pain on their body—each in a different place, just as in analgesic advertising. Men in boiler suits arrive, they move but they are not alive either. Screwdrivers in their hands, they ruthlessly stab at red targets. A silent massacre, not a single sound can be heard. Some sort of sound comes from somewhere in my stomach, the squeak stops under my throat, it does not disturb the scene made of vacuum bricks.

I am still far from the hospital and want to get closer. I walk but am not getting any closer, I even feel that when I quicken my pace I'm lagging behind and move away from it. I start running, my legs are heavy. One after another, they both disconnect from my body and stay behind me. I continue without them, I stroke my arms but they also fall off, disappearing behind me, as if the force of gravity worked horizontally not vertically, they fall back in the opposite direction at about five feet above the motorway, back into the darkness, there, where I stood before. I'm just a torso now, I wiggle myself to the hospital, I can already see the ice handle on the crystal door, I feel like kissing it but hope is deception: I'm further and further away, I only stroke my head now, like a sprinter for the photo at the end of the race.

I am alone in the fading darkness. There are no lamps in this section. The first flashes of daylight can be seen among the clouds. A flock of big black birds crosses the sky, crows or ravens, I never figured out the difference between them. They are beautiful and don't caw; only the flapping of their wings can be heard. They do not fly in regular formation: they first fly straight, but then as if on command, they change the direction of flight almost at a right angle out of nowhere in a chaotic grouping. As if there was an intersection of airways out there, or simply a wind blowing too hard. There is no intersection down here, just a straight road that looks incredibly useless without cars.

I've lost my high heels and my phantom legs are now barefoot. I miss my body but still drag it over the tarmac. It is as clean as if it had just been vacuumed and sprayed with a garden hose. I lick it and it tastes like dry pasta.

Something approaches from behind. I hear a rumble, the sound gets closer, a horn sounds—an illuminated truck at full speed. The driver sounds the horn once more, my ears are buzzing. There is a naked man at the side of the road, his pale body illuminated to the smallest unflattering detail. I slow the scene down: dangling pieces of skin and fat, grey hairs, and circles under his eyes as dark as a hole that could bend the light rays. He steps onto the road and the truck hits him with huge impact. His body dances in the air, as smoothly as a rag, before falling into the bushes behind the crash barriers. The truck doesn't even slow down; it races close behind the cone of light; together they force their way through the dim fog.

The blood is pounding between my ears, the sounds, dull and hollow, are bubbling. I reach the catapulted body and I recognize him right away. I bend down to him. He is not dead; he is even dressed now and smells strongly of sweat, urine, and alcohol.

"Nadenka? Nadenka! My sweet girl, where is your body? Why do you only have a head? I know you; I'd know you if you stood a hundred kilometres away. Why do you cover your mole up?"

Plenty of questions, yet I have more of them. I am just unable to ask.

"Did you get kicked out of the private flat?"

What does he mean by "the private flat?" Does he know where I lived? Or what I did?

"Father, it is *you* who is homeless!"

He stays silent. His calves are wrapped up in chromed magnetic tapes; he pulls crumpled pieces of newspaper out of his trousers and jacket sleeves and clumsily spreads them on the damp grass in front of me. They tear and he swears silently. Those are the cuttings from the chest, I know them by heart. There is also the one that has always stood out from the rest. It is about some accident, but my father was neither the author of it nor mentioned in the article. Mom didn't tell me anything specific about the report. She said it might be in the chest by mistake. I didn't like that. How could it be a magic chest if things ended up in it by accident, even by mistake?

I want to ask my dad but I have no chance—he puts his rough finger over my mouth and shakes his head. His teeth chatter from cold; the insulation made of crumpled newspaper is no longer keeping him warm. His thin jacket and jeans are too big for him, he is lost in them, small and shaking.

"Warm me up," he hugs me, together with my body that has now come back to me. Dad still smells but I don't mind it. His body heat is stronger, stronger than I have ever felt from anyone else.

"You've never given me a hug this tight," Belly says, my father now gone and replaced.

I pull away and Belly nods. Both understandingly and sadly. He sighs and sits down. He sits on the magical chest. He is silent for a moment, he peels off the old paint and sighs at regular 20-second intervals.

The air is not just matter but has resistance and can even break trees. It crawls more ponderously than frivolously and hisses whenever it touches my body. These freezing little sparks illuminate the surroundings so I can see how cold it is, how the coldness crawls under clothes. The cold air has an anaesthetic effect, I am heavier and heavier, my shoulders drop with each inhale and exhale; I am a blade of grass that bends under gusts of the wind and drops of dew. The smell of burnt wood—we are at the cottage! The door is open, the smell that is in my DNA, as well as in my mom's and dad's, the smell from his old things, wood varnish, the wood itself and the dust, all of it strikes my nose. Just a few metres and I am lying on the couch, dying on it from fatigue.

Belly firmly squeezes my arm: "You won't find anyone there anymore. You have to go."

"But I …"

I am at the motorway once again.

I trudge along it and the idea it may be endless torments me, the idea that it goes around the whole world, with tunnels through mountains and bridges over seas. The idea that I would walk for a long time just to circumscribe the giant circle and for what? Just so I could get to the beginning once again? Remission, relapse, a jump from the frying pan into the fire, from hand to mouth, day to day, for one night.

I see another fucking white rectangle and I am already annoyed by it. Let's see what it's going to be this time. What will I follow and what will appear and then disappear? What will scar me? My ability to tolerate surprises is now meeting limits that have been both hard tested and violently shifted.

There is a projector screen and I stand behind the camera, an observer. I see three men, sports shirts, tanned skin, white teeth. They smile, each of them has a joke for me, the best wins. They all court me at the same time, but it is hard to perceive them all simultaneously so I just laugh. When I don't know what to say I pretend to be mysterious. We drink a toast. They pour vodka into my mineral water, it sharpens the bubbles. Their chivalry fades as they vie with each other for my attention.

Me! Me! Here, Look at me! Look, you little bitch. No, not there, here!

It wasn't a good idea, the agent has overreached himself. How do I call the competition off?

I guess with one of them inside me it's too late for that. He has a metal attachment on his penis, almost like a whistle, and thrusts it inside me without protection. Did I take the pill? Cut: In the same rhythm, the knife penetrates the body of one of the men, then the other. Blood spouts out of the wounds and runs down my thighs. The same rhythm, body to body, mating, and killing. And beautiful music, a sighing instrument solo. A camera on a tripod, I don't shoot anymore, I am in stand-by mode. From a height just below the ceiling, outside my body, I resist being in my own body and with somebody else's eyes, I look at the stabbed corpses, at the havoc after the storm of violence. It is not a video from Braňo's computer, it is my memory, which doesn't fail me right now, even if it fucking could.

I am on a motorway. It is raining ink, pouring down from the leaky skies and everything's turning black. I am the blackest tarmac road with no sign of an end.

TONGUE

u-topia

"You seem to be coming apart at the seams, don't you?" Jaro's eyes are too irritated to see his provoker's face, nor does he particularly want to. Nor does he need to—he can imagine his smirk. They have not been friends; in fact, they have had an unpleasant history—Roman was his superior until recently and, because he was his editor-in-chief, Jaro respected him. He used to like coming to this pub, named after the city's Soviet twin town. Things are different now. He avoids the pub, and Roman has been pissing him off.

"I guess you can't hear very well. I said that you're losing it!"

Roman used to have class, but in the course of a few months he has turned bitter and resentful. And to make things worse, he is right. Jaro has been down on his luck lately, which is one of the reasons he is here now. He'd been pushing his daughter's pram in the drizzly weather for an hour before she finally fell asleep, just outside the pub. The wind blew towards them the first drops from the heavy clouds scuttling overhead. The earth felt compressed and isolated; with no crack in the clouds, the depth, height, and width of the universe it had no way of reaching the earth. It was an October both autumnal and wintry.

He felt dry, his head ached and the root of his tongue felt heat-clamped; he had miniature sand dunes rather than taste buds. He deserved a glass of something and sat by the window to keep an eye on the pram under the awning. With a crumpled and sticky cloth handkerchief, he dabbed at his eyes seeping from the wind and cigarette smoke.

He can see Roman's face now. As usual, he is sitting at his corner table by the radiator. Lately he hasn't seen him anywhere else in here. Not going to the gents, neither arriving nor leaving, he always sits there like a small deity—on the table in front of him is a glass of flat beer, an open newspaper, and a smouldering sprat tin full of cigarette butts. He continues to officiate, only now he does it in exile.

"What do you know about me? Everybody's got problems. So what!"

"They say it's already starting. In the Krym café, they've written down the 61 steps to the Slovak independence. One republic may eventually split into two, multiplication by division. I don't want to heat up my own soup, but I told you so. Remember? You all thought I was a complete fool."

The publican chuckles; Roman folds the newspaper and smothers his cigarette in the overflowing ashtray. He looks at Jaro—a challenge or, God forbid, a pity? Jaro looks away.

A year ago he couldn't even imagine his homeland could be divided, and he cannot do so now either. The end of communism was surprising, but not too surprising—many had dreamed of it. But that there might be a border check on the road to Brno? That the plastic stencil that they used at school to outline the land borders would become a torso? A couple of torsos?

They were sitting here exactly like this, he recalls vividly. Roman, rather drunk, was bellowing from the table and fencing with a sheet of newspapers. That it wasn't about competence, about federation, about dashes, or about fucking hyphens. "You've been following the elections, ha? Not a single all-state political party, different priorities in each of the two republics. Nobody says it out loud, but independence hangs in the air. That's the logic of history." Jaro laughed at him, condescendingly stating that his state was Czecho-Slovakia, with or without a hyphen. Only cretins, nationalists, long for secession. Not patriots, not even populists! He was one hundred percent sure that reason and the will of the people would prevail. Now he is less sure. That smart-alecky serpent *must not* be right.

Without the noise from the radio, the pub would be rather quiet. Jaro is looking out at the pram. The publican is washing the beer mugs—twice with a foamy brush, twice with a jet shower, water disappearing down the protruding drain pipe. He shouldn't have come here.

"You have nothing to mourn, Jarino. The Czechs and us might wave goodbye to each other, God's speed and the handkerchief, but what does it matter? We have a new regime here! Both, us and them. And that's what you were pining for, isn't it? Long live liberty!" Roman's fingers mark the air-quotes at the last word.

This is what he and his colleagues were quietly arguing about in the newsroom before November. They even made a bet, and Jaro won—the curbs on freedom were removed. He wanted the farce to end, wanted it badly. He perceived the lack of freedom. Without quotation marks. He wanted democracy—without reservations, without adjectives. He wanted humanity, non-violence, fairness in politics and workplaces.

"The age of oppression ended. And for some, roast pigeons began to fall from the sky. In fact, you're not doing badly either, what do you want? You've got your connections, you've got your slick patron, you're writing celebratory odes for privateers. Except for a few things that have gone wrong, you're basically a happy man. Happy and free."

Jaro gulps down the rest of his beer and signals to the barman for another. He looks around the pub. Not much has changed here. On the wall are the flags of the local football team and its partner clubs. A battered calendar with a titty advertisement for the Jablonec Jewellery, a state-owned enterprise. Old posters, pale next to the new, double-page, ones with pinholes, torn out from the German edition of *Bravo Magazine*. And everything is dirty. Greasy tables, yellowed curtains, dust on the floor, the smell from the toilet, the publican's coat covered in filth. Under the layers of dirt, time has stopped. He wipes the rim of the new pint glass with his sleeve and drinks down the impression, flushing the disgust from his tongue.

"Well, you could at least get a round since you're loaded."

"I'm not loaded," Jaro says, but gives the publican a nod to pull one for Roman.

They raise their glasses to each other from a distance, almost absentmindedly.

"You have a beautiful, healthy daughter," Roman says in his remuneration of Jaro's good fortune. Jaro instinctively peeks out, the pram is not moving, the little one sleeping peacefully.

"And your woman's a looker ..."

Jaro's neck stiffens, he examines the foam, counts the popping bubbles, waits for it to settle.

"Your friend takes care of her too, buys presents for your daughter, and visits her ... especially when you go to Bratislava on business ... I guess it's just a nice coincidence, huh?"

Their gazes meet, the publican pauses. The bad cards have been played, only the high ones remain—aces, tens, and sevens. Mostly sevens. Jaro manages to think of an alternative: to pay and leave without saying a word, but a prehistoric red flush rises up to his head, pushing out the remaining thought. In one leap, he's at Roman's side and punching him. The impulse of self-preservation checks him—his little daughter is waiting for him outside, he cannot fully let loose on Roman—he is holding him by the neck, using his rolled up copy of *Smena* to hit his head with all his might.

"Fuck, guys, what the fuck is wrong with you?" The publican intervenes.

"I've lost my job ..." Roman says, dodging strikes, "prices are rising ... you've fucked it all up. So don't make me feel sorry for your fucked up fate."

"Guys, for God's sake, somebody's got a screaming kid out there!"

Jaro lets go of Roman, takes a moment to breathe, and looks around as if he's just woken up. Why did he come here anyway? He turns around towards the crying, runs out and nearly knocks over a guy in the doorway. Then he hears the publican yelling after him. Christ—he forgot to pay!

* * *

It was foggy and grey, and it was getting dark. He stared ahead, trying to gauge how far he could see—where the limit of his vision was. Maybe, if there had been something in front of him … But there was nothing and so he couldn't determine his limits. He didn't know—maybe he could see five metres into the distance, or maybe twenty. It was not the first time his eyesight had let him down. Seeing a lot, knowing everything—everything on Earth and beyond, he dared to embrace the entire universe. Without fear, convinced that he had the capacity.

He closed his eyes and listened.

They used to laugh at him for hearing things, that he *thought* he was hearing things. And yet, he really could. Even that fog—it rustled quite audibly, and when it was thick, it almost screamed.

"Quiet!" he hushed the barking Duňa, pulled out his tape recorder and started recording.

"Thirtieth of April, ninety eighty-nine, seven forty-six in the evening, by the pond outside of town."

Dozens of minutes on average every day. He recorded everything that caught his attention. He had his trophies.

Raindrops as big as apricots were hammering down; he was standing under the corrugated metal roof of the bicycle stand, crouching like a thief not stealing, though, just borrowing. A thunderstorm, the air charged with electricity, a strike to a tree, a flickering fire in the sound of rain. He could easily have been burned in his ecstasy, but it would have been worth it. The biblical record is unambiguous and harsh.

Pavlína, while she was dancing. He had just pulled the tape out of his recorder at home, sorting through the sounds he'd gathered over the day when she just started to move and pose. He inserted a blank tape and turned on the recording. Subtle sounds.

Soft footfalls, the rubbing of legs in nylon stockings—one against the other, and individually against the carpet during turns, swift bounces, and footfalls. Another man would have no idea what images were hidden behind the sounds. He could hear sequences of frequencies, frequencies of waves, from 20 hertz to 20 kilohertz. He knew exactly. He could see his wife—her foot propped up on the windowsill, arms lifted in arches, hands almost touching above her head, her head leaning back, her expression concentrated. Moving about the apartment, graceful as a peacock. An orphaned animal expelled from the Earth, drawing its own constellation.

Marching soldiers, the sound of dozens of pairs of army boots. Perfect rhythm, yet no content, nothing *meta*. The regular thump, thump, thump, either you join in or you drop out, the parade of time from the past into the future, the endless beat of a heart hungry for conquest. And the memory of his father.

Pavlína, sighing with pleasure. He didn't tell her he was turning on the tape recorder. When she was in the bathroom, he put it under the bed. The next day he listened to the recording—technically perfect. Both the content and the charge immediately gave him an erection. Given how straightforward sex is as an activity, the sighs were varied. A monotonous cadence of mating, but in the sighs there is a story. Gentle whimpering, louder sighs, then singing and the voice testing the upper octaves—head notes and fistula, finally a contented purring in the lower notes. Introduction, rising action, climax, conclusion. One smooth arc, all perfect. The only one thing missing was him. He knew he was being recorded, so he was completely silent, didn't even sigh.

When he couldn't make a good recording, he'd leave the tape recorder at home and go for walks with Duňa. He was afraid he would come across an interesting sound and be unable to immortalize it. But he also looked forward to a world without technology and would just wander around the city with his eyes half closed, guessing what he could hear before he could see it. He would have preferred to walk with his eyes completely closed and secretly wished to have a guide dog.

When he went out into the streets, he was an artist and listener in one person picking up on everyday sounds: a lady in her prime, her face expressionless, but the clicking of her heels sending a clear signal. Shoo! She shooed away people, dogs and weeds in the cracked asphalt. Gold jewels clinked on her neck and arms as she moved to the rhythm of a waltz. Shoo, click, click! Shoo, click, click! In the car park, a man was trying to start a car engine. "You must have a cold engine, use the choke," his friends kibitzed in a disharmonic duet, one with a cigarette, taking a drag all the way to the filter, leaning away from the open bonnet. Then he coughed, tapping out a rhythm perfectly syncopated with the stuttering engine.

Less common sounds: a low-flying fighter jet releasing the same note as the circular saw in a house near his, the saw an octave higher; the clatter of arms on a tennis court—instead of the comforting sounds of racquets and balls, a historical fencing group crossing swords. Metal on metal, skids on clay, muffled sighs.

Then quite extraordinary sounds and situations: a boy with a Walkman, headphones on his ears, music supplemented by his humming, trying to dance with football boots on his feet. He followed and watched him for about five minutes, wondering what he was listening to, unable to figure it out. By the rustling from the foam headphones, it could have easily been metal or Depeche Mode. The boy, undecoded, disappeared into the entrance of the block of flats.

The most bizarre situation—in the lift, a red-eyed elderly neighbour holding back tears for two floors, but on the third, a grotesque sob bubbled up inside her which she literally vomited out. She couldn't withstand the pressure in her rear end either, and the cabin of the lift shook with a sound like the tearing of thick canvas followed by a mixture of choked-up crying, apologetic gesticulation, and attempts to say something with not a word understood. He got out of the lift on the sixth floor and merely waved good-bye. At such moments, he regretted not having his tape recorder on him.

He scorned no sound on his ramblings; together they formed the material for a concert he composed for himself and no one else.

A concert that had never been heard in this version before and would never be heard again. The purest sound, more so than music.

The overture was always difficult. As at ordinary concerts—it takes some time for the audience to stop coughing, settle down, and make contact with the musicians. It takes some time a person lets go of what has been filling their head all day. A whole lifetime. So, he too, whenever he went outside, felt momentarily oppressed by the thoughts of newspaper articles, scenes from the newsroom, ordinary household worries. Now and then, a banal and isolated sound broke through all this, but it was more of a disruption.

It was only after a while that walking put him into a certain rhythm. The surrounding particles of noise began to merge into a more and more homogeneous mass which gradually started to make sense. He could not read music, but he imagined himself skipping like a note in a score, from left to right, to the end of the line, once going up, once down, and then all over again. Leaving traces of notes in the right places, notes of the right length, with mood markings for cheerfulness or sadness. A breath in for every two bars, for every eight crotchets. Harmony out of dull cacophony. The feeling grew stronger, and the notes were soon plucking on his arteries and stirring his blood until his fingertips itched. The neurons in his brain started to flicker and went in search of new connections. He was growing, then floating, moving through the city in an ecstatic dance. He came home relaxed.

"I've cleared my head," he always said to Pavlína.

* * *

Manifesto. The world as we see it is an illusion; the primordial essence is not the image but the sound, a college friend once told him; he was into philosophy and the Indian Vedas. Without an intervention from above, the primordial matter of *pradhana* would remain idle and imperceptible. Only the divine vibrations of sound could stir it into space, time, and the elements, only then things could manifest and literally appear.

He was lucky to have beautiful specimens of sounds capturing the essence of the moment. He caught them in the fragile webs of consciousness, only they then blended and faded away. His ears were the only receptor, his leaky and crooked memory the only repository, coarse metaphors the only way out. He was incapable, mute, disabled. Until he discovered the tape recorder. If sound was the truest evidence of life and the world, then this was the greatest invention in history. With technology, he began to believe in himself. He would catch sound like a shipwrecked man catching rainwater in leaves. He swallowed everything, absorbing tones like a black hole absorbing light.

He loved music, but he only *recognized* pieces and couldn't play an instrument. So instead of playing, he collected and dreamed that one day he would compose a perfect composition from fragments: a symphony that would open everyone's ears, eyes, and hearts. And shut their mouths.

He leans in and pours the nourishing ideas from his head through a funnel onto a long piece of polyester tape with a coating of iron oxide. The mental charges converted into electrical oscillations will magnetize the medium. He selects the best bits and tapes them from a multitude of cassettes onto a single master tape.

A masterful collage. As boys, they would secretly pass around a crumpled envelope with pictures of naked women in it. Among them, one caught his eye—not for the nudity, but for everything else. It was of a figure or statue covered with a white sheet like a monument, a galloping black horse, trees, and a kneeling woman, half-covered, only her belly, legs, and the black triangle between them visible. All this on some sand—or was it on a blanket? His friends were surprised that he had seized on that one but he didn't care. He painstakingly searched for information about the author, found other collages in an old issue of *Cultural Life* and in book illustrations. He pasted them into his notebook, establishing the most precious collection of iconic memory in the visual cortex of his brain.

If he had the skills of the artist, Albert Marenčin, he would have created his own collage: the clippings would show a tilted head, an exposed brain with coils, symbols of signals (many and small), an oversized two-deck tape recorder, and cheering people who understood. The collage would be called 'Jaroslav the Composer' and would depict him as the first collagist of sound.

He temporarily threw himself into speech and words, spoken and written, language and a typewriter. As a journalist, he let experience sonically flow into his head, giving birth to words. First he spoke them to himself, then he pounded them into the typewriter, trying not to distort. Even so, he knew he was only sending a poor imitation of what he felt out into the world. For now, he told himself …

* * *

"Are you okay?" Boris is reaching out towards his face, assessing the damage.

Jaro is trying to push through the pain, not wanting to look like a wimp in front of his friend.

"Sure," he finally manages to say.

Boris sees that it's not bad enough to require the morgue or the hospital and smiles. "Some whack, huh?"

"Fucking piece of wood," Jaro kicks a loose board and almost gets smacked a second time. Boris roars as does Jaro, looking in the mirror at his swollen nose.

Boris called him a week ago: he'd got his hands on some cash and was going to refurbish his grandparents' villa. Jaro mumbled for a moment that he didn't know if he could come, then agreed. In fact, he was looking forward to seeing his friend—even if they'd had to empty the septic tank, he would have gone.

He was picked up at the main station, and they took a narrow one-way road up the hill near the Castle. It was overcast, a grey blanket over the horizon, the cold air clawing at his body wherever it could. It stung under his fingernails; his sinuses were runny, the whole town was damp.

"You'll have a great view from here." Jaro studies the outline of the buildings on the horizon, nods his head appreciatively, has a cigarette lit for him.

"It'll do. I just need to get rid of all the junk inside. I might be able to do it alone, but it'll go faster with the two of us. Don't worry, you won't be working for free."

"I'm not here for money, don't be silly."

"I don't want Pavlína to accuse me of using her husband to do my dirty work. Don't worry, you know I'm all right for money."

First, they sorted out the valuable stuff and took the pottery and antiques down to the basement. Boris looked around the half-empty villa. "And now, we'll bin all the rest—no mercy." Jaro liked the interior of the villa; it had style. But he wasn't going to be living there and agreed in principle: out with the old!

They started with caution and at first it went slowly. But while Jaro was breaking up the banister rail, a loose board smacked him in the face. He is still standing in front of the mirror, examining his nose—blood still flowing—when he hears a thud behind him. Through the whirl of dust he can see Boris laughing. "I'm not fucking wasting time with this."

Boris grabs a loose post from the banister and starts smashing everything around him. Jaro hesitates for only a moment, then joins in. They advance like a tactical unit, pounding down old chairs and cabinets, kicking tables. Soon they are gliding to the rhythm of music, in a dance step, embellishing the ends of the bars with cymbal-like bangs. Shards of worthless kitsch, vases and mirrors fly through the air. They are laughing like fools. Boris then starts smashing the windows, systematically, one pane of glass after another. Jaro hesitates. It's going to get cold outside. The windows have value, he shouldn't really be destroying them. But they've already got into the swing of things. So he goes on smashing and pounding, unrestrained, completely free. They are hollering like beasts, looking at each other during brief pauses and panting hard.

They have saved three items. An unmarked translucent bottle of clear hard liquor; there was nothing else in the bar and they are taking long swigs from it.

An old radio and a record player. They are sitting on the floor, listening to the news.

A former member of the Presidium of the Central Committee of the Communist Party of Slovakia, the Chairman of the Slovak National Council and Chairman of the Slovak Central Committee of the Union of Czechoslovak-Soviet friendship, Viliam Šalgovič, was found by his wife hanging in the laundry room of the family house on Mudroňová Street in Bratislava at about half-past ten yesterday evening. The first findings of the investigation into the circumstances of this tragic event show no third-party involvement. The public will be informed once the case has been closed.

"He was a bastard; he didn't have a clean conscience. By the way, Mudroňová is a short walk from here. Shall we go and sing him a funeral dirge?" Boris giggles.

Jaro's nose starts to bleed again. He sits hunched over, a red stain growing on his white undershirt. A shot straight to the heart. "Come on, let's wash it off." Boris drags him into the bathroom. On the way, they laugh, punching and pushing each other like little boys. Boris fills an enamel basin with water and pushes his friend's face into it. The plunge takes Jaro back twenty years, a scene is being replayed below the surface—his peers are yelling *they're gonna drown you*, the older boys whom he challenged are plunging his head into a garden barrel full of rainwater. It has been used for drowning unwanted kittens and puppies.

Quickly pulling his head out of the basin, he wipes the mixture of blood and water from his face with a grubby towel, his heart racing. He looks at Boris and realizes he doesn't need to be afraid of him.

They walk back into the living room, Boris cleans a Leonard Cohen record with his shirt. The third item they've saved. *New Skin for the Old Ceremony*. He goes straight to playing a song on Side Two: *There Is a War*. "How's Pavlína, anyway?"

* * *

"After the battle, everyone's a general." He could not understand that sentence. The teacher had used it a few times, but he really didn't understand. And he was afraid to ask at home. When they were alone, his mother would tell him with a secretive smile that dad might become a general someday. Then what's so special about it when anyone can be a general? And why after the battle?

Asking dad was out of the question. They hardly talked at all but not because he didn't like him (and his affection was reciprocated, he believed). But dad didn't talk much, not even to mom. He'd come home from work, change out of his uniform, open a beer, and no matter what the weather, he'd go straight onto the balcony for a cigarette wearing just his boxer shorts and a white undershirt. He stared at the horizon, drank, smoked, and sighed. He always threw his cigarette stub into the empty beer bottle. They never noticed at the bottle bank. Little Jaro got a cardboard slip with a number on it in return for the empty bottles.

"Bon appetit."

That was often all he heard from his father all day. A haze of beer and tobacco hovered over the table. They dined in silence. The radio buzzed from the kitchen, the words unintelligible, they digested and contemplated, each of them alone. The silence was neither uncomfortable nor comfortable: they had got used to it.

Only a few times a year, things were different. When dad was in a good mood, he cooked after he got home from work. Most often it was liver and onions with rice. He wore mom's tiny apron, hummed tunes, even made conversation. Innocuous topics—what happened at work or school, what was on TV today, and the football scores. A few times he heard his father sigh: why did he do that job when nothing ever happened.

It was a different story when he came in angry. *Get out of the way*, slap! If he wasn't in the way, then it was a slap and *Where are you going when I am talking to you?* Jaro was silent, only asking himself if now, after the battle, he was also a general. Dad never hit mom. When she got in his way, he would spit out through his gritted teeth *cunt.*

* * *

"Quickly hide it. Dad's coming," Mom whispered in a rush when she heard the jingle of keys at the front door. He was showing her a magic trick he had learned from a classmate and was looking forward to showing it to dad as well. Mom just wrung her hands and nervously scurried towards the door. Reluctantly, Jarko packed up the three mugs and the die and was leaving for his room. It only took a split second for an experienced eye to detect the uncertainty through the partially open door.

"Stop! What have you got?"

He froze.

"What's that for?"

Mom was wiping her hands on her apron, though they were completely dry and clean. She nodded uncertainly at Jarko's questioning face. He placed the three mugs upside down in front of dad and hid the die under the middle one. Slowly, he began to change the positions of the mugs. He alternated between watching his hands and his father. He was sure that his father knew exactly where the die was hidden. He accelerated his movements, but his hands started to shake. The mugs toppled over and the die rolled all the way to his father's brown army boots.

He shifted his gaze to his wife. "Do you want to make a fucking clown out of him?"

* * *

He staggers through the apartment, using doorframes to steady himself as he moves from one room to the next. The bathroom is a church which he enters meekly, his head heavy and bowed. He kneels in front of the tub and heaves, but there is nothing left to vomit; all the blood of Christ has been flushed down the toilet.

His head is splitting, Reims Cathedral towering inside his small skull. The cold shower washes his neck, his hair flowing in strands like plants at the bottom of a creek. He submerges his head into the River Jordan and says to himself *I'm washing off your sins, you drunken shit.* The thought makes him laugh, but a sharp pain in his head turns his laughter into a grimace. He swallows his spittle; his jaw, throat, and tongue ache.

Is it possible for the same square or the same street to look completely different in the course of a month? Leaves have fallen, so has snow, but that's not what I mean. We, the citizens, change our towns—every day we repaint the cold, damp and grey of the December days with the warm and bright colours of the tricolour, the colour of November.

Every morning I pinch my arm, but I'm not dreaming. I took down the kitchen calendar, we are truly in year zero. As a sports commentator, I want to shout out—brothers and sisters, we are the champions of Europe, we are the champions of the world! We've managed to shed decades in record time, in just a few days, with the ease and elegance of the Panenka penalty kick.

Today I got up, had breakfast, and went out into the street. When my neighbour asked me whether I was going to work, I answered: "Yes, there too!" I didn't know exactly where I was going, but I suspected that something was going to happen. A happening, an English word, accurately and fittingly translated by our district newspaper as a spontaneous gathering; in the mini-dictionary handed out with leaflets at yesterday's rally in Bratislava, it was translated as an impromptu citizens' event.

This morning I got up, had breakfast and went out into the street to take part in history, to come across a happening somewhere, to join my fellow citizens, and together we would all take part in the governance of our country and all take responsibility for its destiny. What a beautiful everyday event!

Yesterday, Boris celebrated his birthday, although he had emphasized to everyone that he was not celebrating anything. That it was not about him, that he just wanted to get together with friends and that the anniversary of the atomic bomb in Nagasaki was not to be celebrated.

"Birthdays suck," he said. "If we have to celebrate something, it should be freedom. Sweet life and freedom."

It wasn't the first time Jaro had gone to a disco there, but he still felt a bit like an intruder. The students' residence halls hadn't changed, they were still shabby, the cracks in the panels turned the buildings into an ill-omened, leafless vine. It used to be much livelier—students would scale the high wall in front of the club, jumping, hollering, shoving each other, and running. Now people stood in small clusters in front of the place, crammed onto the three steps below the terrace, as if it were colder outside that space, damper and less fun. Better dressed, leather and silver, economic movements, lazy smoking, less laughter, less noise, and a kind of obvious self-confidence—a demonstrative lack of interest.

Collectively, they exhibited identical features—forming a uniform membrane, a cloud of stench in front of the entrance, so much so it surprised him that he managed to get through to the door with a sign on it: "Private Party."

Inside stood two ticket takers in wide suits, one bald, the other with long hair slicked back in a ponytail.

"Name?"

He glanced at the long list in the ticket taker's hand. "Jaroslav Mišega … from Boris. Here." He pointed to his name with relief. So Boris hadn't forgotten, with all the people from Bratislava, he hadn't forgotten him. In an elated mood, he stepped into the dark interspace, passing into another dimension. Posters whispered a series of messages to him from the walls, without any obvious connection, the advertised events and dates merging into one grandiose show. For a small moment he stepped outside himself, not knowing what year it was, what his name was, how he got there, what language he spoke or thought in. His sensor of time and self-identity had deserted him.

Inside, among the flickering coloured lights, he spotted Boris after a while. It wasn't hard—most people were around his table by the dance floor. Mostly women, pretty women. Beautiful.

He'd never quite understood it—Boris was ugly, as far as he, as a straight guy, could judge. Wavy hair, longer in the back, a round face and very full cheeks and lips. Tall, but stocky, unshapely. Not even fashionable clothes could cover his pear-like build. His dark, shiny shirt was tucked in on one side, hanging out on the other. A huge buckle adorned his belt. Worst of all were the huge hairs growing out of his ears. Even here, in the club, against the coloured lights, they stuck out like antennae. Jaro had never seen such extreme ear hair, not even on scruffy old men, and often wondered if Boris really couldn't see it when he looked in the mirror.

Boris showed no signs of feeling ill at ease, though. Rather the opposite: he acted confidently and without ceremony. Certainly, his status and his money worked on the ladies, but that couldn't explain the attraction. He didn't effuse wit either. But charisma, an inexplicable charisma based on nothing obvious, fuck, he had that all right. Even around that one table, four pairs of light cones shone on him from the eyes of beautiful women. Could it be that what made him attractive was this perverted positive feedback loop? Women loved him, which is why they were attracted to him? Jaro couldn't get his head around it.

In the end, it was a good thing Pavlína hadn't come. He'd asked her, but she hadn't been feeling well in the evenings recently. Boris also mentioned, when they were on the phone, that she'd better not come. When Jaro asked why, he hesitated, started stammering, but in the end he said there would be some chicks there. Jaro smiled; it made sense to him now.

"Jarko, welcome!" They hugged.

"Don't be crazy," he said when Jaro asked the waitress for the drinks menu. "Have whatever crosses your mind. They've got everything here. It's on me!"

"And what are you drinking?"

"It's a red, delicious, Italian." So Jaro drank it too, and he drank a lot. And now he has a bad headache.

I wasn't wrong. As soon as I stepped outside and saw faces lit up not with frost but with hope, I felt a tremendous sense of belonging and wholeness. There were small clusters forming in the streets and people were debating passionately—there were dozens of unfamiliar, yet intimately familiar faces, and I am sure they all felt the same way. When I joined one of the debating circles in the square, an elderly lady put it precisely—on this communal belonging, this holy emotion, the future of the Czechoslovak Socialist Republic must be based.

All of them were particularly kind to one person in the group. He engaged in conversation in a decent Slovak, spiced here and there with Czech expressions, with the nice accent of a foreigner. James, from the University of Montreal in Canada, where he studies the history of Slavic peoples and the history of revolutions—isn't that a beautiful coincidence? When he heard about the events in our country, he immediately flew over. When I asked him why he wasn't in Bratislava or Prague, he thought about it and said that he wanted to see the revolution of ordinary people. I almost wept with emotion—isn't it wonderful to be ordinary and worldly at the same time? James was also on the verge of tears; he said he never dreamed he would be studying history first-hand and patted his backpack full of collected pamphlets. I told him, brother, that makes the two of us who never dreamed of such things. He replied in a beautiful mix of Czech and Slovak: "There is a whole country of us!"

He is standing on the balcony, smoking. Coffee and a biscuit have done him good. Even after he puts out his cigarette in the plastic ashtray, he remains in the damp air. Guilt and religious thoughts are blowing out of his head; God isn't needed anymore. Things are slightly better.

A few moments later, he sits on the linoleum in the room variously referred to as *the drying room* or *storage room*, as needed. An old wooden shipping trunk lies open in front of him and he is rummaging through his old newspaper cuttings. As a student, he was proud that his opinion, something that originated in his head, was read by the whole nation. A grandmother in the lowlands, a worker in the east of the country, or a female doctor in Bratislava. He had his first article framed. Now he hardly ever saves anything, he has written so much.

"Do you want to make some extra money? I might have something for you." Boris surprised him after the first litre or so of wine.

"I work for a smart guy, an entrepreneur, as you know. He's looking for someone who can write."

Jaro had no reason to decline—a few extra crowns would be nice. But now that he's been thinking about it—why did he just smile in agreement, say nothing and pour them both a glass of wine as confirmation—he did it mostly for Boris's sake. He wasn't beholden to him, no. And they certainly didn't agree on everything. But unless it was a matter of principle, if it was just *business*, Jaro wasn't in the habit of arguing back. And that despite the fact that he had once got badly burnt while doing business with Boris. Despite his cardinal mistake and a bad experience, he still wanted to prove to himself that he wasn't a man from the bygone era. Which implied that he wanted to please the new age. And who personified it better than Boris?

"The next time you're here, call ahead and bring some cuttings. I'm sure you have a *portfolio*." Boris stressed the last word and didn't wait for a reply. "I'll introduce you to the chicks …"

I helped James collect the flyers. A difficult task, they are the medium of the day and come in hundreds, in thousands—if an opinion didn't make it onto a flyer, it probably didn't exist.

Posters, too, they covered the whole country like snow. Yesterday they literally took over the capital—as if on a pilgrimage to Lourdes, in the underpass from Poštová Street to May 1 Square and the Palisades, people stopped by the marble columns to view an impromptu exhibition. They were laughing, pensioners copied down funny slogans wherever they could, for example in the margins of the evening paper. There was a spectacular exhibition in the city centre. The fine arts students wanted to give people more than texts written in blue biro on paper, so they put their amateur slogans on large posters and placards, and later pasted them onto a corrugated iron fence around a building site. In their own words, inspired by the poet Mayakovsky and the tradition of the Russian Revolution, they gave their ideas colour and a new form—that of a comic strip, for example. The poster is the most democratic art form, and the street is its gallery, a gallery of awakened folk creativity.

The people have awakened, recovered after a long illness, and now everyone is bursting with energy and creativity. Everyone, to the best of their knowledge and ability.

A downstairs neighbour lit a large mass candle in the window of her flat, because "as a way out of the great darkness, our light will shine into the future". The moustachioed baker at the shop on Radlinsky Street went on strike today by baking bread even more fragrant than usual, and I'm already looking forward to the most festive Christmas Eve sauerkraut soup.

We are all creating a new society, a new civilization, it's a true fermentation! We're feverish, we're in love, we're bubbling like semi-fermented grapes. I see my fellow citizens quite differently, with my eyes open, we are no longer strangers. We are one family, one nation, which has just collectively returned from emigration without ever having left the borders of the republic.

We have rediscovered the ability to act in solidarity and mutual agreement. Even today, without anyone telling us anything, we joined hands, the huddles became short chains, and one short moment later became one big human chain. As one body, we surrounded the town's national committee offices—we built ourselves into a symbol of unity, solidarity, common strength, and firm legitimate demands. A voice rang out: "Throw them out of the windows!" But no one reacted, we had not come to strike or defenestrate. Blood would have tarnished the pure ideal of revolution. It was enough that we sang together, and it must have been clear to everyone that we were morally superior.

History has accelerated and every day is now a holiday because people, every single one of us, have been brought into the spotlight.

He has forgotten the girls' names, though he vaguely remembers that he was with one all night. Leaning against the brick wall, they licked each other's wine- and tobacco-soaked mouths, their hands making the places between their legs feel good. She even loaded him into a cab headed for the main station so that he would catch the first morning train. Or was he just dreaming?

He remembers the job offer clearly, though. Now he is looking for samples of his best work. And again, he returns to the article from eight months ago that he is unable to finish reading in one sitting. His stomach still can't digest it; too much in one go and he would vomit it all up. He can only consume it in tiny pieces. He has a colossal hangover, but it seems to him that the author of the commentary essay that he is holding in his hand—himself—was under the influence. Even though at the time, he'd not touched a glass for months.

He has no idea what Boris's acquaintance, an entrepreneur, would make of his masterpiece—yes, that's how he once described the piece to himself. He doesn't know how he himself would react to it today but is sure he won't be bragging about it. In fact he doesn't even feel that it is his anymore.

* * *

"Did you pick her up with something so stupid? She must be really naive."

"I also thought she had a bit more class."

"Well, first of all, I didn't pick her up. Secondly, she's not naive, just curious. Unlike you two morons."

"Sure, curious. An avid naturalist—her tongue exploring what's in your oral cavity. She probably wants to raise her hand in the anatomy class and improve her grade average before the end of the year."

"And you're a dedicated ufologist, a real Hari Seldon from the Asimov Foundation. I just don't know what alien civilization you wanted to discover in her panties." Jaro's classmates are roaring with laughter, falling against the walls.

"What are you looking so surprised about? The whole class already knows. She told Sedláčková, and she's told everyone else."

"Is she nuts? We agreed to keep it secret." Jaro wants to be upset, but his mouth widens into a proud smile.

Everything he says is true. He wasn't trying to pick her up. He was just looking for some company on his night-time trip to the nuclear power plant. Not to miss anything, and to cover as much of the horizon as possible. First, he approached Aďo and Miloš by the lockers, but they sent him packing. Tamara overheard them, and on the way to class, asked Jaro what was going on. It was suspicious, but he quickly explained, showed her the photos. When she offered to go, his first thought was that she was making fun of him. She was the prettiest in the class and supposedly dating someone from college. She looked deadly serious though.

"So, did you see anything?" Miloš asks.

"Apart from pets," Aďo says.

"What do I know? I thought I did, I was almost sure, but Tamara didn't see anything. Maybe I'll know more tomorrow, I'm going to have the film developed in the afternoon."

"If there's anything there, I'll have to make a copy," Miloš says. "If it worked on Tamara, maybe it will excite Nina, too. She promised me a date for the weekend."

During the math class Jaro is daydreaming, reviewing the scenes from the previous night. Tamara really waited for him, as they agreed, on the dot. He was nervous, but it quickly passed. Along the way, he became a knowledgeable guide. He filled Tamara in on the work of Erich von Däniken, the discoveries of the CIA, the symbols in the crops. He talked about shapes, the most common occurrences, covert operations. She was smiling the whole time, shaking her head in disbelief. She asked few questions; Jaro's explanation was exhaustive.

They were mostly silent in the haystacks; they were *in the spot.* Jaro had his camera in his hand, ready to go. Tamara stared up at the cloudless, star-filled sky. The dampness after dark was opening up new scents in the field.

"My neck hurts." She shook her back-bent head from side to side, her cervical spine creaking gently.

"Then lie down."

That made her laugh. "You're really clever!"

He didn't understand why she was laughing, and she laughed even harder.

She lay back, and he continued to stare into space, a map of millions of stars tattooed into his retina. She closed her eyes, breathed deeply, put her hand on his thigh.

"You really believe they exist?"

"Sure, one hundred percent. There's a million pieces of evidence. But mostly, there has to be something more, more than this here." His gaze traced the horizon from left to right. "This can't be it."

"What do you mean?"

"Well, our world, the world on the Earth. Look around you … History, the present, only wars, hot, cold. Poverty, filth, scarcity. Hatred! We arm ourselves, and somewhere people have nothing to eat. If this is the only world …"

Tamara raised herself up on her elbows and studied Jaro with an amused smile. "You're kind of fired up, be careful the straw doesn't catch fire."

He smiled too. "Guess I'm boring you, huh?"

She shook her head.

"There must be something more, the universe is big, infinite. Apparently we have the gift of reason. But are we using it? Humanity is sick, we are a plague, we are a virus. We are terribly imperfect. We need help. They are surely up there, they must be there." His eyes wandered over the constellations, then looked at her. "Don't you care?" he asked matter-of-factly, out of interest.

"Not really. It's interesting when you talk about it. But I don't normally think about it. I'm more preoccupied with what we have down here." She realized the ambiguity of the remark and laughed. He was not laughing. He grabbed her crotch.

"Do you like me?" she whispered into the night.

"Sure." He grew serious. "I like you very, very much."

* * *

All his life he had been waiting for something major to happen. A miracle. He was afraid to call it that—he wasn't a believer; he wasn't naïve either. But otherwise, it was just the right word because anything less, anything just *partial*, was not enough for him. And not just because of him but because of the seriousness of the situation. In such a situation, no amount of improvement would help. Small progress within the limits of the law? To hell with that! Reforms, compromises would only sanctify the status quo of the system. And the system, the system would continue to rot from within. He couldn't put up with that rot but longed for decisive change. He longed for the absolute. He didn't even dare utter the term out loud, but could he possibly want less?

There was one more thing he wouldn't willingly admit to. He was convinced that it was *either-or*. Either things would be put right, or the whole thing would go to shit. Just let it all come crashing down; it didn't make any sense this way. Because just as he had been waiting his whole life for a miracle, he was also—logically and illogically at the same time—expecting a tragedy. Worldwide destruction, an explosion, a nuclear mushroom, a flood, radioactive radiation, carpet bombing, Napalm. Some kind of blow had to come—followed by cleansing and catharsis. Let the Armageddon come. *Come, come, come—nuclear bomb.*

The other day he met a childhood friend—they used to play football together on the playground between the blocks of flats. He was going to the store and they walked together for a while. He asked him if he liked journalism. Jaro said, half in jest, half seriously: "You know what? If everything was okay in the world, I'd rather do something more creative, something more fun. This way it's more of a mission for me—I'm actually writing about things that shouldn't be. It's a kind of maintenance job."

And the friend, a computer technician—as if apologizing for his ignorance—tentatively asked Jaro: "And … what exactly is wrong with the world?"

"The system, right? The whole system, for God's sake. Politics, the environment, the military, thieves, communists, capitalists … whores!"

"Aha, I see," his friend said, nodding, though Jaro wasn't at all sure he did see. And he wasn't even sure he himself saw anymore.

He fumbled through arguments searching for historical context, analysing the regime that was falling and the regime that was being born, the centrifuge of ideas. He was not sober. On that day, a week before the elections, he started drinking again.

* * *

He went to work at a brisk pace. It was Monday and he was whistling *La Marseillaise*; they must have played it on the radio in the morning. He tripped on a raised kerb and was knocked out of rhythm for a moment. He pushed it away, but it still haunted him— the thought that he was happy. He wasn't used to being happy and to being grateful for feeling well—after all, to whom?

They'd been on a trip over the weekend—breathing free air and swimming in happy water for the first time. Pathetic phrases, but that was how he formulated them to himself, always preparing an article in his head. Everything was suddenly different—they were excited, he and Pavlína. They went for walks, swam, ate *langoš*, drank Kofola. He was staying dry but Pavlína had a small beer after dinner. Every day they went to a restaurant for dinner. It was only Duchonka—the guesthouse was not worth much and the food and services nothing special. But they felt like they were on the Costa Brava, the Côte d'Azur or the Greek islands. They had heard about those places, but hadn't even managed to long for them yet. Happiness and freedom were on tap at Duchonka (*note for the article*).

She doesn't need luxury, Pavlína said, and asked if they had the money for it, going out for dinner at a restaurant for the third evening in a row. An appropriate question for a regional journalist and a woman on maternity leave. No savings, no rich ancestors. A new era, at once longed for and uncertain. You could see it in her eyes: the uncertainty, the shadow of a question mark on her face.

"We do, don't worry. Put on something smart and we can go. I got a bonus last month."

The banknotes felt warm in his pocket; it felt good to be a provider and not just a dreamer. He conjured up his father in his uniform, telling him exactly that, waving the blue bills in front of his nose: Am I really such an idealist? Look at the money I'm making, look!

They had discussed it about a hundred times, and Boris had assured him that it was completely kosher and that he wouldn't leave him alone in it. And that it wouldn't be free. Jaro didn't care about the money in the first place, of course not. He was helping his friend, making a little extra money. He looked at Pavlína—she was chewing, thoughtful, smiling when their eyes met. *I'll provide.*

* * *

"Jarko, listen ... You know that guy that we were doing business with ... You know the one ... Are you there, can you hear me?"

He was holding the receiver, sitting at his desk in the newsroom, not moving at all. *Doing business*, the words that Boris liked to use, and often. Doing business was his job, his pastime, his lifestyle. Classmates, colleagues, friends, girlfriends, lovers, whores, he did business with all of them, nonchalantly and naturally. Jaro felt it had nothing to do with him. And he thought, even at this moment, that Boris wasn't doing business with a malicious intent, but simply because he had to. The way people breathe.

"I am. I can hear you."

"For fuck's sake, Jarko, the fool's done himself in. I don't understand it. We shook hands, everything was arranged. But don't worry, we have nothing to worry about. We've not screwed up. It's not our fault. Do you hear me? I talked it over with him, it looked like ..."

Jaro had stopped listening it in. He *did himself in*. It might still mean that the guy had run away, fled to the Bahamas. Jaro searched desperately for fractions of probability. The second meaning of the word made more sense. He imagined variations of doing oneself in—the motionless scene discovered by the wife and immortalized by the forensic photographer. A body slumped over a chair with its head blown off, blood and other bits of flesh spurted out at the side where the bullet exited. In and out, basic economics. A hanged man with a blue face? Or had he taken some pills? How is it that a lot of chemicals can stop the heart from beating? Is it the molecules, the toxins, that are to blame?

Boris's voice came from somewhere in the distance. Jaro fiddled with the twisted cord of the receiver, sticking his little finger into the holes of the circular dial. A female colleague was pouring coffee, the powder turning into bubbling mud, a hot swamp. Through the open door he had a view of the hallway. People from other offices used it to get to the toilet, but now it was empty. From the ceiling hung a square analogue clock; he remembered its sound from when it worked a few months ago. It used to drive him crazy before a deadline—he would keep the radio turned up loud to drown out the sound. Now it hasn't been working for some time. The glass covering its face was cracked and secured together diagonally, like a cross, with two pieces of grey duct tape.

"Jarko, now it's important not to lose your nerve. We mustn't fuck up. We remain normal and quiet, we've got our version, all right? You understand me—we're in this together."

"Right."

"We can't help him anymore," Boris said.

He had a strong craving for roasted almonds. Salted, oily, he salivated. He went out for some air, his mind far away, and almost walked right under a car. His senses awoke as the horn made his knees buckle, the car's licence plate burning into his memory. He then noticed the red man standing to attention and he had to take a break. Feeling sick, he had to sit down. Beyond the road was a little park, a small space between two roads—three benches, a few poplar trees. He sat down, his head sinking between his shoulders, his arms outstretched and braced against the bench. A couple of pigeons flew down to him just as he vomited up his breakfast. At first they were scared and backed off. But they didn't fly away, they just hopped back a little. Then they cautiously returned, testing the new feed.

"Jardo, Uncle Martin is dying. He has asked for the last rites."

Back in the newsroom, his mouth sour with vomit, he was unable to concentrate on his work. He still has the guy in front of him, can't remember his name or if he ever saw him. A fit-looking guy nearing retirement age. He looked nervous when *doing business* with Boris, but otherwise he looked healthy. Now he's lying somewhere in an autopsy room, a mountain of grey-blue flesh and fat, a plasticine figure. With hairs, blue stains and a hole in his head. With a black-and-blue bruise around his neck or with corroded insides? Maybe he's been cut up by a train and unrecognizable, a mere pile body shreds.

Pavlína is calling him; he hears her voice, but can't picture her, can't recall his wife's face. The projection screen of his mind is still occupied by the autopsy room.

"Excuse me?"

"Uncle Martin, you know how sick he was, they've taken him to hospital. They say he's dying. He's asked for the last rites."

Images of one man dead, of one dying, and of himself all merge: he can't tell them apart. Pavlína says something into the phone, but he only perceives the tone of her voice. She sounds troubled.

"I'll come home." He hangs up.

His uncle has been ill for a long time. He was prepared for such news, so why has it affected him so?

* * *

Jaro and his cousin, Peter, were sitting in a tree, high up in the crown. They must have been eleven years old and it was a hot summer's day, Uncle Martin had asked them to help out in his allotment on the outskirts of the town. They'd begged for a break, pilfered two of his Mars cigarettes, and high up above the sheds, they enjoyed their moment. The air quivered with heat and the irritating smoke shook their lungs when they properly inhaled. Martin called them down when the work was finished. They were rubbing their fingers with the walnut skin and chewing the leaves to cover up the smell of cigarette smoke. From the thermos he served them some lukewarm, horribly spicy venison stew.

"I didn't have any sweet paprika, so I put in twice the amount of the spicy kind. If you are fit to suck on ciggies, you can handle this." He then finished off their portions and gave them some bread with some fish spread on it.

Martin and the last rites—a communist and atheist like him? Jaro had known that about him even before he knew what the words meant. Before November, they had often discussed whether the regime was really based on the ideals it proclaimed. Martin had some doubts, but would not back down. To err is human, he said, and the party will be regenerated. Jaro disagreed, but he respected his uncle's opinion. So why, then, did Martin finally surrender to the church and religion? After all, he had sneered at them all his life ...

Mata Hari, the legendary spy. Jaro had read the story of her execution hundreds of times—she slept peacefully, was awakened, wrote two letters, dressed, and walked calmly to her scaffold. She refused the blindfold and kept her eyes open and head up until her last moment. This is how I would like to die too, Jaro swore every time.

Only death doesn't always arrive in one moment like that but can linger. And not for one morning, but for years of suffering, in which one is not killed by another person but by one's own cells. Which left plenty of time and room for doubt but little for heroism. Jaro was ashamed—he wouldn't bear up either.

* * *

"More, Jerry, more. Come on, more, I'm coming!"

He keeps up the tempo but won't last for much longer. He's sweaty, his gaze is getting fogged up, he can barely breathe. Her mouth reeks of burnt tobacco and the smell blends with her pungent perfume. It's disgusting, it reminds him of garden weeds, and at the same time, turns him on. He licks her neck, bites her ear.

He breathes in, ready for the final push—he thrusts into her with all his strength until a savage animal sound is forced from deep in her throat. In shock, he sighs as if for the last time, and comes inside her.

They lie side by side on the sweaty sheet, and she is smoking again. She's opened the window, there is a draught and Jaro feels a chill on his skin, even though it's warm outside. He waits to see how he will feel, but so far he feels absolutely nothing. Neither joy, nor guilt or fear: there is a void inside him. He raises himself on his elbow, his breathing and pulse already back to normal. Now he is just silently praying for this moment not to end. He doesn't want to hear any more talk, he'd rather not have to get up and go back. Into the street, onto the train, to work, home. Back into his own head and his life. He rolls back down from his elbow. She opens her mouth, about to say something, but Jaro quickly puts a finger to her lips and pleads with his eyes. *Not yet, just a little longer*.

* * *

The guy killed himself by jumping off a cliff. He simply took a train to a town at the foot of the mountains, went for a hike, and jumped. He was mangled beyond recognition, right in front of the eyes of other hikers. The funeral had probably already taken place, a colleague from the editorial office in the capital told him on the phone. Their newspaper had published a brief report on the tragedy, but otherwise no one had done anything about it. At least for now. He heard nothing from Boris.

Jaro only decided to visit Uncle Martin two days after Pavlína's phone call. He was almost unconscious and looked at Jaro as if he couldn't see properly, he had to focus. Jaro stared dully at the diminished body, feeling less sad than he had expected. His head was hollow, full of phrases—how thin the line was that separated a living man from his death. The afflicted body was holding onto this world by a tiny thread. Perhaps, the exact moment of death is just a medical illusion. *Death occurred at 13:45 etc.* Perhaps you can only be so precise in the case of the guy who looks at his watch, jumps, and dies on impact only a few seconds later. Seconds are not given in medical reports, only minutes, rounded up to quarter-hour increments.

But Martin? For him, death was a spectrum. It wasn't a question of *either—or*, but of *from—to*. A few years ago he was closer to life. Now, lying on the bed in front of Jaro, he was more dead than alive. And what if, even in the case of the man who committed suicide, the "spectrum" between life and death had begun the moment he signed those stupid papers? Aren't all the living already kind of dead, getting closer and closer to death, becoming more and more dead? Martin was only a short distance from the doctor's verdict: *Burial within the stat. prd. of time.* It wasn't even worth finishing the words.

Jaro's eyes reflected the poor man's body, and in that moment he had a terrible urge to drink. Just one swig, a proper one. To fill up his mouth. A beer would have been nice but not enough. Wine would have been better but something strong best of all. Louis Armstrong submerged in a big fishbowl, his huge trumpet cheeks full of liquor, a gopher-alcoholic. One minute of holding breath, the liquor irritating the mucous membranes, and drool rushing into the sinuses. When his lungs and mouth start to tingle, he swims to the top, inhales and swallows all at once. The warm liquid then drops down into his guts and warms them, his blood distributing the joyous molecules of oxygen and alcohol throughout his body.

He examines Martin for any traces of the last rites. Is it done only symbolically or for real? And what is he anointed with? What does the fucking priest use to mark the victim? The victim that has been resisting all his life, but in the end—sick and defenceless—waves a white handkerchief, humbled by the horror of death, the fear of the end? The bastard in the cassock, outwardly the embodiment of humility, inwardly gloating with a sense of superiority and triumph. He would have thrown the vulture out through the window.

* * *

A day later he met Tamara—after all these years, the first thing he remembered was her scent, bursting into his head in full force. He remembered it so clearly that he could draw it, play it on the guitar, harp, or mandolin, sculpt it out of plasticine. After the night at the nuclear power plant, he lay in his bed at home, holding his fingers to his nose. He couldn't get enough of her smell. He was afraid that if he washed his hands, he would lose something precious forever.

"Jesus, Jerry, you are alive? This is unreal. How come we haven't met at all? Where do you live? What do you do? Gee, that's sweet," she said over and over.

They talked for a few minutes. They were standing in front of a pastry shop in the centre of the capital, Jaro on his way from a big meeting at work.

She was singing praises about some event related to World Environment Day—everyone went there on bikes, even Budaj was there. They had a vegetarian buffet spread, stalls with information on healthy eating, she bought a soya and grain cookbook. She went on to talk enthusiastically about the esoteric exhibition. Jaro happened to know about it from his colleagues because it was co-sponsored by the syndicate of journalists though he didn't quite understand why. He told Tamara this too, and she began to argue passionately that the world of spiritual mysteries and unexplored forces was important, that parapsychology, Kabbalah, yoga, astrology, and alternative medicine should be studied. A representative of the Mandala publishing house from the Federal Republic of Germany apparently said at the exhibition that one in four books they sell deals with esotericism.

Jaro was fascinated by Tamara's rebirth—he remembered how *he* had initiated *her* into the mystery of extra-terrestrial civilizations. And now they're standing there, and she's telling him how she's bought Tarot cards, essential oils and lamps, and that she can't wait for the healer Kashpirovsky to arrive because he is supposed to be going to Košice. Although he no longer expected salvation from outer space and did not share her enthusiasm for "things between heaven and earth," Tamara's passion was magical, she was all aglow.

She grew cold as she moved on to personal topics. She hardly ever sees her husband, "who is always looking for a good deal of some kind," she doesn't even know what exactly—something to do with foreign currency and the exchange rate. He's been chasing after East German marks and wants to open a private exchange bureau quickly. But the State Bank is slow and he needs it right away, not within thirty days, so he's trying to use his connection to speed things up …

"Well, I don't understand it all … and I guess I don't really want to." Tamara waved her hand and started to laugh loudly and from the heart. It was infectious.

"You know I don't either, though I should." Jaro was laughing too.

"What about you, how are things?"

He didn't know how to answer. He couldn't sum up his situation—there was so much, and yet nothing came to mind. So he recalled a scene that resonated in his mind. He had just seen Lenin's statue being removed in a nearby square.

"And it's a good thing they took it away, isn't it?" Tamara said.

"Sure, sure it is." He was frightened that she had misunderstood him. "It's just that they did it kind of amateurishly, you know. Some tractor came in from the collective farm, they were in a hurry. They toppled the statue, loaded it up, and went off, leaving the pedestal on its side." He was looking for what was bothering him. "They could have done it in a way that was … more official, more precise, I don't know. After all, even executions have a ritual, they follow a precise script. I'm not saying it was supposed to be some kind of ceremony, but this way it looked like a crime, as if they should be ashamed of it, as if no one should see it. A good thing they didn't do it at night. After all, no one even mentioned who had decided to remove the statue and on what basis. I am not sure if it wouldn't have been better for the statue to stay there. To document the past. It's not like it would glorify Lenin or anything … more like it would help us remember things, even bad things, don't you think?" Jaro was getting tangled up and looked helplessly at Tamara, silently inviting her to say something.

"You're right, it's still weird. I was going to give blood yesterday—you know, to help someone, for me it's a physical and spiritual cleansing—and it wasn't until I was at Šmidke Square that I saw that some communists and their sympathizers had turned up to donate blood in response to some pre-election campaign call. So I didn't stay ... nothing against it, but I'm not going to be a useful idiot. Right?"

Jaro was tired, and he didn't like where the debate was going. He'd much rather listen to Tamara talk about something else—how she was going to sprout wheat, how to clear chakras, or where they had opened an acupuncture centre. Anything but politics. Although it was the first free election, he'd already had enough of it all at work. They knew each other from a different era. He didn't want to bring up his dying uncle nor his dead business partner. The next topic that came to his mind—the World Cup football tournament starting in Italy—probably wouldn't interest her, so he just stood there helplessly.

Fortunately, she started nattering again and talked a lot, maybe more afraid of the silence between them than he was. Maybe she also wanted to drown out something inside her. He relaxed and listened, more to her voice than to what she was actually saying. He was watching her. How long was it, ten years? She didn't have her long plaited blonde hair anymore and the pigment spot on top of her forehead was covered by her fringe. She had short hair, her fringe and some tresses on one side dyed purple. She was wearing quite a lot of make-up, but it was nice and accentuated her features. It didn't hide the circles under her eyes, though. Jaro stared at her in elation, mentally comparing her now with how she had been, marvelling at how one woman can be beautiful in a completely different way after only a few years. He didn't listen to her properly until he noticed that she must be asking him something—she was looking at him, her eyebrows raised in anticipation.

"Excuse me?"

"What are you thinking about, Eeyore? I'm wondering if we can grab a coffee." She winked at him.

"Sure, I'd be happy to, we could even have some here, in the pastry shop."

"I have better coffee at home."

* * *

They don't drink coffee after all. Tamara lights a scented candle, pushes away the living room table, and brings in a nicely ironed and folded sheet from somewhere in the back of the flat.

"Will you help me?" She hands him two corners of the sheet, stretches it out, and lays it on the carpet. Jaro cooperates. Tamara undresses, quite slowly and matter-of-factly, not flirtatiously. She smiles at him, but her eyes are serious, maybe even sad. She stands before him completely naked. Her nostrils flare, her breathing deep and fast. Her heart is throbbing, a small mound rising on her chest just below her breasts. As if hypnotized, he watches this pump and feels his own heart pounding blood into his entire stiff body, at full blast, as if it were about to burst at any moment. Their rhythm is completely in tune. A metronome can be heard in the room, 132 beats per minute, pure *allegro*.

Tamara feels his gaze on her breasts and misinterprets it—she covers them, arms crossed, palms over her nipples. He's still not moving. Her legs shake and her knees buckle. She shuffles in place until finally she assumes the position, standing with her legs apart, hands pressed to her breasts, a trace of anger in her face. Jaro is still standing dressed on the other side of the sheet.

He can't hold her gaze. He looks around the room. Lots of framed pictures of the happy couple—Tamara with her husband. He doesn't know him. "So, are you just going to leave me standing here?" she says to him in a strangled voice. She lifts her panties off the carpet and holds them in front of her to cover her crotch, her other hand still over her breasts. Jaro takes the first step, standing on the sheet. He thinks of Pavlína.

"Get undressed," she says lighting a cigarette. "Sorry for this." She takes a drag, hard, as if the cigarette were an asthma spray.

Does smoking go together with esotericism and healthy eating? he wonders, but there's no time to dwell on it.

Quickly and clumsily he undresses, meanwhile she finishes her cigarette in five deep inhales. As Jaro pulls down his boxer shorts, she stubs out the cigarette in the ashtray, and presses a kiss still full of smoke into him, making his eyes sting.

Soon he's inside her, many times in close succession, the metronome ticking faster, 170 beats per minute. All the time he thinks of Pavlína telling him about his uncle and the last rites.

* * *

"Why didn't you want me then?" Jaro exhales the question with smoke. In the short time they've been together, they've finished almost an entire packet. The fog in the room thickens and they're getting lost in the tower block inversion.

"I wanted you, but ... I wasn't sure."

"I could have made you sure. You had your choice ... I probably didn't meet the ideal of a prince, but I wanted you. And I was serious. I mean ... I didn't think so at first, but after that night out there, I expected more. And I could have reassured you that ..."

"I know, but ... "

"I even called you for another stakeout." He last used that word a long time ago, and now a spike of loneliness prickles his heart. There weren't many more stakeouts after that. He didn't ask his classmates to go; Tamara didn't answer his message. And though he gazed up at the night sky during his remaining trips, instead of alien civilizations he was increasingly more thinking of earthly things, though probably even more distant.

"I wanted to go. I had a fantastic time with you back then. But the girls talked me out of it—saying you were a weirdo. And that they wouldn't start anything with you."

"They're bitches. I mean, they were. I could have made you ..." He gets stuck in mid-sentence and waves his hand. "Actually, whatever, it was a long time ago." They lie together in silence. He runs a finger over the scratches on his hands and right hip, caused by her watch. Between sighs he asked her if she wanted to take it off but she just shook her head. He pulls a tape recorder out of the pocket of his trousers and presses the record button. He states the date and time. He inhales the smoke and exhales loudly.

Tamara leans on her elbow and raises an eyebrow curiously but he silences her with a gesture. The silence in the flat is only interrupted by the cracking of joints and the hiss of smoke being drawn into his lungs. Outside, he can hear chirping birds, traffic and trams. Some of it will be heard on the tape, the rest Jaro will remember.

"Weirdo ..." Jaro repeats, shaking his head.

"I also found you strange. But I didn't mind it, it was cute. I just wasn't quite sure about you. I guess I expected you to try harder, too. To get me, I mean. You sent one message ... What did you expect? That I'd go crawling to you? I have my price. I mean, I had ... Actually, I still fucking do. I have my price."

"What price?"

"Sorry?! I mean, I could ... I just want ... even now I can ... And why do you ask so stupidly? You could have tried harder to get me. That's what it's about, so don't shift the focus."

"No, no, Tamarka. My price was certainly lower than yours if that's what you want to hear. But I'm not pleading with anyone. Ever. Either—or. I don't believe in second chances."

"Not even today?" Tamara smiles. "Today happens to be a pretty nice second try." She smothers her cigarette in the big crystal ashtray, leans over Jaro, kisses him on the mouth then on the chest.

He cups her crotch with his hand, strokes it, puts his fingers under his nose. The same scent. "It's different today," he says, just to say something.

* * *

"Double vodka," the voice echoes at the station bar. Fat hairy hands place a glass in front of Jaro. Only now does he realize it was his voice speaking. He fishes in his pocket for coins and pays. He still has time before the train leaves. He is in no hurry to get home and has no idea what he is going to do. What he is going to say, if he is going to say or do anything. Slowly he lifts the glass to his lips; the barman was generous, filling it to the top. He sips the surface of the liquid down a centimetre so he can walk over to the table without spilling it. The small sip fires up the cells in his body—he switches gears and hears a soft click in his head.

It was a strange ending at Tamara's—they were together for about an hour when she told him he should start getting ready to go. She had been trying to warm him up for round three, but he wasn't able to get it up properly.

"Never mind," she said, "at least give me a hug." So they knelt facing each other, hugging tight. She was still holding a cigarette in one hand and smoking behind Jaro's head. His knee ached, but she didn't let go. Still in his embrace, she lit another cigarette with the old one.

"I'm sorry, but I have to go to the loo." He pulled away abruptly.

"Sure, down the hall and to the right." She slumped to the floor. No longer trying to look pretty, she hunched over, her stomach and breasts sagging. Jaro opened the wrong door in the hallway and walked into the room with a crib and a changing table. Then he sat on the toilet and waited for his tubes down there to be switched. There were no toys or diapers in that room, he mused. There was no child in the photos either, just the couple. He thought of Nadenka and longed terribly to go home. When he came out, Tamara was waiting for him with his clothes in her hands. Only wearing a bra herself, she began to help him get dressed.

"You have … you want to …?" He pointed back with his thumb, but she quickly covered his mouth nearly burning him with the glowing tip of her cigarette.

"Go now," she said. She had aged another decade before his eyes.

He stood in the hall, feeling obligated not to just walk away in such a way, in silence. "Sorry, we didn't even get a chance to talk … you know, chat … I wanted to ask you …"

"Don't ask. I'm not asking either."

He wanted to hug her again, but she pushed him away. They stood there for a moment—she was still half-naked, sobbing softly. After a minute or so, she stopped crying and snuggled up to him. Without a cigarette. It took a long time, and it didn't look like Tamara was going to pull away. From behind the door came the slamming of the lift door, startling him.

"Well, I guess I'll be going. Shall we …?"

"No. I'd rather not, Jerry," she said, more warmly now. "I'm terribly glad to have seen you, though. You've been terribly, terribly helpful." But in the lift he wondered how.

* * *

He walked to the station along a wide road. It was stuffy and clouds were gathering, the low pressure intensifying the smell of exhaust fumes. His back ached between his shoulder blades. His shoulders sagged under the pressure of the entire atmosphere, a hundred thousand hectopascals, one bar. At the time when he took off Tamara's panties at the stakeout, he'd built castles in the clouds and could see to the end of the galaxy. Now all he could see was under his feet. Coins clinked in his pocket and banknotes rustled. When he sat down in the station bar and put back a vodka paid for with the dirty Judas coins, he felt no relief at all.

Closing his eyes, he could see Pavlína, his beautiful wife, stretched out on an invisible cross. He stands beneath her and thin streams of milk from her large breasts spill onto him. Outside, it is beginning to rain. The dry season is ending. He orders another double. He still has a little time before the departure. He stopped on a train, on the way to a train he has started. A torrential downpour begins. It lasted exactly six months, half a year, one bar.

* * *

"God bless this country!"

Jaro had just jumped off the train and almost collided with someone—a hulking figure in red and gold attire and a cane in his hand. For a split second he felt scared, the fear of uniforms burnt into the genes of the nation.

"We are with you!" the figure says again in a low voice, and Jaro laughs with relief. It is St. Nicholas, and he is at the head of the crowd, greeting the train's passengers.

"Thanks, we're with you too." He offers him his hand and hands out leaflets to the people around him. It's cold, but nobody minds. Excited faces flicker across the platform—the frost has painted them red and immortalized their smiles. The railway employees are uncoupling the locomotive with the red star. The scene is as if made for a photo shoot and Jaro regrets that the batteries in his camera have died. Maybe one day energy emanating directly from people will be able to power machines and charge batteries. If that were possible today, he'd have shot ten films of thirty-six photos each. If it were possible, this train wouldn't just come to Košice, but would go all the way to Siberia. And even if the sun went out, people would warm and light up the whole world.

A new locomotive is coming, again with a red star. The people are chanting "with the new locomotive, a new government!", but they are cheerful. A bunch of girls want to tape a big poster with a blue and red V over the star, but the tape doesn't stick in the freezing cold and on a slippery surface and the poster falls to the ground. The girls laugh.

A trombone and drum are being played on the platform, and a young accordion player joins in. Jaro is recording, his tape recorder still working. People stomp to the rhythm and sing. He closes his eyes for a moment and it feels nice. Waiting for the train in his hometown, he was freezing. But he warmed up on the way, and now he is outside without a jacket, wearing only a sweater, bare-headed.

"Cheers," the old man says, offering him some beer from his own tankard. Jaro opens his eyes and shakes his head. "I'd like one, but I can't. This is a teetotal train. Nobody drinks now, we're drunk on love and hope."

Over the music, the dispatcher's whistle is almost inaudible. Jaro quickly hops into the nearest carriage. He has put things down in another, but he is not worried about them. He doesn't believe in stealing—today, here—that's out of the question. He pushes his way down the aisle, even greeting strangers.

The students keep pasting more and more flyers on the windows until you can hardly see out. The inside of the train looks like a storefront window during the inventory. *Yes, we're making a big inventory check.* He walks around the compartment, catches a glimpse of the familiar faces of the actors. He can't remember their names, but one of them has a beard like Ľudovít Štúr.

Peripherally, he sees another familiar figure, probably another actor. He is surprised when he speaks to him:

"Jaro, is that you? What are you doing here?"

He recognizes Boris, a friend from college—they haven't seen each other in ages, actually, not since Jaro returned to his hometown. They met in a college club at the beginning of the semester and instantly hit it off. They were together only one year at uni. Boris had just started his first year, Jaro was in his last.

"If you weren't a guy, I'd want you for a girlfriend," Boris said one day; they were already quite drunk.

"Go fuck yourself. What are you, a faggot?" Jaro laughed. But even then, and many times afterwards, he thought there was an atom of truth to it. He hadn't felt such chemistry with any of his friends before. He wondered how it was actually possible that they hadn't contacted each other at all since then and had only met now, by chance.

"Have you stayed true to your journalistic craft?" Boris asks as soon as they find a seat.

"Yep. I didn't want to stay in Bratislava. And it's probably the only thing I enjoy and can make a living from. And you, still law?"

"Yeah, I'm doing law. And I don't regret it."

"Really? It seemed weird to me at the time that you were cramming all that shit. Just communist crap. I mean, we all knew it was bullshit. And you were enjoying it," Jaro said, teasing.

"Well, it wasn't fun, but you know how it is: know your enemy. Besides, even socialist law in the Czechoslovak Socialist Republic provided ways of democratically bringing about change. The problem was the illegal practices of the Communist Party. That's the joke. The law is on our side now, though—people have the power. They just have to know about it and demand it. Why do you think we are distributing all these leaflets about legal ways of dismissing company directors and parliamentary representatives and forming independent unions?"

"You've got it right, my friend, you always did. You sound like a textbook and can go straight into the courtroom." Jaro slaps Boris on the shoulder, winks at him, sips tea from his thermos.

A TV crew walks along the corridor and stops by a group of students. They are filming short interviews and negotiating the format of the interview with one of them. He hides behind a special edition of *Zmena*, turns on a red light, then reveals his face:

"I am a medical student and we are heading east because, as we know, the situation there is different from in Bratislava. We want to support them so that finally there can be freedom in the east too."

Jaro shakes his head condescendingly.

"Explain this to me, Boris. Why do young people in Bratislava feel that people outside the capital haven't woken up, that they need to be told the news?"

"And isn't that so?"

"Not in my opinion."

"Then what's this whole train about? Just look at this headline—*We are carrying love, we are carrying the truth to you!*"

"So what, have truth and love been issued to you somewhere? Do you think people elsewhere don't have any?"

Boris just waves his hand, they both look out of the train window. Like in the old days—they are arguing, but never at knifepoint. As they move north, the snow-covered fields start to come into view. There is more light and they pass towns, villages, garden allotments. A lone old woman stands at a railroad crossing, waving a white handkerchief at them. Jaro quicky jumps up, opens the window and waves back to her, blowing her a kiss.

"Close it or we'll freeze to death in here." Boris shadow kicks Jaro's ass and rubs his arms as if he really was freezing

"Look at him, a star student. On a crusade, he wants to be a Hussite, but he's cold, poor thing." Jaro stands by the open window a moment longer, the wind brushing back his hair. He is challenging Boris with his eyes, who makes a cuckold gesture in retaliation. Everyone in the compartment is laughing, someone tops up Boris's tea from the thermos. Jaro lets go of the handle and the train shakes the window shut.

"I don't think this train is supposed to be a mission," Jaro says after a long pause. "Yesterday I was on the phone with a colleague from the east, and according to him, life is the same there as it is in Bratislava. I don't know how he was able to make a comparison, but he told me about factories on strike, student demonstrations, and happenings—small and big, every day, almost on every street. These people don't need you to preach to them." At that moment, the compartment goes silent and everyone stares at Jaro.

"I don't mean anything bad! I'm really glad you're going ... that we're going. We must all stick together, unite the whole country. It's great that the train connects us." Jaro sounds moved, and his fellow passengers hug him.

"I'm happy that the train has brought the two of us together," Boris says, embracing Jaro.

* * *

"Why are you wearing a Civic Forum badge? Were you in Bohemia?" Boris asks, adjusting his own, with the Public Against Violence emblem drawn on it. He couldn't get an original, he says, so his fellow students made him a badge out of cardboard, with a safety pin and foil and the lettering in felt.

"I wasn't," Jaro says. "We have a Civic Forum here too—we set up our own."

"Are you kidding? I thought we only had Public Against Violence and it was the Czechs who had the Civic Forum."

"A boy from the capital … you see we're doing so well here we have both the Public Against Violence and the Civic Forum."

A rowdy group of students is walking down the aisle led by a saxophonist, playing the traditional protest song *We Shall Overcome*, and the students, harnessed to a *"train"* behind him, are singing the Slovak version *Zvíťazíme určite*. The gospel sounds out of tune, but there is feeling in it. At this time and in this place—complete harmony. Jaro turns on the tape recorder, sticks his hand out in the aisle, hunts for the sound.

They are approaching the next town and the train is slowing. Crowds of people at the station yet again, schoolboys and schoolgirls waving Czechoslovak flags. Someone in the aisle says they won't be stopping for long, so no one should get off. From the window they are handing people flyers and posters, in return they receive a packet of oranges. A camera and a hand with a microphone stick out from the compartment next door. An old gentleman stands nearest.

"Uncle, how do you like the train?"

"Nice. By the way, I have a pension of a thousand and two hundred crowns per month. Hardly a godsend."

"Well, perhaps it will change." The reporter looks sour, the microphone moves back into the compartment window.

The dispatcher whistles, the train is moving. The guy who handed them the oranges raises his hand, his fingers forming a V. When he notices the camera in the window, he quickly lowers his hand.

"What a dick," Boris says. Jaro furrows his brow.

"Isn't he? How long will people be afraid for?" Boris says. "We shouldn't be surprised we have the regimes we do when people are so scared shitless."

"Is it really that simple? You, back then, years ago, did you rebel? Did you protest openly?" They both look out, a blue-and-white microbus overtaking them on the parallel road.

"Besides," Jaro says, "you didn't have it so bad under communism, as far as I remember. You mention fear. And you also talk about how, along with the flyers, you give people instructions how to get rid of their factory bosses. Isn't your dad afraid of losing his job?"

Boris squirms and glares at Jaro. He watches to see if the others in the compartment are listening to what they're talking about. He speaks more quietly: "Are you serious? Why are you dragging my dad into it? Clearly, in his position, he didn't protest, he couldn't. But at least, within the system, he was doing good things. If he hadn't been in charge of the company, there would have been someone else, and believe me, someone much worse."

"I've heard that before. Isn't that what all the retiring communists and secret policemen say?"

"But in his case it's true. If you want to know, he's not afraid of being dismissed. He doesn't have to be. He's been decent to people. Like Baťa or Ford. Nobody wants to get rid of him, they wouldn't even think of it. He was preparing for change and hoping it would come. Every day he saw with his own eyes how inefficient the socialist economy was. Without motivation, without a free market, we could never be competitive and forever remain a backward economy, a hundred years behind the apes. If private and cooperative ownership of the means of production is not allowed, then nobody has any reason to try. Remember Komárek? Have you read anything by him?"

* * *

Jaro hadn't read anything by Valtr Komárek, but he remembers him very well. They met him a few years before at a ball in Prague; you couldn't miss him with his shaggy hair, beard, and genial face.

"Can you see that guy? He's a well-known economist. Do you know where he was before? In Cuba, in the mid-sixties, he was an advisor to Che Guevara. That's something, right? But you know what's funny? Dad thinks highly of him and says he could see him

163

in the state government." Boris lowered his voice, looking to check they weren't being overheard.

"He was behind the reform proposals during the Prague Spring; they're planning something now too. He and the people around him—the clairvoyants. Market reforms to bring us closer to the West." The legend of Komárek intrigued him—he was impressed by a man who could be a communist but also wanted regime change.

The ball and the guests astounded him: he was not used to such things. Everyone well dressed, a buffet, alcohol. Actually, that's how they got there …

"Let's go to Prague, dad needs people to sell raffle tickets at the company ball. We'll make a trip, there's an open bar, quality booze," Boris winked at Jaro, who didn't need coaxing. He loved Prague and with good drinks included and an event with Boris, he could hardly wait.

He was shocked by the quality … He didn't know exactly where Boris's father worked, in foreign trade or something. The ball was a jackpot, he'd never seen such luxury. I guess that's what it's like in the West, he told himself—affluence, cultured people. He was also surprised by Director General. He had seen various communist cadres, all kinds of officials, chairmen of cooperatives, chiefs of staff, his dad's colleagues and superiors in uniforms. One could see Boris's father was different just by looking at him. It was not just his appearance: he behaved quite differently. He had refinement. When Boris introduced them, he greeted Jaro very warmly and asked him where he was from, what he wanted to do, what he enjoyed. He paid real attention to him, even though there were hundreds of other guests. His interest was not feigned, it was genuine.

"Now, please, if you'll excuse me, young man. I'd like to stay in your company longer, but I must go and greet the ambassador." He held out his right hand to Jaro and gave his shoulder a friendly squeeze and pat with his left. He then greeted the arriving pair of strangers in French. Boris once mentioned that when he was little, they had lived in North Africa for a few years.

The evening was wonderful; with Boris they commented on the guests and everything going on, had fun and drank a lot. After midnight they had no more duties and were milling around the hall, trying to pretend that they were at home in that kind of company. Boris was the luckier of the two and disappeared somewhere with a young Czech girl who they'd met outside on a cigarette break. Jaro, meanwhile, moved to the bar. He happened to notice in the bartender's notebook how much their drinks would cost so far and almost choked.

As he went to the toilet, he could smell the pleasant aroma of tobacco in the hallway. He peeked into the lounge—there were a few men standing there, smoking cigars. Among them were Komárek and Boris's father. The latter noticed him and beckoned him to join them. He introduced him to the others, and Jaro was surprised that he had remembered his name. He offered him a "Cuban" and spoke to the others in Czech. Jaro had not caught the beginning of the conversation, nor did he understand everything. He was already drunk and unused to smoking strong cigars, his head was spinning. The men were talking about the Czechoslovak economy, one of them the director of some big manufacturer, an arms factory or car plant.

Boris's father was saying: "Gentlemen, I'm firing on all cylinders. I can do no more, my hands are tied. I don't know about you in production, Peter, but I don't think I can go on like this. Do you know what we could achieve if we opened up? I don't mean sell everything, as some of my colleagues here in Prague suggest. That wouldn't work. But if we brought in capital from abroad, imported technology, improved management processes … you know what we could have here? We could also export and import more from the West. But like this? We're fucked, gentlemen, we're stagnating …"

He looked at Jaro. "Maybe students here will help us." Then he seemed to think of something and looked at him again, this time more reproachfully. "Why aren't you rebelling?"

* * *

"So dad's ready for a change, huh?"

"Always ready!" Boris repeats the Pioneer motto and salutes and they both laugh.

Jaro is relieved that he and his friend are in the same boat. He believes that people are basically good. There are those who would like to start hanging the elites of the old regime but he is not one of them. He is for nonviolence and reconciliation. Everyone must join forces in the struggle for a better new society, even the former cadres. There will be plenty of work.

In the monotonous rhythm of the train wheels, Jaro closes his eyes for a moment. How did this moment come about: what next? He finds it hard to concentrate, the sounds disturb him, the smell of smoked meat disturbs him. The presence is stronger, he opens his eyes. A student beside him frees two slices of bread with meat and a pickle from the foil, offers him some of the fragrant food.

"With pleasure." He accepts with a smile, tearing off a piece. Boris opens his eyes too. What could he be thinking?

"What are you thinking about?"

"Not much, just what is ahead of us. And how much I'd love some champagne." Boris pretends to sabre a bottle of champagne and pours some into imaginary glasses for everyone in the compartment. They are crystal flutes and the sparkling wine bubbles up in them, popping beautifully. Jaro swallows his saliva.

"What are you going to do?" he asks.

"Build and defend ... our new homeland, whatever it's like—a capitalist one, I guess. And why so many questions?"

"I'm here as a journalist, sorry." Jaro puts on a disarming smile. "So what are you really going to do?" And he winks at Boris.

He doesn't mind the question, he's thinking contentedly. "Actually, I don't really know exactly. I want to have a good life. And I want everyone else to have a good life. I mean, all the deserving people. I want to have a good job. I want to work, work, and earn. Make good money. And I want to go to stores where the shelves are full. You ever been to Tuzex? Well, it's nothing compared to what they have in the West. And everybody can get it there, you know? Everybody. Everything is better there, they have democracy, they are happy and free. And they have a lot of money. We could have been there too, if it weren't for the Communists. So, that's what I want to do, get us to where we should have been a long time ago."

"Okay, but do you have any idea how you can do it?"

"Just a vague one so far. Dad still has some connections from foreign trade. There are people in the West who would like to look around to see what there is to buy here, where to invest. I, on the other hand, know the law, it's fresh in my head, I can be useful to them. But I won't tell you any more; I'm going to talk to my father on Sunday."

Sure, always ready.

Boris catches Jaro's ironic grin. "Don't think Dad's going to set me up. He'll just give me some contacts and I'll handle everything myself. I'm not afraid of work or of not succeeding. I don't need leading by the hand. We'll figure something out … From now on, it's every man for himself, no more collectivist bullshit."

Jaro has his own opinion, but doesn't want to argue, not today. For a while they sit in silence, Boris lost in thought, Jaro sorry his friend doesn't ask him what he's going to do. He doesn't exactly know either. But he would tell him his dad won't be arranging anything for him. He doesn't expect anything from a career military man with whom he hasn't spoken in years. And he'd tell Boris that he is afraid of the new times. That he doesn't know what he's going to do, and he's not sure at all if and how he's going to make a living, if they're going to keep him at the newspaper. But that he is happy nonetheless, the happiest he's ever been, because he is free for the first time. And that yes, he too will be happy to fend for himself. But that he's grateful for every moment, every second when he can share the happiness he has been experiencing these days with other people, brothers and sisters. Not because he has to and because someone dictates it; not because it's the first of May or the seventh of November, but because he wants to and because it's as natural as breathing air, every second from birth to death, inhaling, exhaling.

In communion. He wants to tell him what Orwell wrote in *Burmese Days*. That beauty is meaningless until it is shared.

Boris doesn't ask him, though, so he says nothing. Tears well up in his eyes—not because of Boris but from emotion. Finally, he speaks: "Some things you can't do alone, don't you think?"

"What do you mean, like fucking?" Boris responds promptly, and they both burst out laughing, Jaro to the point of hysterics.

The train is passing the Tatra Mountains and the national anthem is playing from the corridor. The friends look out of the window at the snow-capped mountains. The younger one points outside and starts singing "There is lightning above the Tatras," even though there isn't. The older one asks where his home is, though he knows it is with his child and Pavlína.

"Are you still with Pavlína?" Boris reads his mind, Jaro nods contentedly.

"Lucky man. I always liked her. And I'm still doing nothing but fucking around," Boris says, also content. Even though no one asked him.

* * *

"A good journalist shouldn't lag behind but be ahead of the times." An excellent rule, but from Roman's mouth, and now? He sure talked a lot. Just a few months ago, he was spouting ideological lectures and platitudes. He recited them perfectly, although he might not have believed them himself. Even so—there were rumours in the newsroom about where he came from, who he was following, whether he was spying on someone, who had put him there, and what his real role was. Football and weather, those were the topics that came up when he walked into the room. Before November and even now, no one could work him out so nobody really talked to him about serious things. Yet he wasn't stupid at all, on the contrary, he had a perfect knowledge of things. "Nigeria," he didn't hesitate to say when they were discussing in the newsroom the location of Abuja, the city referred to in the agency report. Or when his colleagues from the culture section were sorting through literary news and reviews—Roman casually advised them as if he had read all those books.

"*Life was going on, running up credit/ Only wanting us to have faith in what we'd received and what we owed/ You were brilliant, and decadent, so naked that space went mad, and time went mad/ You were becoming anytime, and something important passed us by,*" he would say, quoting Jozef Urban's lines from memory.

"Beautiful, Romanko, beautiful. You know how to recite poetry so beautifully," young Petra said. She was new to the culture section and did not know her older colleague that well. No one bothered to enlighten her. Why would they?

"Now that verse by Pasternak, the one that you recited last week, please, please." She was fawning over him like a schoolgirl. Roman smiled.

"*The shore is as if trodden by cattle. The waves are copious. The sky without a stir—it had released them onto the meadows and lay on its belly behind the hill.*"

"Christ, how can he remember that?" the sports guys whispered, still finding it difficult that Roman had won the bet about who would score for the national teams in the World Cup qualifiers against Switzerland and Portugal. He even knew the Portuguese guy's name, "for fuck's sake."

He was funny and cheerful. When he said something funny, he started to laugh so contagiously that the others had to join in. With a toothy grin, like a chimpanzee, he ran his eyes over all his colleagues and watched to see if they were laughing enough. With each laughing victim, he too laughed even harder, and that's how the whole editorial staff was laughing as if in some kind of spiral.

That's why his colleagues didn't dislike him. Some secretly called him a police snitch, and nobody defended him—after all, he deserved it ... maybe. At the same time, not too many colleagues went along with such claims. It was quietly acknowledged that Roman's profile might not be entirely clean, but they all knew that the classic communist spy looked different.

He had become deputy editor-in-chief two years before November, having previously worked at a different newspaper. He got along with people; he was naturally friendly. Unless somebody questioned his decision. Which didn't happen often, but when it did, then he became serious within a second, shut down his facial muscles and was utterly cold and to the point in his actions. No one ever heard him say a rude word, issue a threat, or raise his voice. Yet everyone knew who had the upper hand.

After November, no one was surprised when the old editor-in-chief, Julo, was dismissed—the boss had to go, no question about it. And who else, at least temporarily, was to be put in charge of the editorial office other than the deputy? That he was old school? There was a secret ballot in the newsroom and only two votes were against.

* * *

He does not go back to his past; he does not discuss the ideological nature of the regime—old or new. Although it seems practically impossible these times, politics seems not to concern him. He leaves it to the editors and does not interfere with the content. He just professionally manages the newspaper, naturally somehow. And temporarily—just until they find someone new.

"What's on the front page?" he asks the whole room loudly, taking the paper in his hand and murmuring under his breath, "... a balanced anti-inflation budget ... Burešová's judicial rehabilitations ... homeless people at the central station. Well done." He checks each topic with a felt tip pen after a short read-through.

"Next? Anything interesting abroad?" His new deputy, Silvia, the long-time news chief, hands him another list. He repeats the ritual: '... the threat of new attacks by the Irish Republican Army in Britain ... Thatcher asks Saddam Hussein to pardon a journalist ... the withdrawal of the Soviet troops from Hungary ... the resignation of the Mongolian communists, the People's Great Khural announces the first free elections."

"Brilliant." The editor-in-chief thanks the world whenever it delivers a colourful mix of events to his newspaper. Even the details delight, like a "khural," a rarity that both brings attention and amuses; in the newsroom everyone is smiling. His task is to direct the team to portray "the events at home and in the world" faithfully and interestingly, to fashion something out of this pile of often unrelated events, something that will leave at least a trace element of meaning in the readers' minds.

The editorial office becomes a living organism during the big meetings. It was not always so. Not so long ago, because of the regional editors, big meetings were held in the conference room. Everyone had their chair, everyone had their glass of mineral water and their mug of coffee, everyone had to sit through their share of boredom. Julo always opened the meeting and started with general guidelines, often glossing over the situation in all sorts of areas, giving dramatic pauses, which were mostly just pauses.

"That's enough from me to begin with. We'll come back to each point in detail during the discussion, but for now I'll ask each of the editors to give a really concise but factual presentation of your area … time is short," he would say after a good half-hour introduction, glancing at his left wrist, although he never wore a watch.

The new meetings were very different, affected by the time-space compression. They no longer used the conference room but took place in the newsroom. And the regional editors had to fit in. They would sit on the windowsills, lean against desks. Some dared to move off the chairs the "archives"—stacks of paper that the home editors were too lazy to sort through. "There was no time," they said, glaring at the impertinent guests. The latter winked innocently and feasted on the freely supplied pretzel sticks.

Newspapers and meetings were done at the same time; there was an overflow of topics and suggestions. Roman improvised, continuously evaluating his colleagues' inputs and immediately delegating tasks.

"Gorbachev failed in Lithuania, yesterday they declared independence. It's tense in Yugoslavia, too," the foreign affairs editor,

Peter, says. He is thin and has sharp features like a vulture. He was unhappy when nothing was happening abroad; the cold war was killing him. He liked breaking news. When he got onto the Cuban Missile Crisis, his eyes would glitter inappropriately.

"And what, do you want there to be a war?" Julo often asked him.

"No, are you crazy?" Peter said. "But you know how it is, the worst thing is when you have nothing to write about."

Now he is in his element. The whole Eastern Bloc is falling apart, he can smell blood in the air. He says he certainly wouldn't want to be in Yugoslavia now, but smiles as he says it, as if he were looking forward to a holiday there.

"Alright, do a report and try to get hold of some comments. There are some Yugoslavs living here, aren't there?" Roman says, flipping through the previous day's issue.

"Sure, I'll run down to Kamenné for a *pljeskavica* and ask around," Peter says, delighted.

"So what next?" Roman asks, folding the paper and looking at his watch.

"Then there's that Brzezinski proposal again," Peter says.

"What proposal?"

"Well, that Poland and Czechoslovakia should form some kind of confederation or something."

"What, where did he say that?" the sports guys ask, unable to imagine a joint football team. There aren't many Slovaks in the federal team as it is; the Poles would completely crowd them out.

"I don't know, somewhere at a conference back in January, but in April Havel is supposed to be hosting a regional summit with Poland and Hungary in Bratislava, so the word is getting out again," Peter says, his whole body showing that he is only interpreting an idea, not agreeing with it.

"Oh, I've heard that one before," Roman says. "Brzezinski is just reviving an idea from the Second World War. But I'm sceptical."

"Exactly! These days countries are dividing rather than joining, I smell gunpowder." Peter joins in almost enthusiastically, laughing until he notices he's the only one there doing so. Roman is looking at some documents with a stony face.

"Any letters?"

"Lots," Marika, an older editor who started out as a secretary, says. A good soul and tireless worker—and victim of harmless bullying. Her colleagues would make fun of her—as if she were asking for it—but she never made a fuss. She just chortled, *you morons*, and got on with her job. And she did it well, especially research. Like a detective, she'd ferret out any information.

"And? What are people writing, anything new?" the editor-in-chief asks.

"Not really—they're enjoying the freedom but afraid of rising prices." Marika is used to synthesizing, she does it every day. "We have a letter from the Democratic Forum of Communists saying they welcome seeing 'morality spread into political relations'."

"That sounds interesting, put it in there," Roman says. He then opens his mouth to add something, but is interrupted by a voice from the corner of the room.

"Excuse me, may I ask a ... question?" A young intern's hand rises behind the heads of the other editors. She came to the paper late last year from the Coordinating Committee of Slovak College Students. She wore a thick sweater, and her wiry hair, with streaks of premature grey, was pulled back with a rubber band. She was nice, but too nice; no matter the subject, she was always smiling. She looked like a carnival mask.

"Sure, of course. Make it short." Roman's hand indicated encouragement, only it didn't match his facial expressions. Heads are turning. The newsroom doesn't have a strict hierarchy; it's not an army. Yet, it is not customary for young journalists to speak during the meeting, never mind interns.

"I want to ask one thing ... about the evolution of language over time." A grimace, a smirk somewhere, a few pairs of rolled eyes. Roman gives a quick nod with his head—not that he agrees, he just wants to hurry her along.

"I mean, you know, we've had a few months now ... of, what

should I call it … a new era, right? And yet, even in our newspaper, like yesterday, in the foreign section …"

Peter squirms in his chair.

"Well, for example, we use terms like the *South Korean dictator* and the *North Korean leader* at the same time. Shouldn't we, I mean today, use those terms a little more neutrally … or, I don't know, the other way round?"

There's silence for a while, editors umming and ahhing and some clearly thinking about it. But no one speaks up. Peter breathes in as if to say something, wanting to defend himself, but nothing comes to mind.

"Yes, Mrs … Miss, colleague, you are right. Peter, make a note of it." Roman closes the subject, Peter nods almost invisibly, offended.

"Back to the letters, Marika—anything else in there?" Roman would like to end the meeting now, let everyone get back to their work quickly so as to meet the deadline.

"There's one from the prognosticators at the Academy, warning of historically high income inequality in the United States. One that keeps growing."

"Bingo!" Roman says. "Let's do a short report on it."

"Why?" Heads turn towards the voice. It's Jaro. He himself looks surprised that the voice belongs to him. For a moment no one says anything. All that can be heard is the hum of computers and the strong wind from outside battering the poorly sealed windows.

"Why should we criticize America?" His voice is softer, but he can't back down after his incursion. His heart is beating faster and his face is flushed.

"I'm not sure I understand the question," Roman says. "Why *shouldn't* we report this fact? Or perhaps you doubt that it is a fact? We're journalists."

"It's a fact, I don't doubt it. But isn't it enough that you've been ranting against the West ever since you came to the paper? What is it now, ten years?" His mouth twists. "Biased choice of facts"— he air quotes—"they probably didn't teach that at the Evening University of Marxism-Leninism, did they? And you don't have

174

to answer, that was a rhetorical question." The transition from 'we' to 'you' makes it personal; there are now two competing sides on the team.

The reaction is immediate, Roman's facial muscles freeze. Even before today he has never intimidated his staff on purpose or with any pleasure. Through a combination of time, position, and instinct, he has always been on the winning side of conflicts. The magic, however, no longer works. Jaro is clearly nervous, but he is not afraid; he is on the right side of history. He's seen Roman's shut-down face so many times before. It is the same, and yet different. It does not inspire authority; on the contrary, it looks rather weak and old, as if it had been preserved.

"All right, we don't have to write about it," Roman says. He looks Jaro straight in the eye. "Or do you want to include some critical report on the Soviet Union, to balance things out?"

"No. Why kick a corpse?" A couple of colleagues laugh tepidly.

"Then what do you want?" Roman asks.

"What do I actually want?" Jaro repeats the question, thinking. He thinks for a long time, his colleagues fidget nervously. He thinks hard, can't think of anything that would be satisfactory, but knows he has to say something. "I think you should resign."

Roman pulls off his wedding band and rubs the bruised spot on his finger. He's no longer chasing a deadline. The question mark hangs not over one issue of the newspaper, but over his professional existence. In fact, it had been hanging there for a long time, it just hadn't been paid attention to in the speed and rush of work.

No one says anything for now, all in the room are like embryos in amniotic fluid, just blending in. The intern nods her head, grin-ning more than she has so far. Peter lowers his head and slowly massages his temples, his eyes hidden. Marika stares into the upper corner by the window and slowly shakes her head, almost imper-ceptibly. Petra is used to laughing, so she is at least smiling; she doesn't know how to be serious. They all seem to be meditating and taking stock. Suddenly, they are tired and no one is in a hurry to defend either side.

Jaro didn't plan to rebel, nor did it occur to him that he would become the protagonist of an existential dispute in the editorial room. He did not judge his boss, he respected him professionally. About a week ago they had talked openly. Roman overheard Jaro talking about "hard times" and asked him with a smile if he knew what they were. Jaro shook his head, he didn't know. Apparently, they described the city in Doctorow's debut novel, just out in a Slovak translation by Vilikovský—*Welcome to Hard Times*. A western full of violence, a story about the inability of people to collectively stand up to timeless evil, Roman said. Sounds like communism, Jaro tested his older colleague. Yes, that too, he admitted. But also about what was coming. Don't forget, he was telling Jaro, in civilization, regimes change, but people remain the same. *You'll see.*

Jaro did not contradict him. But despite similar wisdoms and editorial hierarchy—was it acceptable for a former … a former party member, informer, spy? … to be in charge of the newspaper several months after the Revolution? Poor old Julo had been deposed to keep up appearances and they put this one in his place? A man vaguely but unmistakably linked to the power of the last regime. A man educated, cheerful, good-natured … but a man of the past era. So much has changed, so quickly, but isn't this going to change? *Fuck, they've been fucking with us for decades, so what is he still doing here, haunting this place?*

* * *

"You're a naive fool! Are you behind the times, or what?" The reproach wouldn't leave Jaro's mind.

He stares out of the train window at the fields all brown after heavy rain. He is feeling fidgety and can't sit still. He'd happily climb out of the window and jump into the bushes, into the thorns, roll in the mud. He needs to stimulate his senses, needs the cold, the heat, the prickling, the wind, the pain. He needs movement instead of sitting in an overcrowded compartment. The heavily perfumed girl next to him is eating an apple, smacking her lips like a cow. When will you finish stuffing yourself, you pig?

The meeting ended awkwardly. After an incredibly long silence, Roman said that he would forward the call for resignation to the 'guys upstairs' to deal with. At the word "resignation" he raised his shoulders, head cocked to the side, a grimace of doubt on his face. Jaro realized at that moment that even he didn't exactly know what the whole process should look like. An employee could hand in their notice or be let go and that way leave their position. But what about the editor-in-chief and who decides it? Jaro has to admit he has no idea.

There is no air left in the compartment. Even though all eight seats are occupied, a mother and her snot-covered child crowd in and squeeze in right next to Jaro. The sausage, the sardines, the stench. The kid kicks him, leaving a dirty smudge on his trousers. The woman apologizes, he says he doesn't mind. He minds the smell of sweat and musty clothes, but he doesn't tell her that. He's not that much of a hero. *A wet stinking Duňa.*

You're a naive fool! Are you behind the times or what? The inside of his bum itches and there's nothing he can do about it, sitting here, sandwiched between two strange bodies. He's gripping his windbreaker—he tried to hang it up, but it slipped off the hook three times, the loop was torn. He would love to throw himself on the hanging jackets and coats of the other passengers, pull them down and kick them all over the train. He wants to cause harm.

Outside, the sun peeks out through the clouds, a ray falling straight on the big rusty water tank by the collective farm.

It then dawns on him. Today was not about Roman.

* * *

"Sure, you can come tomorrow. I've told you a hundred times, you don't even have to ask. Do you have the key? You do. You're always welcome at my place." He is standing at the entrance to the block, about to ring the bell for the third time. He has the key, but hasn't dared use it yet. Didn't he mix up the days? Stupid thought, after all, they talked on the phone yesterday. Since their paths crossed again, they haven't missed an opportunity to get together. Meetings under Julo's leadership had one advantage—they would drag on until the evening, and although he would have definitely caught the last train, it was more pleasant to prolong his stay in Bratislava. "Work, contacts and all that …" he would say at home to Pavlína and also in the district editorial office. After Julo's departure from the newspaper, his habit did not change. A big meeting every month, other *editorial duties* … he was in the capital once a week and always checked in with Boris.

Today, he's here the day before the meeting, digging through his pockets, fumbling for the key. If no one answers on the third ring, he will open the door himself. Maybe his buddy has just run off somewhere. Finally, the buzzer sounds and Jaro goes upstairs. The door to the apartment is ajar, he enters cautiously. He sees a girl with no clothes on, only a sheet wrapped around her body. He is already turning around, thinking he has come to the wrong door, but he notices Boris with a burgundy towel around his waist.

"Am I interrupting?"

"No, no. Come in, put down your stuff," Boris says. "I thought you'd come a little later. This is Jolanda." He points to the girl and smiles. "Nice name, Spanish, I hear."

Jolanda, meanwhile, is already sitting on the toilet, the door open, completely naked, nodding wordlessly to Jaro. He waves back, embarrassed.

"Let's go into the living room. Would you like something?"

"Black tea, if you have any."

"Still keeping dry?" Boris shakes his head and pours himself some brown liquor from a green bottle. "I've given up," he says unnecessarily, "two days after dad gave me a good Armagnac for St. Nicholas's Day—try not having any!" He laughs. "And what did you want? Oh, tea, sure, it's coming."

On his way to the kitchen, he hears a stream of urine hitting the water in the toilet. "Jesus, Joli, can't you close the door? Do you have a nigger at home?"

"No," a voice shouts from the toilet, and a hand reaches out to slam the door shut. "Unfortunately. I wouldn't have to waste time with your five-centimetre …" she says more quietly, but they both hear the remark.

"Unbelievable." Boris is outraged as he lights a match at the stove. "So cheeky. I have a guest and she's giving me lip. Not even whores have any class nowadays." He continues his monologue loud enough for his friend to hear.

"Here you are." Boris comes into the living room carrying a large Asian-themed mug on a tray. He looks like he is serving something rare. Smelling a strange aroma, Jaro looks inside the cup. Herbal.

"Thank you."

* * *

They chat amiably, share a friendly silence, meander through the city every which way, without haste, without purpose. They pass the trilingual wine bar Vináreň pod Baštou-Weinstube-Borozó. They pass the gutter which ends a metre above the ground, a stone pavement underneath has given in to the streams of water. They walk along the scaffolding, and the Czechoslovak flag almost strokes their head—it may be soaked, but it still flies proudly. However, in front of the Forum Hotel, several flagpoles rise up against the evening sky without a single flag on any of them. It's as if everyone has left and no one is arriving.

"Whew, a good thing you dragged me out. It does me good. You can't imagine how busy I am. I don't know what to do first." Boris has one foot propped up on a concrete pot holding a shrub, and he is tying his shoelace.

"Good tits on that job of yours."

Boris doesn't get it right away, but a moment later he bares his teeth. He even wants to add something to explain, but in the end lets it go and just slaps Jaro on the shoulder.

Ivan Lesay

They hike up the Palisades to the Castle. There is a paper sign attached to a pillar with a scrawled inscription *Österreichische Staatsbürger EINTRITT FREI!!!* Jaro thinks of another inscription, on a building further down, below the castle hill: *Bratislava—City of Peace*. He visualises a shabby, poor castle which, fortunately, is now invisible in the darkness. And, thank God, one cannot see the unfinished Slovak National Council building either, the hated monster they are passing just now. *Bratislava—the city of grey hopes*—what would people say to such an inscription on one of the buildings?

He talks about work, what is new in the world, the situation in the newspaper. While doing so, he is watching Boris, who in his black leather zipper boots walks through the puddles and listens thoughtfully.

"So it looks to me like the world is accepting the changes in our country, huh?" he asks, slightly out of breath.

"Jesus Christ, sure, everyone's already taking it for granted. You know the facts—communists everywhere have resigned, some voluntarily, some by force. I can still see in my head the pictures of Ceauşescu's execution. That was powerful, wasn't it? Anyway, we have democracy now. That's the important thing. Why do you ask? Are you afraid of something?"

"Oh, no, no. It just doesn't make sense to me. They were so strong just a few months back and now all of a sudden they're resigning from their positions, almost as if they were looking forward to the elections. Democratic! It's happened so fast it's suspicious to me."

"Tell me! I still have to pinch myself sometimes to make sure I'm not dreaming the whole thing up. It has all happened so fast ... And you, like, what are you doing now? Are you getting by?" Jaro asks, perhaps a little too cheerfully.

"Sure, everything's cool. I've got a lot of work, lots of errands and stuff to do ... there are so many new opportunities these days. I've got some business deals to tie up, so should be coasting soon." Boris winks. "I guess it's going to rain, it's stuffy," he says, changing the subject. Again.

This annoys Jaro terribly. Every time he asks Boris about work, he somehow weasels out of it. Taking care of things, business, meetings ... these are his exact words. General and procedural. *You're taking care of things, but what things exactly? You have meetings, okay, but with whom? Are you dealing in sportswear or nuclear waste?* Jaro has even considered that he has a professional bias, that he's being too nosy. But he's turned it over in his head and decided he doesn't want to know too much. In fact, he doesn't particularly care to know *exactly* what Boris is doing. He knew he was smart, and he had no reason to suspect him. He wasn't investigating him! He just wanted to know, in a normal, friendly way, what Boris was up to, that's all.

When they were at the uni together, it was just the opposite. Boris talked and Jaro was the one who listened. He even learned what he didn't want to. Tiresome detailed stories from the uni— what each professor wanted from them, what they had to cram in. Details about cases and hearings, supposedly fascinating. Boris was burning with a desire for justice. Personal matters. Which girls he liked. What encounters he had with them. Even quite ordinary things—what he ate, that he went to the Inter Club football match, where he was going camping, when the Bratislava Lyre Music Festival was on and who would be performing. Jaro wasn't bored, it was enough for him to listen to Boris's voice. And then plans: Boris talked a lot about them, changing them often, but always talking about them with the same fervour.

And now, nothing. He is just anxiously inquiring if the new regime will last. Regarding work and plans, he speaks only in codes. He opens his mouth and his words disappear in the fog forming around his head. Actually, yes, it *is* suspicious.

"Boris, what exactly are you doing?" They both pause for a moment and look into each other's eyes. Boris slowly moves on, Jaro following a second later. Immediately, they have to stop again, they are at a traffic light. The red light is reflected on Boris's forehead.

"*Exactly?*" he says. "I provide legal services."

They are wandering this way and that, as if deliberately prolonging their journey, and though they haven't agreed on it, it's clear they're headed for the Slavín Memorial. They sense it up above the city, and the city beneath them senses them.

"Fuck, that tells me almost nothing," Jaro says, the green signal lighting up on his forehead. "What's your problem? You've become a real secret monger."

"Not at all, I'm not hiding anything. Anything in particular you're interested in?" Boris tries to speak casually, but sounds artificial and hard. He doesn't even look at Jaro and picks up the pace.

"What kind of services are you providing? And who to?" he asks as the figure enters the shadows of the bushes just below the monument. His voice is desperate; a casual question suddenly becomes an existential thing.

"Wait, for fuck's sake, stand still!" Jaro yells. Boris stops but doesn't turn around. "I don't mean to pry," Jaro says more softly when he catches up with him, "but we used to talk about everything. What's changed?"

Boris turns around slowly so that they are facing each other. "What's changed? Can't you see? Everything has changed, Jarko, absolutely everything. You must keep up!" He steps out again, quickly, Jaro scurrying behind him.

They arrive at the monument to the Soviet soldiers. A dusty fake wreath lies forgotten on the ground. A few candles are still burning inside the glass candle holders, the others have all gone out. Up here, they begin to slow down.

Around them are some romantic couples and a few strange-looking individuals. They both have their hands behind their backs and are shuffling from foot to foot with their heads bowed, like ancient Greek philosophers at the *agora*. Boris spreads his arms and begins expounding:

"Whoever gets his bearings *now* will win. The cards are being dealt at the start of a new game." He waits for Jaro to look him in the eye.

"You're fucking around in the newspaper, you've got first-hand information, but what are you doing with it? You forward it and that's that, right? Otherwise, things are passing you by, you haven't woken up."

"Excuse me?" Jaro is astounded, his jaw goes heavy. He thought he was the one confronting Boris, but the tables have now been turned and his friend is on the attack. And Jaro isn't prepared for it. "I just ... I just wanted to know what's changed *between us*," he says, stuttering. Boris doesn't respond, his teeth clenched. "And now I see a lot has changed. What do you have against me?"

Finally, Boris smiles a little. He beckons to Jaro, takes his hand and leads him down to the lookout. Jaro isn't comfortable holding hands with another guy as if they were gay.

Boris climbs up the wall and pulls Jaro up as well. They just stand there for a while, staring into the distance, the sun has set over the horizon.

"Who owns this city?" Boris asks. "Who do you think it belongs to?" He repeats the question, putting emphasis on each word.

"What do you mean who? Is it some kind of test?" Jaro is huffing. "I don't know ... people?" But he feels like a mediocre pupil letting his teacher down.

Boris bursts out laughing. "Wrong answer!"

"Okay, dickhead, it belongs to animals!" Jaro doesn't like the game. Boris is still laughing and patting his friend on the shoulder. "Don't be angry, I just want to tell you something." He takes a breath, calms down. "This city doesn't belong to anyone. For now." He takes another deep breath and exhaled deeply. "Can you hear the thunder?"

Jaro lifts his gaze to the sky, squints and strains his ears. "No," he replies shaking his head.

"But I can. Things are changing owners. Houses, businesses, everything is changing hands. The old order is collapsing. You see buildings, I see ruins. A city reduced to rubble. Or not rubble, in fact, but a cake. And the cake is going to be divided." Boris's eyes light up, he is enjoying the apt metaphor. "Now knives are being sharpened and the spoons are being cleaned."

An ambulance speeds down Malinovský Street, flashing lights and a blaring siren. Perhaps someone is fighting for their life.

"Nice, Marx and Ferreri combined …" Jaro whispers.

"Who …?" Boris interrupts the observation that is not his own.

"Nothing … Primary accumulation of capital, the Great Pigout," Jaro says.

"Exactly, it's going to be a pigout. Also an accumulation if you want."

Jaro feels dizzy, he has to squat but Boris doesn't notice and asks what November means to him. Jaro is tired and no longer enjoying it. Hunched against a wall, he merely says "Freedom." Boris goes on, wanting more. "Yes, freedom, and that is not to be sniffed at. Some people are satisfied with even less—buying a Ritter chocolate bar at a petrol station in Austria and bringing it across the border … looking forward to the World Cup in football, in hockey, rooting for our team and hoping that all the best players can now go to the NHL and show off in front of the whole world."

Jaro is listening, but doesn't react.

"So let everyone be happy, I wish the best to everyone. But to me, they are drones, people with no vision and no ambition. I want more!" And Boris is almost shouting now, holding his arms out over the city.

Whereas Jaro is curled up in a ball, hugging his knees.

"What do I want, you ask? Well, I'll tell you then. I want to have a choice. In everything. And always."

He lifts his chin, proud of his ambition. He no longer looks at his catatonic friend, the words are rushing out of him.

"Where do you want to be in five years? Ha? Do you still want to be rotting in that newsroom? That's fine, you'll be free to write; I'll keep my fingers crossed for you, seriously." The cracks are deepening with each passing moment.

"And do you know where I want to be? I have no idea, and I don't care. But I do want to be able to lift the anchor, change jobs, change places, work myself to death or take a year off. Do you know what used to be the name of that street the ambulance was going along? Chance Street! This city, this time, this is my chance. I want resources. It's natural, don't you think? Anyway—now is the time when things can be arranged. If you want to know, I work for a rich guy. He used to go abroad even under communism, he's got resources and connections. He's got access to land, vineyards and stuff. He's got other plans, and I'm helping him with them. I'll get a cut of his business. Satisfied?"

* * *

It was about to rain again. They walked down the hill, saying little. They were thirsty, so they stopped at the Funus for kofola and a beer, a quick and quiet sit-down. Boris was now happy to be able to articulate his thoughts—not just to a friend but to himself.

Jaro had poked a hornet's nest—he was curious and now he was all stung and swelling up. He remembered a different Boris. Last December on the train, he wasn't wearing leather boots and jacket. He was wearing a thick sweater then, and it gave off warmth and joy. *Prosperity, delicacies, quality, savour* ... he had used these words before, but now they seemed to be the limit of his vocabulary! *People crave ... luxury, western standards.* How important geography was! History too. Boris was anxious to get ahead.

But Jaro had doubts. Just after the fall of the Iron Curtain, the newspapers wrote that the Austrians were preparing for an onslaught of Czechoslovaks in their shops. They had prepared tents and car parks, volunteers who knew Czech or Slovak. Psychological support, crisis management. But few people came, the tents remained empty. Unnecessary panic. Maybe they were afraid, maybe they didn't have money. And maybe it wasn't that important to them. He remembered the shelves of tinned goods from all over the world, Coca-Cola, Almdudler ... angular sausages lit up like works of art in a gallery. It was beautiful, but it didn't tear at *his* heart strings.

Private property, motivation. Jaro reminded his friend how he had talked about cooperative ownership on the train.

"You're a naive fool! Have you been sleeping or what?" he asked, laughing uproariously. He told him to go down to the collective farm.

On the way back into the city he was thinking whether he, too, was a drone. Passive, merely content with his new life and the chance to speak and write freely. Was he supposed to want more? He hadn't considered that before.

At the beginning of the year, his colleague Elena was interviewing a guy named Vlado Červeň. He had read—and thought—a lot under communism. And finally, he acted—during the May Day Parade in 1987, he threw eggs at communist and state police officials. It was a political protest and personal catharsis—and he served more than a year at the Ilava Prison. Now he's working at the Matadorka. They want him to be a hero because he threw an egg at Šalgovič, but he claims he is not an anti-Communist. Červeň's words even raise a question whether, paradoxically, he is a communist. A real one. Unlike Šalgovič, who was never in his life a communist, just a rat. Is Vlado Červeň also a drone because he lacks the ambition to seize the opportunity by the hair?

His thoughts do not let him sleep and he turns over in bed. He is alone in his friend's apartment. Boris had invited him to a party at a woman friend's place but he'd refused.

Jaro did not have enough strength to resist the twin temptations of alcohol and women so preferred to avoid such events.

"Sure, I understand. You have the keys. It would be a lot to deal with so go and get some sleep."

Was it just his impression or was Boris mocking him?

* * *

Immersed in a hot bath, he scoops a handful of water and slowly dips his nose into it. The warmth and humidity loosen the dried-up blood and mucus from his nose. He shakes his head in disbelief over the gobs of blood, fuck, for the second time this year, his nose has been smashed and swollen, as big as a potato. This time it's more serious. He tries to move it, something in it snaps and hurts tremendously. He stays still for a while, waiting for the pain to subside. The epicentre of his face tingles and burns, small invisible needles prick him under his eyes. It's probably broken.

He reaches out of the tub and from the pocket of his jeans pulls out a crumpled newspaper clipping from January 1990, nine months ago.

"If I exchange 2,000 crowns for dollars at 38 crowns a dollar, it's not worth my while to travel at all. I simply won't get by on it." This is how one of the TV viewers commented on the new exchange regulations for foreign travel. And she went on to ask: "Isn't that discrimination?"

"It is," replied the federal finance minister, Václav Klaus, at the discussion table. "We just need to be clear who is discriminating against whom. The answer: we—against ourselves. And this is due to our inability to sell our work abroad during the past decades." An unpleasant truth. But it needs to be acknowledged. As, after all, a whole host of others. For if we examined, however superficially, the reasons why we ended up the way we did, obscuring the truth and years of circumventing the real state of affairs would obviously rank top of the list. Minister Klaus, one of the most popular figures in the current government, surely knows this very well. Which is why he can often be seen on the television screen, and why he has taken on the difficult task of explaining even the most unpleasant issues of our system.

He caught the eye during his very first television appearance by saying: we must finally stop watching and planning all those kilos, metres, and numbers of items. On the contrary: we should be interested in profits, interest rates, levies, taxes.

Then I remembered how, at university, they used to drum into our heads that finance is not about money, but about relationships. We learned this, but real life didn't demonstrate it to us that much. So only now are most economists beginning to realize it. And not only them. We are all gradually becoming aware how these relationships are gaining strength, how they are beginning—or will soon begin—to work, what mechanisms they use. Meanwhile, most of these mechanisms are not new at all. Apparently, it will very soon be demonstrated that all those past 'magical' routes to efficiency, all those files, experiments, trials—and I don't know what else we have been making up all these years—are a laughing stock in real economics. They were discovering the discovered, looking for the long-found.

"No offence, but this is horseshit. I'm not saying you don't write well, but this is crap. This won't be enough for me."

It could not have been made any clearer—the client was not happy. This was doubly disappointing because Jaro was not thrilled about the article either, then or now. It was an attempt to understand economics, tune into the new era and become friends with it. He wasn't convinced; he was just trying. Klaus was not likeable, but Jaro suspected that he had been the one riding the wave of the times—he was so self-assured that he had considered himself a symbol of the Citizens' Forum's manifesto, which had yet to be written! The article was not received badly at the time of its publication. But today, today it didn't work.

Limescale on the tiles, all steamed up. The steam is conjuring strange shapes. The dots of mould in the grouting whisper to each other, nothing flattering. The moisture is thick and hissing. He lies still, until the water feels lukewarm. He lets it out and runs it again, but only from the hot tap. He is boiling, ready to be skinned. The veins under his ankles are bulging, as if they were on top of the skin and not the other way round. They are the rivers with junctions and currents, gullies and meanders. The heart is an unwilling sea, accepting and ejecting, accepting and ejecting. Tomorrow never comes. Into the steam on the tiles he draws a single line, from the left bottom to the top right. Across the vertical parallels. Just like a waiter counting the fifth pint across the four already finished.

He asked how much he had got for the article then.

"Excuse me?"

The client reluctantly repeated the question, he was not keen on dealing with dopes.

Jaro was embarrassed to admit what had motivated him. That he wanted to provoke his editor-in-chief and older colleagues.

And to prove to his friend that he was marching with the times. "Nothing, it was a part of my monthly salary."

He said he would pay him, even in advance. He nodded to the security guard who handed him an envelope.

"Well, you glorified capitalism, for free. A little *contradictio in adiecto*, eh?" He smiled, allowing the foreign expression to die down. "I don't understand, but it's none of my business. I want a monument for myself. Not the statue of liberty in front of the auto service, but a living monument made of memories and ideas, do you understand? You will be *creating* the memories of me—people will be reading about me, I will create in them my *image*. Do you know that word? You can contribute to it. You will be writing the chronicle of only me, and not of the regime. I am the regime." A self-satisfied expression on his face, as he aptly paraphrased a well-known quote.

The journalist agreed.

The water is getting cold again. There is pressure in his bladder and his urethra is burning. A yellow jet stream mixes up with the water and together they disappear in the swirl of the drain. His nose is clear now, but swelling blocks his nostrils; he can only breathe through his mouth, the hot air irritating his sore tongue. Is he going to choke? He fills the tub again. He closes the little bottles of shampoo and other cosmetics which his wife always leaves open. He is clumsy, his fingers are shrivelled up and slimy, as if infused in ashes.

"What will be the relationship between us?" He did not anticipate the question to be problematic. A friend told him in detail about the negotiations, about *business*, about the need to be straightforward, not to undersell, and so on. The envelope in his hands emboldened him even more—they had basically already shaken hands. He just wanted to clarify for himself how they were going to work together, confirm to himself that their relationship would have boundaries. Understandably, he would write something flattering in return. He was not naïve, he did not doubt the nature of the deal.

The deathly silence could have lasted two, maybe three seconds. The boss glanced with narrowed eyes at the security guard who took a few steps as if serving coffee, and cold-bloodily punched the guest in the face with his fist. The staggering impact pushed him back into the leather chair and his head fell backwards until his neck cricked.

He is lying in the bathtub and quietly sobbing, maybe for the first time since his childhood. He is massaging his nape, his neck and shoulders, moving his head slowly from right to left, forward and backward. He is rolling his head around, there is cracking in his neck. He submerges his whole body, but he can still feel his eyes leaking their salty liquid. He does not even need Epsom salt. The box with the drawing of bubbles that his wife left behind, torn across the sign that says *Solivary Prešov*, the tiny crystals are scattered and sticking to the bathtub and everything around it. He reaches for his toothbrush, scrubbing his teeth and gums with full force. The white foam turns pink.

When he spits it into the sink, there are bright red trickles of blood in it.

The blow to the face switched him to a different channel. He was engulfed by his own body's reaction to it—it inflated a bubble around him in which only a faint whistling could be heard. The room transformed into a flying saucer propelled into the space, the bewildered gravity alternating at short intervals between the extremes of weightlessness and crushing pressure, the astronaut retching, the nut cracking. A sound of the gong in the head, the stream of blood on the shirt, the irrepressible rhythm of his heartbeat, the weight of his breath. The bodyguard walked over to his place in the corner of the room, his stride unchanged from before, his face unmoved. The boss continued to say something, but it had nothing to do with Jaro's question or the punch. As if he were not talking to the man who was bleeding in front of him, as if nothing special had happened in the past few seconds. They were acting in a silent film, behind the screen of sound and picture.

The boss stood up and walked around the large windowless office. Only after a few laps did he stop in front of the painting, illuminated in all corners by the little lamps, yet dark nevertheless. His hands first behind his back, then extended in front of him, he started expounding on its colours, space, technique, *expression*, parallels, similes. Wisdoms and similes, the boss liked that, not particularly caring if they did not fit the reality. Reality can, after all, always be shaped by force.

"Mednňanský, *Evening Mood.*" That was all he remembered from the boss's lecture, nothing else. The scenery fascinated him. The dim sun behind the clouds, the hope behind the walls of this room with no daylight, the journey out in search of the signs of life in the far reaches of the universe. He could hear music, as it trickled out of the hills from the picture all the way down to his shoes.

Wrapped in a towel, he is sitting in the steam on the edge of the bathtub, considering what options he had. To defend himself, to pick up a heavy ashtray from the coffee table and whack it against the bodyguard's head. But realistically? He would probably have received an even bigger beating and the deal would have been off, for certain. All right, he did not have to fight. He could have preserved his dignity differently. Calmly stand up, tell the force that such manners were unacceptable to him, and walk away. The brutish violence and its consequent, almost absurd, ignorance totally paralyzed him. He was not thinking clearly. He continued sitting, switched off, until the boss had stopped talking. Then they stood up, shook hands—he realized with shame that his own was still covered in blood—and said goodbye.

* * *

The wood flies everywhere, falling into the snow and mud. The axe splits one log into two smaller ones, then those into even smaller pieces. The furnace inside the cabin has a small door, big logs wouldn't fit in. He's been outside for several minutes now, and he's been swinging about and chopping incessantly. His baggy sweater moves on his body when he swings down with force; it gets in his way, he wrestles with it. Sweat is pouring from his forehead; he wipes it on the sleeve, but it doesn't help and the wool doesn't soak it up. The fibres from the mangy sweater stick to his wet face and itch. Pieces of wood lie around the yard like fallen soldiers on the battlefield. He collects them in a basket, deposits them in a mass grave before cremation.

It's warm inside, but he's cold to the point of shivering. He feeds the fire and listens to it crackle. He listens to see if he can find regularity in the crackling. He wants to hum a tune to the rhythm, but the crackling always surprises him. He is one step behind. He sings a touch more swiftly, it sounds better. He speeds up, humming until he's almost out of breath. Finally he coughs and laughs, all red. He hasn't held onto the tune, hasn't kept up the tempo—how telling.

There were calluses on his hands and the axe handle quickly brought blood to them. His hands were too delicate for an axe. He sits in a chair, studying the primitive tool. It is a weapon. One can kill with it. But can he use it against himself? How? It's laughable. How come he hasn't thought of it at all? He's already decided *to do* it but until now, hasn't really considered *how*.

He paces up and down the cabin like a caged lion. There's a support pole in the corner behind the Christmas tree, and on it is the thing he refuses to look at. As he keeps walking, each length of the cabin finds him heavier, his shoulders begin to droop. There is hay and straw in the attic; their shadows, soaked with rain, are crushing him. He stops: a metre away from him hangs glass, its back covered with a layer of aluminium and with small rust-stained wounds. He sticks out his tongue, nothing visible in the gloom. But he feels it, feels it grow.

The old couch compresses under the weight of his body, gives way to his pressure. The head is the heaviest, the neck has already slackened. The eyes are closed, only the ears continue to work. The wood in the furnace crackles more slowly and quietly—when it manages to make a sound twice in a row, it's like an old record. It's louder outside, there is a humming thaw. Masses of snow are melting, you can hear the birth of water. There are masses of it, hanging up in the clouds, resting on the ground and in the earth, in all its changing states. A man, for the most part, is also just water. If only he could locate his spigot and let himself out. What would be left of him, a dry mass, a mere 40 percent of his weight? To be ground up and poured in a paper bag. Maybe one day someone will pour hot water over it and steep it in a cup. Maybe he will taste better and more distinctive than he does today. For today, he is mixed badly, poisonous meat and juices, only the earth will digest them. He is falling asleep.

* * *

He walks slowly in the dark, up to his ankles in the water. With each step he sinks deeper, but the shore is shallow; he walks a good distance, still only waist-deep in the water. He has never been at the seaside. Could this be it—finally, the big water? No sky overhead, just water as far as he can see. He doesn't walk alone, someone accompanies him. They walk for a long time, he's already in up to his mouth. They continue, under the surface he feels water filling his nostrils. A second of panic, he's thrashing, drowning.

He's still underwater and alive and can see as clearly as on a sunny day. The brightness does not come from above; the water itself glows, composed of phosphorescent particles. They don't emit light, they can only be seen. He swims with gusto, breathing with his whole body.

He is completely alone in the water. Not only can he see no one, he feels no one. He knows there is no one else with him under the surface. In the distance, there is an outline of a round body. He swims closer, it's a planet. He swims on and discovers another one with a ring, he touches it, he slides down on it. He spirals around it like a dolphin. Is he a dolphin? The planets are attached to a point far in front of him with long poles. He swims alongside the pole, and the water is getting warmer and warmer. At the centre of the world is a ball of hot water, a liquid sun. It lights up and illuminates him. *He has discovered the universe, clearly!* The world on dry land is an optical illusion, as he suspected all along. He's happy to have found out the truth. He screams with joy into the water, bathes in the swirls of his own bubbles, does corkscrews. He accelerates madly, sailing through planetary systems and galaxies. He plays water polo with celestial bodies, sending them into black holes.

Tired with happiness, he descends slowly to the bottom of the liquid universe, sinking into a cabin full of water. Outside, far beyond the courtyard, he sees a giant pillar. He has never seen one there before. He swims out through the window and cautiously approaches it. It is a beam, a column of light, shining like a beacon. It towers to an infinite height, its top invisible. It connects many, many universes. It is *his* ray. He enters it, becomes it. Just before his body dissolves like effervescent powder, he looks underneath and sees feet. They are quite tiny, covered in the knitted baby onesie. They are *his* feet. Slowly he rises, slowly he is pulled upwards until finally, he shoots up like a rocket.

* * *

He sleeps hard with one eye and lightly with the other, waking up just as the sun is setting. Could there be anything worse than waking up to fresh darkness?

He gets up from the table and walks around the room with his eyes closed. It's always been hard to get orientated here using sight—the cabin is on a dark hillside, shadowed by trees, *the light like inside a barn*, his grandmother used to say. It is impossible to recall the interior properly, things have no image or reflection, you only have a hunch. He feels familiar objects, he has known the shape and sound of each of them perfectly since he was little. An old wooden sideboard—he rests his tongue against his palate, creates a vacuum, lets out the sound of a horse's hoof, then taps his knuckles against the hard board. The sounds echo each other, almost perfect harmonies. He squeals and opens the drawer—it creaks exactly the same. He systematically goes through the objects in the room, a ritual from his childhood that he hasn't yet abandoned. He communicates with things, he plays tennis against a wall of identical tones.

His fingers can feel a twin-deck tape recorder. It hasn't always been here; he brought it only a few months ago, along with the tapes—in two full banana boxes from Costa Rica. The cassettes are meticulously numbered, there is a third lined notebook with orange stars open on the table. This was his work at the cabin. More and more frequently he would escape here—to listen to the archives of his memories and compose.

At first, he did it straight into the tape recorder—in the right deck was the master tape, and in the left he inserted tapes he played certain sections from. PLAY and immediately afterwards REC, he played and recorded, a player and recorder in one. But the technology did not withstand the onslaught—tapes became tangled and the rewind button stopped working. And when he changed his mind about something, there was no way to erase the old part or insert a new one—he had to start all over again. He was forced to rely on a pencil. The hexagonal cross-section allowed him to impale the tapes and manually rewind them as needed. With the sharpened tip of the pencil, he wrote down notes in the notebook for whoever would one day take over and finish the work. *Tape #31, Side B, Passage "22 March 1988 17:30 at the playground," from approx. the thirtieth second of the recording to Minute thirty, the sifting of the sand and the rattle of the sand moulds in the sieve.*

He goes out into the light. He can smell water in the air again, he is walking toward the stream. He undresses, folds his things and puts them on a tree stump right on the bank. If someone could see him like that. A naked fool. Whitish body, goosebumps, folds of fat. Hairy, unkempt, circles under his eyes, scars, a winter miniature of a bird. And those folded clothes ... No painter would have been able to paint him. Gothic, Renaissance ... he had no concept. Too ordinary for the avant-garde. Graphically uncapturable. Music, perhaps? That pile of still-warm clothes sings. It plays. The rock organ from the oratory at the bottom of the dam that flooded the human settlement just after Adam and Eve. Bold counter-rhythms, minor keys absurdly variegated by the major, a mini-hymn of hope in the black water of despair. Hope heard by deaf snakes, hope heralded by dumb fish, it is quite distinct. Hope that the stream will merge with the river, the river with the ocean and this to mingle with the milk in the Milky Way and drown out the whole godless universe.

Up to his chest in the stream he must balance himself, lean in so that the current cannot drag him any further. The pressure of the water peels from him the chunks of ice, they crash into each other behind him downstream, he is an icebreaker. His teeth are chattering at a pace the metronome scale doesn't know. He clenches his numb fists, bounces, jumps off of the bottom, he's an icebreaker. The merry-go-round of thoughts stops at the most recent—*he is an icebreaker*. Within seconds his body temperature drops, he can barely breathe, his heart presses against his lungs. Like this? Maybe it's not such a bad idea. After all, they had predicted it for him. *They'll drown you.*

MIND

a-topia

Warmth. That's what I valued the most. They did not let much heat into the dead spheres and zones during the day and sometimes even walking did not warm me up. I walked for five hours, stopped for an hour to eat and to rest, and then walked again for five hours. At the end of each day, I looked for a place to stay overnight. They used waste heat at night. At least that was something.

The last time I slept in bed was before the descent. Since then, I slept at different places but never at the same place twice. One morning I woke up in a heap of tangled synthetic fibres. The evening before I had been fumbling around in an unlit abandoned industrial park with only a little bit of light—more anticipated than real—coming from the megacity overhead. I had lain down carefully and immediately felt warm. As I had rolled over, the fibres had pricked and irritated me. I had folded my jacket under my head and used its faux leather sleeves to cover the hole in my face and the eczema around it. It had been itching even without the fibres touching it. I had had to lie motionless. Somewhere warm and dry, it was possible.

First moments at yet another new place, impressions. It was getting dark Above. In the Underworld, it was almost dark. They chased me off the farm that smelled of pig slurry and manure. There were at least five of them. When they noticed me walking around and checking it out, they started chasing me, screaming, with sticks. And so I ran. I fell down several times—I tripped over a stone, slipped on cow dung, got tangled up in the weeds. When they chased me off to a dense thicket, they stopped and threw rocks at me. One hit me on the head just behind my ear. I began to despair. I did not want to spend another night cowering under a tree. Suddenly I heard a soft female voice singing. It was strange—she was either singing off-key or in a key I had not heard before. It was something between Bizouki Bazou's *African Desert* and Alia Bystrická's high-pitched haymaking songs. I followed the light and found a small house with an old woman sitting in front of it. I greeted her but she did not want to let me in. I hit her so hard she fell off the tree trunk she had been sitting on. Her bed was not very big but we both fit. The blood behind my ear was drying—and so was the blood under the old woman's nose and mouth. Her quiet crying mixed with the sound of wind howling through cracks in the house but I fell asleep at last. Surrounded by warmth.

* * *

In that cold and stale zone between the ground and the sphere I often dreamt about the life Above. I had dreamt about it even in those pricking fibres. In that dream, I made coffee, read about rising sea levels in Northern Europe and about *artificial elephants*—gigantic water pumps built from Damme to Flanders—in my morning paper, drank mango juice, and watched a motionless, sleeping body and when the toaster beeped … I woke up. I woke up at the party in refurbished barracks, surrounded by bodies in coloured luminous coveralls, and I was holding a piece of paper that you put under your tongue and that shook your brain cells loose, catapulting them through your skull and through space and time. I soared on the waves of music without sound, floated like a balloon just under the ceiling of a steel-framed hall. Just a drugged-out brain hallucinating, no big deal, right? I would have agreed if it had not been so difficult to differentiate things.

Cut! From the first row, right under the stage, I watched men and women walk a runaway naked from the waist down. They were only dressed from the waist up—blouses, jackets tank tops, all gaudy, as if made by Maureri. From the waist down, their skin was smooth and they looked just like mannequins in shop windows of bankrupt and abandoned stores. Vacant expressions, icily elegant aura, I felt like slapping them. They stuck in my mind for days, I did not know whether I had really been to a fashion show or had just dreamt it. I had been clean for five days before, had not taken any drugs, and yet my consciousness was jumping back and forth between situations; it was like an annoying advert. Or was being clean for five days also just a dream? Trudging through different versions of reality, I felt lost.

Only in the Underworld had I started to have more or less normal dreams. During the day, it was reality—harsh, sad and depressing but real. It was fantasy only during the night. As it should be.

I also dreamt of Inge.

* * *

Leaving her was harder than I had expected. It hurt. I can still see her face the moment I told her we would not see each other anymore. We had always been cynical about us but she was still surprised. I can't hold it against her, even I was taken aback by what I had said. But time is a convincing illusion that flows in one direction, you can't go back. I lowered myself on a sloped slippery surface, Inge was standing above me—she did not reach out her hand to me, she was too proud—and even though I started having second thoughts about our break up, it was as useless as kissing a dead man's scrapes and cuts better. I was already plummeting and gaining momentum.

It was not the first time I had broken up with a woman. Sometimes, I had not even known the name of a woman I had been spending time with. I had a good memory and adhered to the golden rule of its maintenance—place a filter on the container. What's the point of remembering one name when there were hundreds of different names? What's the point of crying over a loss of one woman when you can find another—for a day, or more like for a night, sometimes for several days and occasionally for a few weeks. One relationship ended when another one began.

First, I needed someone to be with, I needed to touch and to be touched. Second, change was good, boredom was bad. The less I cared about a woman, the easier was to get her. If she was pretty, great. If I did not like her too much, I considered it a challenge and tested my limits. I knew I would not be with her for long anyway. They were all the same—each one reflected the same feminine principle and I was like Plato wandering in that Cave of his and collecting shadows of one and the same idea.

I am not irresistible and I have never thought of women as sluts. Not all women were eager to jump into bed with me, I had to—and wanted to—try hard. Old school. I only used the sexradar a few times, especially shortly after it had been released, but I soon decided to stop using it altogether. It all lost its magic the moment I could scan women's affection in my corner—those who liked me were surrounded by a red aura and those who did not by a brown one. The magic faded when a woman, whose biometric data and preferences were matched with mine by a computer, came to my door. The only thing I had to do was copulate and I wanted more—I wanted to control the whole process from the beginning, I did not want to know the result beforehand. Rejection had to be a possibility, at least theoretically.

As time passed, I found my own way to narrow down my options. I met women several times a day not only at work but at other places as well. If I found a certain woman at least a little bit attractive, I first did the mutual attraction test.

"*You* must've been asked this question a million times," I would say theatrically and sensually. Women would usually warily draw back a little at this, but curiosity always got the better of them.

"What question?" she would ask (she, the lot of them, always) frowning like a little girl who knew her brother was pulling her leg but still hoped there was a slight possibility of finally getting something sweet from him.

"How are you?" I asked and waited. Sometimes it took a while but they usually burst out laughing. Humour could tear down even the most fortified defensive walls and I could tell by the deepness, intensity and honesty of a woman's laughter whether she liked me or not.

After the mutual attraction test followed the accessibility test because not every woman who liked me was sure she wanted to turn her thoughts into action.

"Damn, you have a gorgeous laugh … but I have a girlfriend, you know, so you can't do this to me." The third phrase I would use usually left women surprised. It was important that I do not hesitate and go through all the steps quickly one after another. Altogether, both tests would take less than a minute.

"But I can't resist you so you may invite me for dinner."

It was bold. If at that point three out of four women found me attractive, only one usually passed the willingness test. However, that was all I needed, and at that moment I knew I would not be alone in the evening. Of course, two or three times the selected woman did not show up for the dinner or was not interested in sex. Otherwise, it worked.

I am not trying to boast here. Seduction was to me the same as eating or hygiene—a man needs them on a regular basis and does them without thinking and any pomp or fanfare. A strong need, half-automatic fulfilment, I did not even think about the performed actions, just repeated them. My daily hunt.

* * *

But then I became the prey. Not only me but everyone including me. They were most dangerous before the light set. I would move in the long shadows from one building to another looking over my shoulder and peeking around corners for a pack of hunched primitives led by a straight-standing man with a big forehead and his hands in the air like a meerkat. The leader was usually scrawny and weak but his height, eyesight and sense of smell made him a good tracker. His pack then killed their victims with knives and sticks all while laughing and shouting with joy.

It was the same the day they almost got me. I thought they were after me because they began running towards the old unused slaughterhouse I was hiding behind. But fortunately! Fortunately there was a trembling boy crouched in a cracked wood wardrobe that had been left abandoned on trampled bushes and weeds. He did not manage to stay hidden and began to run. They were fast; they flung a heavy rusty chain through the air, which got tangled around the boy's feet and he fell on the ground. It was a merciful fall, almost knocked him unconscious. They beat him over the head and stabbed him in the neck with nearly euphoric screams. They acted as if they had just scored a goal. Then the tracker came, hissed like a snake and they stopped. Under the tracker's watchful eye, they drained the victim of his blood and carved him. I did not feel sorry for the boy—I was grateful to him for saving my life. The smell of the gutted body was so strong that mine got lost in it and the tracker did not pick it up despite me being only twenty metres away from him. A few minutes later and all that was left of the boy was bones and off-cuts. The hunters left and were replaced by dogs.

People are made of pieces of meat and meat is important and rare—and there is a strong demand for it. It is interesting that dogs in the Underworld are treated better than humans. Well, partly. It is also incredible cruelty at the same time—the Hunters do not always kill dogs. Not immediately. They let them live for some time and use them to grow meat. Some breeds such as Herculebeagle, Superweiler and Whippet are particularly good for growing meat. Thanks to CRISPR genetic modification of the myostatin gene they were specially bred from the most muscular breeds to regenerate muscle tissue as fast as possible. Their owners cut a piece of meat off their bodies, eat it and a week later they can do it again. There were only a few empathetic owners who put their dogs to sleep with gas and cleaned their wounds afterwards. Most owners just tied their dogs up, cut off as much meat as possible and left them to their fate. The wounds either healed or got infected and caused a dog to die. I have seen dogs that were of no use anymore because their bodies were covered in scars. And since scar tissue does not taste good, the dogs were useless. They roam the Underworld and testify to the nature of the world. They are like cities from a drone's perspective. As if they were made of patches. They look like our wrecked planet, patched up horizontally and vertically into spheres and zones where patches were no longer used to fix tears but had become the essential part as the original substance had got lost in them and patches were all that was left.

I have never tasted human flesh, not to my knowledge anyway. But when I lay down in the evening and the smell of barbecue wafted in the air, I could not really tell what kind of meat was being cooked. The thought that I, too, might end up smelling like that popped into my head several times.

* * *

We met on the Regional Peace Conference held in the closely guarded Congress centre on the border of the Bavaria Zone and the Tyrol Special Administrative Region. It was a dark and rainy autumn day. Through the transparent vestibule walls, I watched roboguards patrol the perimeter of the forest in front of the fence at ten-minute intervals. They slid along quietly with raindrops rolling down their rubber bodies and I was telling myself I was happy to be inside and dry. My job there was done and it was up to the principals to finish it. I was optimistically waiting for the result.

"The weather feels quite fitting, doesn't it?" I had not noticed her approaching. With the bright colours she wore and her voice, she stood out against our surroundings as if she had been glued onto a sun-bleached collage; she was the only original and the world was just a rebroadcast of poor quality. She looked like a woman from previous decades in her mini dress made of red and brown faux leather that I had only seen in pictures. Her head was tilted back, her chin lifted and she had a beautiful thick—almost masculine—neck. The statue of revelation, I did not have to touch her to know. She could not have been a hologram or an illusion. There was a green pin on her dress, she must have come from the netswork zone.

"It does, it does." I was nodding even though I did not understand what she meant by "fitting".

"Hello, Adam. I'm Inge." She offered me her hand and fixed me with her stare. I was the only thing in the world for her and she wanted either to eat me at best, or kill me at worst.

"I know…" The stare forced me to look down. "Hi, nice to meet you." I tried to find more information about her but the corner only showed me her name and a question mark after it.

"There's no use searching, I'm password-protected," she said, still looking at me without blinking. I was disconcerted by the lack of information in the corner and was blinking enough for both of us.

"Can you live like this—as a netsworker?" There were few people who did not open up to others. Passwords made people wary.

She did not bother answering and just smiled. I had always liked quiet confidence in women.

"Listen, I have a question *you* must've been asked a million—"

"Don't bother, I'm a lesbian." She cut me off before I even started and I did not even have time to believe her.

She took me by the hand and led me into a lounge with no windows. Furnished only with burgundy red armchairs which seemed to serve more for lying down rather than sitting and a real, glowing, Asian garden hologram. A photon fountain in the middle of the room hummed a pop song with the chorus going something like *Eye Boy, Try Boy, Why Boy*. I couldn't figure out who the singer was, and I didn't like his production or the song itself. An esominimal with two alternating tones, each of them in seven different keys— some of which only animals could hear. Why would anyone write this kind of music, or design rooms like this? Why did she choose to come here?

206

"This place is awful, isn't it?" she asked with a slight smile.

I wasn't used to being teased or feeling embarrassed, not in my own court.

"Who do you work for?" I tried taking over.

"The Free Lance netswork agency." She didn't like the idea. "Is that enough? How about you?"

"I ..."

"I know who you work for. I have some questions for you, you half-blind prince Charming."

I could still just walk away. What was that bitch doing grinding me down like that? Who was I to her and she to me? Who sent her? Was it FemCOREp? Should I call the roboguards? I was both outraged by her audacity and surprised by my affection. Sand kept falling through the thin glass neck of the hourglass as I didn't walk away. I stayed put thinking that inaction is often the best kind of action and that as a human I'm subject to the basic physical principle of stationary action.

"What are they discussing in there?"

"The peace coordination and the trade deal between the Mediterranean Union and Confederation of Central European Na—"

I didn't even finish the sentence. Her eyes were telling me she wouldn't take that crap anyway. And since I couldn't tell her the truth, we both stayed quiet. She must have been pondering how to get under my skin while I was swearing to myself, I won't let her get too close. And it couldn't have been too difficult, nobody was forcing me to stay. All I had to do to leave was simply to enter a zone she couldn't access.

"I've known about you for some time, I've been following you," she said. "And I've been asking myself what happened to you. And the likes of you. How can you do such ... In cold blood, as if your conscience was completely silent ..."

My conscience was silent, I wasn't even sure I knew what she meant. Perhaps I suspected something, but I didn't care. I liked both my work and my life, at least a little bit.

"What do you mean? The quotas?" That was one of our more controversial themes. We had to give the netsworkers and the people something. Nobody would believe that our meetings were just about peace and trade. This way the netsworks were preoccupied with how many chosen ones there would be and which key, which zone and which sphere would guarantee them happy lives.

She let out a disappointed sigh. "You're messing with me. You think I'm a fool. Women are more intelligent than men. For real. And since the Declaration it's been an official and legal fact, so why do you think I'll let you fuck with me like this?"

It looked like she'd just get up and leave. She wanted to give up and I should have been happy about it but instead I wished she would stay.

"What do you want to know? Some information or my motives?"

"I need information. I'm a netsworker, it's my job."

"That I understand, but my job is to provide the customer with strategic solutions, not tell anything to netsworkers."

That was me resigning. I expected her to leave and so I slid down into the chair, put my hands behind my head and closed my eye. In the corner I enabled the resting mode.

My perception of the surroundings became muted. I chose the remix of Shostakovich's fifth in D minor by DJ Baronessy Hal with the entire fifty minutes distilled into ten, inspired mainly by the finale. A few blinks of my eye were sometimes enough for me to switch off and relax. All I could see was fog under my closed eyelid and soon, I was telling myself, I'll be walking out onto a terrace, lighting myself a cigarette, and listening to the crackling tobacco, silent fog or pattering rain. Her face was slow to disappear from my memory. What was I supposed to do? Tell her classified information? In exchange for what? A smile or her spreading her legs? Plenty of other women would do that, even without trading it for information. She was not that special, she could go screw herself. A question popped up in the corner: how to execute this task?

I felt a weightless sink as I slipped into a microsleep. It wasn't rare that I would suddenly not know who I was, what I was or where I was. Was what I saw black or white? Was I inside or outside the dimension of space? Not only would I not know what I knew, I couldn't even be sure about what I didn't know. An existential lapse. I couldn't say how long it lasted because time was also non-existent in this state. What doesn't exist, doesn't pass; what doesn't live cannot last. Only after I woke up did scenes start to appear in front of my eyes, both known and unknown. With Inge in that ugly room and just before I awakened, a display of women's faces circled in my mind. Only a single one could I distinctly identify: my mother's.

A hand on my knee burst my bubble of isolation; Inge was back with a teapot of green tea which she poured into a pair of shallow white cups. She wasn't doing anything. She didn't seem hostile or inviting. She didn't offer me the tea or look at me, instead she stared at the lonely fish in the little pond under the fountain. The fish was still, not dead, just motionless.

"I keep thinking if the fight or the effort are worth it. There are these mentally lobotomized people on the other side, you know. They have always been a part of history." She gave me a glance. "And they always will be."

The fished moved and I took a sip of my tea.

"You guys sure do have balls, no doubt about it, releasing a quota tirade just to create a scandal. Extraordinarily cynical. In practice it's been this way for ages: you simply change the number and the key. But that's the point. You know that this is what people are after—who drops out and who stays. Turning reality into a reality show. You managed to reach perfection, you sorry beasts. You're manipulating people, entire nations of people, admit it! Sophisticated, that language you use. You say fusion and it makes you piss your pants. Putting white gloves on, flaps on your eyes, or one eye in your case. You perhaps even believe it yourself. That there's nothing wrong with what you do. So distanced from the consequences, so disinterested. Not giving a damn about law, or any of the hundreds of jurisystems ... You don't even care enough to create your own legal system but just eliminate anyone who stands in your way. You let one go, fire two others, silence the next three and bribe the last. It's true that there is an extermination pipeline, right? That's how you flush the pariahs? I know for sure that that's how they end up."

A genderless voice spoke through the speakerphone, asking if we wanted anything else and if everything was okay. She said no, sounding both resolute and angry because she had been interrupted. I asked for coffee because the tea was bitter and had a fish-like after-taste. A young, well-built mulatto with a trolley walked in about a minute later, the muscles on his forearm flexing as he poured the coffee from a brass jug. His nametag said Maurice. He tried to give Inge a smile several times, but she kept ignoring him. Instead, he turned to me, so I smiled back at him.

"And you think that nobody knows about the cut-throats you have there? The terrorists you pay to spread fear and settle your accounts. If it wasn't for your support, they would no longer even exist." Maurice silently disappeared with my teacup.

"The secret service used to be misused for that purpose ... terrible, but at least it was the elected representatives who did it. People could at least find out about it and throw them out for such scandals, but you and all the mercenaries you pay, nobody can throw you out or prove your guilt. You even have the guts to bargain about this at a *peace* conference."

I watched her and rubbed my eye. I had to keep blinking because something had fallen in it. She exaggerated, misinterpreted and made up entire stories from hints but I wasn't going to argue with her. Why would I? I was just an animal to her. I knew about most of the things she mentioned but I didn't give a damn about them.

"Alright, so who's in the room? Who sits at the head of the table?" she asked, watching me with a squinted stare.

"It's round."

"Look at that, the pirate has a sense of humour. Wonderful. Don't be a softie, do tell who presides over that reputable body."

"I'd fall a hundred sphere levels down if I told you. Perhaps they would throw me out down that mythical pipeline. You should know." I laughed.

"That's all I need. Only those with secrets hide things. That's it." She finished.

I swallowed as people outside walked past. They were leaving the hall. I leaned over from my chair to see if the eminence I used to work for was among them.

"You're in a rush? Let's wrap it up then. I am interested in understanding the motivation, your motivation for willingly participating in this cynical world management. Yes. I'm interested in you."

She touched my knee, looked me in the eye and gave me her right hand so that our wrists crossed right in the place where we used to have personal sensors before the implayray. My corner lit up when she decrypted herself. A thought rushed through my mind that she was after me. I was not sure for how long, but she had me. She'd had me for ages.

* * *

If the world had a coat-of-arms, it would most certainly have weeds on it. Nothing else. The bottom sphere was drowning in a sea of weeds and the rumours made their way all the way Above. It was in a bar, someplace near Thessaloniki, where I once met a mercenary who bragged about going hunting down there. His face was tattooed and there was an angry vein on his forehead. He was lecturing his audience about the power of weeds, trees, and bushes to overgrow the entire Above world in five years if they weren't cut regularly. A vigorous gesture followed his every word. He cut and chopped the air, made faces and clenched his teeth. Still, it was one thing to hear about it and another to see it for yourself.

I thought I had run into a densely overgrown area after I rappelled down, a jungle of sorts. I wanted to walk around it, but the scenery was still the same an hour later. There were the hints of a well-maintained path around the buildings where people lived; and then 'streets' that the poor slaves made with machetes, as I learned later. Otherwise everything was covered in tall weeds, as far as eye could see. I spent my first night in the ruins of a small town. It must have been beginner's luck that I met this old man who just happened to drop his cane. He looked up at me with a dose of surprise, thankfulness, respect, fear and courage in his face when I picked it up for him.

"I'm old and sick, young man. There is not much you could use me for," he said breathing heavily as if he had just finished a marathon.

Back then I didn't know what he meant. Above we never cared much about what was going on down Under. We didn't know about cannibalism so I didn't react to his comment. Instead, I asked the old man where I could find Okun. He froze for a moment, then he looked around, wiped his drooling mouth with the collar of his shirt and started mumbling. He lived nearby in a block of flats on the ground floor and invited me to stay with him. I stayed for the night. It might not be as bad as I thought, I thought to myself. For a while the old man was the only person I met or spoke to, his words my only source of information. A starter pack for the Overground. Quite funny, what they called the place we named the Underworld. Whenever Martin needed to excuse anything to himself, he would say that it was all about perspective. He would try to smile and carefully examine my reactions. My dear friend Martin, a part of me they ripped out.

I've lived here my entire life, the old man would say. It wasn't too bad after they walled the sky, only gradually everything started to break down. Weeds became the coffin wedges and just like in old westerns the fields swelled with tumbleweed, the weed that ruined everything. All it took was for the wind to rise and the entire town was full of dry stacks of tumbleweed. People filled their wheelbarrows and tried dumping it outside the town, but the weeds made their way there too and there was nowhere to put it. By the time they made it back to town, the places they cleared were already full of weeds again. People gradually gave up on it.

But tumbleweed was nothing compared to preweed. Growing at an incredible pace this invasive and genetically altered weed started spreading across the areas already filled with tumbleweed. It didn't have huge leaves but clambering and prickly stems which first entangled the loose tumbleweed and then hardened into wood becoming as strong as bushes. They grew far and wide and within a year changed the character of the local life in the Underworld, breaking up the already weak structure of society. People struggled to grow crops when their fields and gardens were overgrown with weeds. Robbing the soil of nutrients, water and light, they were nearly impossible to get rid of. Even if someone succeeded in doing so, it would never last long enough. People with guns forced the others to make and maintain makeshift passages with their machetes since it was even hard to walk to places. That is how the class of the slaves of the Underworld came to be. The weeds made it harder to live and breathe freely and the desire for freedom led some to do desperate things, throwing themselves into the thorns, screaming and dying after a few hundred meters of struggle. They hadn't even started to rot when the slaves tracked them down. They would chop their way to the dead bodies and hunters would effortlessly gather them, as if they were picking berries.

It was clearly hard to survive when people only had few kinds of crops and that sorry humanitarian help, in the form of usable garbage, from the Above. That was when meat became the main source of sustenance. First, regular meat, but it was rather odd that people hunted domestic animals. Flocks grazed, gnawing on the weeds, constantly guarded by an armed escort as if the animals were some kind of eminence. Even ten men were sometimes not enough: they might be attacked by a larger group with better guns, there would be rifle shooting, ending in casualties on both sides. The winners took it all: the cattle and the meat of both their dead comrades and enemies. They would feed themselves and keep watch over the flock until a stronger group attacked them. And when they had run out of traditional sources of meat they would turn to all other kinds of animals for their food—dogs, wolves, bulls, birds. And in the end, they shamelessly started hunting human meat. It barely took the old man an hour to give me this lecture on the history of the

Underworld. Since the legend had nothing to do with me, I wasn't moved by it. I only listened with one ear, thinking that perhaps the next day I would get to the spot.

"Why don't you burn it?" I asked to keep the conversation going.

"Do you think it didn't cross our minds?" the old man replied smiling. "But the smoke from the burning weeds stung our eyes and set off the fire alarm. Strong acoustic waves resonated from Above, the pressure cut off supplies of oxygen and the fire went out. As we recovered from breathing in the thick smoke and the ringing in our ears, we realized it was not the way to do it. Those Above … you … are all well protected. Beggars from down here can't hurt you."

The old man had no questions but just kept going with his monologue, so I stayed silent. Perfectly happy being warm and dry, I felt no need to make conversation. It was colder outside than I expected, I thought, sitting in the corner wearing my warmest sweater. Suddenly the old man started sneezing, a fit so aggressive I thought it would tear him to pieces. With red eyes slowly tearing up and a scrunched cloth handkerchief sticky with mucus in his head, he shook his head and cursed under his breath until another wave came around. My eye was getting heavy as I pondered how the old man could live here and the weeds thrive here when the spheres Above absorbed all water, light and warmth.

"The place you're looking for is not too far away. I can give you approximate coordinates. But it's hard to say how long it will take you to get there or whether you even can. It's up in the air and we don't have much of that down here," the old man said before he went to bed.

Ten kilometres was not that much, though; I could walk there on my hands, even through the weeds. It didn't make much sense to me.

The next morning, we barely spoke to each other. The only thing the old man told me was that there are no maps because the passages change so often it's simply useless to map them. He seemed weak, as if he was dying but I couldn't help him. I had no time or will to do so and the old tosser had a certain depressing effect on me; I always disliked people that made a fuss of things just out of principle. I had to get out and focus on my life, not his whining. Anyway who needs maps when there are cardinal points you can use? If you want to get somewhere, you hold your course and try to get there as quickly as you can.

* * *

Dear Adam,

I'm sorry … … ….

I'm sorry about so much I don't even know where to start. I suppose it would be polite to introduce myself first, since we've never met, however I believe you may have heard of me before. I'm your grandfather, your mother's father.

I was supposed to contact you when you were thirteen. How old are you now? About three times that, right? I'm sorry. I lost track.

Forgive me for only writing to you now.

I'm not sure what you know or what your mother told you, but I know what she told me—or rather what I remember of it.

First, she told me about you. She gave you away to her mom to take care of you and told me to find you when you got older. She said that you'd need a role model and that grandma wouldn't be able to raise you properly. It surprised me, made me wonder if Pavlína hadn't hurt her in some way. I couldn't imagine because I never lived with them. Which was another thing that surprised me—how she turned to me, a person who had deserted them.

Adam, you need to understand the situation. First, I'd never met my daughter before this. Second, I was a drunk and kept mixing alcohol and medication … after a time, my life was one long series of (failed) attempts to quit. You can therefore imagine my surprise when a woman showed up at my doorstep in a hostel on the edge of Prague, called me "dad" and talked about her mom, my wife Pavlína, and about my grandson. At first, I seriously thought it was a hallucination: I had experienced that state several times before but this was much worse. Once I realized it wasn't a hallucination, delirium, dream, or nightmare I burst into tears as never before. I was ashamed but I couldn't stop the tears. My roommates stared at me and at the beautiful woman who had come to see me, but they couldn't get their heads around it. I sensed Nada felt uncomfortable—that moment must have seemed like an eternity to her—so I took her outside to get some air. There I managed to calm myself down but a new problem caught me off guard. There was so much I wanted (and now could) tell her and so much I wanted to ask about. A sudden wish to spend some time with her overcame me but I knew I never could. I had so much to say that I knew I couldn't do or say anything. I just stood there, like the wretched, pitiful fool that I was, staring at her as if she was a ghost.

So, when the time comes, will you find Adam and be with him? Will you? Do you promise? She kept asking, very matter-of-fact, and I could sense her hopelessness. I kept nodding until she repeated the same question for about the thousandth time and then I managed to say. "Of course, Nadenka, of course." It took a lot not to burst into tears again.

Where are you going, I asked her. She answered but I couldn't hear her over the noisy emotions rushing through me. I doubted what I heard, thought I'd got it wrong when she repeated herself.

To Arizona? To have herself frozen? It wasn't a joke, nor did I think it was funny. I couldn't say a word. I couldn't even ask her why.

She answered my unsaid questions but still I could barely understand. She said she was sick, tired of all the ups and downs. In the future she'd have a better life, a healthier one with different people who won't know her ... That was about all she told me.

I knew barely anything about cryonics, or even how that was what freezing of human bodies was called. But one thing I did know was that people could have themselves frozen only after they died and not before. Do you know what your mom said to that? That she would manage it somehow ...

I don't know how I'd allowed myself to live without my daughter. Had I been trying to save her from myself? Was that my motive? I realized the scale of my mistake when I watched her there against the sun setting over a Prague suburb and felt the regret and sorrow eating me up as I understood that the very first and last time I ever saw my daughter was when she decided to leave this world. Just like I did years ago. I knew that I couldn't stop her, so I said to myself I would make up for it and be with you.

I was euphoric for the next week until I realized that I would have to wait an entire decade. That was far beyond human ability so I had a drink and after some time fell back into the usual quagmire where I felt at home. Up, down, up, down, day and night, night and day, head swimming, shoulders growing heavy, knees creaking, toes amputated: head, shoulders, knees, and toes ...

But the decade eventually passed and ... nothing. I did nothing. As I realized it, I kept reminding myself—It's time, Jaro, this is what you've been waiting for. Your once-in-a-lifetime chance. But I always put it off and though it might look good in a film, it didn't in real life. I would knock on my wife's door, the wife who I had abandoned and not seen for ages. She was basically a widow. What would I tell her? Hi there, Nada came to see me a few years ago you know and told me to come and see the baby. Baby? You weren't a baby anymore, you were a thirteen-year-old who would have kicked the stranger's ass and certainly not jumped into my arms, kissed me and called me "Grandpa, dear grandpa, I'm so happy to finally see you". Tell me, would that have been your reaction? Of course not, and so I kept putting it off until Christmas, until your birthday, until Easter, until the summer break, until Christmas ...

Now you're all grown up, so if this letter gets to you, you'll surely manage to read it because how could an old drunk possibly offend you? You can burn the letter or reply. We could even meet if you want to. I think that now, in the twilight of my life, I'm ready. I'm not living much of a life anymore, not waiting for anything but I'm still alive. The entire time I've been on this Earth I've spent worrying about myself, my own ideals, my own disappointments, my own failures. I'm responsible for a person's death, can you imagine? I've never reconciled myself to that fact, instead tortured myself with a disease which later turned out to only be a fixed idea. I've wrecked my health with chemicals so much I'm surprised I'm still alive. In the meantime, my daughter became a whore she even said so herself and I don't blame her, I'm simply stating facts. I love her even though I barely know her, I love her and I feel so very sorry for her.

Now she's somewhere in a freezer, dreaming about waking up into a wonderful, perfect world without suffering, where she can live without her disease, forever beautiful, where nobody will know what she used to do for a living. People have invented all kinds of things but that kind of a world exists only in simulations and you should know that even better than I do.

You are my only living offspring, my only heir, my only "blood". You are my only bond with a world I otherwise don't care about. I simply don't perceive it anymore nor understand it. It has become unfamiliar to me. New technologies ... monkeys are better at using them than I am.

I live in a mobile home which offers me more comfort than I need. Nada paid some company big money to take care of me. It's on a lease so those tossers are now just waiting for me to finally kick the bucket. Their motto is "Living as a service". In reality that means they just put my container down wherever it happens to be cheapest. It's enabled me to travel the world but I didn't see much because the time I am allowed to spend outside the box is very limited. They don't want to get in trouble but I don't really mind; I cursed this world a long time ago and there's nothing I'm interested in seeing. I'm telling you this so you know where to find me ... should you ever want to. The company is called Living Industries. I never had the corner installed so you'll have to come in person or send me a letter—a real one in an envelope, if you know what that is.

I'll be waiting for a response; hopefully I'll live to see it for then I'll be ready to go. And if I don't, well I'll be off anyway.

Take care, son. May the sun shine for you!

Granddad (Jaro)

* * *

I rubbed my dry fingers against a kind of paper I had never held or seen before. It was white, very plain but in some way quite different from the paper in books. Thicker, harder to fold, it seemed more important, more symbolic, and more valuable; it discouraged you from only using it for scribbling. I was aware that back in the day people used to write each other letters which would—unbeliev-ably—travel for days even weeks to reach their destination. What I didn't know was that there was a special kind of writing paper made in different colours, patterns, with different watermarks, edges and lines; and that there were whole letter sets. I'd never needed to learn to write by hand but suddenly handwriting fascinated me and I wanted to learn how to do it.

For the first time in my life, I was holding a letter and it felt historic in several ways. Yes, your premonition was correct: it wasn't the contents of the letter that moved me but the form. From my perspective the letter was written by a *stranger*, allegedly we had the same blood, but I couldn't have cared less. There was nothing touching about it because I was constantly in a different woman's body, exchanging liquids and it didn't mean much. Caring for blood ties? Why would I? The only notion of a family I had was from other people's stories. I had never had one nor was I planning on starting one.

I couldn't refresh my memory, everything was mixed up and overlapping in my mind—both real and imaginary. My head started spinning, I waved my arms and tried to find something to hold onto and find out where I was. I had no home of my own, barely anyone had. Wherever I went, I'd rent an apartment from HopTell Homing. Always one with the same parameters and exactly the same furnishing but now not even the familiarity of my environ-ment helped. I was getting more and more of such moments in which I couldn't control my own coordinates and felt some horrible nausea of the soul.

Leaning against an imitation antique dresser I tried to remem-ber when I'd received the letter. It wasn't dated and I'd thrown out the stamped envelope. All I could remember was that I received it during a strange period of life which I only realized was strange when I looked back at it. Even distinguishing that it was a 'period of life' was a retrospective thing since it took some time for me to sort the events into a timeline with a distinct beginning and end. Only once it had ended and a new era begun could I be sure.

Death—an end for some, a beginning for others. Understanding that Martin was dead made me feel as shattered as if lithospheric plates were crushing me, as stirred up as if there was a fusion reaction happening inside my stomach and as split into poles as a magnet. I never saw his corpse or any remains. The explosion was so strong he simply disappeared forever as if he had never existed. His flesh and bones were standing right next to me before he dashed off to a nearby stall for two glasses of pomegranate juice. And then he was blown up by the sheer force of heat and pressure. A smiling face and cautious gait because he had spilled a few drops of juice from one of the cups; arms extended so that he wouldn't spatter his sharply creased beige trousers: that was the last image I had of him. When I opened my eyes, or I should say one eye, he was gone and my other eye had gone to the afterlife with him.

It was a time when our business was thriving. There were four of us running the company but Martin and I always had the decisive vote. We flew around the world and especially around Europe but still couldn't keep up with the demand for our services. Our customers were high-maintenance and wouldn't settle for long-distance discussions: high confidentiality meetings had to be held in person. Sometimes it took us a day to fulfil a requirement, other times it took three but sometimes we might get stuck somewhere for weeks on end. They called us independent negotiators and we didn't mind. Indeed, we were independent—we didn't work for anybody who couldn't afford us, and negotiating was the main part of the job. Martin and I would joke about mostly having to negotiate with our own principals rather than the counterparty but that was the job. On the ecard that people would see in their corner right under my name and the name of the company was my title: Global Head of Division. People would often ask me if there wasn't something missing such as the division I was in charge of. No, I would answer. I ran all the division—when entities were dividing or falling apart—while Martin was Master of Internal and Lateral Fusion, which made sense only with a very broad interpretation and detailed explanation. What was important to him was that the abbreviation of his title was MILF. We were exactly where people, things or regions were connecting or dividing. Sometimes there was need for both division and connection—and sometimes quite the opposite. What was important was that we were good and in constant demand because the world kept spinning and changing.

We started off back in the Acad. Instead of taking all final exams in natural and social sciences, we suggested to our professors that we could perform a twenty-minute play called *The Purpose of the Functioning of the Entire Universe ;-)*. We even kept the emoji and our enlightened professors gave us a chance. The play required us to frequently change costumes and consisted of short sketches in which we demonstrated the dialectics of connecting and detaching, merging and disjoining, exploding and imploding, fusing and separating. From the speakers came the Origamma Rays *I will kill you, to eat you, to be you* catchy chorus, sung in the deep murmur of former teenage pop star, later tattooed rebel, Anita Ray, who everybody knew and soon started impersonating. Our sweaty selves acted out things like nuclear fusion, (me the laser and Martin the burning nucleus of an atom) followed by an international postwar peace treaty with Martin in a black Coalition uniform and me in the light blue colours of the Allies. This was followed by the scene of a pack of wolves sharing a kill with a mother wolf feeding her cub, then throwing the zeros and ones of basic computer language made of letter pasta around like confetti, the mating of banana snails—eating each other's huge penises, the rainbow light decomposition—rainbow clowns doing cartwheels around a glass lens. There was no fear of failure; we were young, spoiled brats who were used to winning. That was why we attended Acad: the school was full of kids just like us. However, we didn't expect the standing ovation we got or the audience shouting *bravo*. Our teachers knew we could study for our exams; idiots would not have got into such a school and they appreciated our creative approach.

We built our business on the same principle. First, we advised smaller businesses, later bigger ones, which earned us good money, and then we started working for corpoments and their principals.

We managed hundreds of the best specialists—and it wasn't a play anymore but for real. Nor was it just some entertainment; things would often get serious and sometimes lives were on the line. We did end up in a war once and though we never said it out loud, we knew things were getting serious, so serious that our names and lives could end up on the other side's red lists.

We preferred more creative assignments with a smaller destruction rate. We knew that damage was an unavoidable consequence of any disruption; we were not naïve. And it was during a celebration of one of those deals when Martin went to get us that pomegranate juice. Rich Lombardy, once separated from its regional neighbours to avoid paying for their mistakes, had been the showcase of innovative industry from transportation to energy. But financial services was its real forte.

The first shock came with the introduction of current-construct. All construction, transport and energy solutions had to be changed completely but Lombardians didn't have the know-how which the East had. All that it took for the world paradigm to change was that in Seoul they built a skyscraper without a single gram of solid material. A pale Korean netsworker reported it from the building on live television in a frantic voice. Touching the floor, she talked about how soft yet firm it was and that it would even clean itself. She described the physical characteristics of the current, reciting words and expressions she didn't herself fully understand. One could see that it was a miracle to her. It didn't matter how but this building was keeping her meters above ground just as well as any iron or concrete would. She seemed relieved once she was done reciting the scientific commentary. She quickly laughed and said that people didn't need to know the details of how such technology worked to use it and that this technology (short pause) WILL be used. Winking to the camera she turned to her guest, Ji-Hun Park, the principal of Soul's corpoment and proud owner of this revolutionary building. The walls behind the reporter changed colour according to his instructions and when he said "clear" they became completely transparent. Those present at the opening ceremony were all shouting with excitement while Park laughed loudly and snorted like a pig.

"It takes a while for people to adjust to a revolution, to adapt to a technological advancement," the fat man said, philosophizing.

Lombardy withstood this first blow, both corpoments and groups focusing on their other comparative advantage. But then their finance sector also collapsed when the new tetra-currencies appeared. This fragmented netsswork system ran unchecked: money was being issued by companies which managed to secure themselves enough users. Corpoments were picky about companies and often changed their suppliers. Later they figured that tetra-currencies worked well for circulation and accounting but creating their own quasi money would preserve value better. The flexibility of the system allowed them to do it because each attempt at a hostile takeover or regulation activated a simultaneous counter system with a range of different attributes based on different grounds but maintaining the same functionality so that people, corpoments and companies could still use it for making payments. It was an unbeatable system, constantly a step ahead of the ones trying to seize it. The desperate Milanese tried looking for its centre, they wanted to destroy both the system and its developers, they wanted to torture and kill them and its code or at least decode and invalidate it. They looked for anything, anything at all but they didn't find it, they wouldn't find it.

Martin and I were laughing about the news of Luigi Calfonso, who first raged in front of the cameras and threatened the unknown tetra-currency perpetrators just to shoot himself an hour later. *Il principe* is dead/Put a gun to his head, I rhymed. Martin almost choked from laughing, food was coming out his nose when we dined in war-torn Riga and watched the women at the bar. Martin would always pick the same old Russian hotel where they had a proper fish in dill sauce. My diet scanner signalized increased danger, calibrated as it was to dislike raw and natural foods, mainly meat, instead it preferred umeat synthetic plant foods, protein cultivars made from mini-insect cattle and stevia and algae as seasonings. No system should be too glorified, though, and so we went on eating, drinking and fucking as before.

I woke up with three naked bodies next to me and a note from the Lyon Administrative Association. I almost flipped over myself—the megacompany worked for the biggest players in the region, from Geneve and Munich all the way to Venice. This was the top game and they wanted to hire us. We were to leave for Lyon that day and so we left without packing a single thing, our suitcases levitated a meter behind us completely empty.

It was a wonderful case, creative destruction, a small death of one branch which allowed another to start growing on top of it. People of Lyon who were the first ones to buy the current-construct patent from the Koreans now wanted the controlling share in decimated Lombardy. The locals were not too keen at first and tried redeeming themselves through making a pact with the northern cantons. A substantive part of land was in the deal, including Solsell, a large transparent solar tiles manufacturing company, and Wirtwin, a top-notch digital simulation center that specialized in simulating physical and electromechanical interfaces of merchandise prototypes. But people from the cantons weren't that stupid. The value of these companies and the land was decreasing every day and when the Lyonaises waved a warning finger at them, it was clear the deal was off.

All Lombardy could do was surrender because if they wanted to survive, they had to accept our offer. The entire process took us exactly four weeks and was later rated the acquisition of the year. We sent generals to Milan to take over the armed forces, key cultural players were relocated to Asia and those who wouldn't cooperate went to the Underworld. We got rid of some of the principals and lured others out to a public open space to shoot them and make them examples of what could happen. Businessmen received good work offers in our partnered South African regions and cooperated nicely; none of them let their pride get in the way. And in the end, we took the best of the human capital for ourselves, which strengthened the Lyon score. The most beautiful women and men, the smart scientists, the elite students and the soldiers who served the Lombardian authorities—after the shareholders changed, they all became ours.

It was essential to rid the region and the sphere in question of their elites and morally devastate them for at least a few years. The ravaged remains could then do nothing but obey us. With a team of no more than three hundred people and a mandate from Lyon's principals we accomplished the task with almost no violence and therefore pleased the majority of people. In their eyes we were artists and even though we kindly declined the epithet, we knew we were artists and we liked it: we liked writing history.

Then one day one of us lost his part in history. I didn't see it coming and it hit me so hard, I had no idea how to react. All I could think of was to reply to your letter. In the anonymity of the hoptell apartment I took a ballpoint I bought a long time ago, from a dresser and put it on the paper.

* * *

Hi Grandad,

It's me Adam. You wrote me a letter. Now I'm writing back even though I can't really write so excuse my handwriting and spelling I have never written anything with a pen before. I'm sure that I'll make a lot of mystakes. You won't guess where I found the writing paper and ink pen. It was in a palentophile and fetish shop. I kid you not—that was its name. They had different test tubes, enemas, handcuphs, globes, daggers, maps, perfumes in flacons, artificial flowers, books written in Gothic script, stuffed animals in gilded displey cabinets, primitive surgical tools—used for example for brain surgery, or even detailed antique sex tools patent drafts. Most of the shops in the city centre went bankrupt because of the entertainment malls and nearly all the showrooms and fitting rooms are now unreal you can try anything on in your corner and they will deliver it strait to you. This must have been one of the very last shops left. I couldn't even find it on the Prague's Újezd. It seems they don't need advertising and it wasn't even on the GPS, I only found it by the adress—Vítězná 16. All the dry and cracked skin around my eye, the eczema, started itching just as I walked in. To my suprise both my good eye and the one I didn't have started watering up. Perhaps there were mites, woodworms, dust, I don't know, it just made me cry.

I'm not sure what to tell you, there's no reason for me to like you. If there's one thing your letter gives away it's that you're just as much of a coward as my mother was. She didn't give a toss and neither did you. She left and you never showed up, not that I ever missed you. There's not much courage in your blood and if that blood is why you're trying to contact me then thank you but no.

Fortunately, I don't believe in heredity and all that I have I faught for myself. Mom may have tried to relieve her conscience by paying for a good school for me and for you to live off the rest of your life comfortably but otherwise I'm on my own.

I'm only thankful to grandma; she was the one who stayed when the rest of the "family" failed (notice the quotation marks). Eventually even grandma and I grew apart. She rarely mentioned you or mom. I guess because she was ashamed of you. Then for my eighteenth birthday, besides a cake with eighteen candles on it, she gave me a note from mom saying that when the world is a better place I should go and have her woken up. Do you get that? What does "when the world is a better place" even mean? Is it when they can cure multiple sclerosis along with all the other diseases, is it when everyone loves one another or when there are no wars? Doesn't matter which way you look at it there is no sign of the world becoming a better place, or even heading in that direction. My mother, your beloved Naďa, has plenty of time, there's no need to disterb her peaceful sleep.

And how about you, do you know what the world is like? It seems to me that you're hiding from it. All your complaining about modular living but I bet that in the end it's not that bad. Sitting in your nice, cosy and warm module without any technologies, using real pens and paper and passing it off as some honourable act of forbearance. It must make you feel like some noble savage but let me tell you that it's no torture, it's luxury, awful luxury, dear grandad. I think I'll do that too; I'll go down memory lane and use that blue liquid to write on some paper. Maybe it'll make me feel important and perhaps I'll even learn to like it. I keep losing track of time and my surroundings and this could help me follow it better. I'll mark every letter in the calendar and on the map, I'll write to you about the present times and what life is like outside of your container. Does that sound good?

* * *

The second time I met with Inge was in the unreal. I swore to myself not to contact her, I wouldn't do what she wanted me to do. First, she password-protected herself and then she undid it. Was that supposed to impress me? I'm not going to lie: I did want to see her, but my strategy is to always let the woman get in touch and be proactive. Eventually it worked, she took things in her hands. After some three weeks she invited me to a game of rawball. Very original. I smiled.

I managed to ignore her message for a full day and then texted her. "Coming?"

A few minutes later she, only as her imbody, appeared in the chambox.

I welcomed her by mentioning that I could see the extra muscles she'd added to herself.

"There's an advantage to this place. The rule of mother nature that gives men a physical advantage over us women doesn't apply here. Hopefully it doesn't scare you. Have you ever been beaten up by a woman?"

I tried to surprise her—I projected a light circle on the wall and sprinted towards it but at the very same moment she projected a ball on the opposite side of the chambox, tripped me up and quickly collected both, gaining two points. The bitch! We'd barely even started. I hated ambitious women and she certainly was one. With all that constant complaining about how unfair the male dominated world was and how badly discriminated they were, women had forgotten to notice that it was no longer true. Thirty years ago, perhaps, but roles had changed and women were now running the world.

I punched her in the throat, exactly where her Adam's apple would be if she was a man. She wasn't here for a fair game and rawball had no rules in but apparently she hadn't expect me to be such a toerag. I kicked the ball, grabbed it, waited for her ball, and scored. Chasing the round shades and lights on the walls of the chambox for about a half an hour completely killed us. She did indeed kick my balls a few times while I kept thumping her like a punchbag and in the end I won, though only by a tiny margin. And it completely drained me. Both our real and imbodied sweaty and exhausted figures were sitting on a mat in the chambox but we were smiling. It took a while before we caught our breath and could talk to each other. Normally, I would try to set up a date at one of our places or a hotel so that this sport savagery would smoothly dovetail into sex and I could finish her off. I even made a move or two but she figured out what I was doing and gave me a look that stopped me in my tracks. Then she stood up ready to leave and asked: "So when can I kick your butt in a rematch?"

"Tomorrow works for me," I said, excited about getting to see her again.

"The day after tomorrow works for me."

"Deal."

It wasn't easy but I eventually won all the three games we played, which was when Inge suggested we place a bet because, according to her, she was going to beat me the next time around. I grinned and asked what we should bet on. Anything, she said, the winner can pick something. I agreed and then was completely thrashed in our fourth game. I suspect she planned it all along but when I brought it up, she laughed and said she just needed a little motivation to raise her game.

"What was your motivation?" I asked. "What have you won?"

"Come to my place at seven tonight and you'll see." She blushed.

Here it comes. This baby girl wanted to have some sex. I cancelled my other date, got ready and came to her place at seven all nice and perfumed. She willingly opened the door wearing only a robe and I couldn't wait, I was certain this time the sex was going to be different, better, just like everything else with her. Her apartment was messy; it was hard to ignore. I noticed clothing all over the floor and take-out boxes with unfinished food as I walked with her through the narrow space. She didn't put much effort into getting ready for me, I thought, but the blood from my head had already made its way down there. I wasn't thinking very clearly anymore. Then she took me to the bathroom where she sat on a wicker chair, laid a towel on the floor and said: "Kneel down and shave my legs." Shamelessly enjoying it with no sign of a blush on her face she handed me the shaver. I've seen worse perversions but this time I started thinking it wasn't going to be some erotic foreplay or our mutual game but her own amusement on my account. I stayed quiet, fearing that saying anything would give away how injured my pride was. Sipping her wine, she was quiet too, maybe slightly purring as I was contemplating what would follow: Will I ever play rawball again with her? What information does she want me to give her? Does she have feelings for me or am I just a tool she wants to use? Should I leave or stay and why would such a pretty woman still use this vintage depilator in times when she could get her body hair removed painlessly, permanently and in a non-invasive way?

"I like pain. Just mild and regulated." She kept her hand right between her eyes and my one eye, showing me the amount of pain with her fingers. The distance between her thumb and finger was miniature. Tilting her head back and crinkling her nose she smacked her lips with pleasure.

"It's been a long time since I had something so sweet and physical with someone," she said laughing at her own joke and gasping.

"No wonder, when you're so repulsive." I said although the pressure inside my trousers was telling a whole different story.

It might have just been my own rationalization, but I was glad I kept my trousers on that night.

* * *

We started seeing each other more frequently. We played rawball, we dined together, we had drinks together and we went for walks together. We mostly frequented the *Individime* gallestra where food consistency wasn't a priority; they only scanned us at the door and mixed us an edible mass tailored to our nutritional needs. The food artists then created a small sculpture out of it, seasoned and coloured it and served it to us. We were eating art, I would say sticking my nose out. Inge would teasingly ask if they could at least make it out of *lángos*. Our taste in alcohol was identical. We would drink anything; and then, drunk, watch silly romantic movies and ridicule them, trying to outdo each other in the nastiness of our comments. We would massage each other's stiff shoulders and stay the night at one another's place. Her dog even started barking *sir* at me.

We avoided labelling what we had but what else was a relationship than a bunch of mutual rituals? I would shave her legs, she would cut my hair, shave me with a straight razor, we would take ten-minute cold showers and then lay in bed in robes and towels warming ourselves up with a hair blower. After we once did it by accident, we started repeating the ritual every night we spent together. Her hair blower was an old-fashioned one, with a plastic grille and, a red-hot wire behind it and a tiny fan blowing sweet-smelling hot air out. I went first and just prayed for her not to stop and always begged for an extra minute. The hot air was melting my light sensor and taking me to a dark void. My body was oozing all over the room, ditching its normal shape and leaking into the outside world through the crack under the door. I suddenly existed all around and nowhere at the same time, my boundaries dissolved. The hair blower made my world warm, supple, both isolated and wide open and safe. Getting perfectly lost in it I was like an embryo in the womb, a red-eyed boy at a swimming pool, in a hallway with grandma—she almost twisted my head off with the towel and then turned the hair blower on. I was a lad who woke up in the lap of his girlfriend for the first time. I was a man getting warmed up by a hair dryer in the hands of his friend. Her smile, her perfume and wet hair was all for real.

Her voice woke me up. "Now you, Martin."

"What? What did you say?" I asked still a little dazed.

I took the dryer out of her hand because she was drying out my cornea with the hot air and turned it off.

"Nothing, it's your turn, Adam. What do you mean?" Was she breathing faster or was I just imagining it? Was I going crazy? Perhaps it was the hormones. Uncertainty must be buried under a meter of concrex otherwise it will grow faster than an Asian poplar. From the very beginning trust and devotion was my ultimate policy towards Inge. That was the basis of this bizarre relationship. The fragile balance left me no time for hesitation so I just kept warming up her feet without a word until they turned from blue to pink. Then I moved upwards to her legs where the light hairs on her knees and thighs changed direction like grass in strong summer wind. I stayed away from her cunt not to push my luck and moved on to her stomach and breasts circling around her nipples until they softened. Her back and buttocks took twice as long to warm up but I liked it when she shivered and when goosebumps showed up on her skin. The tropical breeze I was creating made me feel like a god designing a miniature embossed map of a Philippine Island of Bohol and the thousands of its symmetrical hills. I was a man, too, confining my own magmatic activity under a heavy cover, a cyclops in celibacy, a god and a man, almighty and all-mistaken. Being together without the need for the silly human movements was exhilarating. Then once, as we were watching a movie with some steamy scenes together, she reached into her underwear and did the business. She then bit her lip and sighed heavily. With my heart pounding and an erection like no other I did the same. She then just handed me a tissue and smiled and that was it, our platonic co-existence.

How to define what was between us? A friendship? Perhaps but a rather strange one. Yet still how can a friendship rid someone of that very basic instinct? Before Inge I would chase women almost obsessively and it was utterly exhausting but with her there was no need for adventure. It felt like when you finally cough up that fly that wouldn't stop buzzing and kept draining all your energy. Such freedom, such intoxication.

All the sarcasm, insults, cynical remarks and scornful grins—well it certainly wasn't love. Not even an old married couple in a decades-long toxic relationship would treat each other the way we did. Siblings perhaps but I can't be sure for I never had any. We didn't share the same blood and, although like siblings, we didn't have sex, ours wasn't the kind of love siblings have, nor was it hate, far from it. Perhaps symbiosis? A transaction benefitting both parties? What was in it for me and what did she get out of it? I know I found peace with her, which surprised me because I wasn't aware that I was looking for it. I failed to notice how anxious, irritable, and agitated I had become but seeing her after work made it all go away. We would shower, wash and blow dry each other then sit down on the couch to meditate and fight over what to do next. We would listen to the new classics, the fractal ballads and shimmery pop of Alegro Ellectro and Sonya Gauch and some older things like Queen or Apocalyptica. We would watch the Northern and Russian movies by Zvjagincev, Ahmad, Sewit and Lornakur then talk about work, argue, and swear at each other but always fairly, always fifty-fifty.

What did she get out of it? Information for the netswork about my work? That was why she first came to me but now, our beings having joined together like two trees, close and intertwined, I couldn't believe she felt nothing towards me. She wanted to be with me even though I couldn't give her a single microbit of information.

And even if she had been a spy that whole time, she'd still have deserved a reward. That was why I stopped censoring information and was happy to let my guard down with her. If my colleagues had found out, I would have been a laughingstock and total loser in their eyes—so much pillow talk but NO sex?! But I didn't mind. I valued people's qualities and Inge was different than others, playing a high-risk game, just like me. She had got me and I'd surrendered to her.

A temporary summing up: 1. I wasn't after other women; 2. Inge didn't let me reach the climax nor did I try to get there; 3. There was no view from base camp—which was good because not seeing where it was going to end meant I could stay with her for a longer while.

An end to this provisional balance sheet: I forgot that even when you don't see it, the end always comes around.

* * *

Dear Grandad,

You used to work as a scribe, didn't you? I'm just kidding, no need to answer, I hope you're at least fucking laughing.

Writing on a piece of paper feels to me like I'm leaving behind a record of my existance. I want to believe that this trace of mine is real and tangible, that it isn't just a fantacy. Just for a moment, only until somebody scrunches up the letter, tears it into pieces and throws it down the disintegration pipe ... but still. These aren't those virtual letters that I see in the corner but can't touch, letters which I might not even have written. Ok, it's probably not important but it makes me happy.

I do enjoy writing to you, mainly about things you don't even want to know about. Perhaps this, did you know that the most common cause of death, besides natural causes, of course, was getting killed? Or to be more poetic, getting murdered. Yes, murder, including assasination, these things are killing people just like famine, AIDS or cancer used to. Are you surprised, Mr Humanist? I didn't even know what the word meant, and my corner had to look it up in the dictionary. Based on the letter you sent me you don't really seem like one. What happened, did old age break you, huh? I can help you with that, I'll gladly testify to what you probably already know—people are no good.

We come from animals and we carry the selfish geen. We can both help each other and kill each other when we need to. It's the best of both worlds.

I, too, was a victim of an assasination which killed my friend and cost me an eye. Now I'm left with a teary crater surrounded by itchy eczema. The only thing I know is that the explosion was some religious radicals' doing. I didn't try finding out more about it. What good would it do? I know how things are seen officially. Terrorism is still supposedly carried out by belief-driven fanatics. But I think it's never been about beliefs but about personal problems. For men it's either because they're impotent and women laugh at them or it's because their mothers abandoned them. Women do it too, mostly because they've never truly been loved, have lost their purpose in life or are unhappy with their situation. A person never kills anyone or dies for a belief, there's always some other motivation and reason behind it. Religion is just another word for the sweet hope of an afterlife but it's all rubbish.

All the religious suicide assassins, the Islamists, the Christians, the Salafists, the Adventists, the Hindu Kush and the Antichrists are being replaced by proffesionals. In their hands, an attempt on a person's life is a comission, conducted mostly for secret services. Of course, they too hide behind a symbol—a flag, a cross, a moon or a star but despite that it's still an assasination. I worked for folks that ordered murders. I should know. Perhaps Martin's death and my eye were not accidents either. Who was behind it I don't know, perhaps our competition, a client, someone whose business we ruined or a husband whose wife Martin was fucking. I never thought of it this way, but it wouldn't surprise me.

Murder became highly profitible and the term 'terrorbusiness' soon came into existence. Terrorists became adepts in a field that had originally belonged to organized crime. And since they didn't know how to conquer territories, run institutions or even their own churches and religious societies they developed their own skill set, knowing that their greatest asset was not being afraid to die or to kill. A fascinating proffession. And the best thing is that by blowing up a bomb in some square and sending ten more people to their deaths together with their target, nobody will ever investigate it as an assasination but instead just assume it is a terrorist attack. Remember that economics definition—supply creates demand? It's Say's law of market and I'm not sure if it's universal but it certainly works here. With all those available assasins and such competitive prices, how can you resist the temptation to get rid of someone who's getting on your nerves? It's irresistable.

I can't believe how different it was a decade ago: people killed other people back then too but every assasination and attack made it to the evening news. The netsworks were all flooded with details about the killer, what the motive was, who the victims were, how they lived and so on. Today nobody has time to bother their heads with every murder. People have got used to it—it has become normal. Morality is perminent but how sensitive people are changes throughout history and I feel that now it's almost zero.

Besides, death is now relative, people make copies of themselves and nobody has to die for good.

So, you must be asking why and how is that, right? Am I right? Are you wondering? Well, curiosity killed the cat! Someday, I might write to you about it.

* * *

It wasn't hard to tell night from day down here; there was more light and less light but at a certain point I completely lost track of how long I'd been wandering around. I never actually started counting and assumed I'd find what I was looking for right away. An optimist's mistake. It was easy in the spheres Above because we had GPS and transportation. Moving from place to place was common and happened instinctively. Your corner had a map with arrows and people, using their sixth sense, could move around more precisely. Effortlessly walking to the closest bus stop or simply thinking about it was all it took for a magnetic mobicaps to appear. But there was no such a thing in the Underworld, that was why I spent a long time blundering around like a fart in an insulated room, getting pushed around by an occasional draft from an open door or a giant vent hanging from the ceiling like some fallen god's slit guts. I spent many days, maybe even months there; no, weeks, I definitely spent several *weeks* down there.

I never chopped my way through weeds, I didn't let myself fall so low. Or did I? Not that I remember. I didn't care about social positions, and never analyzed my social status while I was in the upper spheres; my status was a given, though it wasn't until I got down here that I found out I apparently had one. I was a corrupt and spoiled fucking protégé. The decline was obvious, especially when I was forced to eat shit so that my brain and muscles would keep working, just to keep myself alive and survive. Raise a glass! I spent my nights like a dog with warmth its only luxury. I would have easily killed someone just to keep it but would never touch a machete in a million years. To fight the weeds and the bushes was beneath me ... but now I'm just repeating myself.

I was capitalizing on other people's efforts, walking along tunnels someone else has dug before me. But I had always done that, it was my way of life. Some days I would duck down, other times I gambled and walked with my back straight like on a catwalk but it was a bluff. Just like an Englishman straightening his khaki uniform as a man-eating tribe leads him to his death in New Guinea; or a German with a backpack full of clean clothes getting showered with bullets and falling into the rubble of Stalingrad. Or like a Slovak who ... I'm a Slovak but only by origin—my mother was Slovak, I was born in Vienna. I spent a few years of my childhood in Bratislava but now that the two cities have merged I realized I never actually liked it ... Just like a Slovak who thinks he can't lose anything because he never had anything in the first place.

I struggled to advance through makeshift streets cursing like a proper Slovak and only in Slovak. My thoughts switched between Slovak, English and German but cursing was, strangely perhaps, a Slovak preserve. Navigating the streets was very difficult. "*Do piče!*" I yelled into the bushes when I found myself in the same spot after a full day of walking. With no compass nor sun to help me navigate, I could perhaps have tried asking the people around. I guessed they would have either helped or stuck a screwdriver in my throat. So I kept getting lost, kept making mistakes, fixing them and advancing very slowly.

Patience was the only useful thing I learned in school up there that I could use down here; it helped me survive but I had to laugh when I pictured the sweet face of the youngest professor in the school's history. Just five years older than us, her students, she was so insanely smart nobody could be her match. Everyone tried to get her attention, we even competed with one another. We would try to say the funniest one-liner but her comebacks were always so smooth you couldn't tell if she was messing with you or ignoring you; she was brilliant. Both guys and most girls wanted to get her into bed. Martin once told me he had come in her face but I didn't believe him, not that he wasn't capable of it: he sure was an ass, even more so than me, but when I tried hooking up with the professor myself she just said that she was not into sex, and I believed her.

I would often think of her, even back then when I spent the night in a stable, next to a mule to keep me warm. I sneaked in when the guard went to take a dump in the weeds. I rubbed the animal behind the ears to keep it quiet because had they found me, they would have killed me. People down here didn't like pleasantries. No questions would be asked, they would just shoot me but I had my knife with me; I wouldn't give up too easily. I was supposed to be afraid but the smell of death kept me on my toes and kept my senses sharp. I was supposed to be afraid but being alive when you could die any moment was too thrilling. It was that night in the stable that made me realize how unprepared for life I was.

Remembering Gemma, the brilliant professor, and how fervently she explained the benefits of cooperation, saying that compromise is always an option and creative solutions come from open dialogue made me wonder how one talks to a pack of murderous imbeciles. Is there a way to cooperate with wild Amazonians residing in old apartment complexes shooting virus-infected arrows at any men within their range? How do you start a conversation with an assassin whose only commission is to kill anything and anyone but the animals he's guarding? Gemma the smart ass would probably know what to do but I was lost and had no idea how to cooperate with someone in such situations.

We also had lectures on competition and fair play. Professor Fortin, a former member of the elite Montreal and later also

European tactical forces, discharged from duty because of injury and requalified as a business coach, still wearing his uniform, would teach the youth how to mentally ready oneself and approach the enemy. He would teach us how to react to sensitive topics without lying and trick the polygraph without blushing; how to use information about the opposing party gained through industrial espionage; how to mentally oppress; how to muddy the water for ages, make it turbid and cook it until it becomes tasteless, empty soup; how to fog and blur, twist and turn, chew and stretch the band of patience until it snaps; how to lure and tempt, block and hinder and then lead people to the dead ends of the boredom maze; how to blow hot air and fly balloons of emptiness and kites of pointlessness; how to swiftly accelerate, surprise the enemy, stab them, with a pen and frank them from behind the oak table's front line.

Promptly and eagerly improvising, reading, synthetizing, typing, deducing, swinging the arguments around and presenting it in made up situations, mostly stressful ones, haha. We would work on solving fictitious problems, being creatively destructive and resourceful. Getting classmates on the hook and even using blackmail when needed. We had to communicate clearly and be strong to sell it to our teachers.

Cooperation and competition—what a brave concept it was to set up the very first school without a specific focus, preparing its student for *anything* in life. The important part was that that we were getting prepared for the best jobs in the leadership spheres but the tough military drill, which I could really use right now, was not in the curriculum. Our hands were supposed to stay soft, smooth, and clean and our jackets made of the most luxurious striton and fastened at the neck with a brooch. Money was the entrance ticket to Acad. The graduate profile was skills, contacts, prestige: social capital or, in other words, yet again, *money*. An elite education, my mother's gift to me.

But it was of zero use to me down here. Just as my mother had always been of zero value to me not only here but everywhere, and not just then but all my life. As a small boy I must have loved her, perhaps like any other kid. I try to convince myself that I did love her but I would only mumble the words under my breath and still they would trip on my teeth and stagger. I'm just a fraud with marked cards. It's not normal to forget what you feel towards your parents, or is it? I comfort myself by saying it was long ago.

I remember only the feeling I had when she left, the emptiness I felt when she disappeared. Emptiness is not a memory that fades with time; it remains, it is and it isn't. What isn't there can't disappear. She didn't tell me anything, didn't leave a letter I could later read to understand what made her send her child to boarding school and have her mother raise him instead of her. I'm no longer a child and I've seen my share of evil in this world, I've become apathetic. Rationally, I understand her but, in my heart, in that small boy's heart, I don't. She was everything to him, she was his whole world, and it was when she left that my heart hardened. Now it's so solid, it lets nothing in.

I would ask Grandma about it but she would just repeat her hurdy-gurdy: Your mom didn't leave anything behind for you because she hasn't actually gone, she's only taking a nap, waiting for her prince to wake her up. I even think you might be her prince, sweet Adam. Later, when that childish bullshit no longer worked on me, she told me the truth. My mom was sick. Was she dying? I asked. Not entirely, but both her body and soul were numbed, she needed some rest.

Gone for decades, she was dead to me. Perhaps one day they will bring her back, but I won't be a part of it, I have no reason to be. Let Snow White sleep, let her rest in peace.

* * *

Bizarre, very bizarre, a theatrical tragedy, a cheesy picnic and Count Your Simulenemigos—a slow virtual game for autistic children … or something of that kind. Tones of his favourite song *New Your Name* by Šampussy floated through the air as guestesses walked around carrying finger food, coloured water and clear alcohol. A dignified neutral expression programmed on their faces to make them look reverent and sad, specifically for today's purpose. The waiters and waitresses were only minor characters but I found it easier to focus on them than on the main protagonist. Programmed to be genderless according to the latest trends, were they dead or alive? Was it even worth considering? And was anything at all worth considering?

There he was, in a makeshift amphitheatre on a meadow, lying on pine tree branches like a wild boar shot dead, surrounded by a flower bed and red and white checkered tables. A three-dimensional movie sequence of his life projected right above him showed short snippets of his childhood, student years, graduation, leadership at work, with his mother/grandmother, with me and with Ioanna and as a father with his daughter who hasn't yet picked her name. A rubber doll, Martin's impeccable replica, lay there in his stead. Created the previous day for this one occasion was a perfect stunt double playing the part of the dead original. Not a single molecule was left of his body and even the rubber doll was to be burned to ashes within moments so not only was it a flawless recreation of him as a human but also a perfect reconstruction of his destiny—his ending.

Ioanna and the baby knelt tearfully at the bier, whispering to the motionless figure, identical to the original. I walked over and embraced the shaking Ioanna. Her quivering muscles were soothing compared to the feeling the stiff dummy gave me. My arm around her shoulders felt her every movement as she caressed his face so vigorously, his rubber cheeks stretched. It was as if she was pinching him: Wake the fuck up and stop playing dead! Wake up! Don't do this to me! But the body kept still. I felt no emotion nor did I cry and even though I was sad I still hadn't grasped that it was Martin's end and could only focus on the flawlessness of his imitation. The slender scar which made him look like he was grinning stretched out from the left corner of his mouth all the way to his ear. He had a similar grin on his face back in Kishinev when he told me he'd been looking for something wild for the night. I smirked into my crystal glass, then took a sip of the Cahul Merlot and rolled the deep red wine on my tongue long enough to mask any hints of disapproval. I was aware of him cheating on his wife. In the end we were no saints but the fact that he chose to do it in her hometown, in the place where they met, with her waiting for him at home, bearing his child ... call me old-fashioned but I disliked the idea. I tried my hardest not to let it show because Martin loved it when people couldn't define a problem. The last thing I wanted was to give him an opportunity to mock me.

"What exactly ... are you looking for ... some type of hook-up at a bar or something tailor-made?"

He contemplated his answer as a gulp of brandy made its way down his throat. And then he took another and swallowed it carefully.

"I'll go for a guestess. I don't feel like dealing with any romantic crap, I need a bit of rough, you know what I mean ..." He giggled and I felt relieved. Going for a not entirely human person seemed like less of a cheat.

"What about you?"

"I'm feeling pretty tired. I'll switch my radar on a little later and see if some girl comes up." I had two call me, but it was late, and I was sound asleep.

Martin had an ugly scratch on his face the next morning as if from a beast with a single claw.

"Don't worry, she ended up worse," he said at breakfast.

"Not even the clinic can heal that in time. What will you tell Ioanna tomorrow? A shaving cut? A fight?"

"That's a good idea." He raised his eyebrows surprised that I was thinking about it instead of him. We never went back to that conversation and he never had that scar regenerated. His aim was to feel like a military veteran, which he sort of was—and certainly looked like lying in his casket.

The smell of the pine tree was strong, the branches must have been real. I clenched my teeth and prayed for it to be over while Ioanna held me tight around the waist burying her fingers in between my ribs. The pain almost made me let out a whimper. Her other hand reached for the rubber dummy, touched its cheeks, lifted its eyelids, opened its mouth, pulled on its ears and gripped its throat almost as if she wanted to strangle it.

"Should I get his double? Should I program his head with Martin and revive him? Should I bring something like this to life?"

It was a common and well-liked practice.

"Don't. You'll agonize about if it really is him. It will torture you as you keep examining it, trying to decide if the mannequin is authentic enough, if that's what Martin would have said or done. It won't let you sleep because the real Martin is gone. He's dead. Let him go and accept it."

Perhaps I was trying to convince myself more than her and perhaps I was a little too loud because Martin's mom started crying having overheard my speech.

Ioanna kept quiet but her piercing look made me look away. I couldn't bear the searing sorrow of her future, perhaps even the rest of her life. She knew that I knew much more than she did, that I knew it all but she also knew it would stay that way. Her fingers traced the eye patch covering my missing eye. The scar was still tender and tickled a little but I let her. I held it together even as my eye started tearing up as she caressed me for a good minute.

"Won't you get an implant?"

I shook my head. She nodded and stopped stroking me but I still felt pins and needles in my scar for the next hour. I had no good reason to refuse an eye transplant, it was pure bullheadedness that kept me from getting one. But later I had a reason. Apparently, women loved this handicap of mine; perversely it aroused them like nothing else. They all wanted to take the eyepatch off and seeing the scar was something unspeakably carnal. Back then my unwillingness to bother with a replacement eye was an act of defiance. Ioanna understood that and was the only one who could.

"Stay until the end," she said.

I didn't respond.

"Stay, or else I'll lose my mind, I just won't bear it," she said, reading my mind.

"You don't have a choice." Man is a selfish creature, and I certainly was a good example of it. There are times when you must save yourself and not care if others are being saved.

To cover up my lack of empathy I took the baby girl in my arms and kept myself occupied. I noticed that her eyes were more her mother's than her father's. Ioanna observed me for a moment, but she soon gave up and lay down in the coffin next to Martin's replica wrapping her arms around him as if it was her pillow and she was going to bed. An outraged hiss came from the people sitting on the benches but Ioanna had other things on her mind and I didn't care if she was acting inappropriately. All I was there for was to see Martin disappear in flames once again and then leave.

There was no reason for me to rush away from Martin's funeral. I could have easily stayed longer but wait, no, I couldn't, I was going to Rotterdam. Yes, a business trip was my excuse, an alibi planned in advance. I could have sent a younger colleague to deal with it since it wasn't a very important matter but I really wanted to have a cover-up in front of Ioanna. Turning into a total cynic, I told her as I was leaving that Martin would have wanted it that way. Business comes first and even though she didn't mutter a word, her look said it all—she could screw it.

* * *

Greetings dear Grandpa,

I'm only greeting you in my head since I haven't sent any of those letters, they're all just sitting here in my cupboard. You can't write back to me, so I'm not even sure if you're still alive.

There's something in the air and I reckon it's death, I can feel its gross, sweetish, putrid smell in my nose, ugh.

I think the time is coming (or has it already come) when you die of old age in your stinky module and maybe your curiosity has already killed you, who knows?

Have you figured out why people are killing one another more and more? Or why violence has become so ordinary? Let me tell you why. Murderers throughout history have all had the same motives. But the law is weak and even though many have tried to enforce it, no-one has really succeeded.

Since I have nothing to hide I will give you an example. Here it comes. Once, a while back, I hired a highly regarded assasin. She wore a gorgeous ceremonial robe, a skin-tight black dress with white ruffles and a collar. It was way too sexy for a nun but that is not the point. We met in Hamburg's dark but famous Cripple's Bar. Martin had provided both the tip and the contact. So to get to the point, I told her I was being followed around by a competitor (not a very strong one, I have to say)— her hair was blond and short at the sides with a ponytail at the back and she alleged that I was unfairly stealing her clients. I told the nun all that over a large carafe of red wine, adding that she was threatening to kill me. Both statements were partly true: I was indeed stealing her clients but only because I was better; and she really was threatening me. The nun replied with a simple "understood," after which we had some drinks and sex in the hotel room. She was no crude savage, just a truly agreeable and intelligent woman, classy and proffesional.

My rival disappeared off the face of the Earth a week later as I found out from her company's circular which I recieved regularly: A tragedy near the biggest mosque in Brussels; innocent civilians dead. A misfortune, a bewildering act of religious violence. She was simply in the wrong place at the wrong time and will be sadly missed. May she rest in peace.

So one less thing for me to worry about. Do you still think that with today's technology, that nun, or anyone who works for her cannot be traced planting a bomb? All of my comunication with her could easily be traced back. The conversation from the bar, the night we spent at the hotel and even the transaction, since there are cameras and microphones recording everything. Even our corners are wired to the cloud. You're probably asking why the police don't investigate it, right? Back in the day they perhaps would but now with dozens of attacks happening every day, they only bother with formalities. So they classify it as a terrorist attack, an organization claims responsibility and the case is closed. Was it the Cult of the Eighth Day, or maybe the Ninth Night? They are under close surveilance since they're on the list of terrorist threats.

In the past people would riot and urge their elected leaders to protect civilians, safeguard borders, look after private property and public space, monitor criminal sindicates, and use the state's monopoly on imposing violence to prevent violence.

However, there's a catch!

Terms like borders, countries, law, courts, and governments don't have the meaning they used to have. Not that they no longer exist. There are multiple law enforcement units and military forces but they're so hard to tell apart that when they show up you're not sure whether to be relieved or frightened. Documents outlining relations between the armed forces do exist; most of them respect each other most of the time. But sometimes when the hierarcky is challenged and there's a lack of subordination at some level, light shines and knives come out. Unfortunate human soldiers spill their blood, lose their lives and just as history dictates, the stronger man wins and the law obeys the victor.

I must add that the law is constantly adapting to the times. Rules grow old and can't keep up with the changing world. Old ones have to be abolished. Only their texts, some kind of human behaviour methodology, remain and are posted on the cloud. These are based on old laws, they only change according to people's preferences. After all the nation's will cannot only be expressed once every few years in the election as it changes every second. Subjecting it to a lengthy legislative process would; therefore, be nonsensical.

In the end even the original law texts became an obsticle, their rigidness both hard to translate and interpret, the sentimental preferences became harder to express in words, they started forming silly combinations. A set of figures replaced the text which allowed signals from individuals to be proccessed and counted immediately, aiding the contract databank to swiftly generate norms and enable people to know what is currently right and wrong. The algorithm consists of thumbs up and thumbs down signals but you can probably imagine what happens when normotics constantly change, it simply becomes meaningless, less predictable and it loses its point. All of this in the end results in people doing what they like and occassionally recieving a warning red light. Then they just hope that nobody cares about it, which mostly is the case, and move on.

If you're not bored yet, you'll probably wonder, why. It would not be hard to identify, seek and punish those disobeying the normotic algorithm—police stations could have red warning lights going off. But the trouble is that normotics are not uniform: there are several kinds and that is the problem. The entire concept lacks hierarcky, contradicts, and challenges itself meaning that the norms only have an indicative character. Rights and laws exist just for appearance's sake; all laws are "pro forma". Their main contribution is perhaps that people can tell themselves that they at least don't live like savages, in anarchy.

However, we definitely do live in anarchy. The countries as you remember them still exist, but I don't think they hold much power anymore. Their soverignty is only left on paper.

I was born as a Slovak citizen and had a Slovak passport; it certainly expired long ago though I might still have it somewhere. But I guess that a different passport, from some of my other homelands, would still be valid.

Before the eurozone collapsed, when I was a kid, the euro was the official currency. I remember those days and that exciting feeling when you know that history is happening right in front of your eyes. What followed was an incredibly rapid response, you could even call it instinctive. Large European countries introduced their own currencies, and the rest of the union was left with devalued and useless euro. That was when we remembered good old Czechoslovakia and so the Czech crown came into use the next day. At first only unilaterally, but the two nations shortly came to an agreement and reinstated the federation reintroducing the old currency: a rather strange sensation but most people were happy about it. It was just like when a couple break up, both go their seperate ways and they try it with someone new but then realize it will never work and after some time they reunite, have some wine and try to figure out why they ever broke up. They just click back into place with everything perfectly tuned: their conversations, their silences, their touches, even their sex. Everything works as harmonious as a couple of world class ice skaters.

And so, the Czechs and Slovaks were back together for a while. I guess you can imagine Grandma's emotion when she held her new passport with the Czech lion and Slovak mountains on it. She shed a tear when she saw it. However, the upheaval that followed the end of the eurozone was too much for our small federation. Barely two years after our merger, we joined Germany and Austria like a couple of vassals—but it was better than nothing. My most recent homeland is therefore the Confederation of Central European Nations. Anyway, countries and their borders have faded away to be replaced by regions, zones and spheres.

The European Union is still in the minds of people for nobody has officially dissolved it yet. It keeps on as a reminder of what coexistance of the old continent's nations would or could look like. What it could be if … It was an unfulfilled dream.

With the vision of European unity comes a dose of nostalgia. If only Lena had finished medical school then she could have become a medical machinery operator. If only I'd not got drunk and acted like an ass then Laura would have agreed to have sex with me. If only Miro had been luckier then he wouldn't have ended up an artificial intelligence centre operator with robots as his bosses. What if, what if … If only we had wings we could fly …

The important thing for you to know is that the project was a failure but the idea still has potencial. You can find the blue field with yellow stars on t-shirts and cups, but institutions failed to keep the Union relevant. It never stopped existing, and now has a retro feel—people already feel nostalgic about it. It's the same with other states; they exist, have not been dissolved, but their presence on political maps is pointless. Contemperary maps are no more meaningful than historical ones: the latest trend in office decorating among zone and sphere keepers is putting up a large geographical projection with thin lines for state borders but much more important red dots and circles representing buildings, sectors, floors and self-governing territories. These are aquisitions, these are what bosses call home as they lovingly gaze at a red light glowing in a holographic map.

Border control stations and passports are now making their way into museums. Today we have a unique personal code that lets people travel globally. Most of the people in the world, the civilized world, that is, have their code inside them—those that don't cannot leave their sector. The code has all the physical parameters, personal data and identity of its owner—genealogy, status, income, possessions, proffession and even passport. Even though physical passports stopped being issued, the instinct to pull out your credentials stayed with people.

There was an elderly black guy sitting next to me on a flight abroad not too long ago. Both of us were seated in business class and just before take-off, a steward asked him if he would like some coffee. Half asleep, the guy started frantically searching through his pockets for some identification. But when he woke up completely, he remembered that the passport nightmare was a thing of the past and started sobbing. The steward tried to comfort him saying, "It's gonna be ok, sir, it's ok, sir." Rubbing his temples, the spot where the implayray booster was injected, the old man kept wailing and the more they consoled him the more he cried.

People used to dislike and resist both the implants and later the coding solution. The movement fighting for personal information protection called them totalitarian. Bullshit. People had been exposed long before thanks to credit cards, mobile phones, social media, chats and sharing platforms. The coding was here with us, it simply took a while to successfully impliment it. People love their comforts, we've always been lazy bitches and always will be. More importantly you don't really have a choice: you either join the system or stay at home sitting on your butt, both physically and virtually speaking. You can't travel or access the cloud, netsworks, platforms or even the chain systems. You're fucked because none of it is for you—but I don't need to be telling you that, do I? You Grandad, are the perfect example, a living example (assuming you're still alive). You can only go where the Living Industries take you. Otherwise you're knackered.

Both public and virtual spaces are open to all, so talking about dictatership is ridiculous. Only there are less and less of them and they're of poor quality. What people want and need is outside the public sphere.

Human rights still stand so if you meet the criteria, you can theoreti-cally go wherever you want. Private platforms are voluntary: they don't impose any rules on you but if you don't follow them, they won't let you use their services. Most people accept it, saying. "What can anyone do with our data, let them have it." It's progress, it's freedom—travelling without documents—but only if you have good connexions and enough resources.

However, there are some that consider freedom to be the exact oppo-site, i.e. to be disconnected. A movement of the codeless—fools like you. There's only a few of them and they're no threat to the system, so it tol-erates them and can even benefit from them. There are museums of the codeless, showing how people used to live. What a curious thing—this man without a code or corner, working on his computer, holding a small box to his ear.

The majority of the codeless minority present no security threat for they simply dislike the system and their way of protest is to not participate.

However, there are others trying to endanger the system and harm people—terrorists. The massive European implodus has demonstrated that not even a watertight border barrier can stop them. On top of that, many of them were born within European territory; more and more white boys and girls with no connexion to Islam are becoming terror-ists too, which only proves the point. From the disaffected suburbs of relocated aglomerations, they have the motivation and are only looking for a chance—and for that reason safety has become a largely localized thing. Those who can afford to do so create safety zones within states and cities and only let in people with verified identities and entry passes. Hermetically sealed as the netsworkers would say.

The cautious ones know how to eliminate the risk of a violent death almost entirely. The trick is to avoid public spaces but Martin and I were always brave and confident ... Until the moment I told you about. We were defeated ... or rather I was and he was roasted to death.

Oh damn, I'm tearing up. I won't write you a letter in a state like this, I won't give you the pleasure, you pathetic old man.

* * *

I wasn't sure why but the best tridjent scene was in Sofia. The city was full of people willing to sweat in dark pubs and silent sheds. Young Bulgarians had returned to their homeland as the western European economic crisis showed no signs of letting up. And Turks followed suit as their country mirrored Europe in everything, just with a time lag of ten years; their country was disintegrating. All the young people in Sofia brought blood to the place. They hadn't yet succumbed as much to the social interaction of imbodies in their chamboxes. They wanted to clash with each other, feel the sweat and use their senses. Just as I did.

"Hey Ali, how are you going to introduce yourself tonight?" I asked my new colleague.

"What?" He looked at me with the expression of an idiot.

I was good at reading people, but Ali was an exception. When he showed up for a job interview I thought it was a prank. His resumé had all the best references from Acad, which was the only place where I headhunted. His work experience was at top-notch companies, our competitors, in fact. So I seriously thought it was a joke. I looked around the spacious office to see if colleagues weren't covering their red faces and holding back laughter, peaking from behind their desk, the couch or the workout equipment. This bloke just looked dodgy, and not because he was a gypsy. I'm not a racist.

Ali was a product of the Communal Program for Building Capabilities in Marginalized Communities. Struggling parents with big families could give custody of their child to the city or region in exchange for "generous monetary compensation". The dominant population became worried about floods of children entering the program and said it would become too expensive. Their worries, however, turned out to be unnecessary because Romany parents didn't want to surrender their children to the state. Perhaps they didn't believe the people who were behind the project or simply didn't get the memo. The allocated money provided a few disadvantaged kids with elite education and later on institutions started taking children away from their families by force but that's another story. Ali made it to the top of his class in the first wave of the program.

"You could tell girls your name is Sali." Still nothing. "Sali Bari, an Albanian guy from London, he invented tridjent." No reaction. "You could introduce yourself as Sali, instead of Ali."

"Why should I pretend to be some Sali?" he asked as if it was me who was an idiot.

"You know what? Don't bother." And I gave up on the cross-eyed moron.

We walked the city's streets just after an autumn shower when the dry, crumbling foliage soaked up the water and released an earthy smell. Sofia's wider city centre wasn't covered with another sphere, so the sky was real, not just a projection: the rain, air and even smells were authentic. The city's park right beside the statue of an assassinated Prime Minister on Rakovsky street had the odour of bygone days and history mixed with previous night's spew being eaten by stray dogs. I liked the idea of all the fun and dancing that was coming.

Ali wasn't ignorant. Quite the contrary. He only had trouble understanding why he should use cheap tricks, like the "I'm Sali" one to pick up girls when all it took for him was to stand by the bar and smile. In fact even the smile was unnecessary since women would come to him anyway. He radiated a childlike energy, looked completely lost and in need of help. His absent-minded stare combined with cross eyes probably made them think he was blind, which gave him a certain handicapped appearance. Then once they learned he could see (in two directions while only looking in one), could talk and was smart they completely fell for him. Which pissed me off because the eye handicap and quest for compassion was my party trick. His cross-eyed appearance wasn't his fault; he had probably had it since he was a baby but still … a half-blind pirate and a cross-eyed moron, what a duo. Both of us were good but I hated it when Ali could compete with me or even beat me at my own game.

In his first interview, he wasn't particularly impressive. When I asked him what he wanted to do, he made no mention of his skills or the scope of this job, he just said—and I remember this word for word because I found it utterly rude, outrageous, and boastful for his age and with me there (though identical to my reasons for doing the job): he said he wanted to do something meaningful, something that wouldn't bore but challenge him.

After he tried that on me, I said: "Ok, you can go."

"When do I start?"

I shook my head, pointed to the door and rushed to see Klas, the company partner.

"He's good, isn't he? When does he start?" he asked before I could say anything.

Apparently, it wasn't a prank because everybody in the company seemed to like the idea of Ali on the team. I couldn't believe it. We were in need of a helping hand, and I couldn't deal with it anymore so the next day I told Klas to hire whoever they wanted.

Ali eventually ended up on my team, where he proved to be brilliant. Which was good news but none of us wanted to say it out loud. We would beat about the bush, saying things like "we needed an extra set of hands" or "just reinforcing the team."

And even though we all knew that Martin was irreplaceable, Ali actually managed to replace him.

Poor Ioanna! She had no replacement, only grief. Since the funeral I had only seen her once and that was just for some formality. Despite my conscious avoidance of her, she was often on my mind, though; when I was sitting on the soft Persian rug, for instance, next to Martin's work station covered with the small trinkets he had gathered over the years. It resembled the collection of mad Hector, the crazy shaman, with an altar filled with all sorts of pseudo talismans. Our colleagues assumed it was just some strange vice of his and Martin gladly played along, passing himself off as a collector of bizarrerie: A crushed coke can; a rusty microchip; a peach pit; a pair of red pointy tweezers; a lighter with a picture of a skull on it; a dried up rubber tree leaf; a pink artificial nail; a foggy shot glass; a grey wig; a shoe heel; a pill; a link from an old chain; some string; some lady's underwear; a metal lid belonging to God-knows what and hundreds more knick-knacks. They were his sex trophies. When a fat Roman woman once knocked his front tooth out in the heat of her orgasm he kept it, drilled a hole through it and wore it on a leather string. Then he would walk around like a toothless wrestler grinning at everyone and putting off his dentist appointment. Another time it was a white police baton that a Guatemalan woman police officer had shoved down the naked Martin's throat while calling him *hijo de puta*. He'd also kept a pale blue contact lens that fell out of a red-headed lad's eye as Martin was thrusting into him from behind in a Prague gay bar toilet. Or so he claimed. I wasn't there for all his adventures and couldn't know for sure if all his stories were true. Martin loved messing with people. He would tell stories in which he mixed reality with fiction so skilfully, he himself soon forget which of his anecdotes were actually true.

Curled up on the rug I contemplated how to deal with this monument of physical and mental decadence. Should I return it to his grieving family as a keepsake? No, I couldn't. Ioanna could never know about the collection and so I decided to throw it all away. We hadn't talked too much and what does one talk about with a widow anyway? I could talk about work but what would I tell her? That the company had barely noticed her husband was dead so easily had Ali replaced him; that the two of us were slowly becoming a team, one even better than Martin and I had been or that I had showed Ali all the clubs Martin and I discovered together.

Staring at a tridjent club's sign saying *dungeon* in Cyrillic, Ali seemed completely detached, his manner in sharp contrast with that of his sociable predecessor. Small groups of people in tight, black, wetsuit-like costumes hovered around the club's entrance. You wouldn't notice out in the street that each of the suits had something drawn on them but once on the dancefloor, where people dived into a deluge of endorphins, alcohol, drugs and sweat, the lights would reveal all their artwork. Scattered conversations and tobacco smoke rising into the sky complemented the expectant atmosphere. Before a night of interaction and human contact, the tridjent crowd were like focused athletes before a race, fully immersed in the depths of their own thoughts. Silently hovering on the edge of the crowd I lit myself a cigar without bothering to offer one to Ali: he would only give me another of his dumb, are-you-serious looks. My corner detected roughly three hundred people and around seventeen languages. Perfect! The more the cultural and musical backgrounds, the better the tridjent. I remember a tridjent I went to somewhere in southern Africa and it almost killed me; I was the only white guy around. All those African rhythms dominated the place and disarmed and enslaved me. But then it changed and European melodies took over. I felt like a complete weirdo but it was marvellous.

When technology allowed people to create and listen to music in their heads without using their ears, Sali Bari came up with the idea of tridjent. "No hear music" as named by musical theorists, never became a big hit but for Bari, it was a revolution. Unplugged bystanders only watching the mob of people dancing in silence would think us crazy but for us, it was the ultimate fun. No DJ and no setup needed for everyone was their own DJ.

This was Ali's first time at such a party and he didn't seem very enthusiastic about it, which was typical of him. He just nodded when I explained tridjent to him. In the crowded bar I drank Calvados while he had Armagnac.

"You said there would be nice girls here," he said looking around.

Skin-tight black suits made everyone look the same, turned them into a homogenous and anonymous mass. The only things that could distinguish individuals were breast sizes, height and faces.

"You'll find yourself one, or even two …" I said with confidence because that was the standard.

To find someone who really suited you in such a huge crowd was truly wonderful. If it was a man, it was like finding a long-lost brother. We'd dance towards each other, look in one another eyes, examine each other's costume artwork, dance a little, then hug and pat each other's back goodbye. If it was a woman, whose rhythm was like mine and her music the same language, it didn't even matter if she was pretty or what her figure was like. I always clicked with someone and rarely ended up leaving the party on my own.

A couple of drinks later the dark, roofless lounge with dim, yellow light around the walls and emergency exits opened exposing the gorgeous, colourful, multi-dimensional motifs on people's suits.

"Wow, that's beautiful." Ali sighed and I was sorry I couldn't see his face because I had never seen him surprised or amazed before.

"An incredible visual display, that's one of the three pillars of tridjent." I said as the first djent started playing.

"The music is the second pillar. Djent used to be a metal sub-genre with complex rhythms and a crude polyphonic groove. Sali's original production was much harsher—just listen." I joined the crowd and started playing, choosing a cold, sharp sound like from an eight-string under-tuned guitar. Crisp as the Norwegian fjords and deep as the Mariana Trench.

"Later, Sali shifted towards the more subtle type of djent, influenced by electronic and glitch bands like Fuck for Prophits, Mental Hellness and Sho-ho." I switched into the djent's modern, milder version. The room was now filled with some fifty people and I was enjoying my favourite part of the night as more and more "musicians" kept joining to create an orchestra. No conductor needed, though—people did it their own way, some leading, some being led, though the organizers made sure a couple of headliners were in the crowd.

"And here's the third pillar," and I shoved Ali into the crowd and laughed as he crashed into a small group of dancers and fell. They picked him up and the growing crowd devoured him. Physical contact was not only allowed but essential. There were almost no limits, from shoving, hugging, caressing, kissing, holding hands all the way to groping breasts, asses and crotches. If someone didn't like it, they'd give a signal to interrupt the contact. If the other person didn't respect the signal, the first person would then sound a warning tone and a crowd of people would gather to beat the harasser up. Fortunately, it didn't happen very often.

That night in Sofia quickly took off. The ceiling exposed the night sky which showered us with sparkling stardust and a deafening rhythm made your insides dance. I was drunk on strong alcohol and dance, surrounded by sweaty bodies with their pictures changing. Flowers bloomed, trees grew taller, circles multiplied. A woman covered in stars, at least I think it was a woman, almost blinded me—I had to close my eye because her stars were like suns. There was a giant of a man covered in Viking runes, helmets, and swords while I was a small-leaved linden tree with nice and sparkly leaves. Seeing Ali's suit for the first time, I couldn't keep a straight face. His naïve, phosphorescent pictures of a tiny house with fence and smoking chimney, a tree and flower, some clouds in the sky and two wavy-lined crows were sweet and revealed his child-like spirit.

The crowd surged in waves, people surfing on the foamy ocean waters of the sweaty bodies alongside, floating through the shimmering human body forest. Some would climb up and throw themselves into a sea of raised arms, letting their admirers carry them. Thoughts needing to be expressed in words were drowned out by rhythms and melodies. There was no need for verbal communication as spontaneous bonds between people changed swiftly, first thrusting them together, then tearing them apart. It was a democracy where everyone mattered and had a voice, a war where people grouped up and fought over who would set the tone. The sexes were equal as women followed their urges and grabbed men by their asses and balls, allowing them to touch and squeeze them in return. For those trying to keep control, it was hell. A community for one night. A holotropic dive into the womb of the world. A connection hard to part with. Saying goodbye after the party could easily last an hour.

It was a deadly collective adventure that didn't suppress your individuality. And that night was a perfect example. I let myself go but kept my sense of self; though my boundaries became blurred, they didn't disappear. I was everybody and they were all me and suddenly I could see with both eyes. I had no history, no god or father and I forgot I even had a mother. No plans were made, no steps pre-calculated and I had no care for tomorrow. I felt alive like never before yet ready to die on the spot. Brothers and sisters joined together by a mutually tuned inner dynamic. Notes hung on the stave, trembling, rising and falling, growing and shrinking, dividing and merging like cells under a microscope.

As night came on, one voice started to dominate amongst the orchestra of improvisers. At first it was original but died out as it looked for its place. It was a woman's tone and was soon penetrating my spine, shaking my nervous system, overriding my brain, as if a blessed and gifted whale had composed a breathtaking piece. It felt like a thousand volts going straight through me and looking up I saw sunshine through falling rain even though it was night and there was no rain. I felt growing strength and an urge to find this woman. Pushing through the crowd I yearned to put my head next to hers, connect our music centres and feel the vibrations go through us.

Two luminescent crows roused me from my trance as they fluttering over the bucolic scene of a house and tree, coming towards me in their full beauty. Whose home was it and who was smoking out the dance floor through that chimney? Ali, of course, no woman. I was wrong about him, again. He didn't need me, either for work, or for picking up girls—or in tridjent.

* * *

The morning sun shining through delicate curtains blinded me. Inge stood in front of the window with arms above her head, basking in the sunrays in only a vest. She looked as if she was floating, her only point of contact with the ground her left toes, her right foot resting on the other knee, tautened bare buttocks, light hairs on the small of her back and a blonde mane held up by a wooden clip. Motionless she stood there and I could hear nothing, not even my own heartbeat—together with my breath it had stopped existing. The dust set in motion by the open curtains whirled and sparkled in the sunshine then started falling to the floor like snowflakes. I was in a snow glass with a ballerina and someone had shaken it.

"Passé relevé," I said, remembering the phrase from more than twenty years ago. Inge lost her balance and fell onto the bed in a fit of laughter. "Where do you know that from?"

"No idea, from Grandma I suppose … she used to dance."

She inspected my penis with both her sight and touch; it was hardened by the early hour and a night spent with a woman smelling as good as she did. I knew her interest was more scientific than sexual so didn't expect anything. I had come to terms with it long before but when she ran her finger along a dilated vein it was torture. I couldn't bear it.

"Stop, please." I got up from the bed.

"Sorry." She wrapped herself up in a sheet, curled up and turned away. Then the sky turned grey and the room went dark.

I rubbed my eye and my scar, setting free specks of dried-up tears and pus from the infection I hadn't had treated. Moments later, I sat in the bathroom wondering where the fuck we were. A high-pitched sound buzzing in my head blocked location data and prevented me from getting my bearings; the more I tried the worse I felt. The localizing system in the corner wasn't helpful either since I couldn't even ask it about the most basic thing.

Stockholm, I found out stepping out of the shower and noticing Inge's new dress embroidered with the finest thread. It was an unbelievably expensive piece and I remembered that Inge had ordered it from Madame Zhou's traditional salon two months in advance. The old lady didn't take measurements in the chambox, nor did she rely on the imbody or use sewing machines. She had her customers pay for her round trip to wherever in the world they were, would take their measurements, sit down and talk for an hour and then head back to her workshop in Singapore to work on the order. The result was indeed tailor-made and the high price as well as demand for Zhou's work reflected that.

Inge was a professional, always prepared. We attended the global FemCOREp convention together. The most influential women of the world met in the Swedish capital and there wasn't a single man amongst the speakers. I had my own opinions about that but Inge laughed and told me not to be so petty. She said that for centuries men had had the say-so and now was the time to settle the score with exclusion the best way to do it. The women's movement had it all thought out. They started by paving their path with legal suits against violations of equal opportunities. It was cheap, defeatist, and whiney but before we knew, an aggressive corporate strategy had been unleashed following a series of victorious lawsuits. While we were still mocking them, calling them *embroiderers*, women had started banding together in imitation of the male-dominated institutions out there: golf and tennis clubs, cigar bars, strip clubs, brothels and various other forms of networking. Their platforms were different but they had rapid success and a big advantage over men: they didn't underestimate their opponents.

"You should go. Meena hates people coming late," I said breaking the silence. I sat completely naked on a designer armchair in the corner of the room with Inge curled up on the bed pretending to be asleep.

"I know, I'm going. Can you order me a ride?" She stood up to take a shower.

I wanted to enjoy looking at her while I could, so I did as she asked and headed back into the bathroom. Lathering herself with soap she smiled at me and I smiled back even though my insides were drowning in acid.

We spent the rest of the morning in silence and then I accompanied her to her ordered mobicaps.

"My greetings to Meena. I'll pop up in the afternoon, see you then, ok?" She nodded and I kissed her goodbye but she didn't let me come anywhere near her lips and only gave me her cheeks to kiss. It was the way she kissed with strangers or when she was nervous.

It was me who arranged her meeting with the head of the Pacific Chamber of Commerce. A couple of years earlier we had worked on an ambitious project of uniting the southeastern regions of Asia in Palawan for her. She wanted her own satellites orbiting the Earth so as not to have to rely on the traditional Big Ones. Her objective was to make her network reliable to facilitate trade and allow all respectable citizens to access the platform and enjoy the comfort of real time communication. She wanted peace in the surrounding regions to allow her to compete with the northern Chinese provinces and be leader of the force that crushed them.

Meena was a textbook example of one of those few people who cannot be replaced by computers. She was all incredibly powerful, concentrated and direct motivation. Her specific goals weren't important, not even slightly. Her aims drove her forward, they were the impulses that literally kept her moving. And she was always totally convinced of things and would get visibly impatient if people around her were less so.

A system developed for weather forecasting and predicting geological changes made her rich very young. Preventive action which saved people's fortunes was taken based on its prognoses. They called the computer *superintelligent,* but it wasn't clever enough to prosper from its own qualities. It was capable of calculating total precipitation for Montevideo the day after tomorrow, exactly how much wheat the fields surrounding Zhytomyr will yield and how much water from the Teteriv tributary will flow into the Dnepr. I was also able to find out whether the Nojima tectonic crack will create seismic activity at Honshu and when it will. Otherwise, it was stupid because Meena earned from it. The computer was antisocial with no need for a luxurious residence on every continent and harems of young boys who were barely of age. Nor did it long to be admired by the masses—unlike Meena.

Machines were the best at learning to imitate human emotions perfectly, just like apes. There was a fundamental difference between machines and apes, though. Human ambitions are carnal, the result of millions of years of evolution, inherited from our animal ancestors. Our decisions may bear the hallmark of reason but spring from the instincts of our cave life back in the times before we could even speak. Cold microchips made of rock and metal should pulsate and vibrate like full-blooded flesh attached to a bone. But they don't. Even a super-intelligent machine is only a hero when a man (a chump by comparison) gives it a task. A being who doesn't need to be fed by a mother or cry to draw attention, who does not have the need to lick other people's orifices or shove their penises up them, who is not worried about dying ... such a being lacks real motivation and needs instructions to do everything. Every machine is autistic and helpless without its chumpish operator.

Limited in the most ingenious way possible, that's how she was. A small black monkey with ambition gushing from between her white teeth. I didn't like to work or be in Asia, however the Palawan business was good and Meena, the island's governor at the time, grew to like me and appreciated my services. The interview with Inge was arranged for seven o'clock even before breakfast. What did the faces of those two women look like without their polite smiles? I knew but they had never been in such a situation together. I imagined them having a refined discussion over a cup of tea.

I went back into the bedroom, bowed my head to sniff the sheets three or four times then took another shower, alternating between hot and cold water before going down for breakfast. I absently put more fish umeat and plant-based synthetic cheeses on my plate than I could possibly eat then ordered a guestess to rush and get me a triple colourless espresso. Before seven o'clock only one table was occupied. A man with a bony face and bone-like spectacles, most likely a Netherlander, was telling his colleague about something extremely interesting or important. At least the look on his face seemed that was the case—the glowing gaze and stiff smile: the fourth world war has broken out, I'm fucking your missus, someone's invented an immortality elixir, an asteroid will crash into Earth tomorrow, my hometown is underwater, Europe is united, the food on your plate was made from extruded bird shit. But it was none of these—he was talking about his job. I overheard that he built multi-story vegetable farms: immensely effective, he said with a spark in his eyes and a crooked smile. But I'm immensely bored, you moron, and I turned my back on them.

I turned on the news in the corner. Paraguay had a new president, her priority to fight for independence—how many times was that? The Asian trading platform based in Hongkong was already bigger than the European and American combined—congratulations. A new sphere, the size of former Angola, was discovered in Africa where people were being left to die despite medicine being available. Who the fuck was interested in that? The guestess walked around the buffet tables scanning which food was running out and refilling plates. After he was done he stood next to the mahogany counter, white napkin hanging over his forearm and a blank stare in his eyes. I shared his apathy. The boring Netherlander with an interest in his primitive work was still seated behind me and I kept asking why. Why was I still distracted?

* * *

What was that about? What did Ali say? The information gave my brain a nasty sore and deprived me of powers of concentration. I was useless for a month and unable to work. Whenever I was with Inge I would either constantly observe her every move or try to avoid her and for the first time since we had started "dating", after being faithful to her for almost a year despite not sleeping with her, I went looking for other women.

Deborah wasn't one of them; on one hot August day Ali brought her to an interview at our Warsaw branch. I always insisted that our offices looked presentable. They had to be in the Above, never down in the other spheres because I liked real weather with its caressing breeze, burning sun and refreshing rain. This was one of the most luxurious places around. We were one of Europe's top 10 consultation companies, behind the best female-led companies but first amongst those with mostly men. Thanks to that we could afford this place, and I always liked treating our people and myself to the best. We sat down on a terrace of our Warsaw office where I was enjoying my Cuban cigar.

Deborah greeted me in French, and I replied in German. She was the one looking for a job; it was up to her to adjust. Intelligent and very natural, she had a certain charm and a modest yet playful smile. She answered all my questions and had her own opinions ... oh she was simply perfect with her wavy brown hair, tanned and freckled face, emerald eyes, and tiny scar on her cheek. I was amazed and Ali looked happy. He told me that she had almost superhuman powers and could help us close many more deals. I was on board and now that he was practically running operations himself and only needed me to intervene in strategic projects and direct negotiations, I trusted him implicitly and agreed.

After Ali had seen her out, we sat down for a beer.

"She's one of the prefabs, did you notice?" he said trying to sound casual. He knew it was serious and perhaps guessed my reaction.

I stayed quiet for a moment as scores of questions entered my mind. But I said nothing, only motioned to Ali to continue.

"I couldn't tell you about it sooner, I'm sorry. Acad alumni contacted me about half a year ago and insisted it remain confidential."

The sky was clear and cloudless that day: blue as far as the eye could see. We had a wonderful view of the very tip of the Palace of Culture. Recently repainted and illuminated by the bright sun, its white glare dazzled me despite my sun contact lens. I was sitting in the shade, but Ali had picked the sun-lit bench and now the atmosphere was so tense he dared not even twitch. The only movements around us were of the cargo minidrones overhead, drawing lines across the terrace and Ali, buzzing in a heat which hissed and sizzled. Neither of us moved.

"You know that they were working on it, Adam. My old classmate, Sandra Matič ... she worked for us in Bratislava on the Bordel Brothers acquisition ... for the company that makes coloured upholstery from old plastic waste."

"Yeah, I remember that arrogant Slavonian cunt. I have her number." I said tapping my right temple.

Ivan Lesay

"You know the protocol regarding these things, Adam." He said slowly and quietly while I turned red with fury. "She respects you but she came to me first because she trusts me and we know each other. Understand that until recently it was all strictly confidential."

"Six months ago you say…" I reminded him.

The human race had been contemplating it since time immemorial: how to create a person or humanoid without normal means of conception. Technological advancement had now made it possible. People had been talking for a long time about robots and artificial intelligence but ten years ago someone managed to create a very authentic simulation of the human brain and consciousness. Computers with vast amounts of data created such convincing combinations that even I had trouble distinguishing in tests whether the speaker at the other end of the line was a human being or programmed imitation. It had its own made-up past, whims, humour; it could improvise, curse, and laugh … just like a human. Martin and I participated in one of the trials. It was in Geneva's research center where during ten five-minute-long conversations we were both supposed to guess who was at the other end, a human or humanoid. Both of us scored only forty percent—worse than tossing a coin.

An enduring problem was how to connect the operating consciousness with a body or at least faithful replica of one. The guestesses were a successful project—robots encased in something resembling a human body which could be programmed to perform less complicated tasks and could work as shop assistants, receptionists, even prostitutes. They were almost like real people but their fine motor skills, body movements and facial expressions always gave them away.

It wasn't until that hot day in Warsaw that I realized a few things. The exclusive gathering at that conference in Quebec with only a handful of us from Europe was, as usual, a predominantly female event. A North American researcher from Human Societal Advancement Center said that direct implanting of human consciousness into a physiological carrier was the only way forward. I don't know how we got on to the topic (perhaps it was just casual

264

conversation) but I remember she used those very words—'implant' (like a plant?), 'consciousness' (like subsoil from a sack?), 'physiological carrier' (like what: a person dissolved in some solution?). The entire phrase was ridiculous, even more so than the name of the institution she worked for.

"If you need any volunteers sign me up ..." I said trying to be witty but despite the alcohol in our blood (it was an evening reception) we were not on the same wavelength.

"It's not as funny as you might think," she said spitting some red wine on Ali's sleeve. His white turtleneck was now absorbing the droplets, small stains getting larger and paler, like a virus infecting its host.

"Let's get out of here," I said in Slovak and pulled Ali by his sleeve, hoping that Marie-Louise, sure of her importance, felt no reason to install this language into her corner.

We had got used to that technology, to the computer abilities it gave to our everyday existence. Being constantly connected to cloud via implayray meant that speaking different languages was no longer an accomplishment. Anyone could speak any language, all it took was to download it. Nor was playing musical instruments difficult anymore: the computer read the music and sent your hands, mouth, feet—or any other part of you—a signal via the brain, telling you what to do. The only masters of the music industry left were composers, but anyone could become a performer. Only composers with their own stories, personalities and deep fallibility could keep the title of true artists. Computers composed music but their pieces were not born out of errors and anomalies; they lacked that magical and grimy human touch.

Sport suffered even more even though bodies still needed training and their muscles, speed and reflexes were obvious assets. But tactical and strategic tasks were now done by computers. This radical change made purists protest and even try banning technology from sports but the more the people used implayray, a connection via cloud, and their corner screen in their daily lives, the weaker the conservative argument was.

It was one thing to let technology help an individual improve but to obliterate someone's consciousness and replace it with a pre-fabricated one ... that was too much.

"So, you knew it, back then in Quebec. You knew and you've been helping Acad with their research behind my back. So obvious ... why the fuck did I not think of it? I must have lost my mind."

Ali stayed put despite the heat as I opened another beer and passed him a bottle of water from the fridge. He didn't want it so I smashed it against the ground in anger. Staring in two different directions into the distance, the jerk didn't move a muscle.

"How many are there?" I interlaced my fingers and straightened my arms until all my knuckles cracked.

"Certainly a few hundred, maybe even a thousand around the world ..."

He noticed my shocked expression.

"For how long?"

"They started a few months ago, something like that."

I hated him when he spoke vaguely or acted dumb.

"Did anyone notice? Did no-one stop them?"

"What do you think?" he said, smiling.

I remembered perfectly casual and natural Deborah. That fuck-ing gypsy asshole must have programmed her so that I would like her.

"And where do you get the ... those physiological carriers? You call them that, right? Just like that drunk bitch back in Quebec."

"No, they're donors. We call them donors."

A long silence followed; perhaps he realized how bonkers it sounded.

"Alright, donors, so where do you get them?"

"Some of them are suicides taken from psychiatric clinics, oth-ers are from the Underworld. That is the most numerous group. They're all outcasts, tired of their own lives and Acad has given it a lot of thought. They have resources so can offer the donors a decent compensation for their deceased ... I mean, their families, their loved ones." He quickly corrected himself.

"Is there any supervision? You know ... Do they have an ethics code?" I was asking almost automatically but don't even remember if I cared about the answer.

"Certainly. This kind of stuff must have strict rules even if ..." And he hesitated and walked up to the balustrade, leaned against it and looked out. You wouldn't often see him this unsettled. For a moment he watched the city underneath him then turned around, shook his head, grabbed a beer and sat next to me in the shade.

"May I?" he asked and took a sip knowing I wouldn't answer.

"The procedure is very simple and only takes about four minutes, not counting the prepping and formalities. Someone walks in, you reprogram them and then they walk out a different person."

He looked into my eyes, or more precisely, squinted into my eye. I then scratched my eye socket and wiped the discharge from under the eye patch. Warm weather gave it a horrible smell, reminding me of something from grandma's flat. My mind tried to find the source of that memory and as I watched it float around in the hot air hovering across time and space, Ali pulled me back down.

"The weirdest thing is, Adam, that the ones that come to Acad—to the lab, the future donors." He looked at me and looked away again. "They know what they're doing; they're properly interviewed and informed and still have no idea they're going to their deaths. You can see no fear of death in their faces. It's as if they were simply going for a haircut or to get facials. They expect to get improved, undergo a change or some tuning. And there's more ..." He finished his beer and grabbed another.

He got pretty talkative.

"When the procedure is over ... the new ones ... the prefabs don't remember who they used to be. They only know who they are now and believe their newly programmed past and identity so completely they all pass the lie detector. Isn't it crazy? Everyone was worried it would be a failure and like something from a sci-fi horror film, people having flashbacks caused by an imperfectly erased consciousness or something else ... But it's perfect, they have a one-hundred-percent success rate."

Ali took a breath to say something, closed his eyes, rubbed his temples and then waved his hand saying.

"You've seen Deborah. I was there when she was … created and I think I'm in love with her. No, I'm not, sorry. I'm not in love with her. I'm sorry. I just feel something for her. I'm going crazy, sorry."

He pissed me off going behind my back, so I didn't respond but that was the least of my worries at that moment. I was struggling to process the information and the soaring heat was killing me. Prefabricated lives were often on my mind and I'd been thinking about them a lot since the Quebec conference. I was no conservative and lived for new things and trends; once it had even crossed my mind that my wonderful Ali must also be some prototype.

But the truth was I was worried. Above all I was afraid that these new people would be super smart, be better than me at everything—and I wouldn't even notice. Another thing was: what if the reprogramming was done by force—and who knows if it hadn't already happened to the very first people. A thousand is, in the end, a pretty large sample. Screw the ethics, I was worried they might erase and improve me too. Deborah … Inge. I remembered Inge and her old-fashioned hair dryer that blew away memories, inhibitions, secrets. Once my thoughts found her, they stayed, and I couldn't stop thinking about her.

* * *

"Inge … wait up." I grabbed her by the hand and pulled her away from the crowd of people waiting for coffee. I checked if anyone I knew was around, pulled her closer and whispered in her ear. "I'll fuck you tonight, alright?"

"Excuse me?"

"I'm sorry but I need to."

We were standing outside the conference room by the advertising projection stalls when some gender-fluid person approached me asking if I was interested in hormotreatment. I looked at them and pointed to Inge to say: Can't you see I'm talking to someone?

The person had a campaigning partner dressed in a jumpsuit saying *I'MIT* in multiple languages and I waved them away. They turned to pounce on some other poor devil to explain the benefits of a genderless life and sell him their yellow-tablet promo package.

Inge took a deep breath and rolled her closed eyes. I don't think my proposal surprised her but with the summit underway it certainly wasn't the best moment for it as she was deluged with work. Breathing heavily with her eyes closed, it took her a few seconds to absorb what I'd just said and I could see the effort she had to make. But she stayed focused … on me … her partner, perhaps? I guess we both wondered about it at that moment. When she eventually opened her eyes and looked at me, she was quite calm, only her eyelashes were slightly damp when she said okay.

"Hey, what's up you guys?" Meena showed up out of the blue with a smile showing two rows of pearly white teeth.

"Something happened?" She dropped the smile.

The silence was awkward and long so eventually I nodded.

She raised her eyebrows inquisitively but Inge just stood there in silence. I had nothing to say either.

Meena frowned and left saying: "See you around."

As we watched her disappear into the crowd, Inge grabbed my hand and I could feel nothing but pity in her touch.

* * *

"In this pivotal moment in our history let us come together and integrate our beautiful selves by using singularity and technological advancement to improve the lives of our brothers and sisters. Only constant trade—that beautiful interaction where everyone can share something of theirs with the rest of the world—can help us evolve further. Every person can join in because we businesswomen don't exclude, don't compete but instead do business with love and emotion …"

A Serbian woman with fake tan and huge boobs recited her spiel as she looked everyone in the audience in the eye.

Having heard just about enough of love, hope and a bright future, I left the main hall to look for some solitude and privacy, preferably in some dark, impersonal space.

I ended up in a cool, men-filled room where a scatter-brained young lad with dusty blond hair was talking about a capsule he had invented. Programmed to stay close by at all times and in case of emergency pick him up within five minutes, it could fly into the stratosphere, stay there for a few days and then come back down. Stocked with water, food, and oxygen for weeks, it could allegedly handle a free fall from the stratosphere, float on rough waters (even survive a tsunami) and withstand extreme temperature conditions on land. The following presenter was a short Japanese guy who mostly bragged about his global real estate network both for his own and renting purposes. Only for rich people like himself, of course. The word *bunker* must have been his mantra or something because he said it at least two hundred times always with a strange accent, raised voice, and sparkling eyes. They were a bunch of preppers exchanging their survival manuals in the event of natural disaster, civilization downfall or social collapse.

Some short, sickly-looking fellow then stood up and asked: "Don't you think that what you call a cataclysm has already begun, Mr. Whatts?"

The question recipient shook his head and giggled nervously.

"Is there something worse that you think is coming? What could it be?" The young man continued unintimidated. "Aren't you worried that someone with more power is going to steal those bunkers from you, Mr. Hirota? I know what you're going to say …" He raised his voice as the Japanese man raised his finger. "You have guns and guards … More than a small army's worth?"

I burst out laughing, which surprised me, before quickly covering my mouth. All of those preppers shut up and the presenter quickly saved the situation by introducing the next speaker, an

Icelander with a name longer than the polar night itself. He started talking about waking up frozen people and waiting for better times. He began by agreeing with the question from the audience by saying he too believed that society had already failed. All of it reminded me of my mother and I suddenly felt sick. Not even that parade of psychopaths could distract me so I turned off my hearing; I was at rock bottom and went back to thinking about Inge—it was the only thing on my mind.

Our downfall had begun. It was at that moment I first doubted if she was real.

* * *

After the summit we went to my hoptell room instead of Inge's place. A long day behind her and a rough night ahead made her look very tired and her occasional sighs made me feel bad. We walked into the courtyard, through a series of automatized doors and gates and made it to my flat. The door closed, the dim lights turned on and the sound system played moody music. Wasn't all music moody in the end? The thundering bass, the piano and guitar dripping high notes around and the drum brushes rustling like a breeze. A twinkling Jannick Top sat a few metres away playing his bass. And though he couldn't see us, he knew us and our situation perfectly, his music reflecting my sickly but determined mind and Inge's melancholy soul. But though it was supposed to "sync" us, my hatred for this ingenious system that chose your lighting, temperature, humidity, scent and music was overpowering. Did it also know my dilemmas? Could it decide what would happen and make my choices for me? Was my task simply to lie down in submission?

Inge didn't hesitate and undid the brooch on her dress letting the top part slide down to her waist and create a curvaceous line of golden threads. She was like a flower from the north heading into a long polar night after a brief summer, wilting at the thought of the brutal cold. Her slouching figure made her beautifully shaped little breasts even smaller—which made me think of that disgustingly bumper-breasted Serbian woman. All I could see was her tight stretched face and her mouth repeating the word *globally* over and over. I shook my head at Inge saying no, we shouldn't rush it. I helped her with her dress and passed her the satong dressing robe. I was really hungry so I pointed towards the kitchen and she nodded.

I noticed that when people are silent, things start talking. The couch started getting softer and lured our exhausted bodies to lie down. It longed to caress and embrace us, longed to do what it was made for. Inge couldn't take her eyes off it. The copy of my miniature Hindu god statue was grinning and mocking me from its small altar in the hallway by the kitchen. I'd brought it from Sri Lanka and the original resided in my flat in Vienna. This one was teasing me and saying "Look, I have all these limbs and certainly don't need to be sticking them into others."

"You're not even real so what do you care?"

"Why are you talking to me then?" And it laughed, growing more arms and mouths all around its head and showing me copies of the same grin over and over like a broken holoprojector.

"I'm real, I'm real …" It kept mocking me and enjoying itself.

In the meantime, the cupboard boasted about being restocked the day before. It was filled with boxes of freshly conserved ready-to-cook meals that had come just before we arrived in town. I helped myself to some precooked pasta with pear sauce, unwrapped it and tossed the transparent wrapping into the hungry decompost hole which created energy by devouring it, the power going straight into the grid as it gratefully burped. Homecook politely asked if it could scan our body data to prepare nutritious jelly bars and wanted to know what flavour and shape we preferred. Our silence answered the question—whatever … tasteless cubes would do.

"You can melt and pour them over your meal," Homecook said.

The zelone chamber hosted herbs intoxicated by gas, the green leaves planted in brown soil dancing around and singing to themselves. Always delivered fresh to your home, they were grown in skyscraper farms where billions of seeds germinated on shelves. Piled up in layers and exposed to artificial light, they were then replanted in people's homes to stay fresh.

Neither of us however were feeling fresh, not one bit. I chopped some herbs and sprinkled them onto the hot food topped with melting nutrition jelly and poured some wine. Inge was at the table and stared at the spot where I put her plate. We didn't eat very much and had little appetite, instead we sipped the very dry wine and then water. Then I took my favourite drug, the SynTaxOn, which would help curb some of my unnecessary emotions, ease my overbusy thoughts and let me focus on physical sensations or situation analysis, depending on which I needed more. But though it mostly helped, this time it didn't very much as my mind raced with suspicions, doubts and highly intensified hate going both in and out of me. Exhausted from running around for weeks not knowing where I was heading, it was the only thing keeping me conscious and awake.

"Are you real?" I asked as I first plunged into her.

"Why does it matter if even you can't tell the difference?"

Would a human being say that? Wouldn't it be more human to ask ... well, anything else?

Not feeling the need to answer her rhetorical question, I continued with my tedious task. And it was, certainly for me, the worst sex ever.

We were like two beginners at a medical examination or first-aid training session trying to resuscitate a plastic figurine. I had to remind myself that she was what I wanted, she was the woman I'd lusted after because, even with my dick in her mouth, I felt nothing and blamed her for it. It was all her fault. And since creativity is the first thing a fatigued brain switches off, I just thrust into her mechanically as she caressed my face with pity in her eyes. Going full speed and panting heavily for five, even fifteen minutes, I felt the room quake with my frustration and guilt.

And then I thumped her and we stopped in our tracks, both of us in shock. It took her a moment to collect herself but when

Ivan Lesay

she did, she started punching, scratching, and biting me. It actually looked like a game of rawball for a moment and then a drop of blood from a scratch on my nose fell on her face. Again, we stopped. She licked her bleeding lip, wiped the blood off her eyelid and licked her finger while I was still towering over her like a roof that should be protecting her but wasn't. We both started crying.

* * *

A thunderous voice filled the room. Nobody but Lino Sirppo, a Northerner from the highest ranks of the United Union, had a voice that deep. With his thick coal-black eyebrows in sharp contrast to his grey hair, he worked as Sybille Fusatsch's right-hand man and was widely respected. She was the leader of the Regional Assembly and together they contributed to the establishment of the first European armed force and helped unify the corpoments when they were at loggerheads. Many people, mainly men, thought it was Sirppo pulling all the strings but I knew he wasn't that good. The impression of seniority, prudence and power he created was largely due to his stentorian voice, which was also why Fusatsch kept him a member of the Union. The truth was he was a nonentity.

"And so we've decided …" (dramatic pause and high-frequency twitching of his semi-closed eyes)"… that we shall move the back-up data centers from Paris and Frankfurt …" (another pause as he gave the audience a long piercing stare) "… to Slawien, Colmö and Helsinllin". Sirppo proudly smiled at his diplomatic success and the new city names he had invented. Officially, they still had their original names, but he thought that if he kept using his own variations others might join him. But he'd already been doing it for a decade and still nothing. I guess I should have been proud of my city, too, but didn't give a damn anymore; filtering out Sirppo's message, I let his voice carry me away.

A blossoming, bright-green liana was quickly wrapping itself around the ceiling's wooden beams. Sybille, bored by Lino's lengthy

274

speech, slipped out of her iridescent overall and dipped her naked body in the thermal spring running through the room. Despite her grey hair and sagging skin, she still looked attractive sitting waist deep in the water, pouring water over her shoulders and breasts. She then noticed water from the waterfall splashing on Sirppo's head and her laughter filled the room and rippled through my body. A herd of horses and pack of dogs then ran into the room. An Alsatian bitch lay at my feet and I scratched her head as she slipped onto her back and raised her paw demanding more of my attention. A mighty steed lowered his head to snack on some bruised apples. Crushing them with its teeth, a foamy sweet cider formed around his lip and I ran my fingers through his mane breathing in its smell. My fantasy was then shattered when a huge screeching rook suddenly flew down and poked the horse's eye out. I'd done it again; it was happening more and more often.

The conference room changed back in a blink of an eye, becoming as dead as before. The sharp lighting, straight lines and edges, sterile atmosphere and lifeless glances made my eye hurt. I doubted anybody here was truly present but counted myself as the least involved. It was my last meeting before my descent the next day into the Underworld and it shocked me how little these people cared. The talk held was about the second largest data leak since the First Data Revolution.

* * *

Immense amounts of both personal and classified information were leaked including inter-company correspondence, lovers' messages, personal pictures and videos, distasteful messages between colleagues, confidential secret service files, patents, manuals, histories of simulated reality visits, gun and sex toys orders, violent videos from safety satellites, suspicious bank accounts and suspicious transactions with details leading to final beneficiaries, exact coordinates of armed forces bases and access codes to their internal systems and spaces. It was the Great September Intelligence

Revolution, the First Data Revoleak, and netsworkers were going crazy trying to get their bombastic commentaries in first.

Things started happening immediately after the data release. Marriages and other relationships started breaking up; people resigned and got fired; heads, brands and names crashed. There were races involving both cyber and conventional attacks; there were plans for wars, vendettas and settling of accounts. Extortionists and the competitors of the injured parties were delighted but the chaos and malicious joy didn't last long because as more data accumulated and got analyzed, fewer and fewer people remained untouched. Everyone had a secret and a blemish on their reputation.

Many of the events in our history are represented by an image evoking its atmosphere and emotion. A naked little girl with napalm burns running from the terrors of the Vietnam war. An exhausted, famine-struck Sudanese child crawling along the ground with a vulture lurking overhead. A wonderfully peaceful mushroom cloud growing from tens of thousands of souls living through a burning hell: Nagasaki ... Its rhythmic name alone foretold the aesthetical massacre. The innocently blue sky overarching the greatest disgrace and end of the historic era—the leader of European nations signing the capitulation treaty in front of a cathedral in Helsinki, so drunk they had to hold him at the table. And the start of another era: the first man on Mars—a sombre looking Chinese astronaut called Guo who became a sex symbol thanks to his cold expression against an orange background.

The First Data Revolution got its iconic depiction at a fund-raiser for disabled young talents organized by the largest Alpine armaments concern, Heinz-Mutlich. The series of four shots shows the president, Fernanda Heinz and her husband attending the event. The first picture shows them smiling, excited about their selflessness and generous in their show of modesty. The second was taken moments after they received a revealing message on their corners. Mrs. Heinz's open mouth and widened eyes, her husband's hunching and defensive pose, her hand up in the air and he ready to fend off the imminent blow. The message revealed that respected Emeritus Professor Selané used to offer good grades for a certain quid pro quo from his young female students. One of the messages disclosed the sordid details of his assessment methods. "For a blowjob you'll pass, for a regular fuck, you'll get a C and for letting me in through the back door you'll pass with honours." The third snap carried the professor's terrified face and his wife's furious grimace but before they had a chance to process the first wave of bad news, another was on the way. DataLeak portal reported that Fernanda Heinz had held meetings in which she explicitly and repeatedly approved combat gas experiments on Underworld children. Selané didn't seem to mind that too much; it was just the sorry Underworld kids who suffered. Such a matter was deep down his "back door" and he could certainly swallow it and forgive his wife but for the news of her affair with his son from his first marriage and their humiliating sex chats in which they joked about the old man's performance—that was beyond the pale. The picture shows him catching his breath and reaching for his wife while she leans away to avoid him. The last shot was of two expressionless faces looking at talented and happy children without acknowledging each other's existence—but staying where they were, which was the most telling feature of it.

The episode was documented on video and the four moments became legendary. It wasn't unique, though—there were thousands of similar stories. The tabloids were flooded with scandals to report and couldn't pick which ones to cover. For a few days the atmosphere was emotional with everybody planning revenge but as days went by enthusiasm faded. Everybody was equally knee-deep in shit so who was to preach? In the end it was a strange time even if nothing revolutionary happened. But although on the outside, almost nothing changed, the insides of society were turned upside down and all trust was gone.

Five years later when the fibres connecting society had somewhat recovered another massive data leak occurred, this time not as big and as loud but quite the reverse. This time it was accompanied by peace and apathy as if it wasn't really sensitive information that was coming to the surface. It was as if the new undesired transparency had become normal. The netsworkers didn't write about a revolution and nobody drew any far-reaching conclusions. People just lay low. It's happened before, so what? Losing your privacy still hurt a bit but it was bearable since everybody suffered equally. Everybody knew everything but when you put it all together, it didn't mean that much.

Delivering speeches to the anesthetized souls in the ice-cold conference room was an unavoidable ritual but the most important drama took place during the informal parts of the event. A short bald man from Alsace approached Sybille's presiding chair just before they announced a break. He touched her shoulder, leaned closer and whispered something in her ear, hiding the stream of words behind the palm of his hand. I was close enough to hear what he was telling her. A complete banality—an invitation to his daughter's graduation ceremony. A thing he could have easily told her later during the lunch break but why throw away an opportunity to show others how close he was to the boss? A novice diplomat nearby stood up to observe the exchange, surely thinking it was some major side-deal. The Alsatian managed to impress because some people who had dozed off now woke up to watch. One needs to be on guard against potential power grabs.

The fact that nobody actually cared about one of the supreme bodies holding a meeting and discussing a key topic was most evident when lunch was announced. A Yugoslav colleague seated next to me leapt from his chair so abruptly all of us alongside flinched. Stolid and lifeless stares came alive and returned to the conference room from their distant daydreams while a Bavarian at the other end of the incomplete circle opened his eyes and smiled, the moustachioed corners of his mouth springing up to let a trail of drool run down his stubble. Data security was not an issue: nobody could hope to guarantee it anymore and once everything is out there there's no way back.

But food—that was important. And what food there was! They led us out of the conference hall into an atrium where on a long line of dark wood tables covered in starched white tablecloths were vintage-looking stainless steel, gas-heated containers filled with food. Advancing like a swarm of sleepwalkers, we silently chanted food, food, food, food! The smell of roasted meat was in the air and people hungrily swallowed. These instincts couldn't be hidden behind fancy clothing, and nobody even tried hiding them because the huge majority of principals liked their privileges and were proud of their position. A boldly dressed obese woman standing in front of me in the queue helped herself to a pork chop and started munching on it before she even reached her table.

Officially, eating meat was not allowed and plant alternatives and synthetic food were more encouraged since they were both cheaper and healthier. But in these circles such doctrine was null and void.

I was never a foodie and didn't care whether my food came from a plant or animal. Once though, a famous composer showed me what meat obsession was. We dated for a few weeks; she was on the road most of the time but would always carry a container of minced meat with her. I found it strange and asked her if it was necessary when we could go to a restaurant for some umeat or to the chambox where she could eat all the meat she wanted.

"No, it's not the same. Don't you understand?" she would ask me with her thick Polish accent. Speaking in foreign languages made her voice go an octave higher. Her name was Kasia or was it Gosia? One of those, I suppose. I forgot what her face looked like, but I remembered her gasps, which were the same in bed and at the gym where we first met.

"No, I actually don't." I tried sounding like her, but my voice failed.

"An animal died and probably suffered too. The difference is that it died for me, for my pleasure, do you get it?" She emphasized every single word.

I didn't mind the cruelty as much as her absurd sense of her own exceptionalism and entitlement.

I deliberately stood by a table at the side. Thank God for the two Asians, man and woman, who joined me but didn't care for conversation. This room, compared to the petrified conference hall, was full of life, the joy of good food like geysers flooding the space. Dozens of people's forks and knives swished through the air creating an orchestral piece, a baritone of purring exaltation.

The groups of people followed an unwritten rule and faithfully adhered to power orbits, the big names concentrating together because they had stuff to deal with; the staff who occupied the tables around being the closest to their leaders. The middle class claimed the second central circle of tables and while they pretended to have important conversations with their peers, they were constantly eyeing the top dogs, who were too self-absorbed to even notice. From above, it would resemble a concentric firework explosion with the brightest spot in the centre.

Now, on my very last day with them, they seemed like a bunch of clowns and jesters, strange and pathetic, when only a few months and suns ago I was one of them. I was no eager member and didn't care about how close I was with the leaders. Nor did I have any true friends there. And yet I was a part of it. Attending the same events, dining in the same room, smoking in the same yard, drinking at the same bar will make you become a loyal and uncritical part of something that refers to itself in the first-person plural.

Suddenly I saw them all differently—in a slow-motion shot with blurred, unidentifiable faces. Colourful sound waves issued from these human blotches, their tinny voices blending into one unintelligible lump sound of sound. Big, boldly coloured flies crawled and flew around them, laying huge Easter-like eggs painted with skulls and crossbones for the Mexican *Día de los Muertos*. A fake sky projected on the ceiling above the atrium blended with the ground and turned the world into a microscopically thin plate, three dimensions flattened into two. It was one big wallpaper pattern with food, trees, tables and people glued to the cold walls of the universe. Grease dripping from a press searched for the inferno to feed the flames of hell but it was nowhere to be found for hell was the very essence of our flattened world.

* * *

"Should I be thankful or not? I'm not so sure." I told you and meant it; it was no rhetorical question or observation. And I really thought about it even though I knew no answer I gave could make any difference.

"For your mother, for Naďa?" You were a good psychologist. You didn't say much after we started meeting each other and when you did it was always to keep me talking. You'd only get what you already knew and I would just nod without even looking at you. Instead I stared out of the old café window.

I couldn't believe it was just by chance that they parked your home somewhere in Záhorie, so close to where I grew up and worked so often. The reason why I decided to meet you was that the older I was the deeper the concept of providence took root in my mind. But not the one from above, not the all-knowing and all-controlling kind but the one we all had within ourselves. We create our own destiny to give meaning to our lives and when you know that it doesn't make sense, you need to change it. That was my reason for coming to see you although after your first letter I didn't even consider it.

The Avion café was where we would meet because it was in a part of the old town where the sky had not been covered. Even though I'd spent most of my life down in the bowels of the spheres, I still enjoyed the sky and the daylight. My nose identified the smells of coffee and liqueur, of earth and various herbs. Not having slept for two days, a dark bag under my eye stared at me from the glass window. I also noticed your thick grey beard, a lit cigar sticking out of it sending a straight line of smoke upwards.

"That was some top-notch fuckery you did to me, you know. You roused that primitive instinct in me, reminded me of the overrated idea of family by writing to me about yourself and the woman who brought me into the world. Count yourself lucky that I'm conservative and like all things retro. With that nameless sperm donor of a father, my closest relative, genetically speaking, is my distant and hibernating mother so who else beside you, you old loser, am I left with?" We both laughed but I meant it and it wasn't the first time I'd insulted you. But we soon got used to this mostly one-way teasing.

I was genuinely glad. My certainties had disappeared one by one and north was never in the same place anymore. All I was left with was what I used to laugh at: blood and genes.

"Tell me about her," I said without thinking, already knowing what the answer would be.

"I put everything I knew in the letter. There's not much else to say."

"Then tell me about grandma." My empty, tired, and pleasantly dormant head had no restless thoughts anymore and craved only the pleasant and the positive. I wanted to learn about the celestial woman who raised me, about Pavlína, whom I could never quite wrap my mind around.

"You surprise me, Adam," he said, looking truly surprised. "But I can't tell you much about her either. She was wonderful and I loved her, but I didn't deserve her ... God, what a load of crap that is. Is that all I can tell you about her? When I think about it I guess I never really got to know all of her, even though I have so many memories."

"As if a part of her wasn't quite of this world." I knew just what you meant.

"Ineffable," you said and I agreed.

Then you asked me if I thought grandma would've wanted Naďa woken up so she could see her daughter.

"The question is would Naďa want to meet Pavlína?" I did it on purpose, I used their names instead of family relations to piss you off, you old-school bastard.

And so we went on, discussing both the important and the trivial and I discovered that apart from Martin and Inge, I didn't have any true friends.

"We'll never know," you said. "With one of them missing and the other asleep. Unless you were up for finding Pavla ..." And you looked at me with despair in your face. Although you talked about how stoic and balanced you were at the end of your life, I wasn't buying it.

"I have other things to worry about. And it was you who left them, you son of a bitch." I had to dismiss the idea—I didn't want you getting hopeful.

So we went quiet and just sat there, maybe for an hour. And saying little became a habit to us. Occasionally you sighed and closed your eyes; perhaps you even nodded off for a bit while I entertained myself observing movements inside the café and out-side it. Later I ordered an egg sandwich with salmon caviar. As I ate it, I could feel myself destroying the tiny sources of life, crushing them between my teeth like fragile berries. It was a windy day as the pressure between the air-conditioned spheres and the exposed surface searched for equilibrium. All that wasn't tied down or sturdy enough yielded to the wind. A public transport carriage stopped at a tramway stop outside the café and a woman got out, laughing, and trying to tame her rebellious hair which flew upright like a blazing flame. Children ran around throwing cut-up wrappers and packag-ing in the air, while an older boy flew his kite, feeding it the shiny pieces of trash in the air. Then a girl on a bicycle stopped in front of the café and I could hear her scaly dress fluttering and clapping against itself in the wind. The boy behind her caught up with her and she asked him: "Why don't you use the motor?"

"I don't want to." They both laughed and the boy panted heavily from having to ride into the wind. The girl then got back on her bike and rode onwards while the boy, barely keeping his balance, pedalled with all his might to catch up with her.

As the sun set, a wave of depression swept over me which I didn't try to resist. The gloom I felt made me sigh out loud and hum existing and made-up melodies that led into unexpected digressions and dead ends. I was enjoying my out-of-tune jazzy improv, mak-ing mistakes and going nowhere. After days of alertness, coffee and energy bars I was finally tuning out and surrendering to my nightly fate, unafraid of the dark, something which alcohol helped me with. Twilight was my time for sweetened akvavit-enhanced coffee, which

I kept on my tongue for as long as I could, letting it suffuse my oral cavity before swallowing it. In the corner was a notice from the insurance company about the harmful effects of excessive alcohol consumption. Which, of course, I knew all about. Just as I knew that all diseases were treatable, and for that reason paid my insurance. The insurance company, for its part, knew that notifying people at the time of consumption lowered intake by twenty percent. So if you allowed them to notify you, they offered you a discount.

The limbo between day and night was long down here. Floating, sunlight-reflecting balloons (replaced by drones if the wind was strong) allowed sun to shine down on the darkening surface of the sphere even when the sun itself was far below the horizon. It made the day longer but the reflected daylight had a different shade, like that of a million fireflies and a disco combined with a solar eclipse. The world became a stage with the spotlight on the one who occupied the best spot.

Deži Deer, the combojazz master, was playing at Avion that night. Back when he still played with FronTorn band I went to see his gigs in Vienna New Town. Everybody in the band—the Gypsies, the Tiroleans, the Balkans, whoever, they all even knew how to play sad music so that you could dance to it. Here, in the café though, nobody got up to dance. Deži just kept playing the thick bass strings, developing a slow-paced melody, tapping his foot to divide the beats, composing on the spot. At this time of day everything was slowing down, winding down and people going into reset. But why am I telling you about a situation you experienced with me? Surely not because you slept almost right through it.

The artificial lights of this place started outshining the weakening ones from above while mobicaps, magnetis, uniwheels and goods vehicles painted orange lines on the night-time map. Just after my first beer and calvados and just before night completely took over the town, something troubling caught my eye. It was a man, illuminated by the very last sunbeam, smoking a cigarette by the plague column. The highest-flying drone must have reflected the very last slither of sun, which jumped over the horizon and landed on a face ... a face very closely resembling mine.

I stood up from the table, knocking my chair over and ran out of the café. You woke up all drowsy and alarmed as I tried to hurry and see if my eyes were not deceiving me. My legs grew heavy as I sneaked around the old post office and hid behind a fast-food vending machine I felt as if I'd been running for miles. When I was finally close enough, the light went out. The man finished his cigarette, turned around and headed towards a gallery which had once been a church. I saw him up close and in the light for just a fraction of a section: his blond hair, brushed away from his face and tucked behind his ears, a single strand falling down his forehead, his sharp features and ginger-brown stubble, an eyepatch rimmed by a patch of dry and irritated skin. It was like watching a movie about my own future. Or was it my past? It certainly couldn't be the present.

I followed him from a ten-metre distance. Despite it being a warm evening, he was wearing a thin cloak. The wind tossing the three strips of cloth, divided by slits in the back around making him look like a wounded bird that barely made it out an air shaft. All that was an illusion because hiding under the cloak was a very confident tread.

I followed him through the streets of the old town before he walked into an entertainment center at the Tollgate. The front of the sphere in this part of the city wasn't the usual cascade but rather steep and tall. I could have easily seen to the very top in such weather as today's but would have cricked my neck if I had tried.

The place was filled with people eyeing displays of dresses, jewellery, accessories, household goods, exotic trips, and luxury hotels. I kept my double in sight, following him through the room of living canvases. He walked fast into the dining area, apparently uninterested in buying anything, then up to a small, levitating, water-spouting fountain that sang some kind of whale song. The man approached a woman wearing a wine-red costume from behind, then jumped and said 'boo' to surprise her. Startled, she turned around and hit him in the chest only to end up in his arms laughing and tenderly kissing him. It was Inge, or someone just like her and it didn't surprise me, at all. I started suspecting something was wrong when you showed up next to me, I knew that with your slow-paced walk there was no way you could have got there so quickly.

I approached the couple only watching at first because I had no idea what to say. You just blundered around behind me not helping at all. And so I waited for the two of them to notice me because then they would have to say something. I stepped a little closer now, close enough to touch them or for them to feel my breath but they still ignored me.

"What are you two?" I asked quietly.

Perhaps they didn't hear me. I coughed and tried again, this time louder.

Nothing, they just kept chattering about food and where they should go for dinner. Inge mentioned some newly cultivated plant, lustrica, that tasted like seafood and had just as much protein.

"Who the fuck are you? Who prefabricated you and what for? Why do you look just like me and why is she just like Inge? And why the hell are you shoving tongues down each other's throats?" I shouted at the top of my voice.

You kept looking back and forth with fear in your eyes, first at me and then at them, scratching your beard in confusion.

"What was that?" Inge turned my way and so did my lookalike.

I was about to say something, but I had already asked the only question I had for them.

"Probably just a draught," my lookalike said.

"Quite windy out there, isn't it?" Inge seemed like she was relieved.

They stared straight through me for a moment longer as someone walked in and the door closed but then they turned their backs to us and hand in hand walked towards their destination—a shared moment, good food, happiness. Making their way through the crowd, chasing centuries-old desires. It was nothing new, all the same as ever, the things that nobody could hold against them nor which they could surprise anyone with. It had been my life too, until only recently, when I started chasing chimeras.

* * *

The wind outside had calmed down but a hurricane raged through my mind. You followed me out of the entertainment centre, but I couldn't bear you anymore. I turned, sneered at you and stamped my feet, trying to scare you off as I would a stray dog and you even recoiled like one. I couldn't stand you there. I needed to be alone but could barely stand myself either. Unfortunately I'd never learned how to forget myself. I meant to, but never did, and now I wished I had, more than ever.

As a kid I used to crave others, their attention, and their presence. I would run around and always get in Grandma's way, like a clumsy little puppy. If she hadn't had such infinite patience, she would have surely kicked me away. At school after class I would sneak into classmates' groups hoping someone would invite me over to play, knowing I could never return the favour. I didn't have a place I could invite my friends to and I hope Grandma would forgive me for saying it, but I was an orphan; I had no home for a home is only a home when there are parents who make it.

"You bastard," Andrej, my gaunt classmate said after I asked why I couldn't come over to play with them. Unable to form an argument, or even a sentence to oppose me he stood there shaking with excitement. With Paľo and Teo, by his side, both a head taller than him, he felt strong. They had both been invited to his house but he didn't know that in moments like those I knew no fear. I walked up to him, close enough to smell his sweat and see his freckles and the pimple on his cheek up close. I waved the two bodyguards away then bit his nose so hard it started bleeding.

After such—rather frequent—occurrences, I would avoid human contact. Completely. The bottle of liqueur I stole from Grandma and hid under a slab of concrete would keep me going for days. I would always keep my guard up, never drinking enough to pass out and always watching my perimeter to avoid others. Even though I was barely a teenager, Grandma never looked for me or called the police. We were mentally attuned and she knew that I was fine and would come back, that all I needed was some time alone. That was how it always went.

Back then I was my own rock, my only fixed point in a surrounding universe which I could move around in as I liked. I wanted nobody else and was all that I needed but then things changed. Twenty-five years later, I could no longer stand my own company. I made no sense to myself.

Nor did the streets make any sense: simple right-angled streets turned into a confusing labyrinth and each crossroads made my head spin. Buildings tilted down and peering through their windows, I looked at all the sins of the world and they looked back at me. I sat down on a metal flowerpot with wilted flowers which might once have been of any colour—blue, red, or any other for that matter, and I studied my hands. Was it still me? Were these hands mine? What was it that defined me? Was I just a set of cells? Those cells in my tissues that died and those that were born every moment? The skin that was resurrected each month, the blood cells every four months, the bones each decade and the muscles every fifteen years?

Was I still the body I knew from twenty years earlier? Back when I was seventeen, sitting on Shanice's, my then girlfriend's bed. She fell asleep right after sex, but I, despite my weariness, couldn't. We both looked like pieces of carved up meat in the dim light of her purple-decorated room. Touching her thigh, right below her bottom, made her sigh with delight and turn over. What was it that made her wiggle like that in her sleep? I stroked her, running my hand through her hair, sending signals throughout my body, making my muscles and joints move and bend. Fingers, hands, legs and neck ... my heart beating, my penis shrinking, my stomach rumbling, things which I couldn't control. I went to open the window and gazed up at the stars. Closing my eyes I pictured the universe around me, its vast, infinite depths, me as its extremely unlikely

centre and I got goosebumps. Asking myself who I was, I tried
to become my surroundings, see myself from the outside and picture myself standing by Shanice's cluttered vanity table. Is this me,
this piece of something that, for whatever reason, has the power
to think? Does it really believe it can decide about its actions and
understand the motives behind them?

I found no answer. As with many of my reflections, this one had
no resolutions either. Life provided very few stories and even fewer
morals. Mostly it just blew cotton wool into dead ends, alleys and
passages with neither sense nor substance.

Still sitting on the edge of the flowerpot in my town, digging
around in my past and purpose I felt my feet taking root. Their
sharp tips cracked the asphalt and concrete on the surface and
found the nutritious soil underneath. When that wasn't enough,
they kept going further down towards the Earth's core, towards the
furnace and their doom. They grew to die, just like everything, and
everyone.

The air stood still but my sixth sense knew that the weather was
about to go nuts, seeing both its present and future. The cyclone
fraternized with the anticyclone—despite their names, they did not
fight each other. The air and the vacuum coalesced—a molecule of
fullness with a molecule of emptiness. The temperature dropped as
the air mass turned thick and heavy and fell rapidly to the ground.
The strong impact of the high pressure almost squeezed my eye out.

The isobars showed up in my corner. Crammed together, they
told me what I already knew: the wind was strong. Perpendicular
to the isobars was a horizontal arrow, reminding me that the wind
blew towards the place with lowest pressure.

The temperature drop was accompanied by a sharp temperature
rise. The expanding equatorial air soared and carried my consciousness away. As I passed out I could smell all the scents and
smells around going up into the sky: cologne, warm hair, powder
and old-fashioned shaving cream. The smell of horse shit after a
fair, detergent left on the floor by cleaning robots, the cheap perfumes of old sluts from Krížna street who could probably remember

perestroika. The sweat of rootless nomads, standing by the fountain, boasting about their penury when all the money they scrounged made them richer than I was—assholes in torn t-shirts, Greek refugees from the *Saturn's Balls* bistro and their fragrant cucumber yoghurt. Newborns' innocent faces sprayed with milk from their mothers' full boobs and tropical, out-of-bloom lilac. Catching hints of all these, my nose was drowning in the smells of the world as they rushed upwards like an atomic mushroom's stem. God didn't exist but he was gathering up the crumbs of what he had never created.

I gagged and quickly leaned on the edge of the flowerpot I'd been sitting on to vomit over the already wilted flowers. They had no chance of surviving my toxic mixture of coffee, liquor and acids.

* * *

Walking was easier with the night breeze in my face and my insides upturned. Can a person limp with both legs? Mine, lacking any instructions from the brain, led me straight ahead, painfully ahead, right into the sinful part of town. I hadn't been to Majere in a long time but before the Chinese took over the place I used to come here with Martin. As the quarter got more dangerous and we gained more credit we lost the need for cheap fun.

How long had it been, I wondered, passing the first finger-marked shop window displaying underwear on young guestesses. It was just a way of keeping my mind busy; I didn't care about years nor if the owners of the shop sold living meat along with the guestesses nor if some idiot held a knife to my throat and asked for credit—I would just punch him in the face. If my head was going to hurt the next day, I didn't give a damn about what alcohol they offered me either. I stayed away from pills with a monkey logo but alcohol was like karma and would make you pay the next day. I didn't care about the smell hanging over the quarter since I entered from underneath the stars. Just like a person leaving a world they don't care about, I turned off all the warnings in the corner.

Fucking the world without protection is never without risk. I attracted all assaults, both simulated and real, like a magnet. A child approached me, either a real one or not, I wasn't sure and tried to grab my crotch. Fire, like from a dragon's mouth, blazed down on me, and made me strip almost naked, while a single-breasted woman poured bitter ice-cold liquor down my face. I started rubbing the scar around my eye as the alcohol made it burn and itch. This made my vision blurred: the corner in my good eye kept losing reception and my mind's centre of gravity fluttered outside my body. Eczematic, not fitting into my own irritated skin, I was and wasn't myself at the same time. In front of the entrance to a club, I traded punches with some muscly bouncers, spat out blood and teeth, vomited bile, and the coffee I'd drunk with you but hadn't killed the flowers with.

Some random faces pretended to be friendly and took me to a brothel called *Two Hinges*. I could have been completely naked and folks like these could still sniff my credit even from miles away and sense I could be tapped. My corner was bleeping with notifications of all the payments made as these strangers fucked and drank on my account. They even brought me some "stuff" to pick from but at this stage of drunkenness, when I couldn't stand on my own feet or talk, my dick would certainly not cooperate. The brothel-keeper herself came, buttering me up and offering me a young boy, saying: "Look what a nice ass he's got."

As I tried to tell her that I'd been there before but only drool came from my mouth. As I wiped it with the back of my hand, they took the boy away and brought a gypsy girl, who was naked and rubbing herself with oil. I threw a glass at her because she reminded me of Ali, she dodged and the glass hit the wall behind her. Next came Inge, but this time I was sure it was my fantasy and the deactivated security playing tricks on my eye. Grabbing her hand I pulled her closer, kissed her and bit her lip as hard as I could, trying to figure out if she was real. She yelped, hid her bleeding mouth and smacked me in the face ... it felt *almost* real. Despite the alcohol in my veins and my lack of all inhibitions, my eternally cynical and disbelieving nature felt that this was certainly not real.

* * *

Had the previous night only been a dream, then the next day's head-ache, taste of vomit in my mouth, bruises, swelling and other traces of a night of explosive passions were all extremely convincing.

Going back to the original question of why I'm recounting events which you witnessed yourself. Was it just by chance that we only started meeting after my accident, the same accident that caused Martin's death? I have your letter at home and even replied to it several times but never received a response—perhaps because I never sent them, surely, in fact. And then, all of a sudden, we just started meeting at the Avion café. For the life of me, I can't remember how I found you, or whether you found me. Fuck, was it even the real you?

Was I invisible when I yelled at those clones of me and Inge? What's your explanation? Which of us was real? Me, that buffoon or neither of us? I can't recall much of my past: I lose information like I do my hair. My memory has gone bald. What I do have is the notion of the entirety of my life as a continuum. As if it was an axis and the T0 point is the moment of my birth and then a dotted line (T) representing my life, the climax of which is point T1. But that moment is a mystery, for death simply comes and turns the half line into an abscissa.

My earliest memory, the first thing I remember is mom's half-hearted smile and my longing for her embrace. But was it a real memory, or was I making it up? Perhaps it's just my imagination attaching a current emotion to a face from photographs. Bored at school and running home to play, I seem to remember fantasies better than reality. My first girlfriends, the freckled Lily and then Mery, who started crying and made me think she didn't like it, silly me. Synthetical experiments and almost not coming home from a field trip and walking like a zombie through the Small Carpathians. My hallucinations were hard to get over, seeing my own end enticed and frightened me at the same time.

It's blurred and unclear, but I remember my entire life. My memory bends and twists itself, fabricates, swindles, and avoids things; I can't rely on it. The connecting line of the points of my birth and my present is anything but straight. Like a river basin, it changes direction, sends its offshoots to death, claims no right for truth or a just interpretation of my existence. And yet it claims ownership, it is my interpretation and it is authentic. Made of reality, both real and modified; dreams, both night and daydreams; fictions and fantasies, both voluntary and forced, made of those figments of changes in consciousness—fuelled by an alcohol and drug-intoxicated brain and its involuntary changes, caused by thousands of simulations and hundreds of neoreal realities. A nasty mess! The single thing now constituting me is my mind's possession of four decades of time. That's me, nothing else exists for me and nothing else is me. A mind and a memory—I am the centre of what's happening around me, the original of my being, with all its flaws, trips, slips and deviations.

Am I sure I'm the right and original one, the ultra-original?

To leave the comfort of my life was the only step left open to me. To go downwards, into the depths of humanity. It wasn't the content, the good or the evil, the love or the hate, it wasn't truth, the thousand-year brutalized, constantly usurped, conventional truth. None of that was what I was looking for. I just wanted to know if Inge was at least as real as I was. Was she real and was I too? Or were we just another pair of those convincing phantasms?

* * *

What a weird fucking name that was.

"Okun." Some guestess told me a few weeks after I returned from Warsaw.

"Where has he gone to? Okun what?" I furrowed my forehead.

"O-kun," he whispered, looking around to see if anyone was within earshot. "Mister Ali told me to maintain confidentiality when giving you this information."

Sure, let's hide behind the door, I gestured. Following me silently, he was smiling, probably quite pleased with his own execution of the task.

When we were out of sight, I punched him in the stomach making him double up, grabbed him by the neck and pushed him against the wall.

"What else did Mr. Ali tell you? Who do you work for, huh? Me or him?"

For a guestess, his body had quite a range of emotion to express. I knew it wasn't his fault but the rage I had for Ali … His Warsaw confession had disappointed me but it had its redeeming points: I could now exercise my authority because I finally had something on Mr. Perfect. Until then there had been no opportunity: his work was flawless and his commitment total. Nobody said it out loud, but they must have seen that he surpassed even me. But now here it was: a legitimate reason to fire him. Not that I wanted to, but I did like the idea of telling him it was on the table and I was considering it. Then a few days later I would graciously tell him that he could stay but with provisos. The most exciting part would be coming up with ideas how to humiliate and reprimand him. Reprehension, what a great word! He was about to undergo my own private reprehension trial but what did he do instead? He never showed up again and instead had a guestess give me a message to say he'd gone down to some place called Okun. The guestess brought out the worst of me. I left him beaten up on the floor and thought that Ali's smashed up face would perhaps look the same.

* * *

Regardless of what kind of reality you were in, beating someone up would always feel thrilling and liberating. You could always let out steam beating up guestesses but aside from that, there weren't many opportunities up Above. Many, me included, took advantage of the games in the chambox. But they couldn't compete with reality.

Down below I would mostly run away from violence, not towards it. I knew when I was at a disadvantage. But then, soon enough, the tables turned and I felt some temptation. Ripped up tiles, shattered Metro signs, dilapidated buildings with draughts their only residents emitting smells of decomposing carcasses and rat shit; well-preserved, old-fashioned clocks decorating every department store in town; a rusty tram at its very last stop. It was Pompeii, Famagusta, Chernobyl, Mosul and Kiev only with a slightly different landscape. This devastated and overgrown central European city was not a victim of war, natural disaster or nuclear cataclysm, it was just perishing slowly and painfully, time its destroyer and progress the victim. The city Above hogging the sunshine left the place in shadows that brought only darkness and doom.

I watched a slouched, drooling grey-haired old man from my hiding spot. He was standing in the middle of some sort of square and gangs of bandits would pass him by, smelling him and deciding there was nothing they could take—not even his meat. Let their dogs piss on him and leave. And he just stayed put, his only movement an awful and violent tremor, like the symptom of some degenerative nervous disorder or the effect of a hundred volts going straight through him. There was nothing in his hands but there were some scrolls of paper hanging around his neck. When nobody was around, I approached him and grabbed the scrolls after which he fell to his knees, wailed and started muttering something. I bared my teeth to keep the fetid man quiet and stepped away to read. They were full of rubbish, mentioning an apocalypse but also Okun, so I shoved them in my coat pocket. I knew all along that I could beat this guy up and he wouldn't fight back; the letters were an unexpected bonus. In the end, though, I took mercy on him.

He didn't deserve violence—or perhaps violence didn't deserve him. Who knows if blood would have flowed from him. He really was disgusting.

The next day was more generous when it came to throwing punches. After my lunch of a mouldy piece of bread and an afternoon nap, I heard a noise. Standing nearby were two women and two men, the women shouting and swearing hysterically at the top of their voices and holding onto bags of food. There were two things they could do: either leave them there and run or stay and fight. The first option would save their lives until painful exhaustion and hunger killed them somewhere in a bed of weeds; the second meant risking rape, a smashed head or ending up as dinner for the savages. The thought of their roasted meat made me drool; clearly, I hadn't eaten properly in a while.

The women chose to fight, just as I expected and hoped. After watching for a moment, I joined in. The maths was simple—three against two. The killers weren't deterred and merely smiled. They probably just thought what a gentleman I was.

"Take out the one with the big nose," I told one of them. "And you can help me with the other." They got it right away. The first woman threw herself on the guy a head taller than her and almost floored him. Her punches made him laugh until he noticed that the other woman and I were beating the crap out of his colleague. He started returning her punches but once our guy flaked out, we finished him off three on one. Brimming with adrenaline, the women kept kicking the killers' heads even after they were on the ground, completely motionless.

I grabbed a large carrot from the bag on the ground and started munching on it. I wondered whether the women would try to chop up their victims on the spot, take them away or leave them there when something suddenly yanked my head to one side and a heavy shoe struck my teeth. Two angry faces stared down at me. "That's my carrot!" the taller one yelled.

So much for gratitude! I realized too late they didn't like the idea of sharing and knew the basics of maths—two is more than one, after all. I was outnumbered and had to decide. There was no meat to be had, that was certain, but I was not leaving empty handed. Grabbing one of the bags of vegetables I challenged them to a race. The maths was getting complicated; they looked at me, then at the bag, then at the other bag, then at the dead bodies and then at each other. Not so simple now, is it, bitches, I laughed and ran towards the cut-out lanes. They cautiously followed, deciding whether to leave behind the other bag of vegetables and their unexpected prey.

Then as I turned a corner of the old city wall, a good thirty meters ahead of them I run into someone. It was Martin and I almost died of fright when I saw him. He dragged me to a solid building across the street and helped me climb a brick wall onto a metal, moss-covered roof. Barely breathing, we watched the women as one after the other stopped on the corner and looked around, up and even in the bushes by the wall. As my adrenaline levels fell, I realized.

"We're their birds in the bush ... Now they're going back to their birds in the hand," Martin said, smiling stupidly. In my shock, I couldn't even look at him. He sensed it and we both stayed silent for a moment. Then he stood up and pointed to a tall building towering over others nearby, interrupting the smooth horizon line. "Okun, where there's water and fire," he said. I jumped down from the roof and walked away, not looking back at him and not giving a damn about any danger I could possibly be walking into. Why should I when it could all just be another fucking dream? And yet the fight definitely felt real ...

* * *

I've found the place! I've found it! The one I've been looking for. I've finally found it. The excited ink letters spatter the paper as they rush out of my brain.

I almost forgot the greeting.

Hi. Hi again.

I'm confused. I'm overjoyed. You are a part of this, you helped me find it, whoever or whatever you may be. That's why I'm writing to you.

Weeks of going around in circles almost robbed me of my belief. Did such a place even exist? My automatic glances into the corner were in vain, the control panel was blank and silent. I noticed that years of using it had left behind some faded spots on my visual field. Like a wall under a painting or pale skin hiding from the sun under a wristwatch. I even said that stupid name out loud in the past few days, not knowing if it was a building, club or city and getting back only faded white spots and an imaginary echo. Symbols and sounds that didn't really exist.

It's all ugly, reeking and raw with no sugar-coating down here. At first I liked it—it revives your senses. But then ... it's so easy to lose your scruples, you'd be suprised. There are blank spots instead of norms. Standards? You can't fall any lower and going up is an unatainable luxury. The word has no meaning down here.

A few weeks here and you become numb, completely numb. And that's because of the sheer ugliness and emptiness of the place, the absence of any bond that would make things meaningful. Each brick, each cable, each abandoned car exudes lonelyness and a sense of the end. But not only end! Though still and lifeless, they send out signals of shame—but not shame of their end but of their past, their prior purpose. It's as if they wanted to disappear and crawl under the ground. But there's nothing below, this is the very bottom of the world.

Everything is devestated, so much so that a man must crawl over the ruins with only weak light from Above and from guttering candles. The old pedestrian zone sign and a broken city centre sign were the last traces of life before the destruction, life before the sun stopped shining. Was this a department store? It's been a while since I was last here, before it was covered. I can only speculate, desparate wreck climber that I am.

Why did I think a world of virtual reality would be livelier? Nothing I can see here ever seemed intended to enhance or prettify the place or give it a soul. There was no reason or person to do it. The place was a write off, dead, deaf and dumb as a doornail. The real does not equate to the living.

It took me weeks to admit that I was disappointed, even with myself. Believing in a single God of a single reality is impossible when you are used to altering consciousness, switching versions of it like TV channels. You get tired of such an existance, consuming reality as if it was confetti. I suppose you can guess this is about me for even though I'm keeping my distance and calling myself "you" I'm exposed, like a man from thousands of years ago. My corner is turned off and my cloud is out of order. Seeing all this ugliness makes me doubt anyone would bother to simulate the Underworld. And still, I can't help but doubt and disbelieve it. But how would it be? How could one be sure this was the only real world when movement through parallel realities was, dare I say, ingrained in our DNA. Human DNA, just like mine.

What then of Martin? What could possibly explain him appearing out of the blue to help me escape a couple of lunetic women trying to kill me? I felt his hand when he helped me onto that roof, he couldn't have been an illusion, could he? I'd seen him get exterminated in an explosion as if he was just some game character. And what about my eye? I touch the scar. No, that wasn't a fantasy because I am still half blind. I remember wishing, even praying, that it had all been just a simulation. Could it be that the Martin from Above was a fiction and the real one lived here?

Simulations can look very convincing, Grandad, extremely convincing. Back in the day I remember Grandma telling me stories, though she couldn't remember if she'd heard them on television, from a neighbour or just dreamt them. Then she would wink, smile, lean her head back in laughter and dance back to the kitchen to finish her pepper stew. She truly didn't know.

And yet it was still nothing compared to today. Now you don't see it on some external screen but the simulation is actually happening in your head. You see a different world as if it was your own daily reality. The vast majority of people have this non-invasive procedure done as children—it requires no surgery or implants. The result is your sensory perceptions are projected directly into your conciousness. When irradiated, implayray can change your brain waves by connecting you to the cloud and allowing you to play movies in your own head in which you are the main character.

I'm sure that talk of these things reached you. Perhaps you just said to yourself: So what? You can watch TV in your own head but it's not as if bread got cheaper.

But the invention was revolutionery. Old-school reactionaries bewailed it saying that kids would abandon reality and play games the whole time. Yes, that happened but the chambox became a universally personal space which could serve for anything. It was not just for conquering non-existant worlds or kingdoms but also for taking exotic trips, dining in luxurious restaurants, having the filthiest sex, landing on the Moon, Mars or the Seashell Constellation, climbing the highest peaks, the Everests, the Kanchenjunga ... all you had to do to get that authentic experience was make a single eye movement.

Just imagine that when somebody pissed you off, a neighbour, a character in a movie, your girlfriend, son, daughter or boss, you could take the projection you had of them, get into the chambox and beat the crap out of their imbody. Right hand, left hand, bite in the neck, just like a lion. Feeling the sweet blood running down your throat you spit in his face as he lies on the ground writhing. What a sick catharsis, damn it!

Not only that. In the Above, people can use implayray to choose their dreams—all the nice ones, sequels to their daydreams, but not nightmares, of course. For them it's a tool to help them overcome their phobias and conquer their fears: sarmasso, arachno, chirapto, gimno, tropo, megalo, necro. Cacotechno. Each and every one of them. It can strengthen or mute certain brain functions, ease pain or enhance pleasure and suppress everything else, making it a supreme experience and utilitarian utopia.

This ability to fundamentally tamper with human conciousness is revolutionery for ... well human consciousness. What sort of tautology is this? you're asking. Well, you know what I mean. Human mentality, psyche, everything.

Humankind has lost all its sensitivity, for instance. And I'm merely stating here not judging nor pointing the finger at anyone. We're all getting more and more numb, like a freshly anesthetized patient, and it's getting worse by the year. Suffering and pain have become relative and many people have died because neither they nor anybody around them realized it was for real.

You'd stab someone in the throat only to notice it wasn't happening in the chambox but in reality. "I'm sorry, I had a few drinks … I kind of overdid it," you'd say calling an ambulance to save the poor bastard, hoping he had a copy to replace him with.

Death became less absolute and less dreadful. The bereaved family could keep seeing their loved one in the chambox or have a clone with a brand-new purpose-built conciousness. Death was no longer such a loss and only a few people, Ioanna included, were strong enough to choose grief. Non-worlds were places to go when escaping feelings of loss and trying to offset grief. But not only that: gradually any kind of undesirable emotion, not just grief, was being avoided.

Just imagine: you have a whole cornucopia of experience with different versions and levels of reality, drugs, dreams, real life video games. Imagine having all that within reach at all times. Even the poorest people will pay for a dose of a real-life dream: mass delusion has become the most profitible industry. Goods are still a necessity—we have to eat—but services sell more and temporary escapes from reality most of all. The largest corpoments fight to control virtual reality and create the most appealing version—and to attract people who will spend their money, energy, and resources on it. They then reinvest their money to develop even better versions to entice even more sheep and with it take away the sins of the world.

It isn't just escapism—the world is simply not what it used to be but fading away and losing significance. Conventional wars are no longer fought, only mining goes on as before. In the end every simulation needs a tangible base and so they go on mining ores and minerals. Thankfully, nobody fights over them anymore: mass destruction weapons have lived up to their reputation and self-preservation seems to be working. Destroying any part of the data infrastructure is undesirable because everyone benefits from it and the Commons Concensus ensuring this has been a rare, even unique instance of a global agreement of our time. The algorithm world is a battlefield for gygantic platforms in which the winners are those who hack into their competitor's system, steal their innovations and then destroy them. Hacking is the new warfare and cyberspace the new front. Worlds fight then fuse.

The same happens with human bounderies, which almost killed me. I was laughing like a psycho, feeling like it was all a simulation, but if I'd tripped and fell, those two crazy bitches would have beaten the life out of me. Would anyone have stopped to help me? Would anyone have looked for me or missed me? Would Inge or Ali? I didn't really care so had no hopes they would. I didn't believe anyone would have wished to revive me.

Technology is galloping ahead and despite miracles being now possible, you still cannot travel in time, just like you can't bring back a dead fire. You can only make a new one, similar even identical, but still different. I saw a body that went through a turbine being put back together. They saved a woman with so many stab wounds you couldn't even count them. They can heal alkali burns, remove malignant tumours and save helpless cases—almost nothing is impossible anymore.

But once the thin string connecting the living conciousness to dead matter stretches so much it snaps. And when the brain simply shuts off, all that healthcare and science can do is take off their hats and pay their respects. As with Martin, nothing could have saved him or brought him back to life. Well ... if he actually did die but who can tell with so many variables. He was erased by a stupendous blast like some video game character. I guess I told you about this before. Game over for the one and only Martin, irreplaceable by any number of identical extras.

Mom is the same case, her dead body in some fridge somewhere. What can I do? What can anyone do? Her earthly remains were perfectly preserved, she made sure to die and be frozen while still beautiful. Curing her is no longer a problem, they can easily repair a damaged nervous system, but the thing is that she had her body frozen back when transferring conciousness to an extracorporeal medium wasn't possible. Her being was erased the moment her last brain cell fizzled out.

Perhaps in the future someone will come up with a way of reviving those cells, bringing a dead body back to life and resurecting the deceased. But what will that make them? Will they be zombies? I've never believed in a god but the concept of a soul is familiar to me—but in the vitality of the body, its capacity to exist. Once it's gone, though, that's it, the end, kaput. What would reviving the dead turn the world into? It would merely fill the universe with wandering phantoms so can someone tell me why I should want to bring my mother back? What would I do with her and what would she do? How would she live in these times? She died thirty years ago. She didn't want to—all she wanted was to go to sleep for a while and wake up healthy. But does it matter?

Earthly life is no longer the centre of attention. The computer was the start of it. Made by man, it started computing until it learned to learn by itself, to ask questions and find answers a thousand times faster than any person could. Computers concluded that the whole world and its history were anacronisms and that it would be better to move human utopias to a simulated reality. With no attachments to the smell of fresh bread, pattering of rain and physical contact. Making human desires come true in the simulation was all that our species needed to fall for it. They gave us magical powers and turned us into demigods.

Only garbage, the septic tank of demigods' ambitions remained below, down here on the Earth's surface where the entire history of humankind took place before the times of spheres, current-built buildings and digital conciousness extensions. Not so long ago I was still squatting in the Above and now here I am looking for the origin of things, looking at what brought man his certainty throughout history. But instead of stars there is only a giant butthole sending down a toxic bomb.

Leaving everything behind and giving it up, I unwillingly became a monk. I was searching without looking, don't ask me for what. I was drowning, clutching at a straw of poor clues. Martin, or rather someone like Martin gave me directions, telling me about fire and water, or some-thing like that. I climbed up a lamppost in my worn-out shoes and with bleeding feet. The flagpole at the top had no flag on it because what could the Underworld have on its flag if it had one? What symbol would peo-ple here choose? People living in a place they refuse to call home despite knowing they will never live anywhere else. Unpleasant things don't belong on flags or symbols. They wouldn't pick weeds, ruins, darkness, garbage or stink but what else is there to choose from?

From high up I noticed an old smoke-stained water-tower. Fire and water. I started trembling at the excitement. Was it my destination? I was close but it still took me hours to wade through to it. The building was overgrown with bushes and crawling weeds made it almost impossible to advance. Tugging on the loose debris and climbing over the solid pieces my hand slipped straight into a decaying corpse which released a swarm of flies and an awful smell. I almost passed out. It was curious that nobody sniffed out the meat before it started rotting; it was rare for food to be wasted like this. There was barely anyone around, but I noticed a man a few dozen metres away. Again, that's curious. Most people hunt in packs. He didn't seem like an old man but was struggling to climb the debris. His tongue out in exhaustion, murmering something to himself, advancing desparately slowly, he seemed to be crying. Despair was a common thing around here, but this man was the epitome of it. Taking a break from climbing I watched him until he did the same, then stopped moving alltogether. His grey clothes and deathly pale skin matched the concrete rubble surroundings. It was only then that I noticed heaps of dead bodies around. I got anxious in such company.

Taking breaths that felt like my last I took one last leap into space. The air smelled like a Bohemian forest Grandma took me to, of lilac, fresh-cut grass, and dewy nettle back. My nostrils were about to explode—I was gasping for breath, my pupil was irritated by the daylight, my cock started hardening, my fingertips tingling and a bitter taste spread across my tongue. Never have I felt the wave of life shake me so hard, not even when I was on drugs. The contrast with the Underworld couldn't get any bigger. It was as if I'd walked through an invisible membrane beyond which a tunnel wound down further into the underground. I walked in to see a subterranian river with starchy white water flowing right to left and air filled with bubbles of gas which made me hallucinate. I couldn't tell for certain—there was no sign that would confirm it, but everything was different. Yes it must be it.

I did it, Grandad. I'd finally found Okun.

* * *

It was not voices but their absence that was filling me up. Searching for a place and meaning, I was thankful that my brothers and sisters took me back. But as I grew weaker, even the smallest tasks became strenuous. An empty mind full of nothing resembled sorrow more than joy. There were times when I would crowd negative thoughts out with mating, synthetics, or music. To play some simple melody in my head was sometimes all that I needed for things to get better. I suddenly lacked basic creativity and felt more convinced every day that I was finished. The finite world is not an illusion—that's bullshit. It's the single certainty we are all heading towards. Or so I think.

In my dreams I've gone deaf. Colours, characters and plot all play their part, but I can't hear a word. Every single dream is deadly silent. The worst thought, however, haunts me during those long subterranean days. No matter what I do the image of myself floating through space on a comet is with me at all times. But it doesn't feel like if I'm flying or moving at all, instead it's all the celestial bodies around me doing so; I might as well be standing still. All I can do is wait. Wait and not know what I'm waiting for. This daydreaming is killing me. A day goes by but feels like an entire year. And then another day and another until one month is gone but in that time it feels like three decades have passed. That would surely turn a full head of hair grey. Picture being wide awake for an entire eternity without a clue how to end it. Picture being only a consciousness without a body, a cluster of fading memories existing in the present, having nothing to give or contribute, only consisting of time. This fat and decomposing time passes ever more slowly until it almost stands still. Except it's only an illusion because time decomposes for eternity. Without a body, you can't die and consciousness is permanent. Or perhaps it's false ... is only ephemeral and easier to refute than to prove the existence of. What hardly exists can hardly end.

Spending my last hours on the top of the sphere, observing the world around from the highest rooftop, I hope these are the last images to enter my wretched memory's mosaic, one that will soon break up into a million tiny fragments and shoot out in every direction flying fast enough to disappear completely. Mom is going to be on the first fragment. How else could it be? Her fragment has long lost its sharp edges; time has smoothed it out to resemble a cobble stone. The kind that children build stone statues with on beaches or skim across the water. I bet mom's fragment would skip ten times before sinking. Down to the very bottom of memory beneath which lies total oblivion.

The last, razor-sharp fragment will cut everything it sets its sight on. That one will not belong to any of you, not to my mom or my father, who I only know to have conceived me, not to you, Grandma, Inge, Ali or Martin. Nobody who's close to me, nobody who's distant, no relative and no stranger. Because this last fragment will carry me. It's Good Friday tomorrow and the last person will soon leave the corpoment's military units headquarters below me. Only roboguards guard the building at night and there's no-one to pity them.

The part of my memory containing the current-built buildings' destruction manual has thawed out. Almost every building above the original Earth's surface was current-built but there was never a need to use the manual on our zealous expeditions from the underground. The reason was the same as the one that kept us from using bombs: they can't differentiate between things. That doesn't trouble me today, though, because I know that tonight I'll be the only living soul in the administrative district. My unique suicide attack will blast me through the collapsing walls, floors and furniture of this building. It will become my own little history junkyard. I will make a point of killing nobody else. It's taken me weeks to prepare this plan and learn about the building. Had I switched off all the walls, floors and ceilings a few hours ago, it would have been the greatest terrorist attack in history. Hopefully they will gather what my intentions were for I myself am starting to lose track of them.

The sun is flooding the world with its array of sunset reds peeking through the clouds while I'm flooded with inexplicable joy. I decided long ago, subconsciously when I was coming down perhaps but certainly by the time fire was melting my still memory, frozen like permafrost, releasing like methane gases of despair and sorrow. For the first time now, the thought that I should fear the end crossed my mind, but I feel no fear, none at all. It was mom who did: she feared old age and death, but my fear is not dying. The idea of my consciousness staying alive, of someone keeping it alive to wander around time and space forever. That is my only fear.

Crawling to the edge and staring, focusing and zooming in. My eye once again has its corner back and I can see a handful of people going in different directions as they leave the building, some riding their uniwheel, some their mobicaps and others walking. Counting down the people leaving, I was soon approaching zero—simple mathematics. Before long the last one would be on their way.

I am the first human. The first to undergo a partial conversion voluntarily and purposefully, the first who partly forgot and partly gained, the first who went Above to destroy evil and lost his way. I resign to the future, reconciled to the dead ends of time and memory, the single solution to which is to find a way out. That's me. I'm from the same line as Martin, Inge, Aladár, my siblings, my blood brothers and sisters. Going Above was my idea. It was me who put on the disguise of half oblivion and infiltrated with Martin by my side. Inge and Ali only joined us after I had lost course and dismissed my original purpose after forgetting I was on a mission and had to go back. However, the fault was not in my scheme: there were things I wished to forget, mostly abandonment, painful emptiness and my mother. I wanted to forget about them from the very beginning, throughout this hybrid halftime right until this moment. I wanted them *completely* wiped from my memory.

With nobody underneath me I look up. There, beyond the roof of the sphere is the sky. It would surely be clear and I will see the lights. The weight of all the stars, the black holes, the clouds of gas, the dust, the black matter and all the rest of things we haven't named yet must be heavier than seven billion Suns, only thinking about our own galaxy. Was the existence of the universe only an accident or someone's creation? The amount of imagination such a deed would have required! Wow, was the closeness of death bringing these religious shortcuts and illogisms? I wasn't sure but the thing I was certain about was that I could no longer bear looking into the vast, cold, distant and swelling heaviness. It made my eyeball want to burst so I hid it behind my eyelid to keep it in one piece. At least for a moment, at least until I come crushing down into the oblivion, the graveyard of history and I shall sing the song Grandma used to sing to me as I fall:

I have hidden the ring
And covered your face.
Beyond the broken fence
Lies a frosty space.

You can tell me your secrets
(God is so far from here)
Chimneys are cold
But the heart does not fear

In the blackness of fields
Are candles without flames
Spaces are burning
Losing their names

Happiness is an illness.
And people don't lie.
Shadows on the nail.
Oh why do they die?

* * *

Your jaw was crushed and there is a tiny trace of dried old blood in the corner of your mouth. The scorching sky and the still air got me asking myself how long it was since we were basking in the warm Warsaw sun. You've grown old. The stubble on your narrow, thin face with grey hair catching up with the dark and the dark knowing it never equal the grey. Is it still you, Adam?

It's not too bad for falling from such height. Your head is fairly well preserved, your face however seems a bit crooked, and I don't dare to look under the sheet covering the rest of your body. The medical record says you suffered devastating injuries and what I imagine by that is a crushed cluster of meat. And yet you survived.

You intended to leave without a goodbye and I should probably be angry with you and guess I am. I don't want to resist anger since it's the most authentic human emotion. We taught the prefabs a multitude of feelings—love, fear, affection, stress, even humour, those were not particularly hard to do but anger was. That authentic human anger that makes every cell of your body rise up till you're about to burst, when your body stiffens, becomes completely autonomous and takes flight like a runaway carousel as your blood starts to boil. That was extremely hard. Leave it be, they used to tell me. It's the way it's supposed to be, they don't need to know how to be angry. But I was persistent—anger is productive, it can't be overlooked. Isn't that what makes us human? Human?

New humans. You used to call them that and how did we never think of it? Prefab is such a stupid term. You were their co-creator, you partially became one of them and yet you never liked them. Why does it always surprise me when I know you feared having children of your own. You figured out almost immediately that there is no difference between a biological parent and a prefabricator. The responsibility stays the same. We procreate, we form a tissue out of two cells, then we pack it with values, opinions, likes and dislikes and all sorts of impressions by our parenting, environment, chance, intention, and error. The same goes for new people. Becoming a parent means stretching consciousness over the shell of muscle, bone and brain. What held you back was a reluctance to replicate the evil you carried inside.

Do you remember? You found us in Okun and after a couple of days of roaming around the camp as if sleepwalking you were curious about everything, and it was all so new to you. You asked me why I was so excited about creating new people and so I took you for a walk to the Haunted House. Nely gave it that name.

I took you up to the second floor, walked around it and lit the candles illuminating a hall filled with paintings.

You stopped right before the first one, one of a girl grimacing, either in pain or delight. You touched it. There were pale white semi-circles under her sore red eyes and a space between the lips showing her teeth. Was she inhaling, exhaling or holding her breath? There was no background, body or ornaments—only the pencil strokes were visible. The second painting also portrayed a woman, her face hidden in the shade of her cap, holding a black horse by the reins, an oil painting.

Beautiful, you said despite your innate cynicism. We stood in silence and in awe when you suddenly understood. Nely? You asked me and I nodded. My eldest daughter and the gallery of her creativity. She always cried when painting. Maybe it was a fault in my programming or maybe she just turned out that way regardless of my intentions or mistakes, I don't know.

They're our creation. They're like us.

You had concussion and I wonder how your skull managed to keep the brain inside. How did you survive that? Do you even remember anything? You probably don't, certainly not our youth together, you erased that before you went to the Above. I'll remind you of what you were like and what we were like. Marauders—that's what your grandma used to call us.

We focused on technologies which were about to undermine the old industries and weaken the order of society. Disruption of law, medicine, economy, administration. The final solutions in justice, health and freedom. You really don't recall? You were one of us before you left. More cynical and sceptical than the rest of the party with ideals in second place, you took delight in doing mischief. But we worked together for a better society however pathetic it may sound to your deaf ears.

Our first attempts didn't work since we both under- and over-estimated humanity. No system can override its essence and no technology change its nature. You laughed at me asking what I expected. You ignored how hurt I was and made fun of me.

Transporting fresh tulips from Northern Europe in cooling boxes to customers in Asia or the New World was perfectly normal but loading up ramen soups and purification tablets into a truck and sending it to poor and famished countries was a problem beyond solving. Visions from a century ago about work time with machines and robots doing everything for us while we relaxed and spent our time doing whatever we liked …Well you knew what would become of it. A decaying humanity living off a minimal wage inside a four-by-four metre dungeon. Videogame heroes, seducers, and Olympic winners, all virtual of course. A nation of obese idiots with nothing to do, a daily dose of prescribed entertainment, evolutionary boredom and humanism on its knees.

We were desperate but didn't give up figuring out how to fix the problem and right the world. Our analysis had two different possibilities. We were either disgracefully wasting the potential of a large group of people or, and this is said without any prejudice or emotion, humans are garbage, organic waste, a material that can be either taken advantage of or discarded depending on the sheer luck of a particular human. And whether we leave them to decay in a casket with their throat slit to be eaten by worms or to rot more slowly in a reeking tomb, with smiles on their faces or a head full of illusions and games it's all the same.

Once the road to progress failed and technology fixed most of mankind's practical problems, uncovering human incompetence and our inclination to self-destruct at the same time, we stopped asking ourselves whether people had potential or were to be thrown away. Our plan B was to *come up* with a conception of a human that wouldn't end up being just space debris. The question wasn't if a good old fallible human or an errorless machine, a computer without feelings or reason was better. To that we knew the answer: it was a humanity programmed to a better, more sustainable mode.

However, another question emerged during the process. Wasn't humanity, the old, original humanity also just an experiment or a simulation? Weren't we only a creation of some other beings from beyond our world? Our own prefabs are not aware of who they used to be until we tell them otherwise. They think they are the originals.

Can you remember anything or anyone? Martin or Inge? As I see your barely alive remains, I doubt that you do. What is memory even and can any definition of it be applied to a brain in a vegetative state? Does it make a difference talking to an unconscious body, recapping its history, the supposed course of its and your existence? And is there a point in not doing so?

You pushed a great deal of memories out of your mind but coming back to Okun refreshed your memory, or so it seemed. I'm hesitant to evaluate the current state of your brain's capacity. No reaction. You're not nodding or shaking your head. Can I go on?

I was slow to realize that it was never about making the world a better place. Your thing was only learning if it was real and then one day you lost it. Our gang was on a mission Above and that day ten of our brothers died there. They had their throats slit like a bunch of pigs in a slaughterhouse. It came out of the blue and the other side was prepared for us while we were not. Spending the night hiding in some lousy boarding-house outside Dresden we drowned our sorrow in liquor when you suddenly flew out of your seat and ran towards the sphere lifts. There was no chance of stopping you and we thought that was your end but two hours later you were back, soaked to the bone and delirious with a teary eye. You demanded to know if everything was a dream, if you were floating through some parallel reality or truly alive. You asked how to tell the real, original truth from anything else. You wanted to know if it's real when you feel a sip of wine roll on your tongue, tickle your tastebuds and warm up your throat as you swallow. You insisted it would be a slap in the face of mankind if it wasn't real. All the wind and rain on the sphere's rooftop tilting you from side to side couldn't just be your drugged and programmed brain's imagination.

Shaking your head, you watched us when Ingrid approached and hugged you whispering and asking why you even cared about reality when you couldn't distinguish it from hallucinations. There was no way you could know if any true reality even existed. Maybe they were all real and fake to the same extent, she said consolingly, and the only way you could be free and happy was to accept that everything was futile. Then she covered you with a blanket and caressed your hair as she asked you to stop searching for the one finite truth because that was just humanity's illusion. Everything else in the universe was constantly changing and shifting. She repeated those words making it sound like a lullaby. I tried to soothe you myself repeating that there still was a chance we indeed were one of a kind and therefore no simulation.

You managed to persuade us to put all our effort towards finding out. Putting everything else aside we unsuccessfully tried to crack the code with only few clues and a suspicion but no key to help us expose the world outside our sensory perceptions and our perceivable, definable, measurable, and observable parameters. Calculating all the data of the world, crunching it a thousand times, distilling it into the ultimate spirit of knowledge and conducting our experiments only brought us to a simple conclusion. If our creators were behind the simulation which we exist in, they designed it so well we stood no chance of decoding it. They gave us some suspicious discrepancies to make it more entertaining but the chance of meeting them face to face—should they even have faces—is point zero while the likelihood of never learning about the virtual, beyond earthly place is, on the other hand, huge. That notion was killing you. You craved to find out what those creatures that created us were like—if they had ever existed.

I had no idea, I never found out but perhaps they lived among us without us ever seeing them, invisible. I reflected on all that to please you rather than to quench my thirst for knowing. Or they used to be among us and then disappeared, got bored or died and left the simulation running with us forever stuck in a loop or impasse. My pondering was of no use to you.

No, it's only on our own heads, you would counter. There's nobody up above, that's only our own imagination because we don't like the idea of being responsible ourselves. It's simply us using third person non-beings, our so-called creators, to distance ourselves from all the misery.

The past saw plenty of such conversations between us. They were futile and led nowhere; in the end, there was nothing more to say so we agreed to give up on the big issues and without ever saying a word about it we started pillaging, going up into the Above and spontaneously killing fiends, criminals, and terrorists. This was no new concept, we simply took the good old morality guide, good versus evil, black versus white, the modern day Robin Hoods.

Many found themselves in this new mission, but you grew more resentful, your ideals were now a mere excuse for violence since it was more acceptable to kill the bad guys than to kill everyone without exception. Violence became your drug, you craved hurting others and loved risking being hurt yourself. Martin then got the worst of it and you lost your eye although I remember you yelling out another version of the story.

Your mom was gone too and regardless of your tough guy face and claims that she was just a stranger to you, every Christmas you would disappear for a few days, and I was sure it was to sit by her side. Just like I am now sitting next to you, next to the snarl of bones, nerves and limbs that's left of you. I believe that had you any consciousness left you'd be groaning with pain.

Always wanting to do it, I lift the gauze off your eye. I imagine putting my finger into the void of darkness inside your head but the mere idea of it cause me such sharp pain I almost faint. And perhaps that's it: maybe only excruciating pain can reveal what is true and what is not.

What do I do with you? I found you but now I'm losing you again and will miss you. But I respect your decision: you must have had a good enough reason to throw yourself down from such a height and bury yourself under a mountain of ruins. Even though it didn't kill you, even though you might be suffering and the doctors could probably bring you back to life I'm only giving them one instruction: not to let you die.

I will leave you as you are.

About the Author

IVAN LESAY (1980) was born in Trnava, (Czecho-)Slovakia. He studied and taught political science and political economy at universities in Trnava, Budapest, Bratislava and Vienna. His professional career has been centered around European investments and green energy. Lesay made his literary debut with a children's book and has authored short stories, including some for radio. His debut novel *Topography of Pain* was published in 2020 and received the prestigious 3rd place in the Slovak National Book of the Year 2020 award.

About the Translator

JONATHAN GRESTY (1965) grew up in a British town in Cheshire but has lived more than half his life in Slovakia. He is a university teacher but has also worked as a translator from Slovak into English for many years and has several translations of novels to his credit. He has written several short stories and theatre plays, in which he has also acted. He is married and has two grown-up children.

Printed by Imprimerie Gauvin
Gatineau, Québec